C.M. Elliott was born in the UK, educated in Australia and has worked in the safari industry in Zimbabwe for many years. She took up writing in 2010. Sibanda and the Night Adder is her forth novel.

Also by C.M. Elliott

Sibanda and the Rainbird
Sibanda and the Black Sparrow Hawk
Sibanda and the Death's Head Moth

SIBANDA AND THE NIGHT ADDER

C.M. Elliott

First published in Great Britain in 2023 by:

Carnelian Heart Publishing Ltd

Suite A

82 James Carter Road

Mildenhall

Suffolk

IP28 7DE

UK

www.carnelianheartpublishing.co.uk

Paperback ISBN 978-1-914287-30-5

eBook ISBN 978-1-914287-31-2

A CIP catalogue record for this book is available from the British Library.

This novel is entirely a work of fiction. The names, characters and incidents portrayed in it are the work of the author's imagination. Any resemblance to actual persons, living or dead, is purely coincidental.

Editors: Samantha Rumbidzai Vazhure and

Lazarus Panashe Nyagwambo

Cover design: Rebeca Covers

Typeset by Carnelian Heart Publishing Ltd

Layout and formatting by DanTs Media

For Oskar

Chapter 1

'Has anyone touched the body?' Detective Inspector Jabulani Sibanda crouched over the corpse of a well-dressed man. The dead man's shirt, although grubby, appeared stylish, buttons done up at the neck and around the wrists. He wore gloves, black ones, odd given the heat. A couple of dirt marks scuffed the knees of his trousers, evidently not bought from Barghees General Dealers. The cut and fit were too tailored. The body bore no marks, no signs of violence.

'We were waiting for you, sir.' Sergeant Ncube glanced at Sibanda, expecting questions he couldn't answer and twisted comments he wouldn't understand. The sergeant regretted he'd come across the scene. The discovery of the body would cause tension at Gubu police station; barked orders and horrible conflict between DI Sibanda and the officer-in-charge, Stalin Mfumu. He sensed dyspeptic days ahead.

The sergeant had left home early in the morning to welcome the gathering storm. The downpour would be the first of the season. An atmosphere was building, inky black and beautiful with all the sensuous promise of a pot of bubbling mealie meal. Ncube wanted to be part of the rain, to rejoice in the puddles and rivulets, to watch as the dust dissolved on the leaves like salt in a biltong brine and most of all, to breathe in the riches springing from the earth with each drop of the precious liquid. No one could fail to be excited by the smell of new rain on parched land after such a bleak and wistful winter. Ncube was trying to decide if the tang of fresh raindrops thrumming on the ground as he walked was more thrilling than the waft of a simmering stew when Mama Elephant barrelled down the alley way and nearly bowled him over. The two large bodies shared an unwanted embrace in a tangle of limbs.

'Oh! Sergeant Ncube, ayi ayi, thank goodness. I was running to the Police Station.'

Sergeant Ncube glanced down the alley expecting an angry bull to be chasing the flustered eatery owner, 'What is it? Have you been robbed?'

'No, there's a dead man outside the diner.'

'Are you sure? Not someone sleeping off a heavy night?'

Mama Elephant's voice changed from alarm to cynicism. With one arm on her hips, she sashayed her head, 'his eyes are wide and staring and there are flies all over him. Believe me, he's as dead as the black cow Mpofu slaughtered last month for his father's *umbuyiso*.' Realising the impact this disaster would have on her business, she bleated, 'My breakfast customers will be put off their Russian sausages.'

'Calm yourself, Mama. Show me where he is.' As the words left his mouth, the thought of Russian sausages invaded his brain, a treat with all those organs and gizzards and tasty bits from who knows what animal - some claimed dead donkey - minced together. It didn't matter what flavoured the mix, the ground and seasoned body parts were mouth-watering. He gave up on this fantasy when they reached the body. The man was dead alright. Blow flies, lazy from the heavy weather, clustered in the still moist eye corners and open mouth of the victim.

'Cancel breakfast Mama,' he sighed, all thoughts of sizzling sausage, Russian or other nationality disappeared. 'This will take hours to sort out. No one can pass this way until we have investigated.' The sergeant ran thumbs around his waistband. His trousers grabbed and pinched as his stomach expanded to house his stress and he mourned the loss of his rain celebrations, his personal rain dance. The sergeant's leviathan body hardly left the ground anymore, but his feet could still tap, and his hips remembered with nostalgia the gyrations of his youth. He sent Mama Elephant on her way to alert Detective Inspector Jabulani Sibanda, the cause of all his woes past, present and no doubt, future. Mama Elephant hurried towards the police station, elbows tucked in to minimise the sway of her pendulous breasts, hands splayed for balance. Her legs windmilled at the knees whilst her double-shovel buttocks rippled in synchronicity with each foot fall. A few minutes later the tall, lithe detective jogged towards him with the ease and strength of a cantering zebra stallion.

Detective Sibanda crouched for a closer look at the dead man. A roll of thunder rumbled amongst the anvil shaped clouds. The devil's blacksmith was planishing his blades with enthusiasm.

'Run and get a tarp, Ncube.'

'Run, sir? I ...'

Sibanda looked up at Ncube's less than athletic bulk, his portly stomach, and jowls that disappeared in a concertina of double chins. 'You're right. On second thought, let's get PC Tshuma to bring some cover. Phone him.' He handed his phone to Ncube. 'He might get here before next week. For now, I want the crime scene left untouched.'

Sergeant Ncube wasn't built for speed, but he did know everyone in the village of Gubu, and the dead body in the alleyway next to Mama Elephant's diner was most likely a local. 'Do you recognise him, Ncube?'

'No, I've never seen that face before. How did he die?' Ncube, rather than look at the dead man or give further thought to the cause of death, concentrated on the detective's phone. Having barely come to grips with mobile technology, he handled the device as though it were a snake.

'Too young for natural causes, I would think.' DI Sibanda was scanning the body for an obvious cause of death. The victim lay on his side, his face stared upwards, his wide eyes reflected the passage of clouds skittering like goats fleeing the klaxon of a speeding truck. Ncube took a closer look, avoiding further engagement with the phone. The distaste of a corpse to prod or the intricacies of a smartphone to negotiate was a choice between a scorpion sting and the deadly bite of a six-eyed sand spider. He chose the body.

Sibanda leant and touched a patch of wet earth near the victim's head. He rubbed the grainy sand between his thumb and forefinger and brought the resultant mud to his nose, 'Blood. Where's that tarp?'

'I, er...' the sergeant shrugged.

The detective snatched the phone, glared at the sergeant, and made the call himself as the first drops of rain tapped on his broad shoulders.

Ncube again lamented bad timing. If the rain had come sooner, the dark patch would have been a puddle. With no cause for further investigation the body would have been sent for a post-mortem and become somebody else's problem. He could have been at the Police Station enjoying a few quiet moments with Miss Daisy as she received a well-deserved shower at the end of a bitter, dry and dusty winter. The old Land Rover needed a good wash. This pleasant thought dissolved with the rain. The detective was as wily as a jackal with a ferret's nose. He would have unearthed a clue whatever the weather - a wisp of grass pointing in the wrong direction, a bird flying north instead of south, a piece of clothing swinging from the branches of a tree. At least the body wasn't found in the middle of the bush with herds of wild creatures prowling to devour anyone who approached.

The rain pelted harder, 'Ncube, stop daydreaming, grab something from Mama Elephant's diner to cover the body.' Sibanda mantled over the corpse with his jacket, flaring it to cover as much of the victim as possible. When Ncube returned with a red gingham tablecloth, the rain, still yet to crescendo, bounced off the ground with such ferocity that each spaced droplet created its own exploding crater in the sandy earth.

PC Tshuma and the tarpaulin arrived in the nick of time, the tablecloth was sodden and dripping. Together, the three managed to fashion a low-slung tent, tying corners to convenient door handles, veranda posts and an electricity pole. The covering would protect the body and some of the surrounding area. Sibanda crouched and slithered under. Tshuma sheltered on a veranda, but Ncube stayed out in the rain, his face turned to the heavens to embrace each drop, each delicious sting as the rain hit. This is what everyone waited for, a blessing, a baptism of riches. The fields were ploughed, the seeds were in, the speculation done, and a bounteous season was predicted by all the old timers who herded cattle through the dusty roads of the village and congregated for a morning *imbodlela* of beer at the Blue Gnu cocktail bar. Every few seconds the flash on the detective's phone camera lit up the dark tent, the flare distracting Ncube from his bliss.

'Ncube,' the detective's voice bellowed above the hammering rain, 'get under here.'

'Are you sure, sir? There's not much room.'

'Now! Ncube.'

The sergeant crouched in the mud and entered on all fours. Poor light hampered his vision. Blow flies multiplied, enjoying the rising gases and sheltered environment where they hovered, miniature iridescent helicopters on the updraft of decay. Ncube batted them aside as he crawled further in. The space was intimate and stuffy. The canvas forced his head low over the corpse.

'Sergeant, pull the body towards you. I want to check something.'

'We shouldn't move him...' Ncube's voice trailed off. Experience taught him the detective manhandled corpses at will, any protestation would go unheeded.

'I want to examine the back of his skull. There's blood.'

'Couldn't he have banged his head as he fell?'

'Or maybe he's been bludgeoned which is why he toppled over in the first place.'

'Not another murder, sir.' Ncube gulped and stifled an unwanted expulsion of air.

'I don't know yet, that's what I want to find out. Pull the body over.'

Ncube's knees were stiff, the joints creaked and complained. The bones articulated more flesh than the average kneecap. Now the full force of the sergeant's bulk bore down on them. He edged the body towards him, trying not to embrace the poor man, trying to keep death at a distance. He failed, or rather his knees did. As he rolled, the victim rolled with him. Ncube ended up under the body. Escaping corpse gases gurgled and sighed as the weight of death bore down on the sergeant's delicate stomach.

'Help! Get this thing off me, I'm going to explode!'

Sibanda never commented on the obvious, 'one minute, Ncube and I'll be finished. Hold him still, stop jiggling.'

Ncube lay for what seemed like hours under the corpse as Sibanda examined the back of the victim's head. When Sibanda lifted the body with the ease of an Armenian weightlifter snatching the Olympic record, Ncube babbled gratitude even though the situation was engineered by his rescuer in the first place. 'My tongue does not have enough words to thank you, sir.'

'Then give it a rest. You won't be so grateful when you know we do have another murder on our hands.'

'What have you found?' he shouted above the din of rain on the canvas roof.

'There's a bullet hole in the back of the victim's head.'

The sergeant sighed and understood any suggestion of taking leave in the next couple of weeks would be impossible. He had planned a trip with his wives and children to his home village to plant a crop. His family would have to travel alone to prepare the lands. This rain could not be wasted.

'Why so little blood, sir? It's lucky you saw that drop.' Ncube suspected the observation had nothing to do with luck.

'The killer used a low calibre pistol at close range. The subject died instantly, no time to bleed. There's some odd skin flaring around the wound. The light is so bad in here, I can't make it out.'

'But there's no exit wound. Is that possible at close range?' The victim's face, planted on his, was untouched, no hideous hole in the face.

'Hollow nose bullet.'

'A hollow nose bullet?' Ncube narrowed his eyes. He could have kicked himself for asking a question instead of repeating the statement. He supposed the nose referred to the pointy bit at the end that pierced the target.

'You must have completed the firearm's course, Ncube, it's part of the sergeants' qualification.

'Er... yes, of course, sir, some time ago, but I'm as rusty as old man Gumede's plough on these matters.' In truth, Ncube had paid little attention to the details of the course. He had bribed the firearms instructor with a long string of smoked fish to sign his papers. He hated guns.

'A hollow nose expands inside the soft tissue; the slug causes maximum injury.

Ncube's face drained. He hated slugs and snails, pests that ate through his wives' vegetable patch. Did this bullet somehow contain a slimy creature in its empty nose that ended up in the body? 'What do the *iminenke* do in the body?'

'Snails? What have they got to do with anything? Has the sun got you? Concentrate Ncube, we have a murder on our hands, not a gardening lecture.'

'Sorry, sir, I wandered off for a moment Nomatter has problems with pests in the garden...' Ncube hoped he had disguised his ignorance. 'Carry on about the sunken nose. I am listening with all my ears.'

Sibanda threw his hands up in exasperation, 'the hollow nose mushrooms because it's designed to decrease penetration, prevent collateral damage and avoid a ricochet that could double back on the killer. Whoever killed this guy knew weapons.' He wanted to add: 'which is more than I can say about you,' but he reined in his sarcasm.

Ncube's stomach groaned, all this talk of mushrooms made him hungry. If the coming season promised, he would be eating *makowas*, giant mushrooms that sprang up overnight on antheaps during the rains, some almost as big as umbrellas. But *soft tissue, maximum injury* and *collateral damage,* whatever that meant, didn't mix well with mushrooms. His stomach groaned again. 'Yes, of course, hollow noses.'

Sibanda looked at him askance, 'Maybe you know it as a Dum-dum?'

Ncube's tongue clicked in ridicule, 'All bullets are dumb sir. Has this one been loaded with a double dose of foolishness?'

'Ncube, have you eaten your own brains for breakfast?'

Too late, the sergeant realised he'd dropped himself in a hole again. *When would he ever learn to keep his guard up around the detective?* 'A joke, sir.' He forced a laugh. Suko, his third wife had come up with the strategy. 'Pretend you are playful if you don't understand.'

'Comedy doesn't suit you,' Sibanda snapped, 'your timing's way off. The reason they're called Dum-dums is after the Dum Dum arsenal near Calcutta. The bullet was developed by the British Indian Army.'

'To keep the poor population under control, I suppose.'

'No, to better kill large game. They're no good in war or for crowd control. In conflict and riots, you want mayhem, multiple injuries, and suffering soldiers. The enemy wants you to tie up personnel carrying the wounded to field stations. Hollow noses are the preferred bullet of hunters and murderers because they kill on impact, hit the target, and cause no ricochet.'

Sibanda felt around in the dead man's clothing as he spoke. He found a small magnifying glass that slid in and out of a black casing. He pocketed the device.

'We've got an anonymous victim, Ncube. You got close to his face. Are you sure you don't recognise him? He's of mixed race.'

Ncube had tried to avoid the dead man's piercing, unblinking stare, but with the body on top of him and noses almost touching, he had had a close view. 'No one I recognise, sir. He must be a visitor, not from around here. Very dark skin and straight hair for a local man of colour. I don't think he even comes from Zimbabwe. In fact...'

Sibanda looked up, 'What is it Ncube?'

'Nothing, er... nothing at all.' He'd dropped himself in it again. Why had he opened his mouth? Now the questions would begin. He feigned his practised look of understanding, a tight mouth and narrowed eyes, but the detective didn't give up.

'Ncube, what have you noticed?'

'His eyes,' he offered, 'they seem too light, streaked with green, like slime on churned up mud and yet his skin is so dark, and his nose...'

Sibanda manoeuvred in the tight space to get a better look at the victim's face. The eyes, still wide, had clouded over with the onset of rigor mortis. Ncube was right, they were unusual and now, up close, the face looked too perfect, almost without pores. What was he missing? Where had this man come from? Maybe West Africa or somewhere to the far north-east of the continent. The victim was cold and waxy to the touch, but even given the changes wrought by death, the texture of the skin didn't feel normal.

'Touch him, Ncube,' the detective said, rubbing his fingers down the sides of the body's nose and across his cheeks. 'Is he wearing make-up?' He spat on his fingers and began to rub the skin

Ncube drew back, 'sir, this man's been murdered. I don't think you should spit on him.'

'The rain's already done that.' The detective grabbed Ncube's hand and pressed his fingers onto the dead man's skin, dragging them up and down. 'That's not skin, is it?'

The sergeant snatched his hand back as though burnt, '*Hau*! This thing is not human, get it away from me.' Ncube started to scrabble out of the tented space. 'We cannot stay in here sir. This creature has been sent from the spirit world.

Sibanda grabbed Ncube's fleeing shirt and hauled him back into the tent. 'This man is as human as you are, but he's gone to great lengths to disguise his identity.

Ncube shook. He didn't believe Sibanda. The corpse was a creature, maybe an alien from outer space come down to inhabit some poor soul's body. 'Why?' he croaked.

'Not sure, but I think we're about to find out. Sibanda began to unbutton the neck of the victim's shirt. Halfway down the chest, the man's skin turned from black to coffee. Having found the seam where pale olive met black, the detective began to roll the skin. He worked upwards until the black covering over the face was unpeeled and underneath lay a man with features that didn't belong to Africa.

'A mask, Ncube, a sophisticated silicone mask. Why did this man feel the need to cover his tracks?'

There was no reply from Sergeant Ncube. He'd passed out when the peeling skin reached the nostrils.

Chapter 2

The rain found its stride, pummelling down, spear-hard, lashing everything in its path. Sibanda and Tshuma battled to manoeuvre the sergeant out of the makeshift tent and over to the veranda where he now sat, propped against the wall, soaked to the skin. Ncube was drinking a bottle of his favourite orange fizz. Sibanda had dispatched Tshuma to Barghees to buy it, knowing a whiff of the liquid would get the sergeant back on his feet.

'Sorry, sir,' Ncube apologised as he gathered himself, 'but that skin stripping was a little too close to the last murders. It brought back memories.'

'This isn't skin, Ncube, it's a clever mask.' Sibanda rubbed the silicone between his fingers. 'So perfect, fitting like the casing on boerewors and turning a white man black.'

'I didn't know such a disguise was possible.' Ncube wished the detective hadn't mentioned boerewors, the delicious spicy, traditional sausage would have gone down a treat, might have settled his stomach.

'These kinds of masks are developed by the movie industry, Ncube, to create those ghosts and ghouls you are so in awe of. Criminals got wind of the technology early on. The world outside Zimbabwe is plastered wall to wall with surveillance cameras. The old-fashioned method of disguise, a balaclava or a stocking over the head, flags a crime about to be committed. In a silicone mask, a felon can be an ordinary citizen going about his business, never to be recognised in a line-up.'

'But why would an almost white man come to Gubu disguised as a black man?'

'If we knew that, we'd know why he was murdered.' Sibanda massaged the tension building in his jaw. 'These custom-built masks aren't cheap. Our victim has money, look at his clothes. He was either running from someone and chose to hide in Gubu, the most unlikely and deserted of backwaters...or he was planning a crime.'

'What do you think, sir?'

Sibanda stared into the pounding rainstorm, not flinching as lightning tore across the ominous sky. He rubbed the old wound in his thigh. It stabbed every now and again, often in wet weather and always in a thunderstorm. His fingers strayed to the object found in the pocket of the dead man. The detective had theories, but the less Ncube knew, the better for him.

'No idea, Ncube.'

The sergeant was silenced by the startling admission. The detective was usually one step ahead like an impala catching hyena breath on the curl of a breeze. The ancients whispered solutions to him. He always understood what to do. Had the ancestral spirits abandoned him? Ncube didn't have much longer to dwell on his thoughts as little Shalotte Ndebele came skipping down the laneway from her mother's diner, a large plastic bag across her head and shoulders, barefoot and dancing through the puddles like a water sprite, laughing as though she'd never set eyes on standing water before. PC Tshuma stopped her before the roped off area then led her to Sergeant Ncube. Her face shuttered and her natural shyness descended as the rain began to soften.

'What is it Shalotte?' the sergeant asked in a child friendly voice.

'Mama said I should give you this. She found it near the bins at the back. Maybe it belonged to that man under the tent.' She handed him a backpack.

'Thank you, *mntanami*, and thank your mother too.' He watched as the young child skipped back up the alleyway, splashing and stamping in the muddy pools. He smiled at the carefree joys of youth that had once been his.

'Sir,' he disturbed the still and silent detective, 'Mama Elephant found this behind the diner. It could belong to the victim, but it's been picked through.'

'A mugging, Ncube?'

'Looks like it, sir. Someone wanted the bag and our man resisted.'

'Yes, open and shut case, now we have to find the thief.'

Ncube looked again at the detective. *Open and shut case* sounded far too much like Chief Inspector Stalin Mfumu, the officer-in-charge at Gubu Police Station, aka Cold War who was obsessed with wrapping up every case in a hurry. Had it rubbed off on Detective Sibanda? Surely not. This man walked on hot coals to solve crimes, didn't care about treading on political toes and took far too many risks to be a safe companion. And yet he stared into the far distance, to the very end of Mother Earth's outstretched fingertips, agreeing this murder might be a mugging gone wrong. The detective must be sick. He would talk with Blessing, his senior wife. She would know what troubled him and would have a bottle of healing *muthi* to get the detective back to his familiar, difficult, bad tempered and worrying self.

'Let's get on our way, Ncube. Go home, get dried off and change. I'll head to the station. Tshuma can stay with the body.'

'What's in the backpack, sir?

'The usual: a change of underwear, a spare shirt, some curios. Anything valuable must have been stolen. Maybe when you get to the station have a look under Miss Daisy's bonnet. With all this rain, she might have got water in her... her...'

'Injectors, sir?'

That's it... injectors. Spend some time checking her out.'

That last conversation nagged Ncube as he made his way home. His wives fussed but he remained oblivious to them, worried instead about the detective. To have suggested he work on Miss Daisy was as far-fetched as a lion becoming vegetarian or a hyena swearing off bones. Sibanda was usually rude and dismissive about the old Land Rover.

'Lovely rain, so precious and valuable.' Suko, his third wife, greeted him with a wide smile. She offered him a dry towel and set off to attend to a squealing baby.

'You seem distracted, my dear. What is wrong?' Blessing, his first wife, possessed second sight. Nothing could be kept from her.

'It's detective Sibanda, he's sick.'

'Is it the flu?'

'No, not any sickness of the body. There is trouble in his head.'

'Never, not detective Sibanda. His strong spirit is blessed by the ancients.

Ncube should have known he wouldn't be believed. Detective Sibanda cast a spell over any woman whose eyes fell on his chiselled features and tall athletic frame. His own wives were not immune. 'He is suffering from an outbreak of niceness.'

Blessing raised her eyebrows which Ncube could never argue with. They were thick, shapely and with the slightest movement, could send detailed messages on all sorts of matters. No one argued with Blessing's eyebrows.

'I know, he's always nice. Perhaps it's me that's sick.' Ncube sighed.

'Your stomach again, no doubt. Have you been taking the drops?

'Always, dear wife. I never forget.'

Sergeant Ncube made his way back to work. He left the detective's worrying behaviour behind him. The downpour lifted his spirits and quenched his winter restlessness. Rain meant food. He rubbed his stomach and smiled at the thought of a morning with Miss Daisy.

Sibanda examined the backpack, flicking his eyes up to his office window from time to time hoping to catch sight of a bird in the frame. Spotting birds helped him think. Checking the pin feathers, the primaries, the secondaries, the beak adaptation, searching his brain for feeding and breeding habits, visualising nesting sites and nest architecture created a welcome distraction from focusing on depravity, and crime. His avian ramblings helped his detective's brain to focus. Right now, he sighted a red-backed shrike, the butcher bird who impaled its prey, skulking in a thorn bush on the edge of the station yard. Through the leaves, he could make out a handsome grey forehead and russet back. This specimen had flown in from as far away as northern Europe. Inter tropical migrants arrived ahead of the rains, tweeting the onset of weather fronts, chasing food, adding a whole new cluster of population groups to keep watch for. The detective liked to keep a date record of the first arrivals of the year. This murder couldn't have come at a worse time for a dedicated birder.

Sibanda unzipped the backpack's front pocket and pulled out a Congolese passport in the name of Laurent Kasongo. The photo showed the man in his mask and disguised. The passport appeared to be a fake, but it was an open secret that African passports changed hands for money. Civil servants everywhere were underpaid. Home Affairs officials from Abuja to Ouagadougou weren't immune.

'So, Laurent Kasongo, who are you and what have you been up to? Why are you in Zimbabwe? And who were you running from?'

Sibanda knew the murder was an execution. A gunshot to the back of the head, to that exact spot where the neck joined the skull and the brain stem was at its most exposed, suggested familiarity with this age-old method of killing. The victim fell onto his knees hence the dirt on the trousers. His killer turned him over after accessing his backpack. Laurent Kasongo was hunted and targeted. Had a professional assassin been paid to do the job? This murder was stamped with the hallmarks of a hit man. What did the victim do to bring down the wrath of someone wealthy enough to hire a gun? Sibanda sorted through the rest of the backpack. In front of him lay a wallet with seven hundred dollars and a handful of bond notes, Zimbabwe's latest attempt to create its own currency. No one trusted the stability of the new money. The US dollar was still king. He rummaged further. Down the side of the bag, he discovered a folded sheet of newspaper, a page ripped from a recent Bulawayo Chronicle. Sibanda put it aside to read later.

Most of the backpack was taken up by a stone sculpture wrapped in clothes. He placed the carving on his desk. Now that the bag lay empty, he could see another item had been removed, maybe stolen at the time of the murder. The lining showed an indent where a hard-edged object had frayed the fabric. The damage wasn't from the sculpture, which had been well wrapped, and was rounded and polished with sensuous curves and no sharp points. Was this man shot because he carried something desirable? Money wasn't the killer's target. This murder was no mugging gone wrong, no opportunistic theft. Seven hundred dollars was a fortune in Gubu, more than most villagers would see in a year and yet it wasn't stolen. The sculpture was not shabby either, not the usual airport art, the likes of soapstone elephants turned out by the hundreds for tourists smitten with their safari, or the ever-popular sinuous mother and child arrangements of hollow ellipses with heads. This sculpture had style. Sibanda looked for a signature.

'*Qoki, qoki*,' Sergeant Ncube put his head around the door, mimicking the sound of a knocking knuckle with the glottal Ndebele click, 'you called me, sir?'

Sibanda looked up. 'No.'

'Oh, I thought I heard you shout.'

'Voices in your head. What do you want, Ncube, have you come to tell me a joke?'

Ncube didn't get upset, even though everyone knew Sibanda heard voices in the head, not him. The detective's sarcasm was back, a heartening sign of recovery, 'Checking to see if you've come up with news on our victim. Is that his passport?'

'A Congolese fake, in the name of Laurent Kasongo.'

'Is he from the Democratic Republic of Congo? Or The Republic of the Congo?

'He's from the DRC.'

'Do you want me to check up on the real Kasongo, see if he exists? Could be a lead.'

Sibanda fingered the metal object he had taken from the victim's pocket. He turned it over and over. The lens told him a story and he wouldn't involve his sergeant in the tale, 'I doubt we'll get satisfactory communications with Kinshasa, but you can try. How is the old Land Rover?'

'Miss Daisy?' The sergeant double-checked the query. Sibanda nodded and Ncube's words on his favourite subject ran like free-flowing water, almost lyrical as he itemised each detail of the vintage lady's parts, what he had fixed or replaced. Sibanda appeared interested but blocked his ears to Ncube's eulogy, all the while staring out of the window, considering the treacherous implications of the murder in Mama Elephant's alleyway.

When Ncube stopped to take a breath, Sibanda encouraged his departure, 'Finding the original Kasongo could be important, Ncube. Get to it! ' Sibanda tossed the fake passport over the desk.

Ncube left the office more confused than ever. Why was the detective taking an interest in Miss Daisy? He never had a good word to say about her. The sergeant scratched his head, convinced the detective was straying from the connections to his forebears.

CHAPTER 3

Sibanda sat for a few minutes, staring through the window for another bird to help focus his attention, but the red-backed shrike had flown away. The area appeared devoid of life. The downpour created puddles elsewhere for the birds to bathe. The station yard, despite the heavy rain, remained as hard as rocks. Noah's flood wouldn't penetrate that patch of baked earth. He picked up the sculpture and turned it over. The carving was in good condition apart from a few nibbles around the base. A sense of lightness and movement radiated from the stone. Depicted was a dancing lady, a comely woman, with a baby strapped to her back, frolicking as though her life was a party. Stubby hands flung in the air, feet kicking. The figurine brought a rare smile. The baby lay swaddled in a polished cocoon. The artist highlighted the infant, allowing the colourful striations of the stone – pomegranate, avocado, mulberry and lemon – to suggest the movement and rhythm of the mother. The dancer's dress stippled in places, adding pleasing texture and fold. 'Anonymous Ecstasy', would be an apt title, he thought, observing the merest suggestion of a nose, the shallow eyes, and the wide smile that stretched like a statement of joy across the flat and otherwise featureless face.

'Now, what have you got to dance about, Mama? What in this hard, forgotten landscape has brought you such delight?' Sibanda placed her on the corner of his desk and watched for a moment as she gambolled in the morning light. 'Did you bring a smile to Laurent Kasongo's face? Is that why he purchased you? And where did you come from?' If he could pinpoint the travels of this lady, she might shed light on Kasongo and even the murderer. Mama Ecstasy said nothing. The dancing lady must have begun her life in Zimbabwe, the sole country on the continent to have deposits of stone suitable for serious sculpture, genuine art. It was a start.

Sibanda took the magnifying glass from his pocket and gave it the name he'd been repressing - a jeweller's loupe, the indispensable trade tool of every diamond dealer worth his salt. 'Why did you carry a loupe, Laurent?' he spoke to the deserted office, 'What have you been up to?' He slid the glass from between metal arms and used its optic accuracy to take a closer look at scratch marks he detected on the planted foot of Mama Ecstasy. The morning's pewter light filtered through thunder clouds and played with her toes. Sibanda's mind strayed to Zimbabwe's involvement with the Congo. Politicians lured by the country's diamond riches rushed troops to assist in an internal war without so much as a nod to parliamentary approval. The political elite had an eye to the main chance.

Sibanda would never have seen the marks without the loupe clamped into his eye socket. Someone had tried to erase them, scratched over them. The signature ran deep, chiselled by an artist who wanted his work recognised for eternity. Sibanda spat on the roughened area. His saliva seeped into the grooves confirming the initials T. M. He was lucky he knew how to use a loupe, a skill which required practise. Nottingham Police Academy had sent him on attachment to various fraud squads. The art mob were interesting although he doubted he would ever tell a Klimt from a Baines. Even if he could, the forgers were great masters themselves. The skill lay not in detecting fake brush strokes but in the minutiae of dealer's stamps or whether a tint correlated to the artist's unique recipe and if the canvas was contemporaneous. Investigation occurred under a microscope or by chemical analysis. He learned nothing. The gemstone experts were different, they'd opened his eyes. Fraud in the diamond trade was rife.

Belgium, he learnt, was the centre of the world diamond dealings, the ex-colonial master of the DRC. Belgium was one of Europe's tadpole countries, small, quiet with the occasional wriggle from the European parliament. That's how the diamond dealers liked it, a gelatinous blob avoiding the radar. The ancient, secretive city of Antwerp lay at the heart of the trade, keeping to old ways established over the centuries - a wink, a nod and a wad of cash being the preferred transaction. With the recent discovery of diamonds in Zimbabwe, Sibanda was both interested and shocked to learn how poorly the trade was regulated, how open it was to money laundering and tax evasion. The cases being investigated by the UK Diamond Squad made Zimbabwe's commercial corruption look like kids cheating at marbles.

'Billions of dollars each year come out of the ground only to disappear back into the murky underworld.

Some stones never see the light of day.' Damien Bartle, the officer he'd been attached to, had given him an eye-opening take on the trade. 'Diamonds carry convertible wealth in an indestructible stone. Small enough to fit in a hand, better than cash, easier to smuggle, diamonds have a ready market, yet avoid a paper trail. They don't rot, can't burn, and survive inflation. They're a fraud cop's nightmare.'

'But you're on to the dealers. You've got massive resources. The big guys can be trailed, their bank accounts monitored,' Sibanda's rookie naivete showed.

'Don't get me started on the banks,' Bartle clamped his hand to his forehead in despair, 'many of them are aware the large deposits in their vaults are dodgy, but they don't delve too deep. Do you think they care?'

'Don't they?' A young Sibanda still believed Europe held itself to the highest standards, and thought only Africa embraced corruption.

'Bankers are all about the bottom line and to hell with the morality of the money. But God help the poor punter who misjudges his overdraft. You're from Africa, Jabu, did you know half a million people died in Angola because of war fuelled by illegal diamond deals? Sierra Leone, Congo are the same. The continent's a mess and all that mess ends up in Belgium. Antwerp is the real centre for ethnic cleansing and the banks are accessories. They've all got blood on their hands.'

'Conflict diamonds?'

'Too right,' Bartle threw a pile of papers onto his desk, 'and whatever you do with your career make sure you never get assigned to the Diamond Squad, it's a minefield. You'll end up bitter and disillusioned.

'And I thought this posting was a cosy number,' Sibanda enjoyed his time with the squad which was less confrontational than domestic violence calls on the streets of Nottingham.

'No cushy number, trust me. We're investigated regularly after that fiasco with the Diamond Squad in Belgium. None of us sleep at night. Here, this case makes shocking reading.' He threw Sibanda a file, 'and then go talk to Cartwright over there. He'll fill you in on cut, clarity, and carats. You need to be able to use a loupe and recognise a real diamond, although distinguishing the genuine article from synthetics these days is nigh impossible without hi-tech equipment.'

'Sir, are you busy?' Ncube popped his head around the door, rousing Sibanda from his memories. He placed the statue back on his desk, having taken a photo of the dancing lady and her marks. 'What have you got, Ncube?'

'Nothing from The DRC yet, PC Khumalo is still trying to make contact. We don't seem to have any numbers for Kinshasa and nor does Harare Central. Laurent Kasongo entered Zimbabwe from Zambia through the Livingstone Border Post. Look at the entry stamp in his passport.' Sibanda took the passport,

'When did he arrive?'

'Five days ago, on the nineteenth.'

'Any other entry visas?'

'Some to Malawi, Tanzania, Angola and Kenya. He's even got one from Ethiopia.'

'Are they real?'

'I can't say, sir. Trouble contacting those countries as well...' Sergeant Ncube shuffled uncomfortably. 'Kasongo entered Zambia on the fifteenth. He must have flown into Lusaka, made his way by road to the

Border Post at Livingstone and through to Victoria Falls.'

'Where has Laurent been for the last five days?'

'It doesn't say in his passport, sir.'

Sibanda stared at his sergeant and wondered if it was worth persisting with someone so unworldly. The sergeant would be of no use on this case. He didn't want him sticking his nose in the wrong places for his own good. 'They don't stamp passports in hotels, Ncube,' he snapped.

'Of course not, sir, ki ki ki,' Ncube chortled, hoping he'd camouflaged his mistake. Suko's advice was proving to be a godsend.

'From now on, Ncube, be warned. Keep that pathetic sense of humour to yourself,' Sibanda slammed the door as he left his office.

The sergeant was more comforted by this retort than might be imagined. The detective was snapping like a crocodile with a cavity. Perhaps he was out of sorts with the thought of all the form filling involved in the murder of a foreigner. His hatred of paperwork was well known. This victim died by gunshot and there hadn't been a gun crime in Gubu for some years unless you counted the poacher murdered with the ancient muzzle loader. Maybe the thought of a weapon on the loose caused the detective's concern.

Sibanda reached the reception area and found PC Khumalo documenting a complaint. Old man Moyo's cattle had been harried by old man Ndebele's dogs. One of the cows had aborted, a huge loss to the traditional herder who loved those *izinkomo* more than his wife and children. His herd were his life and at 83, poor as a fire without a pot, thin as a whipping stick and battling to breathe, his humble herd of five beasts kept him alive. PC Khumalo looked from her meticulous form filling into the impossibly handsome face of the detective, 'Can I help, sir?' She smiled at the first pleasing thing she'd seen all day.

'Log this statue in as evidence.' He handed her Mama Ecstasy. 'Cold War in?'

She nodded towards the door of Chief Superintendent Stalin Mfumu. 'He is. But be careful, he's not in the best of moods. His application for a transfer has been turned down again.'

Sibanda tilted his head towards Zanele Khumalo as if to ask how she knew this.

'No river runs silently, sir, not even the deep and treacherous ones.' She shrugged and returned to her forms. You couldn't blink in Gubu Police Station without the whole world knowing.

The detective knocked on the OIC's door and entered. There was nothing cold about the war he and Chief Inspector Stalin Mfumu waged. The barely disguised hostility between them was an open secret. The difference in their respective approaches to policing was as wide as the Limpopo in flood. Mfumu favoured a quick, clean, and orderly solution to crimes. If the wrong man got convicted, it mattered little provided the paperwork was completed and filed in a prompt and tidy fashion. Sibanda sought the truth and if the pursuit of it became messy and took time, he didn't care.

Mfumu looked up from his desk and scowled. Another plague, his nemesis, Detective Inspector Sibanda, come to spread dung on his face as threatened in Malachi 2:3. The Bible carried the most appropriate passages to deal with moments like these.

'What do you want, Detective?'

Sibanda downplayed the murder and kept the briefing minimal, 'A fatal mugging outside Mama Elephant's diner last night. A man killed carrying a fake passport. He came in through the Vic Falls border post. I'm heading up there to investigate with immigration to see if they remember him, find out who he is.'

'A mugging? Don't involve Chanza, he has more important matters to attend to,' Mfumu kept his bungling nephew away from Sibanda. The man might taint his godliness.

'I'll take Sergeant Ncube.'

'And you can't have the Santana,' Mfumu said, referring to the station's most reliable vehicle.

'We'll use the Land Rover.'

'There's no money for food and accommodation.'

'We'll be away a day. Sergeant Ncube's wives will keep us well provisioned.'

Mfumu frowned at the plural. The Bible did not sanction multiple marriages. Didn't St Paul suggest that a priest should have only one wife? The saint didn't mention laymen, but it was understood they should follow the advice. The thrice married sergeant was the perfect companion for the devil himself – Detective Inspector Jabulani Sibanda. He cast around for further obstacles to Sibanda's journey. Pointless; the man could hurdle high hedges. One day he would find some way to trip him up and there would be no God for the detective to lean on, to make his path straight as Proverbs exhorted, he would see to that. But not before Sibanda solved this latest death. A few words of praise attached to the letter rejecting his transfer pointed out that Gubu station appeared amongst the most efficient in the region and as soon as a posting became available, Mfumu would be considered. 'Make sure this mugging murder is wrapped up by the end of this quarter. The details must be included in my report.' He buttoned up the pocket of his stiffly ironed shirt and patted it flat for good measure, a signal for Sibanda to leave.

In reception, PC Khumalo completed the paperwork on Ndebele's cow and shoved the statue under the counter. She'd log it later. No-one else was in the waiting room. Crime and minor complaints fell off when the rains came. Everyone busied themselves planting or planning, scheming how to inveigle Confidence Dube, the sole man in the village with a tractor, to plough their lands for barter. Most sharpened the old hoes that had done many years' service. Women liked a keen edged *ikhuba*. It made hoeing of the still-hard clods less back-breaking. A good husband sat and honed the implements, watching from the shade of his veranda, full of beer and satisfaction as his wife turned the earth and planted the crops. Rain brought joy for many.

'Zee, I need your help.' Sibanda passed by reception again, 'Our murder victim was in disguise. Probably doesn't even come from the DRC. Get some copies of this passport photo and enlarge them. Door knock around the village, see if anyone recognises him.'

'There's a photocopier at Barghees, but he charges like a King's impi.'

Sibanda rummaged in his pocket and produced a handful of bond notes. 'That should be enough. Find out if Kasongo stayed in the village.'

'Couldn't this have been a random attack?'

'We still have to identify him. His family have the right to know he's dead. See if you can winkle Detective Chanza from Mfumu's grip. You've a lot of ground to cover, you'll need him. Sergeant Ncube's coming with me.'

Sibanda left reception before PC Khumalo could ask more questions.

Chapter 4

'Caro, are you still up there? What's keeping you?

'Enough dust to carpet the Kalahari,' she coughed, 'and an old trunk wedged under the eaves.' Her voice faded and wheezed with each tug on the handle.

Caroline's husband, Rupert, stuck his head into the loft space and frowned, 'Leave it, we've done enough. This old dump might collapse if you move the trunk. It's been jammed up there for years.

'But it's stunning,' she fingered the banding and the lock, silver and probably worth more than the house.' Her laughter underlined an apology. Rupert had put great store on the value of her inheritance. She tugged harder. The trunk slid a few centimetres.

Rupert retreated down the ladder and waited for disaster. His wife never listened. *Let her put her back out.* He would do nothing more in this ruin. It had been a huge and costly mistake to come to Zimbabwe, to Bulawayo, of all places, a mouldering backwater. On the upside, only one of his London creditors knew he was here which offered some respite, at least, from the constant dunning. He'd been relieved at the thought of money coming in, joked with Caroline that she was an heiress blessed with the unexpected windfall of a house, but if he'd known this ramshackle shanty was the outcome of that lawyer's letter, he'd have saved the long-haul airfares and gone skiing instead.

'Come down, darling,' he yawned, 'you've done enough. Let's get back to the hotel.'

'You go, Rupe,' Caroline shouted from the attic, 'didn't you say you had some business connections to catch up with. You can pick me up in a couple of hours. I'll phone.'

Walking out to the hired car, Rupert Templeton flicked through his phone looking for the number to contact. Somehow, Bilal Haddad had got wind of this trip to Zimbabwe and asked for a 'favour'. He wondered how the bastard had become so enmeshed in his life. Bilal started as a more than useful business associate until everything went pear-shaped. The ancient firm of Templeton Investments began to fly after their link up. Word was Rupert Templeton had the touch, inherited his father's and grandfather's skills and the company had landed in safe hands. Bilal seemed the broker from Heaven. Every new start-up he brought to the table looked gilt-edged and risk free. Where did it all go wrong and how come the business now teetered on the point of bankruptcy?

Haddad's hands, he learned, were in every dodgy deal around the London money market. He seemed to have siblings and cousins all over the world with access to banks that never asked too many questions. How had he not seen the obvious? The answer, two words: fear and greed. Two words that ruled the money markets and the fund managers who manipulated them. The start-ups he embraced whilst others rejected, made him look like a hero. Other hedge funds cursed their caution, but then his over-reliance and trust in Bilal turned rotten. Deals started to fail, become suspect. The company's funds were plummeting. The bastard had sucked him in with a few sweet plumbs and now it appeared Templeton Investments was funding fraud and criminal dealings. When Rupert tried to pull out, Bilal threatened and became ugly. The man had originally told him his commissions weren't urgent. 'Hang onto them for a while Rupe,' he urged, 'I'm not short. You can put the money to good use whilst you're building your portfolios.' A sneaky move because as the firm began to fail, retaining those commissions helped. He now had men the likes of Bilal Haddad threatening him to pay up, or else. He found himself in the middle of a B movie - in debt to gangsters and terrified for his life. If his mother ever found out the ancient and well revered firm of Templeton Investments was about to collapse, sending seismic shock waves through the financial world, she'd have his guts for more than garters. Rupert could feel the steel grey eyes of Bobo Hudson-Templeton boring into the back of his neck. He shuddered and scrutinised his phone.

What was that name? Another Lebanese cousin, no doubt. Getting Haddad off his back was his priority. 'Collect a small parcel,' the broker insisted, 'no drugs, I promise. Bring it back and we can talk, get over this little...contretemps.' And then he'd placed his hands on Rupert's shoulders and squeezed hard to underline his strength, hard enough to leave bruises. Right now, Rupert Templeton couldn't sleep easily in his own bed. He had listened for every footfall outside his London home, made sure he had a companion on entering the underground car park, flinched at an exhaust backfiring, had even taken to carrying a weapon, his grandfather's old 9 mm from the war. Rupert had shot it a couple of times; the weapon still worked. He'd scrabbled around the family attic looking for it when Haddad started his nonsense. The thug delivered veiled warnings with a lizard like smile and a malevolent glint in those ridiculous hang dog eyes. Bilal was connected to the Lebanese Mafia and if there existed one mob you didn't cross, it was the Lebanese.

Caro screeched. The blood-curdling yell of terror highlighted thoughts of the Lebanese gangs and their legendary reprisals. Rupert ran into the crumbling house, took the stairs two at a time and reached the attic.

'Are you okay?'

Caroline had retreated to the far corner, 'I'm fine now, I got a shock that's all.' She had gathered herself but was still shaking. 'I moved the trunk and there's a snake behind it.' Caro pointed to a small snake hugging the sloping eaves and trying to stay far away from danger.

'Is it poisonous?' Rupert, a city dweller since birth, was wary of insects let alone an African snake.

'How would I know?' Calm now, the creature didn't appear to be a threat. Caroline was fascinated. She'd never seen a snake before except in a zoo, a huge coiling rope, not this slender worm-like creature with pretty scales and black diamond markings.

'Because' he accused, 'you're the African.' The words fell between them, icy shards tumbling into a chasm. Caroline stared at her husband and then looked back to the motionless snake curled and minimising itself in the corner. She didn't answer. She had her own questions, had been churning them over since they'd arrived.

'He's rather handsome, don't you think, all those diamonds running up his back?' she defused the subject.

'It's a snake Caro, and the only good snake is a dead one, diamonds or no diamonds.'

'I wonder what sort.'

'Who cares? Don't move or do anything stupid. I'll call the neighbours.'

Caroline had no intention of moving. The snake remained in one corner, she in the other and the situation appeared under control. Or was it? The snake might no longer be a worry, but her current situation puzzled her. Why had she inherited this cobweb infested cottage in Bulawayo and who was Isiah Jacobs who'd left it to her? He must have been a relative, they shared a surname, but how distant? No one in her family had ever spoken of Africa, ever visited, or mentioned any connection. She ran her fingers through tangled hair, black as night and thick as weed and considered her olive skin and coal black eyes and wished her parents were still alive. They would have known something. Did she have African blood running in her veins? Oh, how she hoped she did. Since setting foot on the tarmac at Bulawayo airport, Caroline felt a pull, a sense of belonging, a tug in the soles of her feet, a lightness of being as though she'd sprouted wings. The trunk, before she discovered the snake, offered a glimpse of dusty old papers and books. Maybe the answer nestled in there. She was determined to find out.

'I've brought Godwishes, darling,' Rupert shouted up, 'he's the odd job man from next door.' A young man crept up into the loft space. Caroline was taken back by his appearance. A strong, wiry looking young man popped up, dressed like an urchin. His upper lip was split, eaten away, festering as high as his nose. Well brought up, her face remained unchanged. Poor lad, she thought. When Godwishes turned his attention to the snake in the corner, she mouthed to Rupert, *leprosy?* Rupert shrugged in ignorance. The gardener carried a spade with a lethal looking edge.

'Are you going to kill it?' she asked.

'Mama?' the urchin turned towards her. She had spoken to him.

'The snake, are you going to kill it?'

Godwishes stared at her blankly. He could speak English even though he had not gone to school growing up. When his parents were alive there was never money for education. But no one ever spoke to him. He was ignored, invisible, most likely because of his looks he supposed. As an orphan, he was grateful to have been taken in by his uncle, an important man, part of the Government. Godwishes now worked as his uncle's gardener for food, a bed and the occasional dollar thrown in his direction. Sometimes, he filled in the potholes on the road outside. The driver of the odd passing car threw him a few coins. In the evening, he excavated the potholes again ready for the next day of filling them in. He knew his appearance helped with the begging. Life was simple in a leaking hut at the bottom of the garden and now a simple choice lay in front of him. With one slicing blow he decapitated the snake, shovelled the still wriggling body onto the spade and backed towards the ladder.

'What's it called?' Caroline asked, shocked at the violence of a life snuffed, even a terrifying one. The snake had seemed more frightened of her and now she had caused its death.

'Its name?' she repeated loudly and slowly as though Godwishes was deaf or stupid. 'I'm Caroline.' She hit her chest, 'this is Rupert,' she pointed to her husband. 'What is the name of the snake?' Godwishes, his feet already several rungs down the ladder looked up at the loud, crazy woman,

'*Inhlangwana*,' he said, 'the night adder,' and smiled through teeth with no covering. Caroline thought the deformity made him look like a chipmunk, a rather cute one. *Did they have chipmunks in Africa?*

'*Inhlangwana*,' she repeated, trying hard to replicate the Welsh-like lisp of the 'hla' sound.

'Caro, do you still want to stay on your own up there?' Rupert headed back down the ladder.

'I'll be fine. There's no other junk up here for anything to hide behind. I'll finish and give you a call. Do what you have to.'

Caroline tried to manhandle the trunk for a while and then gave up. She would need someone to help her pull it from under the eaves so she could open the lid and examine the contents. She climbed down the ladder, out of the attic and headed next door. She had seen something alive and life affirming in the snake killer, Godwishes. How charming to have a name with such meaning and pathos. European names were a collective of sounds, some pleasing, some not, some a ridiculous concoction of empty, hollow syllables. No one knew the meanings anymore. Godwishes attracted her despite his affliction. His eyes were large, bright and full of intelligence.

Next door, she encountered a guard hut, housing an armed guard. Seated, bored and unobservant, his weapon leant against the wall of little more than a tall dog kennel built of overlapping wooden slats.

'I'm looking for Godwishes,' she said.

The guard, seeing no threat to security, took his clipboard and noted her name and time of arrival. He waved towards an old brick hut at the lower end of the garden.

'Thank you.' Caroline picked her way down a crazy paved path to a wooden door. Most of the wood had rotted. The door consisted of more holes than door with rags and old paper stuffed in the gaps.

'Godwishes,' she called out.

The door swung open. The young man appeared. 'Another snake, Madam?' he asked.

'No,' she smiled, 'but I could do with a hand to shift that trunk if you've got time.'

When Rupert drove away from the red brick, overgrown colonial wreck he thought about Caroline's words, *do what you have to.* He lived in constant dread of the phone call he had to make and kept putting it off. He'd located the name and number while Godwishes executed the snake - Madani Haddad. Whatever Bilal and Madani Haddad were up to, he was about to get sucked into their murky world.

At the Holiday Inn, Rupert poured himself a stiff whisky from the mini bar and sculled it in one swallow. Years ago, his mother introduced him to 'scotch' as she called it, pronouncing it more like 'scartch' than anything that might be associated with Scotland. Bobo Hudson-Templeton was American. Rupert dialled the number on his phone and waited. His hand trembled. He wasn't cut out for skulduggery.

'Hello.'

'Madani Haddad?'

'Yes.' The voice sounded curt, clipped, accented and unhelpful.

'I'm a friend of Balil.'

'Yes,' he snapped in a tone overlaid with 'and what's that got to do with me?'

Rupert floundered, 'er, he asked me to phone you.'

'And you're phoning me, don't waste my time. What do you want?'

Rupert began to sweat, 'Balil says you have a parcel he wants taken back to the UK.'

'You can come and collect it from me.'

'When can we meet?'

'Soon,' the monosyllabic replies continued.

'Whereabouts?' Rupert attempted his own version of curtness.

'In Gubu. Don't phone me again.' Madani Haddad ended the call.

Chapter 5

Miss Daisy preened. As her new wipers swept away pounding drops, she threw them to the side and dismissed their attempts to cling to the window. The view of the road ahead was as perfect as possible. It wasn't the old lady's fault there were a few chips and scratches in the windscreen and the beginnings of an ominous crack in the left-hand corner. Over recent years, potholes and general road crumbling attacked her with tarmac hand grenades. Speeding slag carriers shot coal hard bullets like rockets, and in her middle age, some bored village child even catapulted a heater plug at her which caused the chip that started the crack, adding insult to injury. Being wounded by your own spare part was no joke. Road travel these days was a war zone and the man in the driving seat, the detective, a boots-and-all sort of driver, was the General Patton of the steering wheel with no thought of diversionary tactics or taking cover in the trenches. With him, it was 'over the top lads and die like a man.' Miss Daisy was a card-carrying pacifist.

'More rain, sir. This weather might continue all the way to Vic Falls.' Sergeant Ncube stared through the window at sheets of water lashing the teak forests lining their route, 'Madhlodhlo heard from Mamoyo, whose daughter heard it from a man who consulted *umlimu*. She's been saying for months we would be blessed with good rain this year. I watched *amatheza* shoring up their mounds and collecting dead grass.'

'Termites are a good sign, Ncube, but the long-range weather forecast is more accurate than a ventriloquist in a cave or any other sort of rain god. Madhlodhlo has access to the internet.' Sibanda stabbed the accelerator harder, Miss Daisy lurched forward. 'Cold War won't be happy though.'

'Why not?'

'Because he can't take the credit. This water has fallen before he got the chance to start his praying for rain.'

'Maybe this bounty is a carry-over from last year's prayers, a build-up of enough good will.'

'Procrastination by a higher power, a sort of spiritually controlled water tap, you think?' Sibanda raised his eyebrows.

Ncube had no idea what the detective meant so he clamped his mouth shut, squinted and changed the subject. 'What will we be doing up in Vic Falls, sir?'

'I'll drop you off at the border post. Take Laurent Kasongo's passport. See if the officer on duty when Kasongo came into the country recognises him and if he travelled with anyone else. Check if those other stamps are valid.'

'And you, sir?'

'I've got a date with a dancing lady.'

'But, but... Miss Barton?' Ncube was shocked the detective might be two-timing his girlfriend.

Sibanda looked at his sergeant and cursed that he had brought up Berry's name. He had been trying for some time to banish her from his thoughts. 'Keep your nose out of my personal life, Ncube. Stick it in this investigation.'

The words hurt the sergeant. A stony silence descended on the deck chair striped cab. The rain stopped, and with it, the teeth-setting squeal of the windscreen wipers. The rain, for all Ncube's enthusiasm, was still patchy. Ncube shuffled in his seat. He shouldn't have mentioned Miss Barton, not his business, but the detective would be happier settled, and Miss Barton, until now, had seemed like a front runner. He sighed, pinched in a post breakfast buttock squeak and watched as the refurbished airport flashed past. In his wildest dreams, he couldn't imagine himself on a flight to anywhere. Holidays for a police sergeant with three wives and eight, nearly nine children would always be on the ground close to home, preferably near a fishing hole. In his life, he would never see the ocean, feel the icy kiss of snow, or taste exotic foods. But he had no regrets. Those dreams were never his. This was Zimbabwe, a full belly and a happy family were enough.

Sibanda tried to keep his mind on the job ahead, that of tracing the artist T.M., whoever he was. Laurent Kasongo must have spent some time playing holiday maker in the town before he left for Gubu. Sibanda suspected Mama Ecstasy started life here since most artists washed up in Vic Falls. But the memory of Berry invaded like an antbear raiding a termite mound, digging away with long claws, scratching down the hard clay built up over the last few weeks, unearthing pale, vulnerable grubs.

Xolisani, his brother, had caused the problems. He let it slip to their mother that Sibanda was dating a white girl. It had happened during a family gathering at their rural home to celebrate his younger sister's place at university in South Africa. She and his mother were leaving to stay with a cousin in Johannesburg. Sabatha, named for the Sunday of her birth, was to be settled in for the new term. When his mother spoke to him, he recognised the pain in her eyes, and it tore through his heart. He owed his mother everything. She worked like a span of trek oxen to keep he and Xolisani in Marula Tree School after their father died, sacrificed any future for herself and, he suspected, looking at her as she confronted him, gave up her health and strength as well. When had she become so frail?

'Your father...' she had wiped tears from her eyes, shaken her head in bewilderment and clasped his hands in hers. There had been no anger in her voice, only love, pride and tradition welling up.

'It's a fling, nothing serious,' Sibanda had lied. He never lied to his mother.

'Promise me Jabu, promise on your father's grave you'll give up this white girl.' She had glanced towards the cattle kraal where his father lay buried.

'I promise, Mama.' As soon as the words left his lips, he understood his happiness was over. He thought a family could be his, that he had found his soul mate, but his life would have to take a different path. His mother had made countless sacrifices for him and now he had to repay the debt. He cursed Xolisani. Given time and a few meetings in the right environment, his mother would have come around, seen beyond Berry's skin colour and crystal eyes, got to know a girl as African as herself.

The following night had been the hardest conversation he'd ever had. Berry arrived at his house with wine and the makings of a meal. She often came for the night. They would spend time in the kitchen, she chiding him for his lack of culinary skills and he watching her fuss around, glass of wine in hand, stirring some delicious sauce, educating him on the finer points of dining, laughing, flirting in a preamble to a night of lovemaking. This time, as she flung herself into his arms, he disentangled her embrace.

'Sit down, Berry.'

'What's wrong, Jabu?'

'We... we have to talk,' his jaw ached with the tension of what was to come. 'We... this can't go on. You must have known. I have a demanding job and...'

'...Is there someone else? The clinic sister?'

Saying yes would have been easier, a less complicated excuse, but he loved Berry Barton, had loved her for years without her knowing, without him knowing and now he was giving her up. 'No one else. I'm not ready to settle, my career has taken a backward step being posted to Gubu. I need to reverse that without any distractions.'

'So, that's it? I'm a distraction?'

'No... Berry, you know what I mean. I have to focus now. Look, this has been great, but...'

'... great but time to move on,' she finished the sentence. Sibanda could still remember the look she had given him. Her bright cut sapphire eyes had bored into him as if she were examining an unpleasant stranger or something stuck on the bottom of her shoe. She didn't cry. He was grateful he hadn't hurt her too much. He couldn't have borne her pain. He'd done more harm to himself. He hadn't spoken to Xolisani since. This murder case saved him from wallowing in a quagmire of misery.

They were almost at Victoria Falls town, Sibanda mulling over his despair, Ncube still licking the wounds inflicted by the detective and Miss Daisy contemplating her imminent, well-earned rest when a car hurtled towards them on the wrong side. The oncoming black Mercedes overtook one of the many overland trucks plying the route, misjudging both the distance to Miss Daisy and the state of the road. The vehicle hit a pothole and careered towards them, out of control. Sibanda slammed on the brakes. Miss Daisy skidded and squealed in terror. Ncube's gases exploded from every possible vent. The speeding vehicle braked hard, squirming across the road like a fish out of water, flapping from one side to the next and then aquaplaning, side-on, hidden behind a wash of its own making and heading towards the old Land Rover. Sibanda jerked the wheel hard to the left to avoid the out-of-control Mercedes. He steered onto the shrub-lined verge. They dodged tree trunks, mowed down bushes, Miss Daisy threading her way through the wooded maze with more agility than she thought possible. Not too far ahead, two trees grew close together, blocking her path. Sibanda wrestled to avoid a head on collision, but Miss Daisy was travelling too fast. The escape route required too acute an angle for the arthritic steering column now bellowing like a cow desperate for milking. The groans were silenced when the Land Rover's left wing smashed into a large Mopane tree, bringing her to a shuddering halt.

'Are you okay, Ncube?' Sibanda checked on his sergeant before glancing in the rear mirror to see the black saloon speeding towards Bulawayo.

Ncube gathered himself, 'Ayi, ayi I thought we were all dead. That vehicle travelled like a whipped donkey galloping down a hill. Blessing will find something for my bruises and bumps but poor Miss Daisy... I must look at the damage.'

Sibanda was shaken. They had come close to death. As the black Mercedes skated past them with less clearance than the whisker on a caracal, he'd recognised the driver – The Honourable Cuthbert Muchacha. He might have guessed it would be someone of his ilk, careless, entitled, arrogant with no thought for the welfare of others. But why was a prominent government minister driving a vehicle on his own and racing in such a hurry? Where was his chauffeur? What underhand nonsense was he up to that had to be conducted in private?

'Sir, I need a hand,' Ncube, on his knees, tried to yank out the crumpled mud guard pressing on the tyre.

'Will Miss Daisy get us to Vic Falls?'

'If I can free up the wheel. We've lost the lights though.' Ncube stared at the pile of broken glass at the base of the tree. What would he have to produce in the way of smoked fish to replace headlights, sidelights and indicators, never mind the wing, now a study in concertinaed aluminium, and a bumper curled like a corkscrew?

They both heaved on the collapsed bumper, peeling it back like the lid on a tin of sardines. Freeing the wing took more grunt. Together they prised and manhandled the mud guard, levering it away from the tyre until the wheel could move.

'She is now utterly dirigible,' the sergeant proclaimed with pride. Dirigible had a strong ring, suggesting power and command. This special find in his prized dictionary awaited its moment. Blessing, his senior wife, had said 'utterly' was a smart English word spoken by smart English people and he should trot it out from time to time. Such a word would add taste like a teaspoon of salt in a stew, she added. Ncube's English vocabulary expanded daily thanks to his Oxford dictionary. He was proud of his learning.

'The Land Rover's not a bloody blimp, Ncube. Miss Daisy isn't going to float away,' Sibanda snapped, his patience was wearing thin. The sight of Cuthbert Muchacha's yellow face had ruined his day.

Chapter 6

'Make your way back into town. I'll be at the curio market.' Sibanda dropped Ncube close to the border post. A bridge, over 110 years old and guaranteed for 100 years, arched in steel chevrons across the narrow gorge separating Zimbabwe and Zambia. Laden trucks, stacked back for hundreds of metres at either end of the bridge, dribbled across one at a time. Infrequent freight trains inched along the tracks, hoping their weight wouldn't be the one to put the expired guarantee to the test. Ncube walked towards the Immigration office.

Sibanda watched him disappear into the grubby building before he turned Miss Daisy in the direction of the town. He waited for a gaggle of backpackers to cross the road on their way to a historical tour of the bridge. Cecil Rhodes ordered the structure to be built as part of his Cape to Cairo vision of train travel up through Africa. A bridge sited so the trains should catch the spray of the Falls as they passed, whilst the mighty Zambezi, freshly fallen over the chasm, thundered and churned beneath. Rhodes might have been something of an old romantic, but the bridge remained in his dreams; he never made it to the Falls.

Sibanda headed for the area where he knew the carvers and curio touts hung out. He pulled up in the car park at Elephant Walk Shopping Mall. The security guard hardly gave him a second glance. No one would steal a wrecked old Land Rover. The driver of such a beat-up looking vehicle wouldn't give him a tip for watching it, not worth his while walking over. As Sibanda strode to the cluster of curio shops, the guard looked again. He noted something in the swagger of the man, the length of his stride, the tilt of his head and the breadth of his shoulders that indicated he might not be a fit with the old *skoroskoro* vehicle. Maybe he'd missed a trick.

Curio shops filled the space ahead of the detective, coloured fabrics and wall hangings, wooden carvings, beaded bowls, wire sculptures and jewellery to suit every taste and budget. Sibanda avoided the shops and veered to the back of the complex, past a larger-than-life-size rhino made of cool drink cans featuring many flattened tins of Ncube's favourite fizz. Sibanda allowed himself a wry smile and wondered how his sergeant was faring at Immigration.

The ranks of curio sellers behind the complex were far from smart; no artistic displays and arranged shop windows, no exotic imports from the north or south, or copies churned out in China, just items crafted by talented Zimbabweans, polished and marshalled into ranks. The name, 'Arise and Shine Flea market', more than fitted the bill. Rows of curios stretched into the distance and then curved to form an L shape. Each vendor was allotted their place, some on cemented floors, thatched and shaded from the sun, others out in the open. Sibanda surveyed the scene. This would be a bigger job than he'd imagined. The first vendor he approached with the photo and initials shook his head, 'there are many of us here, but I can show you something better.' He took Sibanda by the arm and led him through a maze of elephants, giraffes, warthogs and rhinos to a section of carved figures. 'See, I have everything, I'll give you a good price.'

'I'm not buying.'

'Something for your wife.' The man picked up a mother and child composition, polishing the stone at the same time while trying to thrust his work into the detective's hands, 'special price for you,' he cajoled, 'times are hard, sir.' Sibanda sighed as he rejected the piece.

'I'm looking for this particular style and this artist, T.M.'

The vendor gave up; besides he'd seen an overland truck pull up into the parking space. Foreigners, young ones at that, were much easier meat than grumbling, penny-pinching locals.

By the time he was given his first lead, Sibanda had been shown numerous chess sets, a mountain of beads, enough bracelets to encircle the earth and more wildlife than in the whole of the park, but nothing resembling Mama Ecstasy.

The stall holders became less enthusiastic as they realised there was no sale on offer. 'The only T.M. I know of around here is Thomas Mabiza. He's about six stands down, the one with the dreads in the yellow shirt.' This was from a vendor who grunted as he herded his large flock of soapstone Zimbabwe birds into neat rows.

'Ever seen this man?' he showed the photograph of the dead man yet again.

'Hard to say. Many tourists visit. I don't remember this face.'

Thomas Mabiza wore his acacia yellow football shirt with arrogance as though he had scored the winning goal for Real Madrid. The name Ronaldo and the number nine were emblazoned on his back. Long dreads fringed with beads, red, yellow, and green, chinked as he walked. The colours of Rasta and the Zimbabwean flag were conveniently similar. His stand was colourful, peopled with giraffes cut from cans and wound around a metal armature.

'Thomas Mabiza?'

'Who's asking?'

'I hear you're good with stone carvings, the man to buy from.'

'I have a few,' Thomas Mabiza showed less enthusiasm than his fellow vendors.

'Can I see them?'

Mabiza walked to the darkest corner of his display. A few serpentine sculptures clustered in a huddle amidst debris - failed carvings, split, shattered, and discarded. Several of them were Mama Ecstasy lookalikes, chunky and roughed up in places, but none of them glowed with her lightness of being, radiated her inner bliss or the pleasures to be found in a spot of cavorting. They stood, or rather squatted, like lumps of stone that should never have been chipped off the mother lode. Thomas Mabiza picked one up.

'Is this one of yours?' Sibanda showed him the picture of Mama Ecstasy on the phone.

'Where did you get that? Not from me.' Thomas Mabiza's alarmed eyes darted around the market, 'I have nothing you want, try further along.'

'Look again,' Sibanda flicked to the close-up of the initials, that's your signature, isn't it?'

'No, I don't sign my work. Who sent you to bother me like this? Who are you? If you are not buying something I have other customers.' Mabiza walked away. The overlanders were beginning to filter through the stall, some handling the metal giraffes.

Sibanda grabbed him by the arm. 'Detective Inspector Jabulani Sibanda, Gubu police. I'm investigating a murder case. Did you sell this carving to this man?' He produced the dead man's picture.

Mabiza stopped in his tracks, 'Murder? I have nothing to do with any murder. Gubu? Never been there. I've never seen this man.' His eyes were still darting and the stone curio in his hands shook. 'That's not my work and that's not my signature. Why don't you talk to the twins? That mama looks like their creation.'

'The twins?'

'Yes. Talkmore and Talkless Manhombo.'

Sibanda was mulling over the familiar surname when Sergeant Ncube appeared, hot and panting. He hadn't walked from Immigration, instead flagging down a local car to transport him up the hill from the river. The airless, humid day played heavy as the Zambezi Valley worked up one of her energy sapping sweats.

Sibanda ambled over to the sergeant. As he approached, Ncube wondered what magic kept the detective looking so cool. His forehead remained dry, his breathing even, and his shoulders hadn't even slumped a rib's width. Ncube straightened himself as best he could and threw back his own aching shoulders, causing a shower of perspiration to shake from his body like a dog escaping an unwanted bath. He couldn't speak, and he was holding words that needed to form.

'A drink?' the detective offered.

Ncube nodded. His tongue was glued to the roof of his mouth and the information he'd come by stuck in his mouth like burrs to a blanket. Sibanda ushered Ncube towards a cool drink stand in the middle of the market. He bought three bottles of water and ordered his sergeant to drink two of them.

'Water, sir?' he grimaced between swigs, eyeing the colourful cans nestling in the cooler box.

'Drink, Ncube.' Sibanda turned to the refreshment vendor, a young woman with two children playing at her feet, 'Do you know the twins?' he asked.

'More, or Less?'

'Either.'

Ncube planted the water bottle on his lips and drank. This conversation sounded as strange as a two-headed lizard, but he dared not risk appearing stupid again.

'They aren't here today. They go home often. That's their patch over there.' she pointed to a heap of rocks, littered with stone chips and dust and a collection of sculptures that bore the skill, technique and artistry of Mama Ecstasy. A tribe of fat ladies frolicked and danced with delight in the hot summer sun, as if they had not a care in the world. He smiled.

'Where's home for the twins?'

'Not sure, over east somewhere... Marange, I think.'

Sibanda's hand went to his jaw where the muscles clenched. His other hand fingered the object in his pocket. Marange was home to the largest diamond find anywhere in recent years and the loupe was the indispensable tool of the diamond trade. Everyone knew Zimbabwe's alluvial diamonds were disappearing faster than rats down a sewer. Even the President lamented that diamonds to the value of fifteen billion dollars had been mined but only 2 million dollars could be accounted for. Half the alluvial rich soils were shipped out unpanned, with diamonds still buried in the exported dirt. Airfields appeared, built to accommodate huge cargo planes that swallowed up earth, tonnes of it shovelled into aircraft holds as fast as the dozers could operate and then flown to eastern countries for panning. There were rumours of violence and shootings of local, artisanal prospectors. Anything left was being scrabbled over by those with a link to the powerful.

Sibanda had had his suspicions with the discovery of the jeweller's loupe and the Congolese passport, a country that traded in blood diamonds. Now there was the Marange connection and, even worse, he remembered the Manhombos were close to the Muchacha clan. Why was Cuthbert Muchacha, ex minister of mines here in the Falls and how were the Manhombo twins involved? Pieces were falling into place, and he didn't like the picture one bit.

'Ever seen this man?' Sibanda produced the photo of the masked man.

The vendor scrutinised the face. 'Maybe,' she said, after a minute or two staring at the image. 'There's something... Did he come in an overland truck?'

'Yes, that's it.' Sergeant Ncube wheezed in between gulps of water, his gathered evidence making it past his parched tongue. 'The officer on duty at the border post thinks he recognised the face as one of the travellers on a Rugged Rascals truck that came through a few days ago. He stood out – the only black man on the trip.'

'Where's the truck now?' Sibanda looked across to an overland rig in the car park, but the name Afrexplore was emblazoned on the side.

'The next stop is an overnight near Gubu. At Gubu Safari Lodge, I think, and then into the park. Most of the overlanders stay at Thunduluka Lodge. There's a backpacker's camp behind the main buildings. That's where they'll be now.' Before they left the curio market, Sibanda glanced back at Thomas Mabiza talking on his phone and waving his free arm as if trying to swat away the sins of the world.

Chapter 7

Ncube reckoned they did the road trip back to Gubu in record time, for Miss Daisy that is. She didn't rank in the black Mercedes's league, but she was older, wiser, more composed and seemed to know where the potholes were hiding under the rain-soaked tarmac, which is more than could be said for the arrogant Teutonic madam that had forced them off the road. Once in the park, though, Miss Daisy began to misbehave on the corrugated roads leading to Thunduluka. At first, the slipping and sliding was hardly noticeable as she waggled her tail from time to time and shimmied across the washboard bumps. Ncube even managed a few mouthfuls of his much-awaited sandwich. A recent fishing and foraging trip with his family had been bountiful. He'd caught a bucketful of bream and his wives and children, led by Blessing, came home with baskets of wild herbs and fruits, including *umkozombo*, monkey fingers, the jam from which now soaked into Sukho's fresh, sour dough bread - almost as good as his Gogo used to make. He took a mouthful. The tart, red jelly swam around his teeth causing his eyes to wince with pleasurable memory and his stomach to grumble with delight.

'Would you like one, sir?' Ncube was reluctant to share his special lunch, but it would be rude not to.

'No thanks Ncube, Miss Daisy's playing up. She's dancing over this road like a drunkard at a wedding. I need both hands on the wheel.'

'Perhaps a bit slower, sir.'

'I want to make sure we catch that truck. Once it's back on the road south...' Sibanda didn't finish the sentence. Miss Daisy sashayed a little too enthusiastically.

'What the hell is wrong with this tin of trash, Ncube?'

Ncube almost choked on a crunchy bit of crust as he gasped in indignation, 'Tin, sir? That's like mistaking a pointed stick for a spear. Miss Daisy is aluminium through and through. I suspect she damaged a tyre when you crashed her into that tree trunk,' he glowered, 'she's suffering a slow puncture, a bit soft in the left front.'

'A bit soft in the head if you ask me.' Sibanda was forced to slow down. Had he given Miss Daisy a brain? Was he the one going soft in the head? This case was heading into murky waters, clouding his thinking. He would have to pull himself together, keep his wits sharp.

They turned into Thunduluka Lodge without having stopped once to look at wildlife. Ncube understood this must be an urgent visit if the detective sailed past muddied elephants, relaxed and bathing, kudu nibbling on shrubs, a herd of sable staring at them with round coal black eyes, and who knows how many birds. The detective never paused once to point out some long-winded detail about habits or diets or populations.

Miss Daisy rolled to a halt in the lodge car park. Sibanda leapt out and strode towards reception. He threw the keys to Ncube, 'Get some air in the tyres, then come and find me. I don't want to have to skate all the way back to Gubu.'

John Berger, the manager, saw him from reception. He admired the detective, but every time Sibanda arrived at the lodge he brought a problem. What trouble was he carrying to his door this time? Arrivals were already down. He had only recently managed to persuade a major French tour operator that all was well in Zimbabwe and at Thunduluka Lodge. He sighed and rose to greet the detective.

'Rugged Rascals? They're in the camping ground. Scheduled to leave tomorrow. Off down through the park, then on to Bulawayo.'

'Can you take me to the truck?'

'Of course. And all the overlanders should be in camp, the game drives are back from the morning safari. Buff and Berry are here by the way. You might want to pop in and have a chat before you leave.'

Sibanda faltered for a minute, 'No time, I'm afraid.' He lengthened his stride, the manager battling to keep up with him.

The overland vehicle was a home-grown affair, some kind of truck with a cab plonked on the top, but although it looked safe and comfortable enough, Sibanda couldn't imagine weeks sharing a glass and steel cage with a bunch of strangers, pounding the rutted roads of Africa.

'Detective Sibanda, we meet again.' Barney Jones walked towards him, hand outstretched, 'What brings you here?'

Sibanda shook the hand firmly, feeling the pleasing crush of bone against bone. Now he understood why Berry and her father were here. As soon as he'd broken off their relationship, Berry ran back to Barney Jones, aka Rubble, a man far too assured for his own good.

'Is this your rig, Jones? I thought you'd gone overseas?'

'I did, worked every hour of the day over there, and night sometimes. Saved enough to start this business. You can't keep a good man out of Africa,' he quipped.

'Rugged Rascals is yours?'

'It is, and so far, I'm the one employee and this is the only truck,' Barney Jones laughed. 'Hard work but loads of fun, a party every night.'

'You've lost one of your revellers.' Sibanda did not want to be drawn into the light-hearted banter. He didn't want a relationship with Barney Jones; he loathed the man. He didn't even want to emphasise the alliteration - Rubble of the Rugged Rascals, although the put down might have been satisfying.

'Lost...? I'm not sure I'm with you.'

'Laurent Kasongo. He came through the Zambian border on your vehicle.'

'Ah, him, yes. Tricky customer.'

'In what way?'

'Kept to himself. We saw little of him in the Falls. When we reached Gubu he said he'd had enough and left the trip. He travelled with us for three days. I told him there couldn't be a refund. I mean... Has he complained?'

'He's dead.'

'What? How? Poor bloke.' Jones seemed shaken, but murderers were masters of deception in Sibanda's book.

'I want to speak to your clients.'

'They're all here. Five of them since Laurent left. Dead, you say?'

Sibanda strode past the safari guide towards a group of three sitting on camp stools and chatting, all young, carefree, waiting for their lives to start.

'Marlie, James, Rebecca, meet Detective Sibanda. He wants to ask some questions about Laurent...'

'... that asshole, good riddance he left the trip. I knowed he was a wrong'un, didn't I tell you Becky?' This from Marlie whose high southern US accent grated like long nails on a chalkboard. The lilt of the slave owner set off the go away birds perched in an overhead teak tree. A jackal who heard the unappealing notes as far away as the valley responded with an echoing howl.

'You didn't like him, Marlie?'

'Like him? He was a weirdo, pinned him as a pervert from the get go.'

'Why?'

'He sweated a lot, changed his shirts, always in private, like a big girl. Those shirts wuz drenched soon as he put 'em on. Why wear a black shirt in this African heat? And he never took those gloves off, some kind of fetish I guess or else he suffered from OCD. You know those people are obsessed with cleanliness and order. And jittery – the guy seemed as nervy as a long-tailed cat in a room full of rockin' chairs.'

'Did he talk to you?'

'Some, normal stuff like, "gimme the sugar," otherwise kept his distance.'

'What accent did he have?'

'We thought he come from France or somewhere from North Africa, didn't we, Becky? But he never said.'

'No, he didn't give out much personal detail at all.' Becky spoke with a softer mid-Atlantic accent. 'He was real possessive about his backpack, as though we were a bunch of thieves. Kept it close to him, never put it in his truck locker like the rest of us.'

'Yeh, remember when I picked it up because I mistook it for mine?' James was English, 'God knows what he carried in the backpack, so flipping heavy.'

'That's when he showed his temper,' Marlie added, 'like a snarling wild cat. Had a duck fit over that bag, grabbed the straps, hollered at James and skedaddled. Didn't come back for hours and then said he was leavin'.'

'We decided the backpack was full of gold and he was a smuggler.' James adopted a gothic voice from the crypt, wiggled his fingers like long-legged spiders and then laughed. 'Where is he now? In jail?'

'Dead.'

'That can't be. When? How? You need to talk to the Van Dalens.' He pointed to a tent where two girls lay reading, 'He spent more time with them. They'll be upset.' James shook his head in disbelief.

Barney stepped in, 'Geneva and Alair. I'll introduce you.'

The girls were certainly sisters. They both wore short, thick yellow hair with jaws that gave new meaning to the definition of 'square' and eyes that did the same for 'narrow'. When they stood, their solid muscular frames were evident. Sibanda now found his own hand bones being crushed by their welcome.

'Genny and Ally, this is Detective Inspector Sibanda. He has some questions about Laurent.'

Unlike Marlie, neither offered an opinion.

'Did you talk to Laurent much, spend time with him?'

The girls looked at one another, deciding who would answer. 'Not a lot, he was a loner, but we are French speakers which helped. His English was very broken.' Geneva took the lead.

'Where did he come from?'

'The DRC. Kinshasa, I think.'

'Unusual for a Congolese to be on an overland trip.' Sibanda now addressed Barney.

'This is my first trip, Detective. I'm not sure yet which nationalities travel, and which don't.'

'He was making for Johannesburg, leaving the trip in Bulawayo and heading south from there. Cheapest way to travel, he said,' Alair added.

'My first trip, so I offered knock down prices, a sort of test run,' Barney apologised for his rates.

'How did you two hear about Rugged Rascals?' Sibanda asked.

Both girls spoke together, but Geneva grabbed Alair's arm and took the lead again, 'We happened to be backpacking in Livingstone, Zambia, and saw the Rugged Rascals' vehicle at the campsite. We negotiated a last-minute deal.' They both smiled.

'Shhh,' Barney looked around, 'The others will kill me if they know you have a better discount.'

'Anything else Laurent discussed? Anything at all you remember?'

'He wasn't married, no children.' The sisters looked at one another, 'Travelling to Joburg to get work, said he was an IT man.'

'Thank you for your help. If you think of anything else that might be useful, please get in touch.'

Sibanda and Barney walked back to the truck. 'How did Laurent Kasongo book this trip?'

'My website.'

'How long ago?'

'A couple of weeks. These late bookings have helped.'

'You'll have to stay in the country until Laurent's death is sorted out. You and your guests were the last people to see him alive. What's your planned itinerary?'

'We move on through the park to Bulawayo for a couple of nights, then into the Matopos. After that, we head east for Great Zimbabwe and the ruins, north to Lake Kariba and then back across the country to Victoria Falls. How did Laurent die, Detective?'

'Murdered,' Sibanda was curt. 'I'll need all the passports. No one is leaving the country without my say so. Break it to them gently.'

Sibanda walked towards the car park, hoping Ncube had inflated the tyre, hoping to skirt the lodge and avoid Berry and her father, his head full of questions. The explanation that Laurent Kasongo was headed to Joburg for IT work seemed feeble. He didn't even have a computer in his bag. Kasongo wasn't popular on the trip. No one liked him. The Van Dalen sisters didn't bother to ask what happened to him and Marlie and friends thought him strange. He'd heard rumours of overlanders resorting to violence over girls and chores and choice seats, but Laurent Kasongo's murder was not the result of a fight gone wrong or petty retribution. His murder was an execution. Someone knew Laurent's true identity; someone knew he was in disguise.

He saw her from a distance. She turned, saw him, he waved, the least he could do. She didn't acknowledge him, looked through him, turned back and continued talking to her father as though he didn't exist.

Chapter 8

They had been at Gubu Safari Lodge for three days now and Caroline loved it. A safari was not planned when they left England to take ownership of the house, but Caroline was delighted with the outcome. 'I thought we might go and look at a few elephants since we're here,' Rupert had said the night she found the trunk and the snake was killed. 'There's a lodge near Gubu with great elephant viewing. I've been checking on Tripadvisor.'

'Sounds wonderful. Such a treat, thank you, darling.' She gave him a hug and hoped the excitement of a safari would be the start of a rapprochement between them. She understood he was having problems at work. She'd stayed as calm as possible when he brought his stress home. But she started to notice a chill and an off-hand manner in his dealings with her. The secrecy hurt. The way he slammed his laptop shut when she entered the room, or shredded correspondence as though it contained treasonable secrets made her feel excluded. Worst of all, he came home later and later with more than a whiff of alcohol about him. Arguments rose to a level of aggression she had never experienced in her life. Was he having an affair?

When Rupert first took her home to meet Bobo, his mother, she knew she would never be good enough, knew her pedigree was not long or revered enough for the likes of Bobo Hudson-Templeton. Even a PhD in microbiology from Oxford was no substitute for selective breeding. According to Rupert, his mother had been manoeuvring a union for him with Sappy Washington of the Back Bay Washingtons. No relation to the great man, of course, as Bobo was quick to point out, but a daughter of the Revolution, nonetheless. Rupert sneered when he told Caroline even though Templeton Investments was experiencing a rough patch, he would swallow razor blades before he laid a hand on squint-eyed Sappy Washington. Templeton's fortunes might be waning and the Washingtons' waxing with all the shine of a furniture polish factory, but she was not his type. Had Sappy Washington become his type now? Caroline wouldn't bet against it.

Whenever she thought about the past, Caroline twisted the engagement ring on her finger, a perfect cushion cut diamond weighing four carats surrounded by sapphires. She'd never wanted the valued family ring in the first place, but it seemed to satisfy Hudson-Templeton tradition. Sometimes she thought the ring was more of a nose ring than an engagement ring, a hoop to rope her up and control her life. It was made clear, if the marriage failed, she would have to return it. Family tradition and the mythical history of the stone dictated the ring remain a Templeton possession. The gem didn't belong in the African bush. Such crass ostentation clashed with the simple life she observed around her.

Caroline sighed, adjusted her toned body on the pool lounger, ordered another Rock Shandy and watched as the sun began to set. Rupert should be back soon. His business associate in Gubu was giving him the run around, but maybe this evening all would be sorted, and they could enjoy the elephants together. In the meantime, rifling through the old journals and papers from the trunk would keep her occupied. Initial investigations proved to be a revelation; the sort she was sure would turn Bobo Hudson-Templeton's dreams into nightmares.

'Enjoying the good life, I see,' Rupert arrived back at the lodge bitter and nervy. Nothing was going to plan.

'This is not champagne…' She swirled her glass of soda water mixed with lemonade and a shot of bitters, 'a Rock Shandy…more like liver salts if you ask me, and I think it's about to rain. There's nothing insipid about this African weather. Looks like a humdinger of a storm blowing in.'

Rupert glanced at the ominous build up. Blue-black clouds brushed with lavender were gathering over the valley and the wind was lifting. A crack of lightning shafted from a low drifting nimbus to the trees on the other side of the waterhole and made them both jump and then Caroline gathered her papers and ran as a roll of thunder bellowed and bawled with such volume, she thought the skies were collapsing. 'Come on, Rupe,' she called over her shoulder, 'you're going to get soaked.'

Rupert remained and watched her skittering away like one of the antelope they had spotted. He couldn't remember the name, but all long legs, big eyes and a glorious rump. The creature distracted him from the terrible mess he was tangled in. He could see only one solution to extract himself. Unpalatable, but there was no other way out. He took one last look at the valley before joining his wife. A herd of elephants materialised like doves from a magician's sleeve. Where did they come from? How could such huge creatures conceal themselves and then appear with the stealth of a submarine pack running on silent? Rupert watched in fascination, wishing he possessed their finesse. This whole Madani Haddad business was turning into a nightmare. The Elephants lumbered towards the waterhole, feet shuffling, heads nodding like a chorus line bobbing to the beat of gentle but persistent music. They picked up pace now the water lay close; they could smell it, imagine the first trunkful, dream of a soothing mud bath. Rain began to pound, streaming and steaming down their hides as they dipped their trunks into the water, darkening their bodies from grey to black before his eyes. Rupert turned and sprinted after his wife.

Chapter 9

'We'll have to get Detective Sibanda involved. I won't have my statistics ruined by your incompetency.' Chief Inspector Mfumu strode about his office readjusting any object that dared to defy regimentation. His current focus, a book of official papers which didn't match the others. Why in the name of all that was sacred had the government stationers decided on a larger size of charge book? And why was his sister's child such a liability? Assistant Detective Inspector Chanza had wrecked two vehicles, one he'd crashed into a cow and the second he'd burned beyond recognition leaving them exposed to ridicule in the form of an ancient Land Rover. Now he was here with some cock and bull story about a suicide. But, Mfumu supposed, if an elephant couldn't be burdened by the weight of its own trunk, then an uncle could put up with a stupid nephew. Such a pity Prosper took after his mother. Didn't the bible have something to say about sibling tolerance? Ah yes, Matthew, always a good man to turn to: *Why do you see the speck that is in your brother's eye, but do not notice the log that is in your own eye?*

'Tell me again about the scene.' Mfumu sighed, took out a starched handkerchief and prodded the corner into his tear duct.

'Well, Uncle....'

'...How many times have I told you not to address me as uncle at work?'

'Sorry, sir. I arrived at the house at 8.47 a.m. I walked around the house to see if anyone was home and spotted the body through a window. I proceeded to the front door which was unlocked and then to the bedroom door which was locked as were all the other doors and windows.

'Yes, yes,' Mfumu waved his hands, 'get to the body itself. I don't need a run down on every step you took.'

Chanza prodded at the glasses sliding down his nose on a tsunami of sweat. Clouds were building outside. The morning was closer than hidden lovers in a cupboard. 'The bedroom door was locked as were all the windows....'

'...You've said that. Now get to the body, Chanza,' Mfumu's irritation levels were reaching breaking point. The oppressive weather affected everyone's equanimity. The Lord asked a great deal on a day like this.

'The body lay on its back. A few minor injuries to the face and a bitten tongue. He must have choked to death on his own blood.'

'This is a mess, another foreign national dead in Gubu and you say it's suicide? Who commits suicide by biting off his tongue?

'But, Unc... sir.' Another nudge at the glasses battling against the tide. 'Suicide is the correct outcome. It can happen from a tongue bite. I've heard of it. The man locked himself in and then....'

'....chewed away at his own tongue until he choked? Even I couldn't pass this off as suicide. Get out of here!'

Chanza made it out of the office just in time to hear the offending oversize charge book clatter against the closing door.

Sibanda heard nothing. He stared through his window and planned his next move. Was it back to the Falls to try and find the Manhombo twins or should he concentrate on the overlanders, none of whom struck him as murderers? They would be on the move from Thunduluka soon. If he could discover the identity of Laurent Kasongo, it might throw up a few more promising leads. He picked up his phone, entered credit from a couple of recharge cards and hoped it would be enough for the overseas call he was about to make. He was skint this month, having given the better part of his salary and whatever was in his account to Sabatha and his mother for their trip to South Africa. University fees and living costs for a three-year degree would take the whole clan chipping in and more. This was how it was done in Africa, no loan schemes or bursaries, no social security or unemployment benefits; just the bank of family paying forward to the next one down the line whose need was greatest.

'Jabs, that's got to be you. Long time, how are you? Still in Zimbabwe?'

'Still here, Eddie, and rubbish at keeping in touch.'

'You can say that again. Sarge says you've disappeared into the jungle. He thinks you're Tarzan swinging through the trees. He'll be made up you phoned.'

'How's everyone at the station – Robbo, Bumper, Casta, the whole crew?' Sibanda felt an unheralded wave of nostalgia for the easy camaraderie of Sherwood Police station where he'd been on secondment.

'Still the same, missing your wild sense of humour.' The phone went quiet. 'Just joking, Jabs,' he guffawed, 'but we could do with your instinct right now. We've got ourselves a serial rapist on our patch, a real bastard of a headache. Don't suppose your intuition works from a distance, does it?'

'Eddie, I'm looking for your help.'

'Ah, now the truth comes out. I thought you were phoning 'cos you missed my blue eyes.'

'You've got brown eyes, Eddie.'

'Still as sharp as ever, Jabs. How can I help?'

'I need background checks on a few names.'

'Can't be done from your end?'

'No.'

'Okay, fire away. I'll do what I can, but we are flat out here with our own problems.'

'Appreciate it, Eddie. Three Europeans: James Templeton from London, and Geneva and Alair Van Dalen, sisters from France or maybe Belgium.'

'What are you looking for?'

'It's a murder case, so any criminal links. In particular, any connection to the diamond trade?'

'Diamonds? That's dodgy in your part of the world, isn't it? Don't get in too deep, Jabs.'

'I know what I'm doing, Eddie.'

'That you do. But African diamonds are covered in blood. Keep yourself safe. The mobs dealing in stones are brutal.'

'Thanks for the reminder.' He rubbed his chin. 'One other thing...'

'... Why did I think this sounded too easy?'

'Can you check on a couple of American nationals as well? Communications with the USA aren't too good at the moment...' Eddie had become well informed since he got to know his Zimbabwean friend. He understood what a nasty political sinkhole Zimbabwe was in.

'I'll see what I can come up with. Give me the names.'

'Marlie Scalzo from Arkansas, and Rebecca Grasston from Springfield Illinois.'

'Is that it?'

'Yes, phone me as soon as you have anything, Eddie. I'm getting nowhere with this one.'

'Will do, and don't you be a stranger. Seriously, Jabs, we all miss you. Casta hasn't smiled since you left.'

The niceties of the phone call over, Sibanda turned his attention to the page of the newspaper found in the backpack. He read it over and over until the print faded and his head was filled with the crushing doom of current affairs. There had to be some clue in it, otherwise why did Laurent fold it and keep it? The page held stories about car theft, a hammer attack by an enraged husband, and a murderous fight over five dollars. Stories now emblazoned word for word on his brain, but no names in the reports rang any bells. A large advert cautioning the shareholders of a failing bank and an even larger one offering the chance of winning a fridge in exchange for patronising a local supermarket could not be the reason Laurent Kasongo kept this specific page. On the reverse, Sibanda was confronted by column after column of classifieds, the majority of which were estate notices. He scrutinised every single one. Most of the names had waited for death to achieve this microscopic notoriety. Another depressing thought. He decided to give the classifieds one last going over. Perhaps Laurent fingered one more than the others. He scrutinised the columns. Yes, there was something. A faint ink mark, next to the estate of Isaiah Jacobs who died at Hillside, Bulawayo, seven years ago. Could it have been an accidental smudge? Why did it take so long to track down an heir and wrap up the estate? He took a note of the address of the house, a long shot but worth keeping in mind.

He stared through the window looking for inspiration. Not a single bird in sight. Then he spotted the culprit, a night adder skulking around the bird bath. Sibanda had heard a few toads about, croaking ahead of the rain. Toads were the night adders' favourite feast. The snake slithered off, unfed. A pink girl with a large, round, bright eye, her diamond markings undulating down her fat viper body as she moved. She was off to lay eggs.

Someone tapped on his door. Not Sergeant Ncube, he'd been fussing over the Land Rover since their return, getting the tyre fixed, bashing out a few dents. As to the rest of the damage, repairing it wasn't worth the effort.

PC Khumalo popped her head in. 'Sorry, to be the bearer of bad news, but we found a body on our rounds checking for Laurent Kasongo earlier this morning. Cold War wants you to handle it, says Chanza has another case to deal with.'

'What? I'm up to my eyes, Zee.'

'Truth is, Chanza's messed this one up and Mfumu needs you to sort it out. His statistics might suffer otherwise.'

'Is the body still in situ?'

'PC Tshuma is guarding it.'

'How did he die?'

'Bit off his own tongue. Chanza thinks it's suicide.'

Sibanda didn't hide his incredulity. 'Do we know who the victim is?'

'The neighbours say he's a foreigner, been around for a while. His name is...' PC Khumalo checked her notes, '...Madani Haddad, a Lebanese national.'

The house lay not far from Sibanda's own, two roads down on Duiker Avenue. A crowd of onlookers gathered outside. While PC Tshuma kept them at bay, PC Khumalo led the way inside. 'We'd been knocking on all these doors, as you asked, with no positive feedback about the dead backpacker. No one at this house answered. Detective Chanza went around the back and that's when he spotted the body through an open curtain.'

'You broke the door down?'

'Chanza and I did. The front door was open, but the bedroom door was locked. The key was on the inside. We charged the door together, with our shoulders. There's more muscle under the detective's scrawny jacket than you might imagine,' she chuckled. 'We both heard the key drop on the floor as the lock splintered. That's why Chanza thought it was suicide. The key was found on the inside. No way in or out of that room unless there's an *isipuku* about that can float through walls.'

'Don't catch Ncube's disease, Zee.'

'Ncube's disease, sir?' She spoke with distaste as if the sergeant had the clap or infectious pustules at the very least.

'Belief in the supernatural. There are no such things as ghosts.' Sibanda walked towards the bedroom. The corpse lay face up in the gap between the bed and the wall. Sibanda leant down to take a closer look at the injuries to the body. The bridge of the nose showed damage. His right eye was bruised, his lip split through to the teeth and his tongue almost severed. Sibanda stood and surveyed the room. There were no signs of a struggle, no displaced furniture, except the bedside table, a heavy teak affair on its side.

'Did he kill himself, sir?'

'By biting off his own tongue?'

'I saw a movie once where a female boxer was paralysed and on a ventilator. She almost committed suicide by gnawing her tongue. Chanza must have seen it as well.'

Sibanda shook his head in exasperation. Typical of the incompetent detective to base his theories on movies. 'Unlikely,' he mocked, 'unless this victim suffered from haemophilia. Clots would form long before he lost sufficient blood to bleed out.

'And choking to death?'

'He would have to be unconscious or paralysed for that to happen. Natural reflexes would cause him to cough and expel the blood. Not unless....' Sibanda paused.

'Unless what sir?'

'Have you heard of epilepsy, Zee?'

'When people have convulsions?'

'Yes, and tongue-biting is a characteristic.'

PC Khumalo beamed. She knew the detective would get to the bottom of this death behind locked doors. Calm would be restored at the police station and Cold War could get back to bashing his bible and tidying his desk. 'I can see what happened, sir.'

'Tell me what you think, Zee.'

'This poor man suspected he was about to become ill and have a fit, so he locked himself into his bedroom for privacy. No one wants to writhe around in public.'

'There is a stigma attached to epilepsy. Do you see that tiny sliver of skin on the corner of the table?

'So, he could have fallen during his fit, cut his lip, knocked himself out and then choked to death.' PC Khumalo chided herself. Why hadn't she noticed that clue before? 'Not suicide at all, but an accident.'

'No, not suicide but....'

PC Khumalo's face fell. She suspected complications were about to follow. 'Sir?'

'Where's his medication? Did you find anything?'

'No pills anywhere. We checked. Chanza thought he might have drugged himself.'

Sibanda shook his head, 'A serious epileptic would have them on him always.' He knelt again and examined the speck of skin on the table edge. 'Why so little blood on this table? How did he land on his back and why is there no blood on his face? A smashed lip would stream with the stuff.'

PC Khumalo didn't answer, the questions were not for her.

Sibanda checked the body again, 'Someone has cleaned this face, Zee, wiped away the blood.'

'But, sir, the door was locked from the inside, the key was still in the lock. How could anyone come in and out again?'

Sibanda straightened, surveyed the room. The windows were fixed with brass catches which were all latched. The key lay amongst the wooden debris and the remains of the latch from the splintered door.

'There has to be a logical explanation. Somehow, someone came into this room. This is not suicide or an epileptic attack. We have a murder victim.' His hand went to his jaw. Two murders on the same day in Gubu. There would be a connection. Was this the break he needed to find Laurent Kasongo's real identity? Madani Haddad was swarthy, with greenish eyes, a similar look to Laurent.

'Weapon?' Zanele Khumalo was studying criminology. The murder weapon was the most important find at a crime scene. She wanted to be a detective. The knife wound in her thigh from a previous sleuth attempt had healed and she couldn't see the scar on her scalp. Although she had made mistakes, her contribution to the last case the detective solved had been important.

'Nothing obvious. Take a look at the fireplace, too hot for a fire but there are fresh ashes in the grate. Someone burnt something here, got rid of evidence.'

'I did smell smoke when we first broke into the room.' PC Khumalo's eyes fell. 'I didn't mention it because Chanza was convinced Madani Haddad committed suicide, said he'd burnt incriminating documents he didn't want found after his death.'

'Paper ash is white, this is black and there's an odd smell.' He rubbed a portion of the ash between his fingers. It felt gritty and brittle. 'Smells like celery' PC Khumalo shrugged her shoulders. 'Forensics will have to sort this one. I'll check the room again. Get back to the station and send Sergeant Ncube if he's finished tinkering with that old wreck.'

'He'll be finished, sir, there's nothing much he can do. Miss Daisy's for the scrapyard this time. She's a goner. No matter how many times you wash a goat, it'll still smell like a goat.' She headed for the door. 'Odd man, though, this Madani Haddad.' She gestured towards the corpse.

'Uh?' Sibanda was concentrating on the room.

'I never met a man who plucks his eyebrows.' PC Khumalo pointed to a pair of tweezers on the bedside table before heading off to the police station. Sibanda began a meticulous fingertip search of the bedroom. If Madani Haddad had something to hide he would have kept it close. Everyone stashed their hoard in the bedroom.

Sergeant Ncube arrived as Sibanda finished. He was spared the sight of a corpse beginning to bloat by a bedspread the detective had used to cover the body.

'Nothing else out of place in here, Ncube. I've been over it with a nit comb.'

'Time of death, sir?'

'Yesterday afternoon or early evening. Backpacker man was killed later, after dark. Two to five hours between murders if I were to hazard a guess.'

'Did this one commit suicide, sir? That's the rumour.'

'No, he was murdered. Beaten with a blunt instrument and the killer got in and out of this room leaving the door locked from the inside.'

'A magician?'

'Not a bad guess, but there's no one with magical powers, so don't get carried away.' Sibanda glowered at his sergeant. 'A clever, tricky adversary. What was this Lebanese man doing in Gubu, Ncube? What have you heard?'

Ncube didn't vocalise his thoughts of magical tokoloshes who could walk through walls, 'A loner who didn't socialise much. Rented this house a few months ago. Visitors passed by at night. Single men, not from around here. There were rumours... Some say he paid for favours.' The sergeant coughed to hide his discomfort. 'PC Khumalo said he, er, plucked his eyebrows.... What is it, sir?'

Sibanda swivelled on his heels and headed for the bedside table. He picked up the tweezers and ran his fingers inside the pincers.

'Not for eyebrows, Ncube. How could I have missed them? These tweezers are an expensive piece of kit, satin brushed, stainless steel to avoid false reflection and they're grooved on the inside.'

'Why, what for?'

'To better hold and examine gemstones, and I'd stake my life it's diamonds.'

Ncube's eyes grew round. His mouth fell open. 'Diamonds?' he gasped. His hands went up as though to distance himself. The story of Zimbabwe's diamonds was fraught with political and military involvement. Any person in their right mind, at the very mention of the stone, turned their eyes backwards like a chameleon, zipped their lips and threw their ears into the deepest, darkest pit. 'Diamonds?' he stuttered again.

'I don't like it any more than you do, Ncube, but we have two murders on our hands, at least one of them linked to diamonds. Our first victim, Laurent Kasongo may also be Lebanese. He has a similar look to Madani Haddad.

'What have the Lebanese got to do with diamonds?'

'A lot. Their arrival in West Africa coincided with the discovery of diamond fields in Sierra Leone in the fifties. That's where they began their dealing. Those early smugglers learned the trade, how to spot a fake, got to grips with the four c's. They've expanded into Zimbabwe.'

'The four seas? But we don't have a coastline...'

'Colour, clarity, cut and carats.'

'Carrots, sir?' Ncube was in too much shock to monitor his questions for possible ridicule, too stunned to narrow his eyes and shut his mouth, too horrified to pretend he'd made a joke. Muddling was the least of his worries.

Sibanda shook his head and allowed his lips a wry smile. 'I'll explain later, Ncube, but this case has nothing to do with root vegetables or oceans.'

Ncube was dazed by the lack of sting in the reply. 'And why that nationality? Why the Lebanese?'

'In Sierra Leone, the Lebanese were already trading other goods. The move into illegal diamonds was a natural fit, but they needed to get up to speed on diamonds. They soon dominated the trade.'

'Why not the locals?'

'No capital to invest. Banks would never give credit to the diamond trade. It's a skilled business; not for amateurs. One bad deal, one fake or occluded stone could wipe out a dealer. The clever boys honed their skills. Didn't take them long to match the expertise of the best gemmologists and cutters in Antwerp. If necessity is the mother of invention, Ncube, then proficiency is the father of survival. The Lebanese learnt how to survive. Their diaspora has been worse than ours.'

Ncube didn't understand a word. What species of ant was a twerp? This time he held his tongue. If Sibanda wanted to babble long, tangled words about slicing up insects and mothers and fathers, he understood. The detective must be in shock as well.

Sibanda continued, 'My guess is, Madani Haddad is an itinerant miner-dealer, murdered for his troubles.'

'What now, sir, shouldn't we pass this case on to....?

'...Who would you trust with this?'

'This business is too dangerous for a small rural police station to investigate.'

'Sergeant, I understand if you want to back out. You have a family.'

The temptation to quit was as mouth-watering as PC Khumalo's buttocks bending over the bottom drawer of the filing cabinet. The detective was a rogue in the force, never followed protocols, always on his own mission, but he couldn't abandon him now. Who knew what trouble he might get into without a sensible head by his side? Ncube took a moment before replying, 'I'm with you, sir.'

'Thank you, sergeant, I appreciate that.' Sibanda let slip a hint of rare emotion and then he turned back to business. 'You check out the neighbours and onlookers Ncube. Find out what they know about Haddad. I'll scout around the house. The murderer got into the bedroom somehow.'

Ncube took a notebook from his pocket and walked towards the gathered crowd. Sibanda edged around the building checking for spoor and any signs an intruder may have found entry. He followed Chanza's footprints, an easy track in the rain sodden earth. His heavy heels and toes pointed like watch hands at ten to two, but the rain had done a great job of obliterating earlier marks. He reached the bedroom window. An overhanging sill protected the area beneath from the rain. The dry, bare ground was churned with activity. Under Chanza's tracks were others laid down hours earlier, maybe the previous evening. These were more difficult to read. The tread was smooth and featureless, possibly leather, and the step was light. A careful stalk by someone who didn't want to be heard or seen, but he loitered at the window. There were faint traces of yet another set of prints. Chanza did his best to wipe them out with his pacing back and forth. The man was an ineffectual clod with crime scenes. Part of one footprint survived in the soft, ungrassed sand. A scuff, but distinct enough. This peeping Tom was taller, a broader, larger shoe size. Excluding Chanza, at least three people, including Bigfoot, peered through Madani Haddad's window on the night of his death. Was this the work of the same hit squad who shot Laurent Kasongo? Had they come for Haddad first? If so, why wasn't Haddad also shot? Why was he clubbed to death? Was he dealing with organised assassins? He walked to the front of the house giving the area a last glance. Chanza was right about one thing. No one had opened or entered through this window for some time. The dust on the sill had been there for weeks.

'Anything?' Sibanda and Ncube strode back towards the police station, Ncube having spent half an hour questioning bystanders and neighbours.

'No one heard or noticed anything unusual, but they all noted a lot of visitors in recent days. Young men who always came after dark.'

'Anyone they recognised?'

Ncube coughed and mumbled and then spoke up with enthusiasm, 'A white man who came earlier yesterday evening.'

'Do you have a name?'

'No, he isn't known around these parts.'

'A description?'

'Yes, but it's as woolly as the coat of a goat. You know all white men look the same unless they're fat, bald and have skin dappled like boerewors or hair the colour of pumpkin.'

'Something other than food descriptions? Some detail to go on?'

Ncube shuffled and consulted his notebook, 'Tall, light skin, blondish, blue eyes, long pointy nose, ears that allow light to pass through and shine red...'

'That description would fit every *mukiwa* from here to Cape Town.'

'I did say the report was unclear, sir.'

'Unclear? More like a thick September haze after a bush fire. Come on, Ncube, I can tell you're hiding something; your gut is sloshing about like fish in a bucket. What else did you find out?'

The subsequent explosion was of such force Sibanda thought his sergeant would be propelled to the police station without his feet touching the ground.

Ncube ignored the digestive detonation, looked around hoping to blame someone in the dispersed crowd, and patted his trousers as if the slapping sound could disguise his embarrassment. He did feel better, but he suspected his recovery would be short lived once the detective heard the name he was suppressing.

'An expensive car...' the sergeant stuttered and took a deep breath, '...with a deformed boy in the back, with no top lip.'

'Don't make a meal of it, Ncube. Who was driving?'

A meal is what Ncube could have done with right now, a delicious blob of stiff maize porridge, *isitshwala,* covered with lashings of thick, meaty gravy, laced with tomato and onion and a hint of garlic to appease his nervy system. 'The car was parked outside Haddad's house yesterday afternoon,' he continued, his head buried in his notebook, avoiding the detective's eyes.

'What sort of a car?' As the question left his lips, Sibanda already knew the answer. 'A black Mercedes.' They spoke in unison.

'Did anyone recognise the driver?'

Ncube gave up ever knowing a calm, compliant stomach again, 'Minister Muchacha.'

Chapter 10

'What? Now?'

'Yes, now, Caro. We have to leave.'

'But why? I love it here, love the bush. We're not in any rush to get back. Our return tickets aren't booked for another week.'

'I changed the tickets. We're leaving for England the day after tomorrow, first flight I could get out of this god forsaken hell hole.'

'It's too soon. I've still got to…'

'… and I have a business crisis to attend to.'

'Crisis? Oh no! Can't Bilal handle it?'

'Bilal Haddad?' Rupert almost choked on the name.

'What other Bilal do we know?' His wife ladled on the sarcasm. 'I thought he was a partner in Templeton's.

'No, he can't, and don't stick your damn nose into my business,' Rupert snapped, his nerves shredded.

'Can I at least have a shower, wash off the suntan lotion?'

'Did you need to tan? Your skin is dark enough. Hurry up.'

Caroline slammed the bathroom door and ran a shower. Rupert's comments were becoming pointed. She was hurt and angry and as with every argument, she twisted her engagement ring around her finger. The ring's exquisite beauty sparkled under the shower water. Caroline resented the ring. More of a millstone than a token of enduring love. She wished Bobo hadn't found it again.

The story of the diamond's survival was part of the Hudson family mythology. Bobo Hudson, according to Rupert, turned into a bloodhound when the ring disappeared. Grandmother Hudson passed away in Boston and the Hudson diamond, her engagement ring, couldn't be found. Bobo searched high and low, rifling through her mother's drawers, ransacking every cupboard. She became frantic when the family discovered the jewel was under-insured. According to Rupert, his mother wittered endlessly and since his father had died the previous year, he was on the receiving end of the anxiety. Months later, a casual conversation with a cousin reminded Bobo how fond her mother was of incinerating waste. She flew back to Boston on the earliest plane. In a pair of overalls never worn before or since, Bobo sieved her way through years of charcoal and ash like a forty-niner panning for gold. She picked over anything solid, sluicing the debris like a professional. Nothing missed her eye. She struck gold after two weeks. The gemstone, born in pressure and fire, survived the second conflagration of an incinerator. Newly polished, the diamond caught the light once more and tossed it back with the brilliance of witty dinner party repartee. Bobo insured the ring for its real value and locked it away in the bank safety deposit box along with a few other baubles.

The conversation where Rupert asked his mother for the ring was the focus of much giggling pillow talk between Caroline and Rupert leading up to their wedding. Rupert imitated his mother's Boston drawl to perfection. He was in the wrong profession. He should have been an actor or a stand-up comedian. Lately, his sense of humour and the boyish fun she'd fallen for had disappeared, like the wretched ring, in a smouldering fire of sour throw away lines.

'I didn't realise you would need it so soon,' Bobo had said, handing her son his drink. 'Will it be...?' she rarely swallowed her words, but this negotiation required delicacy. The thought of the Hudson jewel encircling a lower-class finger incensed her.

'...Safe, mother?' interjected Rupert.

'The Hudson legacy is of consequence, darling.'

'Caro understands this,' he replied, looking into his mother's face, 'She has agreed to return all valuables should the marriage break down without issue. She will sign a document to that effect.'

'You've thought of everything, clever darling.' His mother's shoulders relaxed as the amber liquid from the peaty bogs of Scotland swirled over her ceramic teeth.

The engagement party was the talk of the shires. Caroline remembered with satisfaction the satin bias-cut dress she wore that caressed her Monroe curves. A revealing simplicity seduced every man in the room. Tasty Miss Jacob's working-class origins never peppered any male conversations, but Caroline knew from stolen glances and hidden whispers they certainly salted the female ones.

'Hurry up, Caroline, I'm leaving now,' Rupert banged on the bathroom door, 'I've thrown your stuff in the suitcase.'

Caroline sighed, stepped out of the shower, gave the ring one last twist, and smiled.

Chapter 11

Sibanda never slept well, but that night he tossed and turned more than he usually did. The rain on his tin roof was a lullaby. The hollow tapping ranged from a gentle persistent patter to a loud drumming, an effective sleeping pill. Tonight, the rhythmic serenade gave him no relief, and when thunder began to rumble and roar like a pride of lions, he gave up, got up and threw a pan of coffee on the stove.

His thoughts on the two murder cases were tumbling around his brain. He couldn't make the links, couldn't seem to fix on a frontrunner for the murders. The trip to the Falls turned up little of value. Thomas Mabiza, the vendor at the market was up to no good, wore his guilt with the sweaty discomfort of vinyl Chinese shoes, but with no obvious tie to Laurent Kasongo or Mama Ecstasy. Sipping a thick black coffee, Sibanda turned his attention to the Muchacha clan, the sculpting twins and their high-powered rural neighbour, Cuthbert, ex Minister of Mines, current Minister of Cultural Affairs. Motive, geography and a sculpture linked them and Mama Ecstasy was the work of Talkmore or Talkless Manhombo. Muchacha, in his black Mercedes, ran Miss Daisy off the road. He was travelling down from the Falls. Could have been there at the same time as Laurent Kasongo. Was there a connection between Muchacha and this second murder victim, Madani Haddad? The Minister was present at the victim's house on the day of both murders. Did he kill Haddad and then linger until night fall and shoot Kasongo. If not him then maybe his henchmen? Time and place fitted, but what was his motive? Diamonds? The Manhombo twins hailed from the diamond fields. Were they the mules ferrying the precious stones to Vic Falls? Was Gubu somehow at the centre of a smuggling route? What evidence did he have to sustain that theory? Nothing, a few clues; the gemmologist's loupe, the tweezers, some dodgy demographics, and a bit of geography. If the diamonds were clearing through Gubu, and the comings and goings at Haddad's house indicated nocturnal and underhand dealings, where were the stones now? Haddad's house was as whistle clean as the polished Ncube household. Sibanda scratched his chin. His thoughts were turning to the motley crew on the Rugged Rascals truck and how the overlanders might fit into the picture.

A flash of lightning lit up his yard as though day had arrived under a harsh blue-white flare. He flinched, rubbed his thigh and wondered if he would ever get over the instinct to duck. That thought vaporised as he caught the hint of a movement through his open window. Something was circling his house. An outline, highlighted as the last of the murderous light swept the earth, told him the silhouette wasn't an animal. Sibanda was being watched. He'd done too many stake outs himself not to recognise the signs – shadowy figures, more than one, skulking behind cover and using sign language to communicate. These two were careless or bored, or skittish because of the storm. Watchers, he figured from their body language, and not about to move in on him. Sibanda switched off the light, doing nothing to alert the stalkers he'd seen them, and assessed the risk. He watched until the pair moved off in the light of dawn.

They'd left their departure late, made the rookie mistake of overestimating the gloom cast by a threatening storm. When the sun broke through the layered corduroy clouds, fluorescent as a bubble of cheap gum, the snoopers hurried. The pair scuttled from their exposure, woodlice looking for another rock to hide under. Sibanda recognised one. He'd worked with him in CID and heard he'd moved on to Police Internal Security which meant this stake out was officially sanctioned. Once again, he was being hounded. Memories of the last time he fell foul of officialdom flooded his early morning. Cuthbert Muchacha, Minister of Mines, had sewn him up then, had him demoted and transferred and Cuthbert Muchacha ex Minister of mines and current Minister of Rural and Cultural Affairs was after more than his skin this time.

As the pink bubble floated higher and began to moulder to a jaundiced yellow in the damp and muggy morning, Sibanda made his way to the police station. At reception he greeted PC Khumalo.

'Morning Zee. Good crowd in this morning, I see.' Sibanda gestured to a number of head holding, hand wrenching unfortunates awaiting their turn.

'You know this weather sir, it gets everyone's nerves on end. No one can sleep for the heat and humidity. We're all tense getting the lands ready for the crops, plus,' she gestured to the sorry mob, 'pay day and too much beer. Bit of a punch up at the Blu Gnu. All petty stuff but it'll keep me busy.'

'Where's Ncube?'

'Haven't seen him. He's not in yet.'

Sibanda turned on his heels and headed back through the door. 'Unlike him to be late. Have you tried his phone?' he called over his shoulder.

'What phone? He hasn't caught up with technology yet...' Her words were lost as Sibanda sprinted back towards the Ncube house.

He could hear babies crying and women fussing as he approached. Ncube was sitting on the stoop, head in hands, blood pouring through his fingers, trickling onto the polished red floor and camouflaging itself as water.

'What happened Ncube?' Ncube's gate was open, the twist of wire acting as a latch had been cut.

'Intruders, sir.' He looked around to check none of his wives were in hearing distance. 'I couldn't sleep because of the heat and caught them in my yard before dawn. I *tshayaed* one, a fair punch to the gut, but I didn't see the other until too late. He flayed me with the butt of a pistol, grabbed me around the throat. I couldn't breathe.'

'That's a bad cut, Ncube.'

'Blessing has been trying to stop the bleeding. I may need stitches. I'm off to see Sister Angel.' He lowered his voice to a whisper and looked around, 'This wasn't an ordinary burglary attempt.'

'Because they carried weapons?'

'They didn't look like robbers. Wore suits. Who robs a house in a suit? My next-door neighbour arrived with a baseball bat and his two sons. Before the thugs took off, the one guy with his hand around my throat asked me where the diamonds were. You haven't found any diamonds, sir?'

'No diamonds, Ncube, but someone has them and your intruder friends will do anything to get their hands on them.'

'Could they have been taken from Laurent Kasongo's backpack? Is that why he was murdered?'

'Or was there a stash at Madani Haddad's place, or both? Whichever, it makes life dangerous. I want you to get your family out of Gubu, Ncube. Send them home to plough your lands. Well tell everyone at the station you tripped and gashed your head. I don't want this made public.'

'Are we in danger?

'You have children. These guys will stop at nothing. I know how they operate. If you want to leave, I'll understand.'

'I said I'll stay, and I will.'

'When you're stitched up, come to the station. We have planning to do.'

'Sir, you know I said I couldn't sleep last night.'

'Yes.'

'I was thinking about Madani Haddad's murder. I've come up with a solution. I know how the murderer got in and out of that room.'

'What's your theory?'

'The murderer jacked up the roof, just a little, and then sent in a tame baboon to kill the victim. A cornered baboon can be murderous.'

'If I didn't know better, Ncube, I'd say you'd been reading Edgar Alan Poe.' The tone of Sibanda's quip should have warned Ncube.

'Reading, sir? Me? I swear I haven't read a book since grade seven. Everyone knows baboons are the familiars of the spirit world and can hide in cupboards. You don't have to read books for that. Remember the poaching case? Yes…' The light of understanding flooded Ncube's eyes, 'That's it, maybe the baboon was hiding in the cupboard all along…'

'…Or Ncube, how about this theory?' The irony was so thick in Sibanda's voice it could have plastered an entire hut, 'our murderer pumped a gas so awful, under the door, it caused the victim to go mad, bash himself in the face and choke himself to death.' Sibanda could feel his empathy for the injured sergeant waning and his sarcasm rising to bursting point.

Ncube laughed, 'That's a bit far-fetched, ki ki ki.'

Blessing arrived just in time. Sibanda's tolerance was stretched to its thinnest. 'Why are you laughing, Ncube, I have told you to stay calm. Is the head wound making you stupid?'

Ncube's senior wife was quite sharp with her rebuke. 'Oh, detective, I didn't see you there. Greetings. Stay for tea.'

'Sorry, I must go now, Mama. Look after your husband, that knock to the head has rattled his brain. I've told him to take a break and take it easy for a while, but he's insisting on coming into work. Such an outstanding officer.' Sibanda clapped his hand on Ncube's shoulder, hoping they'd been able to keep the situation light. Blessing was nobody's fool.

Ncube's gaze followed Sibanda as he set off back to the station, not sure if he'd been praised or insulted but knowing he would have to keep his wits about him. 'Get the family organised, Blessing, and let them know it's time to plough our lands. We can't ignore the riches of this rain.'

Sibanda was halfway back to the station when his phone rang. 'Jabs, is this a good time?'

'If you have news for me, it's always a good time, Eddie.'

'What's that noise in the background? Sounds like a jet coming in to land.'

'Rain, Eddie. Downpours come in a deluge in this part of the world. Hang on while I find some cover.' Sibanda ran to Barghee's veranda and watched as sheets of water streamed and pummelled in a continuous flood.

'Did you get that? Are you still there? I've dug up stuff on a couple of the names.' Eddie was having to shout over the rain. 'James Templeton was employed by a brokerage firm of the same name for some years. I've had the word they're in trouble, up to all sorts of shady deals. The main guy is overseas. The authorities are on to him. Word is James Templeton is getting out before the ship sinks. He won't be clean as a whistle. Everyone in the City has their hands in the pie.'

'Any diamond connection?' Sibanda was straining to make himself heard.

'Can't say, but the firm has broken every rule in the book. The banking and investment sector is rotten over here. Africa isn't alone in corruption. All I have on the Van Dalen sisters is that they are some kind of circus act. But I do have a diamond connection for you.'

'Who?'

'Marlie Scalzo.'

'The American girl?'

'Easy to trace with that surname. She's a park ranger in Arkansas.'

'What's that got to do with diamonds?'

'The park is the Crater of Diamonds State Park.'

Sibanda took a moment to absorb the information. 'I didn't know they mined diamonds in the USA.'

'Not mining exactly. The park is a small area, around thirty-seven ploughed up acres. Pay the entry fee and you can search for diamonds. The rangers assess finds. Punters keep them. Scalzo is one of the experts who gives the Certificate of Authenticity. Knows her stuff.'

Sibanda mulled over his next move. Two leads were in his sights; James Templeton and Marlie Scalzo, one attached to a corrupt firm, probably on the run and the other a diamond grader or at least familiar with the gems. James even had access to Kasongo's backpack. Did he see diamonds and scheme with Marlie to get his hands on them? The pair seemed cosy together.

Sergeant Ncube, caught up with him. 'Stitches?'

'No, I didn't go to the clinic. Blessing staunched the bleeding with leaves.' He pointed to a large bandage around his head with a few green leaves poking out. Sibanda noted they were from a species of combretum, *umbondo*. The leaves were soft and velvety with a furry underside. The old time *sangomas* knew they worked best to staunch bleeding when fresh and moist. Blessing had used the traditional Ndebele wound dressing of King Lobengula's warriors.

'And your family?'

'Packing up to leave for our rural home. My wives didn't want to go on account of my injury, but I am, after all, the husband and for once I made my wishes clear. I don't like anger but there's danger about. I feel as stressed as a dung beetle pushing an oversize dung ball uphill only to have it roll back down again. My wives got the message. I want them to prepare the lands. They'll be on the bus in half an hour.'

'Good. And how's Miss Daisy?'

'We are both in the same state, a bit battered and bruised but able to move.'

'Then we're off to Thunduluka to talk to the overlanders again. There's more to them than meets the eye.'

Miss Daisy trundled through the park gates and assessed the road ahead. The first part of the journey to Thunduluka was notorious after a heavy downpour. Unlike later parts of the road where sand wicked away the standing water, this stretch drained badly, was as treacherous as thin ice and required skilled driving. She knew from all the pumping and wrenching of her bits and pieces that the detective was behind the wheel, the self-same driver who'd driven her straight into a tree. The pain, discomfort and disfigurement were distressing. *Oh dear*, she seemed to sigh, *here we go again...*

'Ncube, what's all that huffing coming from the engine? '

'Nothing serious, sir. I've checked Miss Daisy out since the accident, but it might be better not to drive fast... this road...'

Sibanda never commented, his eyes glued to the rear-view mirror, a shiny survivor given the age of Miss Daisy. The detective's view was crazed and vibrating but he could make out a vehicle approaching from behind at a mad speed, 'I think we have visitors, Ncube.'

'Visitors?'

'We're being followed, hang on.' Sibanda slammed his foot hard on the accelerator. Miss Daisy leapt forward, throwing up mud and slurry, her threadbare tyres doing their best to grip the treacherous road. As she lurched and skated, so did Ncube. His already damaged head hit the side window and the wound re opened.

'Sir, this is a dangerous speed!' Ncube was alarmed; his head was aching, his stomach gassing up. 'Are we being chased by an elephant?' his voice wobbled.

'Behind us is the deadliest species on the planet, Ncube. A dust-up with an elephant would be the least of our worries.'

Ncube clung to the seat, the tension in Sibanda's jaw emphasising the danger. He glanced back to see a pick-up pursuing them at speed. 'People sir, and they're catching up with us.'

'We have to shake them.'

'How?' Ncube's eyes were now on the temperature gauge which was starting to rise. 'Miss Daisy can't outrun them. Are they after the diamonds?'

'Either they think we have the stones, or they want to stop us investigating the syndicate. We're getting too close to the source.' Miss Daisy's steering wheel was swinging from side to side as Sibanda wrestled to keep her on the road. He hoped he could get her to the better drainage ahead. The easier road would allow him to think.

'Can't we pull off and hide in the bushes, sir?'

'No use Ncube, the road's wet. We'll leave tracks a blind man could read.' Sibanda glanced overhead. The sky was heaving with thunder clouds; black, water-filled balloons ready for popping. Would the weather do them a favour? If they could get far enough ahead, a downpour might wash out their tracks.

'Sir,' Ncube's voice was beset with fear, 'I can see their faces and… and… they have guns pointed at us.'

The first shot whistled past Miss Daisy. Sibanda swerved once, then again. The pursuers were aiming for the tyres, a hard enough target on a steady road. Sibanda pumped the accelerator. Miss Daisy had no more oomph to give. She was flat out and failing.

'How many of them in the vehicle, Ncube?'

'Two in the front. The two shooters are in the back.'

On his own, Sibanda would have slammed to a stop and skipped into the bush. He could outrun the goons and outwit them. The bush was his territory. But Ncube didn't stand a chance. Another hail of bullets skimmed past the Land Rover. Sibanda heard the ring of metal on metal as a bullet sliced through the back door and ricocheted through the roof. Ncube was crouched as low as his bulk would allow, head in hands, blood pouring through his fingers. The shooters were targeting the cab. Sibanda and Ncube were caged lions in a hunter's paralysing spotlight.

Miss Daisy was coughing. The chase was coming to a close for her, for all of them. Sibanda was beginning to think ploughing into the bush might be a last resort when a herd of cow elephants appeared on the road ahead.

'Ncube!' he yelled, 'hang on tight. We've got a chance. Close your eyes and don't open them until I tell you.' What he was about to do was idiocy, sheer madness that went against every belief he held, but it was their one chance to escape the lethal pack following them. In a flash, he picked out a mother and calf on the right of the road. 'Come on Miss Daisy, a bit more effort,' he mouthed, as he, Miss Daisy and a quivering, sightless Ncube hurtled towards the herd. The mother, sensing danger, screamed at her calf to run ahead but she was too late. Sibanda slammed on the brakes, slid towards the pair, gliding between mother and son. Miss Daisy delicately brushed the baby, nudging him further from his mother. The calf bellowed in distress. Sibanda accelerated through the rest of the herd, pushing Miss Daisy to her limits, haring down the road like a cheetah at full stretch.

When Sibanda looked in the jiggling rear-view mirror he could make out the chaos left in their wake. The pursuing pick-up drove straight into the milling herd and the eye line of the angry mother. With Miss Daisy out of reach, the cow turned her attention to the next best thing, another growling metal creature about to threaten her offspring. The pick-up came to a screeching halt. Mud showered and spattered the windscreen but didn't obscure the terrified faces in the front seat. The car was now reversing as fast as possible, zig zagging with the cow in hot pursuit until the vehicle hit the side of the road and toppled over. The two shooters in the back, thrown out, were running. They had the sense to know a low calibre handgun was no match for a charging elephant. The angry mama would keep the remaining two occupants pinned for some time. The unharmed baby was trumpeting at the runners, taunting them with new-found bravado.

A couple of kilometres further down the road, Sibanda drove a wheezing Miss Daisy into the bush and negotiated the trees and fallen logs until he felt he was a safe distance from the road. The heavens opened with monsoon ferocity. Their tracks would be obliterated.

'What happened back there, sir?' Ncube opened his eyes one at a time in case full vision was too alarming. 'How did you give them the slip?'

'Don't ask, Ncube. We'll hang around here until Miss Daisy recovers and we're not being followed, then it's back to Gubu.'

'What about the overlanders?'

'They'll keep. I've got their passports. I'm beginning to think we have bigger fish to fry.'

'Fish sir? Do you have fish? I'm feeling as though my ribs have collapsed into the hole that is my stomach.'

Sibanda controlled his desire to snap at his sergeant. Instead, he removed his shirt, ripped it and rebandaged Ncube's head. Rain dripped through the new bullet hole in the roof and fell between them onto the deck chair upholstery.

CHAPTER 12

Extract from the memoirs of John Jacobs:

Lo Bengula had been 20 years on the throne when he employed me as the Royal Secretary. He learned I was educated in Holland, Scotland, and the Cape. I am classified as cape coloured, a proud ethnic group descended from a mix of European settlers, Khoisan, Xhosa, and slaves from India, Indonesia and Malaysia. My father, I'm told, was a European shipwreck survivor. My mother soon abandoned me, her light skinned child, to the streets and the missionaries. Pastor Asseline rescued me and took me to his orphanage. I learned quickly. I shone. The Pastor sent me to Europe to further my studies, at first, to a Dutch Seminary which time is best forgotten, although I profited from the spiritual knowledge. Later I was sent to Scotland.

How did I enter Matabeleland? For a few years, I was the self-styled pastor of the Ethiopian church, but religion did not pay well. It might sustain the soul but did little for the mind and body. I heard of riches and opportunities to the north. I set off, trading a few diamonds here and there, and for my sins, spending some months in prison for crimes best forgotten. After much adventure and acquaintance with life's vicissitudes, I entered Matabeleland. When King Lo Bengula learned of my skills, that I could read and write and speak many languages including English, Dutch, and Zulu, I was summoned to his employment.

The King was being hounded, at that time, by the English and the Dutch for mining concessions. After the duplicity of Rhodes, Rudd and his cohorts, he needed someone trustworthy to write agreements and translate intentions. He learned the English were ruled by documents, legal terms and signatures, but not by words. The Dutch were a bunch of thieves who never kept their word, spoken or written. The King knew where he was with the Dutch. His advisors counselled he play the two rapacious nations off against one another. Enter his new Royal Secretary, me, John Jacobs.

I crossed the Limpopo into the kingdom of the Matabele late in 1888. Too late to have any effect on the Rudd disaster that was to steal a kingdom by stealth. It would be another six years before I crossed back. Had I been at the King's side a few months earlier, when those devious and scheming negotiations took place, the map of Africa would have been much changed. This is an account of all that happened in those years. I made a promise to recount the events truthfully. The memories remain clear, despite the passage of time. To all the gainsayers and disbelievers, to the treasure hunters and government officials who have doubted me, I stand by the truth of my words. My honesty is all I have left.

My first task on arriving at the King's kraal of Bulawayo was to document all his possessions. A large journal was at my disposal. I carried with me powder to make ink and a sharp knife to pare the quills of which there was an endless supply. The land was plagued with eagles quick to make off with fowl, or the kids from the King's goat herds. The herd boys are accurate with sling shots, and eagle feathers make fine writing implements. I began my accounting with those herds, documenting every single beast. The cattle were Lo Bengula's pride and joy. He oversaw them himself, from time to time walked among them, stopping to admire the red and white markings of a fine Nguni bull or the gleaming black hide of a healthy cow, commenting that the shields of his regiments would never be few. There were often feasts when the slaughtering of forty cattle would be ordered. The hides were sorted and taken to be made into the distinctive shields of the differing regiments, each battalion denoted by a different colour or pattern. The king was proud of his army. In the year of our Lord, 1888, he feared no one. His warriors raided the neighbouring tribes and stole their women, children and cattle with impunity. But times were changing. The British were about to woo those tribes with promises of protection and sovereignty. Ha! Those fools were duped as easily as the king.

Every day, the King partook of vast haunches of beef swilled down with millet beer. When I arrived to take up my post, he was already a large man, perhaps larger than anyone I had ever met. When I left, he was so obese and riddled with gout that a million maggots would take years to eat through the mounds of flesh that hung off his body. But I am getting ahead of myself.

One evening, when the reckoning of cattle was done and written up in the ledger. The King called me to his palace. This was not a palace as I had seen in Scotland with towers and curlicues and all manner of ornamentation, but a collection of large, well-constructed mud huts clustered next to one another and surrounded by a thorn picket. The King's bodyguard saw me approaching and led me to his door. I came prepared to write a letter.

The hut was dark, filled with smoke and stinking of fat. A single candle burned. The king lay on a bed of furs many hides thick. On top was a leopard skin kaross made from the pelt of four animals sewn together with sinew. Lo Bengula's large body sank into the bed, 'I wish to write to the white Queen, Jacobi, take down my words.'

'Queen Victoria?' I queried, for I was shocked to be asked to write to such nobility.

'Do you question me?' he snarled, raising himself up on his elbow.

'Never my King, Black lion of Mabindela, spoor of the leopard that disappears in the river, destroyer of the commoners, he whose path is winding like that of ants.' I recited some of the King's praise poem. With hindsight these may not have been the best lines to repeat. They reminded him of his wariness, his lack of military victories, and his tendency to have difficult policies to follow. Lo Bengula may not have been as sadistic as his father, the great King Mzilikazi, but I witnessed his justice when displeased. It was brutal; severing of lips, gouging of eyes and cutting out of tongues I saw with my own eyes. Yet, his warriors still muttered, called him a weak woman with not enough bloodlust compared to the old king.

Lo Bengula sank back into the furs, 'Translate what I say.'

'As you wish, my King.'

These were his words, so few as to be easily committed to memory: "the white people are troubling me much about gold. If the Queen hears I have given away my country it is not so." The Rudd Concession had become a millstone around the King's neck, deliberately misinterpreted by the colonialists. He was appealing to their paramount chieftain to intervene.

I wrote in my best hand, for this was to be read by the Queen of the most powerful nation on earth, changing not a word. When written, I took the letter to the king. He scrutinised the writing, my perfect copperplate, and asked me to read it back to him. He seemed satisfied.

'Place my seal on the letter and send it to the white Queen.'

He watched as I melted the wax and sealed the letter. The King's seal was oblong bearing the imprint of an elephant with the words King of the Matabele and Mashonas *written underneath. He had the stamp made for him in England which is why the elephant looked Indian with small ears. The seal maker had no idea what an African elephant looked like.*

When the Queen's reply arrived a year later, these were the words she sent: "A King gives a stranger an ox, not his whole herd of cattle, otherwise what would other strangers arriving have to eat?" *Clearly, she was a woman who dealt in enigma and riddle, but the reply had no currency anyway. By then, Rhodes had trampled on the Rudd Concession and the verbally agreed appendices to limit each mining concession to ten men. He flooded the country with over 200 pioneers, giving each 3000 acres of the Ndebele Kingdom. There was....*

The rest of the page was illegible. Water had seeped into the journal at some point. Caroline rubbed her eyes. The spidery writing had given them a workout. Was she related to John Jacobs? It looked like it. Did that mean she had an exotic mixture of cape coloured in her blood? What a thought. When the lawyer called and told her she now owned an old house in Bulawayo, little did she know she would be reclaiming her birthright and discovering her true heritage. She twisted her engagement ring round and round until she worked it off her finger and placed it on the bedside table. Caroline's mind and body were cleansed with a lightness she hadn't felt for ages. In a reversal of roles, she seemed to float from the bed as a free African woman who looked down on the chained European girl, heavy and laden below.

CHAPTER 13

Sibanda made his way back to the park gates, taking every side road, every little-known track, every navigable game trail until he was certain they weren't being followed. Miss Daisy made slow progress, but the gentle, circuitous journey gave her time to recover. The same could not be said of Sergeant Ncube. He began shivering, and as Sibanda recounted the full horror of the event and the encounter with the elephants, he set to shaking, his large body undulating in panic, his jowls quivering and his stomach promising an event of unrivalled precedence. The only positive in the assessment of his health was that his head had stopped bleeding. The bandage applied by Sibanda was bound so tightly no blood dared seep.

'Settle, Ncube, we're safe now. Those guys will be in no state to come after us.'

'There will be others.'

'We'll face that hurdle when we get to it.' Sibanda's immediate concern was Ncube's unreliable digestion. 'Haven't you got one of those lunch boxes your wives prepare, or a can of orange fizz?'

'They left in too much of a hurry, I wanted them away from the danger as quickly as possible.'

'We'll pick something up from the kiosk.' Sibanda brought the Land Rover to a halt at the park gate.

'Is it wise to stop here, sir? I thought we should try and sneak though unnoticed. The boldness of a lion does not protect it from the hunter's spear.'

'We aren't going to be speared, Ncube. I'll check in with the warden. You go and buy a pie.' He handed some money to the sergeant.

'I'm not sure my legs....'

Sibanda got out of the vehicle and strode towards the warden's office, leaving Ncube testing his unreliable muscles. Approaching the office, the detective became aware of bustling activity. Multiple vehicles were starting up laden with kit and men.

'Ah, detective Sibanda, you've come about the incident.' Edison Bango, the warden barked instructions, pointed to vehicles. 'Terrible. Two men are badly injured, their vehicle squashed by an elephant, another broke a leg and knocked himself out running away. Tourists came upon them. They were lucky.'

'Where are they now?'

'Transported to hospital.'

'Do you know who they are?'

'A couple of civil servants on a jaunt. Up here for some reason and with time on their hands to go game viewing.'

'And the fourth man?'

'Still running. We are off to track him down now.'

'Then I won't keep you.' Sibanda looked to the sky and raised his eyebrows.

'Yes, in this weather.' Warden Bango pointed to overhead clouds about to burst, 'It's going to be almost impossible. I hope he has the sense to keep dry and stay in one place. This could be a long search.'

'Good luck. Keep me posted.'

Bango replied with a thumbs-up as he headed for his vehicle. The rain started again, lashing the ground ferociously, unrelentingly. Sibanda sprinted to Miss Daisy. Ncube waddled back a few minutes later, half a pie devoured and another waiting. His equilibrium restored, he smiled at the detective, 'Have you heard?'

'Yes, we're in the clear for now but there'll be replacements. Keep your wits about you. We might not need the courage of the lion, but we will need the wiliness of a jackal.'

Miss Daisy pulled into the Gubu station yard, rain streaming through her new plug hole. 'Get that leak fixed, Ncube. We'll need this old crate. I don't want to be swimming on this seat.'

'I will congestion her, sir.'

'Congestion her, Ncube? What are you rabbiting on about?'

'You know, sir? Bung her up.' Ncube allowed himself an inward triumphant smile. He had once again flummoxed his boss with his learning from the Oxford English dictionary.

Sibanda slammed the Land Rover door, shook his head, rolled his eyes, and made for his office. As he entered reception, one look at PC Khumalo's face told him there was trouble.

'What's up, Zee?'

'I don't know. Minister Muchacha was in Cold War's office for at least an hour. After he left, Mfumu looked like the toad that got the dragon fly, strutting around the office with a smile so wide it cracked the creases in his shirt. He wants to see you as soon as you come in. They're cooking something up.'

'Where's Muchacha now?'

'Gone up to the Falls, I expect. Aren't all the politicos going to be up there? Party Conference this week?'

Sibanda strode down the corridor to his office. The minute he opened the door, he knew his room had been given the once over. The search had been subtle, but his dishevelled and unfiled papers were in a changed state of dishevelment. The detective had an eye for his own mess and his own arrangement of dust and chaos with a memory bordering on the photographic. He could smell the intruder; a cheap, thick, oily scent pervaded his office, meaning whoever did this came in early, freshly showered and too enthusiastic with the body lotion. Certainly not the night shift who beat up Ncube. How many teams were after them? One lot were put out of action by the elephant but there would be others on the prowl. He and Ncube needed to watch their backs. At a glance, he could tell they searched with care, thoroughly and professionally. Laurent Kasongo's backpack was gone. What was in there? Not Mama Ecstasy, PC Khumalo had her stowed away safely; not the money that was in Cold War's safe. Just Laurent's change of clothing and the folded newspaper page. If Muchacha's men - and he was certain the minister was behind this raid - found the address, then whoever was in that house in Hillside better be armed and ready. Muchacha did not take prisoners.

'Zee, who was in my office?'

PC Khumalo was on the phone taking notes. 'No one,' she mouthed, 'not since I've been on duty.'

'Who was on the early shift?'

'PC Tshuma, why?'

'Evidence has been removed from my office under his watch.'

PC Khumalo put the phone down, shrugged her shoulders and handed Sibanda her notes, 'From forensics,' she said. 'Mfumu knows you're in.'

'I want a word with him.'

Between reception and the Officer in Charge's office, Sibanda managed to digest the contents of the note. The ash in Madani Haddad's fireplace didn't come from paper, as he suspected, but from a lycra-based fabric and a piece of sponge. A minute part of the garment remained intact, a rounded edge, the finger end of a glove. Whoever killed Madani Haddad used tight-fitting protection to avoid leaving fingerprints on the murder weapon and in the room, then burnt them in the fireplace. He had found no discarded heavy object used to bludgeon the victim. The murder weapon was still missing. Indications were Madani Haddad was murdered before Laurent Kasongo, a few hours at most. What did that mean?

Chief inspector Mfumu looked relaxed when Sibanda entered.

'My office has been rifled and vital evidence removed.' Sibanda was on the offensive, 'Who's been in there?'

'You have bigger problems, Detective Sibanda. You are suspended from duties until further notice,' Mfumu smirked as he added, 'without pay.'

'On what grounds?' Sibanda kept his voice low and measured.

'You are a suspect in a country-wide diamond fraud and your very presence in Gubu Police Station would compromise the furtherance of the investigation.'

'What evidence do you have?'

'Diamonds are missing from the house of a suspected diamond dealer, Madani Haddad. You are the one person to have been in that house on your own. When detective Chanza and PC Khumalo entered the scene, they were together the whole time. You, on the other hand, spent an hour alone checking over the room.'

'Who knew Haddad dealt in diamonds?'

'The CIO, they've had him under surveillance for some time.'

'They must know who murdered him then.'

'According to the Central Intelligence Organisation, he wasn't murdered. He committed suicide. The net was closing in. He killed himself. The door was locked from the inside, impossible for anyone else to enter. He bit off his tongue.' Mfumu began to fiddle with his pens, aligning them like a regimental parade. His discomfort was obvious. The OIC was lying. Someone was leaning on Mfumu, and he was happy to be the prop.

'What have they offered you, Mfumu? A posting to Harare? A cosy station in Kadoma? Madani Haddad was murdered, and you know it.' Sibanda rested his clenched knuckles on the desk, his face inches from Mfumu's.

As he stood to avoid Sibanda's glare, Stalin Mfumu's chair fell backwards, clattering in the awkward silence. Sibanda had crossed a boundary. 'This conversation is finished, Detective Sibanda.' He pointed to the door, his index finger quivering. 'Take your personal belongings and leave this police station until further notice. I require your I.D and keys.' He held out his hand.

'You have no idea what you're getting yourself into, Mfumu, and when you do, you'll need more than a dose of the Old Testament to get you out of it.' Sibanda threw his ID and keys on the desk and stormed out of the office.

From his own office, Sibanda picked up the overlanders' passports and put them in his pocket. His office was bare of personal belongings. He'd learnt long ago to keep his private life separate from work. No photos, no trinkets, no good luck charms. Eddie from Sherwood kept a half-clad Barbie doll on his desk. Some remnant from an early case he'd solved. A complete red herring he claimed, but he kissed her lips before every investigation, said she reminded him he wasn't Sherlock Holmes and could make a complete balls-up of things if he didn't focus. Too superstitious for Sibanda.

'I won't be in for a while, Zee, but keep your ears open for me.'

'Going on leave, sir? Off to plough?'

'You could say that.' He forced a smile. 'Where's Ncube?'

'Out in the yard, tinkering. How he keeps that wreck on the road, I'll never know.'

He found Ncube on top of Miss Daisy's roof. The sun came out with blistering intensity and the earth was steaming. The sergeant looked up, his face a sea of dripping sweat and determination. The humidity was heavy and energy sapping.

'Fixing the *congestion,* are you?'

'Yes, sir, all done. Pratley's putty,' he waved a tube of instant cement. 'Miss Daisy will stay dry until I can patch her up with a bit of welding.'

'Time to leave, Sergeant. Get out of Gubu and join your wives.'

'But...'

'...No arguments this time. I've been suspended. Things are heating up around here. The CIO are involved. They're after the diamonds.'

'The CIO?' Ncube trembled. 'Suspended? Why? There are no diamonds.'

'Not that we know of, Ncube, but they're convinced there are and that I'm involved. Go home, see to your lands.'

'What will you do?'

'Take a break, catch up on some sleep, do a bit of birdwatching. This could be the enforced breather I've been looking for.' He placed a hand on Ncube's shoulder, 'Look after yourself and that family of yours.'

Ncube was both moved and alarmed by the detective's affection. He watched Sibanda walk away. Taking a break? That would be like a vulture eating seeds. The detective wasn't a man to holiday. He would never abandon an unsolved murder case, let alone two. Thadeus Ncube didn't believe a word of it.

'Well, Miss Daisy,' he patted the old Land Rover on her remaining mud guard, 'I don't think we'll be moving far. Do you? The detective will need us even though he doesn't think he does. Better get you fixed up. Now where did I put that spanner?'

Chapter 14

Sibanda placed a pot on the stove and shook the remains of the coffee grounds into the filter. He screwed up the empty packet and threw it into the bin. He was broke after giving the last of his money to Ncube to pay for those pies. His bank account was flat and this month's salary, due tomorrow, was to replenish supplies and pay bills. He boiled up the last of his mealie meal and rinsed out a tomato sauce bottle for gravy.

If Mfumu thought he was abandoning those murder cases, he was mistaken.

He sat at the table, swiped a mound of isitshwala into the watery tomato sauce and began to list all the suspects. Cuthbert Muchacha and his cohorts were top of his list, an ex-Minister of Mines involved in lining his pockets on a daily basis, reshuffled to Cultural Affairs as punishment for his part in underhand schemes - suspect number one. Ncube mentioned an accomplice with a deformed top lip. Could he have been brought along to do Muchacha's dirty work? Muchacha was looking for the diamonds. If he was behind Haddad's murder, he had left empty-handed. Had someone got there before him and made off with the stash? A non descript white man had been hanging around the house. Who was he and how did he fit into the picture? And then there were the overlanders. Marlie Scalzo knew her diamonds, James Templeton worked for a firm in trouble. They were in the mix. Nothing yet on the Van Dalen sisters, the circus act. He wanted to call Eddie back for information but there was little airtime on his phone. Not enough to make an overseas call. He would need that credit for emergencies. He couldn't decide if Barney Rubble Jones turning up like a bad penny was a blessing or a curse. How he would love to find he played a role in the diamond story. Being back in Zimbabwe put him too close to Berry. Sibanda knew he couldn't lay claim to her, but, selfishly, he didn't want anyone else in her sights. He threw his dishes in the sink with more violence than was necessary, poured a coffee and sat on his veranda, staring into the bush. He looked for something, anything, to distract him from thinking about the woman he had loved and lost.

The following day and night passed in a blur. He was getting no closer to any kind of solution and the lack of coffee and proper food was beginning to take its toll. His irritation levels were toxic. He sat again on his veranda, nursing the dregs of a whiskey bottle. The setting sun was excluded from the horizon by a stew of dark, dumpling clouds; the evening mourned the absence of light. Heavy, sticky gloom trickled like treacle, weighing down the world and scrubbing out all colour.

When Sibanda's phone chirped its night jar call, he was so far away in thought, he scanned the bush expecting to see the bird close by. He didn't recognise the number and was instantly wary.

A woman's voice asked, 'Detective, Sibanda?'

'Yes.'

'Thank God.'

'Who is this?'

'Nokhuthula Nxumalo... Thula.'

'The girl from the nail bar in the village?' Sibanda pictured the disabled girl who'd helped him before.

'Yes, you remembered...' She was both grateful and flattered, 'but we haven't much time to talk.' Thula took a deep breath. She would have loved to chat with the handsome detective, but she needed to warn him. 'Are you at home?'

'Yes.'

'Get out now. They're coming for you.'

'Who?'

'I don't know. They were standing under the tree outside the nail bar. Guys in suits, talking as if I didn't exist or was deaf or stupid. But I heard it all. They have guns, were talking about how they needed to get rid of you. They know you aren't at work. I called as soon as I could. Please hurry, get out.'

'Thanks, Thula.'

Sibanda pocketed his phone, grabbed the one-eyed binoculars and headed for the bedroom. He checked the cupboard. His emergency backpack was there, sitting in the corner, almost invisible under folded winter blankets. A dirty shirt lay on top of the laundry pile. Sibanda stuffed the crumpled garment in a zipped pocket. He exited through the back door, was over the fence and sprinting before the door swung closed.

The first shots pinged into the front door as he raced towards Duiker Ave. His killers were using a silencer.

They meant business. He skirted the main thoroughfares, leapt a few back fences. Reaching the railway line, he took cover behind one of the rotting, discarded carriages. The ballast between the rails was perfect to hide his tracks but the village was still busy with the comings and goings of the day. Someone would spot him. Gubu would be alive with the news of a felon on the run. Sibanda understood his tribe well. There was nothing they liked more than to catch a baddie and give him a thorough beating. Many of the villagers were outstanding trackers, involved in hunting and tourism. A group of vigilantes, whipped up by the CIO, would be on his tail and with a probable reward on his head, doubly motivated. A rogue police officer? What a catch. Using the bush parallel to the railway line as cover, he reached the sewage ponds. Other than elephants, few people came this way. He shinned up a large acacia until he was well hidden high in the thickly leaved summer branches and wedged himself in a fork. Satisfied he was undetected, he switched off his phone and removed the sim then placed both in the inside pocket of his jacket. They couldn't track him with mobile technology. Next, he familiarised himself with the contents of the backpack. He'd stowed it months ago when he'd first arrived in Gubu knowing he would need it one day, knowing his enemies hadn't gone far. The contents were sparse, but they'd do. His main concern was money or the lack of it. He knew where to get his hands on some, but that would have to wait for the cover of darkness. In the meantime, this was as good a hiding spot as any.

The night was moonless. A steady drizzle fell, Sibanda picked his path with care. In the dark, he moved once again using the railway line to disguise his tracks. When he reached a suitable point, he left the line and headed towards Gubu village. Sibanda jogged through already ploughed lands, his body bent and his profile low. A couple of dogs howled and barked in the distance. Did they sense his presence? Or were they throwing their echo against the night sky, seeing how far the sound carried, baying for the excitement of a reply, a challenge? He slipped to the back of the building, wanting Thula to be there. He passed by often, late in the evening to see her light still on. She was a worker, studying, saving hard for a future.

The detective reached into his backpack for his panga. Shorter and sharper than the average slashing blade and the most useful piece of kit he'd ever owned. Stealthily, he prised a rotting back window frame, splintering and fragmenting the wood until he worked his finger through the gap. He unlatched the clasp, hauled himself through the opening and into a room so small his shoulders almost touched both walls. Once his eyes became accustomed to the dark, he picked out the door in front of him leading to Thula's little shop. Squeezing on the handle, he opened it. Thula didn't notice him entering. She was pouring over a text. Last time, he remembered, she'd been studying Shakespeare. He crept up behind her and grabbed her mouth, putting his finger to his lips, signalling her to stay quiet. The fear and panic faded from her eyes when she recognised him. She nodded her head. He ducked down behind her chair

'Pretend you're still reading,' he whispered.

Thula stared through the open door of her shop and then back down to her book.

'What have you heard?' he asked.

'You've murdered two people and stolen diamonds. The rumour is all over Gubu. Everyone is in shock. You didn't do it, did you?'

'Innocence is no defence in this game.'

'What are your plans? Those men are dangerous.'

'Have they been here?'

'No, no one takes any notice of me. I'm crippled remember. I don't exist.'

'You exist Thula and one day the world will know. For now, I need a favour. I want to break into the police station.'

'What!' she twisted her head to look at him. 'I can't help with that. I want to study law. I can't have a criminal conviction on my record,' she spluttered, even though in her heart she would do time for the man crouching behind her.

'Keep your eyes fixed on your book, Thula. I need a diversion.'

'How?'

'Go to reception at the police station. I don't know who's on duty but tell them you've seen me running east through the forest towards the main Bulawayo Road. If they chase, I can be caught. Make a big enough scene so if any officers are still at their desks they'll head out after me.'

'What are you going to do?'

'Better you don't know. I need to get into the station. Buy me some time, please.'

How could she resist? 'Will you be able to clear your name?'

He shrugged. 'Give me fifteen minutes and then go in all guns blazing.'

'Perhaps not the best figure of speech, Detective,' she chided.

He never heard the reprimand, having already left the room, thrown his backpack through the window and wriggled out. He fell to the ground with feline stealth, grateful there was no moon.

The screaming and yelling coming from the police station was such that Sibanda couldn't believe Thula's delicate frame could produce such volume. She was clever, he thought. Any potential suspicion cast on her role in the robbery would be dismissed as the ravings of a hysterical half-wit. Her disability, for once, was in her favour.

'Help!' she screamed, 'He's here, we'll all be murdered in our beds.'

'Who? Where?'

'Detective Sibanda, the murderer. There, can't you see him, running towards the road.'

'I can't see anyone.' PC Tshuma was peering into the darkness.

'There he is. Look!' she insisted. Thula spun the wheels of her wheelchair and set off down the road at a fair speed. PC Tshuma was having some difficulty keeping up.

'I can still see him, come on.' Her voice was fading as she drew PC Tshuma further and further from the station.

Sibanda was sheltering behind the syringa tree in the station yard. As soon as Tshuma was through the yard gates, he dashed into the police station, a piece of wire at the ready to pick Mfumu's lock. The officer's door was loose, old and not fit for purpose. The lock was worse. Sibanda opened the door in seconds. He knew where Mfumu hid the safe key; the OIC was a creature of far too much habit. It hung from a paper clip inside the file marked 'cases pending M-T.' Sibanda breathed a sigh of relief. Laurent Kasongo's money was still inside the safe. He pocketed the $700. 'Expenses,' he muttered, closed the safe and replaced the key in the file, wiping away any fingerprints. Relocking the office door took longer than he bargained. PC Tshuma's size tens pounding the earth, announced the policeman's return. In his hurry, Sibanda dropped the wire and fumbled to reinsert it.

'Come on,' he exhorted the bent wire. Beads of sweat broke out on his forehead as he battled to keep a steady grip, trying not to panic as he jiggled the makeshift key. He removed the wire, re- moulded the hook and reinserted it. He was ready to give up when the lock clicked. He released the breath he was holding and flew behind the nearest cover – the open station door. If PC Tshuma was more observant, he would have seen Sibanda minimising himself against the wall. But as the constable returned to the desk, clicking his tongue and shaking his head, Sibanda slid out from the shadow and out of the station.

The detective melted into the bush. Three options lay before him: south to Bulawayo and a large population where he could disappear, west to Botswana, with nothing but bush between where he stood and the long, unpatrolled border, or north to Victoria Falls. The first two options were the safest. He wasn't taking either. Victoria Falls was in his sights. His pursuers wouldn't expect that. He was certain the tourist town held the answer to the two murders. The overlanders would be back up there in a few days, the sculptors were permanent, and Cuthbert Muchacha would be at the conference. Most of his suspects in one place. He liked that.

Sibanda jogged at a fair pace to put as much distance as possible between himself and Gubu. Avoiding paths, he took off through the tall wet grass.

Chapter 15

Sibanda ran through the grass until he'd pushed his luck as much as he dared. His journey was through big game territory, anything could be lurking in the cover of the heavy undergrowth. Buffalo worried him most. Running into a herd at night would be certain death. At the speed he was travelling, his hearing was blunted by the swishing of the grass, his jogging footfall and the pounding heartbeat in his ears. With no moon to light his way, he had to get to safer territory and that was the railway line with a cleared verge on either side. He zig-zagged back until he reached the open ground. He'd left a trail in the grass a child could read. His pursuers would soon be checking. He couldn't follow the rail track for long.

After a couple of kilometres, a gravel pile next to the line gave him a get-off point. Leaping from the rails to the stones, he landed softly, scuffling the indent of his foot to hide his landing spot, picking his way across the gravel until he reached a low hanging branch. From a standing jump, he grasped the limb. Hand over hand, he edged his way towards the trunk, clambering higher up the tree. His plan was to leap across a gap to another branch on a nearby tree taking him further from the rail line. He launched himself. The ground beneath stretched into the night. The branch was further than he'd judged. He landed heavily, and for a moment, felt safe until the branch swayed and he lost his balance. As he fell, his fingertips latched on to a clump of twigs and leaves, clawing for grip. The twigs broke, the leaves shredded with his weight. He was in danger of tumbling to the ground. At best, both his ankles would break, at worst he would smash his skull. With the last off his purchase, he swayed his body to the side. His right foot found a toe hold on a stubby, broken spur. The clump disintegrated as his hands found the trunk. He clung on like a monkey embracing the rough bark. Steadying his breathing, grateful for safety, he slithered down to the next branch, knowing he was pushing himself. One false move and he might injure himself, be unable to escape. This strategy was dangerous lunacy, but he gained at least fifty metres of clean ground, the difference between throwing off his pursuers for a few hours or constantly looking over his shoulder.

Another hour of careful anti- tracking; staying away from worn paths, using the sides of his shoes when the earth was wet and soft, walking along as many fallen trees as he could and strewing dead leaves in his wake, saw him a safe distance from Gubu.

Jagged lightning in a molten silver chevron lit up the night sky, followed by thunder screaming the pain, the fury and the disappointment of Africa like a wounded elephant trumpeting its last. Another storm was coming. Sibanda didn't want to get caught in a downpour. Time to find shelter.

The detective picked his spot, avoiding tall trees; the memories of being impaled by a lightning-splintered branch still haunted him. He chose an area of low growing shrubs to make his camp. The early storm flashes provided him with enough light to slash the undergrowth and hollow out a bush. Mud mixed into a paste made with crushed seeds of wild basil rubbed over his face and hands would help repel mosquitos. The resultant smell was pungent, an effective deterrent. He lined the roof of his shelter with a sheet of plastic, another backpack inclusion. The excess, he slid under his body to keep himself dry.

Summer could be a strange season in Zimbabwe, some days and nights so hot and oppressive as to sap a person of their will to live. Others, when the rain-soaked earth, low clouds and racing wind colluded, would plunge the mercury and emancipate a nation's woollens from their winter mothballs. Tonight was such a night. Sibanda buttoned up his jacket, turned up his collar and caught sleep in snatches. Through the constant whine of mosquitos and clicking of cicadas, he tuned in to the sounds of the bush – the stammering trill of a female white-faced owl, the spooky, liquid '*kyoo-kyoo*' of a freckled nightjar and further afield, a sound he'd been hoping for, brought to him in broken stanzas on the gusting wind: a hyena. Was she hunting, scavenging, or nosing in old bones looking for sun-dried hide and a chewy morsel? He slept again. Next time he woke, the hyena had grown more vocal, tittering and chortling, whooping, laughing. She'd caught something herself or had come across a lion kill. He listened harder, waiting for a break in the wind and driving rain. Could he hear the tell-tale moaning of a lion or was the stiff breeze playing tricks? He marked the direction. Man could be a scavenger too.

Whatever was left of the night gave him intermittent sleep and between dozes, his brain searched among the clues to try and solve the two murders. The resolution of those killings would bring him closer to getting to the bottom of this mess and clearing his name. Laurent Kasongo, real identity still unknown, was executed, but why? Did the deal go bad, or had he double crossed the diamond mafia? His face was a liability otherwise why did he go to such effort to conceal his identity? Something in Kasongo's backpack had been removed after his murder as evidenced by the damaged lining. If Laurent had been couriering gemstones, maybe someone shadowed him from Vic Falls. Did they murder him for the package before he could deliver it to Madani Haddad? Was Haddad killed because he, in turn, failed to produce the goods for the man up the chain. Who was the mysterious white man? Plenty of questions but no answers. Those ghost diamonds were missing, he was being chased, shot at and accused of stealing them. Finding the diamonds would lead him to the killer.

Dawn came late, smudged, dull and suffocated by heavy cloud and drizzle. Sibanda stretched his aching muscles, retrieved the plastic, and disguised his sleeping spot. He carried with him the chopped branches, using the leaves as a brush to obscure his tracks in the soaked earth and then scattering them as far into the bush as he could. He jogged in the direction of the hyena melee, pushing himself hard, taking care to minimise any trace of his passing.

Within fifteen minutes he stopped to examine tracks. Distinct claws marks, fat banana toes and a larger front print confirmed a spotted hyena. The species killed most of its own food and devoured every trace, but Sibanda suspected they were practising their cunning thievery. As the super kleptoparasite, they stole from other predators or at least harried them as they ate. If they were doing their job well enough, keeping the big guys distracted, he might steal some breakfast. Hunger was beginning to bite. It had been days since he'd eaten a decent meal. More tracks appeared. The clan was small, good news for him. He read excitement in every footfall. A kill lay ahead, and this little band knew it. No vultures were soaring. The keen-eyed carrion eaters would have to await the arrival of thermals later in the morning as the air heated and rose. He squinted through his single lens binoculars and checked the crowns of trees. The vultures should be roosting nearby, keeping an eye on the possibilities, awaiting the warmer air to swoop in. When he found the birds, he adjusted his direction. Vultures didn't cluster close to a kill, perching up to a kilometre away, their eyesight such they could keep watch until they took over the baton from the predator and cleaned up the pickings. The smallest of the vultures, the hooded, were no party goers like their weighty cousins who danced at the wake. The little guys were so used to being shooed away from kills by the larger species that their talons strengthened and sharpened over the ages, adapting to catching small rodents and lizards to compensate. A metaphor for life in Africa, he thought; adapt, or get shunted by the big boys. He would do well to take heed of that lesson himself.

The scavengers were thick in the tops of the trees. The predator must be still with the prey. Sibanda tracked the hyena, the more reliable indicator of direction and distance. Closing in on the kill site, he heard bones crunching and smelt the feral reek of blood, fear and adrenaline - a lion kill. Panga in hand, the thick bush would be his ally. He had to stay downwind and hidden if he was to get a chance to carve off a hunk of meat. Timing was crucial. He would wait until the lions left for their morning drink, the hyenas took over and the vultures harried and distracted them in their turn. Speed and bravado were essential. He crept closer.

From behind a sturdy camelthorn acacia on the fringe of a clearing, he found an uninterrupted view of the carnage. Two lionesses with half grown cubs growled ownership next to a large kudu bull. The kudu had headed to an antheap hoping the higher ground would guard his back and put him in a position to joust with his magnificent cream tipped, corkscrew horns, offering him a chance at survival. From the churned-up clay on the side of the antheap, he could see that the bull had put up a spirited defence. In the end, the lions and their progeny brought him down. With faces pasted in blood, the cats seemed to have eaten their fill. There was no sign of a big male lion which made what he was about to attempt less dangerous. Even better, the lions left good sized portions of Kudu flesh untouched. Sibanda noted the large number of uneven white stripes running down the sides of the antelope's half-eaten body, could be as many as fourteen, he heard, but he wasn't about to count them. The V-shaped band on the kudu's face was stark-white and sharp. In life, he was a handsome male; in death, his eyes stared, fixed in horror. His tail curled, exposing the powder puff underside and the pellets he defecated as he succumbed.

The hyenas were keeping their distance, shaggy ginger manes fluffed up, heads down, darting like wary mice checking out the cheese in a trap. One of them had caught a serious claw gash down her rump in a previous sortie attempt. Sibanda cast around for a weapon. His panga wouldn't suffice against these hungry bystanders. He found a club-shaped log, weighed it up in his hand. This is how the Paleolithics did it, he thought.

The lionesses wouldn't stay long, they needed to drink. Their cubs were too young to be left alone to guard the carcass against marauding hyenas. As dawn stripped her drab grey clothing to reveal a pretty pink underslip, the sated lionesses and their cubs rose as one and headed off. The vultures were ready. The hyenas were ready. Sibanda was ready.

He had a millisecond to race to the kill site, leaping as he went, making his profile as large and threatening as he could. The hyenas were taken by surprise and stuttered in their tracks. The vultures halted their swoop. Sibanda slashed at the meat, slicing off a couple of wedges of rump before the hyenas regathered their composure and came in to attack the intruder thieving their spoils. Muzzles bared, they exposed ferocious bone crunching canines attached to the most powerful jaws in the animal kingdom. This was life or death. Sibanda wouldn't survive a fight with a hyena clan. The band were closing in, darting in his direction. His imagination ran riot with the thought of his flesh being torn from his bones and his guts disappearing into the stinking mouths of his attackers whilst he still lived. He'd seen too many hyena kills to fool himself into believing his end would be peaceful. Sibanda yelled at the top of his lungs, standing and waving the lump of wood in the direction of his attackers. His heart was pounding. Would his strategy work? The sudden height and bizarre noise caused the hyenas to hesitate and, in that moment, Sibanda made his escape. He dropped his club, grabbed the booty, and ran like the wind. The hyenas wouldn't follow. They had what they came for and began to giggle and titter in triumph. In front of them lay a free feast.

As he ran and despite his pounding heart, Sibanda heard a noise not associated with the bush, a human yell in response to his. When he bellowed at the hyenas, it had been a last resort. He knew his voice would carry. If his pursuers were near, he would give himself away, but he had to take the risk. Living off roots, grasses, and whatever bird eggs he could scavenge would keep him alive but slow him down and leave him lethargic. He didn't have time to hang around in one spot to check traps and snares, he had to be at the top of his game in the days ahead. The kill had been too good an opportunity to turn up.

At a safe distance from the scene, he stopped and listened. There it was again, a distinct wailing. Had some wood collecting woman become lost? It wouldn't be the first time. But so deep into the park? Or could this be an ambush? He stuffed the kudu rump into his backpack and headed in the direction of the howling. As he approached the noise, he picked up a single set of human tracks on an elephant path. They were imprinted into the wet ground. Another storm and they would be gone. The pace was erratic, staggering. Blood, plenty of it, had dripped along the trail. Still wary, Sibanda skirted the crying, did a three-sixty-degree circuit checking for tracks or signs of a trap. When he was sure the distressed person was alone, he closed in.

Propped up against the base of a tree, limp, wet, bleeding, torn, shoeless and tattered was a man moaning and wailing with every last drop of energy. He looked up, saw Sibanda and, with recognition, the glimmer of hope in his eyes faded. He dragged himself upright and stumbled away trying to escape. He collapsed after a few metres and lay on the ground curled in the foetal position, keening and shielding his head.

Chapter 16

'Time to get up.' Rupert pulled the bedclothes off his wife.

Caroline dragged herself away from her dreams. 'I thought the plane left at midday.'

'Change of plans, I've had second thoughts. It's such a pity to come all this way and miss Victoria Falls. We can stay another couple of nights.'

'Really?' Caroline perked up briefly, 'Could be a second honeymoon in the most romantic spot in the world.' Her words were heavy with irony. The look on Rupert's face told her this was to be no honeymoon. He was sweating and agitated despite the cooler weather brought on by the lashing downpour the previous night. His skin shone pale through his dark tan. He'd worked on bronzing himself since they'd arrived, like a lizard basking on cement. She'd always known he was something of a narcissist, but his relentless exposure to the sun was over the top. He was shaking.

'Yes, yes,' he blustered. 'Let's hurry up. It's a long way.'

'Are you okay? You look peaky.'

'I'm fine,' he snapped, wiping sweat from his brow. 'Maybe I'm coming down with something. I shouldn't have eaten the prawns. Never order seafood in a landlocked country.' He forced a smile.

'A pity you didn't think of this trip sooner. We'd already have been halfway there when we were at the game park.'

'I know, silly me. But it's four or five hours at most. Get a move on, hop to it.'

'At least I'm packed,' Caroline chirped, as she made for the bathroom.

Rupert paced the hotel room. His stomach churned. Nothing to do with dodgy prawns. He'd received a visit from Godwishes in the morning whilst Caroline was still asleep. The police had been sniffing around the wreck of a house and asking questions. They wanted to know who owned it. Godwishes had said he liked the madam and boss Rupert because they were generous. He didn't want them to come to any harm. Rupert thanked his lucky stars Caroline insisted he pay Godwishes over the odds for killing the diamond backed snake and was amazed at the gratitude shown for the $20 he had given him along with an old pair of trainers and a shirt he no longer liked. But how did the police get onto him? He'd left no trace up at Gubu, taken great care to leave his rental car a long way from Madani Haddad's house and worn a hooded rain jacket. How did they even learn about Caroline's house? Godwishes told the detectives he didn't know where Mr Templeton was. And he really didn't. The police told him they would keep an eye on the airports since he was a foreigner.

'They are armed, boss. I saw their weapons bulging under their jackets. They were in a hurry to find you. I promised to phone them if I saw you again, but I won't do that.'

'Why are you doing this for me, Godwishes?'

'Because no one likes the police, do they? Go well, boss.'

Rupert had no intention of taking the flight from Bulawayo airport today, hence the change of plans. He'd find some way to cross the border at Vic Falls either into Zambia or Botswana. The trip was turning into a nightmare. He didn't know how much more ducking and diving he could take.

Why the hell did Caroline have to spend so long in the bathroom? 'Hurry up for God's sake, Caro. I want to go.'

Caroline had run a bath and was enjoying the hotel-supplied bubbles. Rupert was in a state. What was wrong with him? He was rattled before they went up to Gubu and the park but since they had come back to Bulawayo he had been jumping at shadows. She felt relaxed despite having read John Joseph's journals late into the night. What a story they told. How would she absorb everything he'd written? She hadn't been able to concentrate as she paged through the journal because Rupert had been sleeping uneasily, moaning, tossing and twisting himself in the sheets like a restless mummy. At one point he had even yelled. Something disturbed his peace of mind. A few days up at Vic Falls in a glamorous hotel would relax him.

'A taxi?' she queried.

'Just as far as the bus.'

'Bus? Why can't we keep the hire car?'

'I returned it and there are no more to be rented. The bus ride will be comfortable.' Rupert had phoned the hire company to tell them their vehicle was in the hotel car park, keys in the ignition. They could debit his card. Was his credit still good? He was maxed out, but a declined card was the least of his worries and a hire car wouldn't be safe anymore. The police roadblocks were numerous on the last trip. He couldn't risk them checking his licence, noting his name. This way he and Caroline were an anonymous tourist couple.

'Not like you to slum it, Rupert,' she chided.

'Tired of driving on these potholed roads. The bus might be fun.'

'As long as we're making up for it with lobster and champagne tonight.' Caroline laughed, her eyes, the colour of ancient amber, sparkled. Rupert knew a moment of regret. Whatever happened after this fiasco, his marriage to Caroline was over. Squint-eyed Sappy Washington and her fortune were looking more promising by the minute and the returned engagement ring would give him some money. Two hundred thousand at least, enough to help stave off the collapse of the firm. Life would never be so easy with Sappy holding the reins. She reminded him too much of his mother in the pitch of her voice and the paucity of her breasts.

'Anything you want, my darling?' he sighed.

The bus was more comfortable than Caroline had imagined. Rupert immediately fell asleep as though he hadn't slept for weeks. Caroline retrieved the journal from her bag, pushed her seat into the recline position and began to read.

... Some weeks after this incident I was called again, at night, to the King's kraal. He was drunk, 'reet bluitered' as they say in Scotland. Through the smoke-filled hut I could make out large gourds of millet beer, many of which were

empty. From one of them, he was swigging and swallowing without taking a breath. When he came up for air it was to belch a cloud of fumes so rancid, they could have come from the foulest latrine.

'Ah, Jacobi', he slurred, 'I am a wealthy man, with the strength of a thousand oxen. No one can challenge me.'

'You are alone in greatness, oh words of a mountain, King of Mgabi Ndwandwe.' It did no harm to praise the king, to remind him of his legitimacy to reign, particularly in this moment. We had visited the sacred oracle, umlimu, who spoke from the cave in the hill of slippery sides, Mt Injelele, deep in the Matopos Hills, the very mountain whose words foretold his ascension to the throne against all odds. The spirit crowed like a cockerel and barked like a dog from the depths of the cave and the priests interpreted the prophecy. The omens were poor. The white man was coming and not with the bottles of golden water the King so favoured but bringing war. Lo Bengula had dispensed far too liberal prospecting rights in return for the Scottish nectar, learned too late that the spider's web was more than a sleeping mat. The King had been in low ebb since our return from that cave of gloom and foreboding, not calling on a single one of his favourite wives to help with his mood, barely leaving his palace.

'Jacobi, bring me my gold sovereigns,' he mumbled, his alcohol-swollen tongue finding difficulty in expelling the words.

Lo Bengula's wealth was fabled. Each of his subjects who left to mine in the Kimberley returned with at least one stolen diamond, smuggled out in any body cavity they could use. The King also instructed that each subject return with a weapon, a Martini-Henry or a Mauser, no old-fashioned blunderbuss would do. He amassed quite an armoury. De Beers understood their diamond losses and, in

March 1883, set up searching houses to find the hidden diamonds. Production increased. It is said 100,000 carats a year were being uncovered during the searching of African contract workers leaving the compounds for home. In the years prior to this system, many of those undetected diamonds made their way to Lo Bengula's kraal.

The miners used the diamonds to buy sovereigns for the King. The petitioners and those seeking hunting and mining concessions offered their own British sovereigns when they visited, along with crates of whiskey. Lo Bengula stashed raw gold too, plenty of it, dug from the old Mashona workings and some inherited from the old king, Mzilikazi. As I said, his wealth was fabled.

I had never entered the King's treasury before. The building was guarded night and day by men who would rip your heart out if they suspected a thief. If one ounce of gold went missing, the speed of death caused by an absent heart would be a blessing. The guards' deaths would take days of slow and exquisite torture; the thief, if caught, could expect far less mercy.

I began to transfer the bags of gold sovereigns to the King's sleeping hut. Many trips were required even as two of the guards assisted. The King snored throughout like a leopard with the grippe. When he awoke, it was with a start. He reached for his beer and began imbibing once again. Struggling to sit, in which manoeuvre I assisted, he pissed without aim into a large gourd set next to the bed, before falling once again on his karosses.

'Cover me with my gold, Jacobi,' he mumbled.

Not wishing to question the King's wishes, I began placing the gold sovereigns over that mountain of a body until not a patch of skin remained unadorned. He lay still, only the rise and fall of his vast girth dislodged any coins. I replaced them as soon as they fell. The King resembled a gilded Indian god on a sacrificial altar. There was irony in the truth of that image. This was a ceremony I was to repeat several times over the next few months. As Lo Bengula's stress grew, so did the repeat performances of the laying on of the gold. The precious metal appeared to draw the toxins from his soul and the anxiety from his body...

'Oh my God, Rupe, you should read this.'

'What?' Rupert stirred and looked through the window at the tree lined road dotted with picturesque villages, a snapshot of rural simplicity and tranquillity. He almost envied these people and their lifestyle. No guns, no subterfuge, no bodies, just waiving fields of maize, donkey carts ferrying water and children running barefoot to and from school with no expectation of the latest phones or an account to fuel them. Under any other circumstances this would have been a special and healing holiday. 'What should I read?'

'This journal written by John Jacobs. I think he must have been my three or four times great grandfather. The stories he tells are fascinating. I never knew any of this.'

Rupert lost focus when he saw the police road block ahead. He sank into the seat, pulled up his collar and pretended to sleep.

Chapter 17

'Don't gulp.' Sibanda proffered the squirming man his water bottle, filled during the night. The man was parched, didn't even have the wit to keep himself hydrated in the overnight deluge. He patted him down for a weapon.

'I lost the gun... somewhere... when I was running from the elephants... tried to drink at waterholes,' he gasped between gulps, 'but at one, I was charged by buffalo. I managed to escape by diving into a thick outcrop of thorn bushes. After that, I ran. Have you any food? Do you know where we are? There were lions last night, weren't they? I'm terrified of elephants,' he babbled.

'Let's get you fixed up first. Sibanda dabbed at the wounds as best he could from his makeshift first aid kit and bound them with strips from the man's own shredded clothing. The operative had hurtled into branches and trees, impaling himself and slicing open nasty leg wounds. The scratches and grazes would heal if he could keep them dry, but the bigger lacerations needed stitching and one large hole in the side of his gut was beginning to ooze pus or something more ominous. Following Blessing's lead, he stuffed the wound with picked leaves from a nearby *umbondo* and hoped both sides of the veined leaf were as effective.

'You're from the turned over vehicle in the park, the one shooting at me.'

The man cringed like a whipped dog, 'I was doing what I was told....'

'It's okay, I'm not going to hurt you. Who sent you after me?'

'Have you got anything to eat? I'm tired, I haven't slept.' The man was pale, shivering and in shock. Sibanda realised they wouldn't have a meaningful conversation until he had something inside him, something warm. His own stomach was grumbling. They couldn't delay for long. Half the district was out looking for this man and there were some excellent trackers in the team. The other half, armed and dangerous, were out looking for him.

The detective foraged under bushes for the driest twigs and grasses. One hint of smoke, and their position would be given away. He took time and preparation, building a small wigwam structure of kindling with an opening to the breeze. He picked a few bush fruits, 'Eat these, the sugar will help.' The man grabbed the fruit and rammed it in his mouth, almost choking in his efforts to swallow.

'Go easy... what's your name?'

'Patson Mwembe.'

'CIO?'

Mwembe nodded. The wind gusted. Sibanda relaxed. It would take a keen eye to spot the smoke and fix their position and this enemy from the feared Central Intelligence Organisation was at his mercy. He chose the wood for the cooking fire from a Chinese lantern bush, *ugagu*, the ultimate in smokeless fuel. With a stiff breeze carrying away any tell-tale signs, he fed the flames with more dry twigs, larger and larger each time until he encouraged enough fire for his purpose. Retrieving an ex-   baked bean tin from his backpack, he cleared it of the scraps of wire, string, and other useful odds and ends and set it to boil. Next, he cut off a couple of hunks of kudu rump and skewered them on bark-stripped sticks. He would wait for the flames to die and then roast the meat on the coals. He had planned his emergency backpack well.

'So, Patson, what did they tell you? Why did you come after me?'

'You murdered two men, stole diamonds and were armed and dangerous.'

Sibanda rose. Patson cowered. His cratered face crumpled, his fleshy lips stretched over unbrushed teeth like a cringing cur, but the detective was moving to a nearby bush to collect *inandinandi* – bush tea. The leaves were a mild stimulant, similar to khat, with a slight liquorice flavour. The leaves he collected, past their juicy chewing best, had turned brown. He threw the dried leaf tea into the now bubbling water and added Kalahari currents to take away the bitterness. 'How did I get into the locked room?' he asked, as he stirred the brew.

'You… you have magical powers. Everyone says so.'

'That's rubbish and you know it, Mwembe. '

'But you could have murdered the man in the alley way, Jaafar Bastany.'

'Jaafar Bastany? Hmm, so I could. How do you know his name? He entered the country on a fake passport as Laurent Kasongo.'

'I was told.' Mwembe's hooded eyes took deeper refuge under their lids.

'Who passed that information?'

'Higher ups... my boss, I guess.' He looked away, using a twig to doodle in the wet sand, avoiding the detective's laser-like eyes.

'Higher up than that, keep climbing.'

'I don't know about anything further up the chain. I just know his name is Jaafar Bastany and he's a Lebanese national.'

'Was he related to Madani Haddad?'

'They had a deal going.'

'Diamonds?' Sibanda picked up the boiling drink from the fire and set it to cool.

Patson Mwembe stared at the hot drink, 'I've revealed more than I should.'

'You haven't begun to tell me what I need to know and if you want a share of this meat and the road home then you'll open up.'

The kebabs were grilling above coals. Searing juices spattered and sizzled on the glowing embers. The smell of cooking meat spiced the air. Mwembe could have ripped into the meat raw. He was starving; the berries had only tantalised his stomach.

'Why was Jaafar Bastany in disguise?' Sibanda continued his questioning.

'His face is well known. Interpol have a warrant out for him. Bastany was involved in some scandal in Antwerp. He had enemies everywhere as far as I can make out. Been in the diamond smuggling game for years.'

'Why did he come to Zimbabwe?'

'Diamonds. Haddad was a clearing house for both Zimbabwe diamonds from the Marange fields and DRC diamonds from the north.'

'Why bring Congolese diamonds into Zimbabwe?'

'Their diamonds are tainted - blood diamonds. Ours,' he snorted with derision, 'are clean according to the Kimberley lot.'

Sibanda had heard of the Kimberley Process, enacted to regulate the diamond trade. Guidelines had been set in place to ensure conflict diamonds weren't being used to fuel rebellion and oppression. But the convention didn't drill down into the nitty gritty of vote rigging. Guns were one thing, skewed, diamond-funded elections another. Nor did the penalty of being excluded from the diamond cartel hold much fear. If money could be made illegally from the stones, and it appeared an easy trade, why bother with the Convention at all? The whole process was hampered by the secrecy existing at the heart of the traditional trade. The short time he'd spent with the diamond fraud group in the UK taught him Antwerp was far from squeaky clean. Damian Bartle was clear on that, but Africa bore the notoriety for the squalid end of the dealings. De Beers, the monopoly in the African diamond trade, had manipulated the market for over a hundred years, playing with supply and demand to elevate the price, alarmed at every new diamond discovery in case the market became flooded and those hard, sparkling stones that seduced the world, worthless. The whole set up was cleverly done. Men who controlled the trade convinced women that a diamond was a rare, enduring, must-have accessory, a declaration of love, a promise of forever adoration ensuring a bigger, better, longer liaison, a measurable, public display of passion and devotion. He wondered if universities offered the marketing scheme as a case study in successful business practice. Manipulative profiteering came close to a racket in his books.

Sibanda handed the drink to Patson, 'Madani Haddad must have been in league with someone, and that someone has enough status to steer those diamonds back into a legal channel, piggyback the endorsed Zimbabwe system and reap the rewards.'

Mwembe sipped the warming drink, 'I don't know about that, but whoever is leading this operation has it in for you. We were told to shoot on sight.'

'I've got a good idea.' Sibanda handed the cooked meat to the hungry man and a twist of salt from his kit. The starving man's attack on the food would have given the hyenas a run for their money.

'Cuthbert Muchacha?' The food and mildly drugged drink were beginning to loosen Patson's tongue.

'Why did you think of him?'

'Rumours.'

'Go on.'

'About a year ago, there was talk Muchacha was trapped in a sting by an officer in the CID. He'd wriggled his way out of it, pulled strings, but lost face. The CID officer has disappeared. You're that officer, aren't you?'

Sibanda chewed on his meat and spat out a piece of gristle. He didn't answer. 'We need to move soon, can you walk?'

'I'm tired and sore.'

'It won't be far. I know of a well-used road about five kilometres from here. I'll get you there. You'll be picked up soon.' Sibanda busied himself putting out the fire, burying the ashes and obliterating any trace of the campsite. He refolded the tin foil, flattened it and returned it to the pocket of his backpack. As he did, the action dislodged a childhood memory. Something he'd read in a Famous Five book, part of the gang's emergency kit. He smacked himself on the forehead in exasperation. What an idiot. The solution to Madani Haddad's murder had been staring him in the face for days. It took a piece of flattened tinfoil to jog his detection skills. He now knew who must have murdered the Lebanese diamond dealer and how the killer got in and out of that locked room. He even had a fair idea of the murder weapon. So simple, so obvious. How had he missed it? He should have been on to that straight away. Was he getting slack? One murder down, one to go.

'Let's go Patson.' There was a renewed spring and determination in Sibanda's step.

'Where did you learn all this bush stuff?'

'Here and there.' Sibanda was vague. He didn't know if he'd 'learned' bushcraft. Surviving in the bush seemed natural to him since he was a youngster. The properties of plants and trees, the habits of animals and birds were second nature to him. As much as Patson Mwembe was terrified of this environment, wondering about the next threat, Sibanda felt at home, relished the wilderness, the challenge and the solitude. A person could do well to get 'lost' in the bush from time to time. The experience was restorative for the soul. Not that he could indulge much on this outing. Survival ranked above bird and tree identification.

Despite being fed and having his wounds tended, Patson Mwembe was struggling. Sibanda held onto the CIO man as he tripped and stumbled. By mid-morning, Sibanda had located the dirt road.

'Rest here for a while. When you can, head in that direction,' Sibanda pointed east.

'You can't leave me, I'll die.'

'If you can't make it today, take cover at night. Don't ever walk in the dark. This track leads to the tourist roads and lodges. You're within half a day of rescue. The whole of the park is out looking for you, so listen for vehicles and animals. Keep your eyes open for elephants. If you hear or see them, climb a tree until they're gone. Always have a good tree in sight to retreat to. And check for fresh spoor. The track ahead will tell you what's going on.'

'Can't I come with you?'

'No, I'm heading west, to the Botswana border. It's a long hike, you'd be an encumbrance.'

'I'm sorry.'

'For the long hike or being an encumbrance?' Sibanda smiled to reassure the terrified man

'For trying to kill you. I was ordered to. I've done things...' he shook his head as if to obliterate uncomfortable memories, 'This country's politics are a mess. Everyone is jockeying for position, using government resources as a private bank or in this case, as a private army. Will we ever get it right?'

'The people can be the judge of that.'

'They don't have the gavel right now, do they?'

'They will. Keep the faith, but in the meantime, do your job and keep shooting with the same accuracy. You can't go wrong.' Sibanda raised an eyebrow to underline the irony. 'Take this water bottle, refill it from puddles when you can, but don't leave the road.'

'What will you do for water?'

'I'll manage.'

Sibanda melted into the bush, became one with his environment. Patson Mwembe stared at the empty space and wondered how it was done. So little effort, so little noise. An illusion? The pursuers were wasting their time. They would never find him. The rumours were right; this man was a sorcerer.

Chapter 18

'Sergeant Ncube, my office, now.' Chief Inspector Mfumu was on the prowl since arriving at the station that Monday morning and, as was his habit at the start of the week, checked the wall safe. The safe was empty, yet the key was still in its hiding place in the filing cabinet. The money was missing. Both PC Khumalo and PC Tshuma were on duty during the weekend and Sergeant Ncube had been around tinkering with that ridiculous vehicle, Miss Flower-something-or-other. His nephew, Chanza, popped in and out, investigating a spate of thefts in the village. Little deduction was needed to understand the money theft was an inside job. Gubu Police would be a laughingstock if word got out they were robbed under their very own noses. This crime could not be publicised. No transfer would be offered to an OIC who allowed in-house theft. Someone's head was going to roll. He needed to work out whose thieving head that would be.

To add to his woes, his phone had been ringing hotter than the sizzling rivers of hell. Those same rivers he promised his backsliding congregation at The

Brethren of the Lord's Blood. His conversation with the chief of CIO was brutal and to the point: find Jabulani Sibanda or face censure. Mfumu calmed himself by reliving his powerful sermon from Sunday, based on a verse from the Book of Revelation : *But the cowardly, the unbelieving, the vile, the murderers, the sexually immoral, those who practise magic arts, the idolaters and all liars – they will be consigned to the burning lake of fiery sulphur.* A huge success. His faithful quivered in their pews, wails of despair echoed. Madlodlo even fainted. What had she been up to? Nothing like a bit of good old-fashioned terror to get the congregation motivated. New Testament brimstone always proved a winner. Next week, his church would be packed.

He immediately regretted reliving his triumph because it brought to mind the biggest backslider of the lot, Detective Inspector Jabulani Sibanda, notorious dabbler in the dark arts, now missing. Everyone knew he was in league with the Devil otherwise how did he solve so many cases? Mfumu was hoping to see him hanging around the village, humiliated, brought to his knees, snivelling like a sinner in a popish confessional, but he had disappeared. Shots were fired. The report said Sibanda took aim at a CIO delegation sent to question him. No doubt he used the same weapon as the one he'd used to murder the man in the alley way. Mfumu fiddled with the pens on his desk. Something jarred with that scenario. He didn't believe Sibanda, for all his faults, was a gun-toting murderer. Ah well, you could never tell sometimes. What did Luke have to say on this: *For nothing is hidden that will not become evident, nor anything secret that will not be known and come to light.* Luke always was the man for the moment.

'You called me, sir,' Ncube coughed.

'Sergeant Ncube.' How long was he loitering there? Had he voiced his fears aloud? These were stressful times. He would pray harder for success and focus. 'What do you know of this theft?'

'Me, sir?'

'Yes, you, Sergeant. It happened this weekend. You came into the station, didn't you?

'To work on Miss Daisy, I never went past the reception desk. PC Khumalo on Saturday and PC Tshuma on Sunday can vouch for that.'

Mfumu now toyed with the arrangement of papers on his desk, aligning the pages until they seemed like a new ream, fresh from the honed edge of the manufacturer's guillotine. Of course, this overweight, unironed, multi-married dolt in front of him hadn't done it. He didn't have the wit or the guile. 'No word of this must leave the station,' he snarled, 'there were top secret documents in the safe that could compromise the safety of the nation.' A lie, but Mfumu knew the Lord would forgive him since it was told in the defence of a reputation – his.

'Yes, sir, not a word will escape my mouth any more than the unwary beetle escapes the foot of the elephant.'

'Er, right. On another matter, Sergeant, you work with Detective Sibanda. I must contact him. Where is he?'

'He has a phone, sir, have you tried that?'

'Of course, he has a phone,' Mfumu spat in exasperation.' He's not answering or he's out of range.' Mfumu was becoming agitated. 'Where did he say he was going?'

'Home to relax.'

'There's been an incident at his house, shots fired.'

'I heard about that.' Ncube was in anguish since he learned of the shoot-out. No one could tell him if Sibanda was safe, injured or arrested. 'What happened to him, sir?'

'The detective is on the run.'

'Then you'll never find him.' Ncube collapsed with relief without moving an external muscle. But his insides appreciated the release of tension and a gentle *mfushwa* exited in a long and continuous stream of anal vapour wafting through the open office door. Ncube was grateful for both the silence and the ventilated region of the event. 'That man can disappear like a solitary tear in a river, like a grain of maize in a pot of porridge, like a blade of grass on a football field, like...'

'...Like a needle in a haystack, yes, yes, I get the idea. Don't get carried away, Sergeant, but if you value your stripes, you'll let me know if he contacts you.'

'I will, sir.' This was a lie, but Ncube didn't care if the devil himself put him on a spit or Mfumu demoted him to constable. He would never betray a friend. Detective Sibanda couldn't technically be called a friend, but he was as close, in a way, as anyone he knew. 'And to remind you, sir, you have approved my leave starting tomorrow. You said I could take Miss Daisy as long as I got her fixed at my own expense. I'm joining my wives to plough in the fields.'

'Get that wreck out of the yard, the Land Rover is a disgrace. I have important people visiting. We can't afford to look like a neglected backwater. This Sibanda case is high profile.'

Ncube left the office. What didn't show on his face was the mixture of relief, tension and ongoing worry building once again in his stomach like a boil gathering pus prior to an intervention by Blessing's hot needle.

Detective Sibanda was alive and had escaped. This was excellent news, the best he'd heard since his solitary, skinny, infertile cow produced a calf. Ncube knew exactly where Sibanda would be. Well, not exactly. The detective was somewhere in the park, in that vast and frightening wilderness stretching from Gubu to the Botswana border in the west, south to Tsholotsho and north almost to the Victoria Falls. Sibanda would be safe there, he knew how to survive, to turn twigs into fire, grass into food and animals into friends. Even lions and elephants seemed to bow down to him. And he had money. As soon as Ncube knew Sibanda was free, he realised he had taken the money from the safe. The robbery was flawless, no clues left behind, as though *isipoko* entered the police station. That was his man - no spook - detective Jabulani Sibanda, the last word in stealth, a leopard in the dark, a chameleon in full camouflage. And what was it Mfumu said? *A pin in the fodder*? Very perfect.

The detective would not be thinking of himself or his own safety. He would be heading into the hyena's lair. Ncube planned to follow. He and Miss Daisy would travel up to Victoria Falls and wait there. He suspected the detective would be chasing the overland truck, the curio carvers and the politician. He would be chasing the real murderers. Ncube knew him too well. Somehow, he and Miss Daisy would contact the detective because the fugitive would need allies. Ncube glanced towards the west and the heavy low clouds gathering over the park. The swollen shadows spoke of navy bruising on an angry fist, hissed the venom of a cobra and prodded with the sharp prongs of the devil's shining pitchfork. Ncube shuddered. 'Stay safe, sir, wherever you are.'

Once he left Patson Mwembe, Sibanda made his way west, towards Botswana, leaving a track in the sodden ground that tried to show some concealment but left just enough signs for an expert tracker to follow. He stumbled from time to time to indicate he might be in distress. Then he turned north towards his destination employing every skill in the book, every anti-tracking knack he possessed, to hide his direction.

The weather began to close in. Dense cloud blanketed the area, painting the bush in a grey sameness. After an hour, Sibanda came across a pile of giraffe bones he had passed a while back and realised he was walking in circles. The southern and western part of the park were featureless, no hills to speak of, no vantage points, just millions of acres of flat, summer-overgrown Kalahari woodland. The sun provided a rough directional guide, but the bright weathervane lay smothered behind a sky of rhino-hide dull. Much as he wanted to press on, it would be folly. He cursed Patson Mwembe who had lost him so much time. The longer he was stationary, the quicker the trackers would find him. Mwembe might even now have been rescued and could be squealing to his colleagues. He didn't expect gratitude. The moment of regret would disappear in the safety of civilisation. He would regale his mates with stories of his bravery. Once Sibanda's fake westerly track went cold, the pursuers would circle. He wanted to press on but navigation in these grey-out conditions was impossible. He would wait until the clouds cleared and the sun got a moment, or until evening when the moon rose in the east, or night when he might be able to navigate by the stars. Right now, the weather threatened. Laden clouds blocked the sun, moody and ominous. Sibanda felt a tightening in the pit of his stomach. Lightning almost killed him once and he didn't believe in the second-strike rule.

The storm, when it broke, was amongst the most violent in recent years and Sibanda was at the heart of its fury. At first the wind came, harsh and fast, tumbling leaves and undergrowth in its path, bending and cracking anything offering resistance. When the thunder rolled like a thousand bowling balls on the teak floors of the old Gubu clubhouse, Sibanda made for a clearing. He lay flat on the ground, wrapped in his sheet of plastic. He didn't have long to wait. He timed his protection to the second. Lightning hit in multiple strikes. He watched the jagged spears descending like the fluorescent tentacles of an alien landing craft, lashing the earth, painting the underbelly of the clouds in a ghostly green. Africa was boasting. 'Look,' she said, 'I am the lightning capital of the world, no one can beat me at this,' and she pounded her chest. Sibanda gambled that the plastic and his low profile would insulate him from the strikes. The wind picked up, howling and moaning, swinging through the trees and brushing the high grass. Sibanda clung to his covering. The plastic tried to fly.

Then came the rain, hard and relentless, crashing in a waterfall on his flimsy shelter. The water streamed in rivers on the already rain-soaked ground, found the weak spots in his plastic armour and soaked him to the skin. He could barely breathe beneath the pounding. The deluge went on and on. Sibanda felt he was adrift in a bubble under the sea, almost at risk of drowning. He lay still, cut off all the mayhem, took shallow breaths and tried to focus. He now knew who murdered Madani Haddad and how, but who murdered Jaafar Bastany

AKA Laurent Kasongo? He must have been carrying diamonds, but the gems were never delivered to Madani Haddad. Was he executed for failing to deliver by the overall puppet master? Patson Mwembe said Bastany had many enemies. Did one of them catch up with him? Or was it a case of out and out theft; someone learned he was carrying diamonds, trailed him and robbed him? That put the overlanders in the frame.

When the rain stopped, the sky fell silent and the peeping sun had knocked the burnt skin off the rice pudding clouds, despite all his musings, Sibanda was no closer to the murderer of Jaafar Bastany. But he made short work of getting back on his feet and heading north. The going was heavy. The rain had been so severe, temporary pans had formed shallow lakes. Water pooled ankle deep. In places, he was wading.

In a couple of difficult hours of striding out, Sibanda reached mopane veldt. The butterfly shaped leaves of the park's north gave him encouragement. The vegetation was becoming less dense, but the going didn't get easier. Underfoot, the ground was changing. The poorly drained soils formed mud. His already soaked boots were sucked and caked, impeding his progress. After some kilometres, he slowed, tiring from the constant effort of dragging his legs through the uncompromising terrain. Scooping a tin full of water from a nearby puddle, Sibanda sat with his back to an antheap and took a drink. He was exhausted.

He heard the helicopters before he spotted them. They were returning from the west, two of them, their blades chopping the freshly minted air, flying low, skimming the tree canopy. An armed combatant hung out of each door. Mwembe must have made it back, passed on his direction. His pursuers, having found no trace of their quarry towards the border, were swinging further north, scouring the ground, ready to shoot on sight. From that height they had a panoramic view. Open season. The choppers were almost on him. Sibanda had seconds to react. He scrambled into the nearest bush.

'Did you see that?' the left-hand side rifleman on the lead helicopter shouted over the stuttering thump of the rotor.

'What?' the pilot cursed the crackling internal communications.

'Over there, I saw a movement. Could have been a man. I caught a flash of something dark running off.'

'Probably an animal. I'll look.' The pilot swung the helicopter in the direction of the soldier's pointed finger. The second helicopter followed. The pair hovered for a while, buzzing like bees choosing their pollen. The displaced air tousled the bushes.

The choppers were close. Too close. The pulsing drum of the blades screamed in Sibanda's ears. When he dived into the bush, curled into a tight ball, knowing his chance of evading detection was minimal, he didn't know the shade was already occupied. His fellow fugitive, a snake, uncoiled and slithered across Sibanda's ankle. The detective lay motionless, willing himself not to move. He identified the reptile as the rhombic night adder, the demon night adder – a snake by any other name. Every instinct screamed to kick at the slithering viper, to get the hell out of that bush, but if inside lay horror, then outside lay certain death. He watched, almost in fascination, as the adder's slender, cylindrical body undulated. The satiny texture of the scales reflected jade light filtering through the leaves. The sinuous movement was fluid and muscular; a squeeze here, a relaxation there and the diamonds on the adder's back sparkled in their rose gold setting like a treacherous anklet. A bite would be debilitating rather than fatal, causing dangerous tissue damage from the cytotoxic venom, but if Sibanda survived the helicopters then he would need every muscle working and every ounce of energy he could muster. The fully grown, metre long snake could damage his survival prospects. The adder hesitated midway across Sibanda's exposed ankle and stared with large, round, unblinking eyes. Sibanda held the gaze as steadily as the snake. The movement he couldn't control was the furious pounding of his heart and his pumping pulse points. The adder's sensitive scales would pick up on that.

'Can you see anything?' The pilot yelled.

'I'm not sure, maybe. I'll let off a few bursts. That'll move whatever's there.' The soldier clicked off the safety catch and engaged automatic mode. He sprayed the bushes. His partner on the opposite side followed his lead. The soldiers in the next helicopter, caught up in the excitement, did the same. The ground exploded in a hail of bullets, shredding all vegetation in their sights.

Chapter 19

Sergeant Ncube and Miss Daisy chugged to Victoria Falls. He watched the rear-view mirror with vigilance to see if he was being followed. Detective Sibanda would have been alert, but the pair were alone on their journey. The trip was not without its hazards. Rain bombarded the old lady, squeezing past her door rubbers, hammering her windscreen and playing havoc with her less than appropriate footwear, a little short on tread. Sergeant Ncube, as concerned as he was for Miss Daisy's welfare, was preoccupied with thoughts of his boss. Where was Detective Sibanda, was he safe? Impossible to stay dry in this storm as brutal as any he'd witnessed. Everyone knew lightning flashed to warn the deaf while thunder rumbled to warn the blind. Would the detective have taken heed of nature's alerts? He doubted it. The man's senses were numbed when it came to danger, he'd plunge ahead without thought. When the storm let up and the rain stopped, Ncube breathed a sigh of relief, 'Do you think he's made it through, Miss Daisy?'

Miss Daisy rather hoped he hadn't. The detective was a vehicle-abusing brute and she for one would prefer he melted in the rainstorm like pistons in an overheated system. Ncube took Miss Daisy's silence for agreement. He caringly cleared her misted windscreen. The world loved rain and Ncube loved it more than most, but right now he wanted the detective to be safe and dry. When the storm drained its last drops and the sun bounced with joy off the wet tarmac, painting the sky the yellow colour of hope, Ncube took it as a good omen. The sergeant's spirits lifted. His relief was short- lived.

Two military helicopters swooped low over the road heading west into the park, their occupants armed.

'Oh! Sweet sunflower seeds!' Ncube slammed his foot on Miss Daisy's accelerator. She lurched forward. The sooner he reached Victoria Falls and found out about the detective the better. The suspense of not knowing was worse than not eating for a week and then being fed lettuce.

Sibanda remained curled up in his bush. Bullets pinged and burst around him splintering branches, exploding into the earth, showering him with debris and deafening brutality. The night adder slithered off, making for a safer shelter. As abruptly as it started, the firing stopped. The helicopters moved off to his right. He worked out his saviours were a herd of wildebeest stampeded by the pulsing blades and screaming engines. The panicked beasts were running and snorting. The helicopters were following, picking off a couple of prime specimens like fish in a barrel, wounding others. Sibanda waited, listening, even though the din from the blades and the bullets out-gunned any other sound. The pounding hooves faded.

The helicopters whined to a stop and landed. He peered through the leaves. Not far from his hiding spot lay a dead warthog, a colander-like carcass riddled with bullets. The animal may well have saved his life as it ran from a neighbouring bush. The soldiers ignored the shredded meat of the warthog, targeting the beefier wildebeest. With binoculars, he watched the men hacking up their trophies and loading the meat onto the choppers. The survivors of the silver-blue herd stopped and gathered, looked back, peering down their roman noses, fascinated at the butchery of their companions, their black bearded throats twitching, their skinny shanks unmoving, their long sweeping tails flowing in the stiff breeze. And then the helicopters were gone like sunbirds darting into the distance.

Sibanda waited until the thrumming died away and reflected on his luck. How the bullets missed him he didn't know but the intensity of the attack seemed to be aimed at a clump of bushes some metres away, the warthog their unwitting target. Gathering his belongings, he ran north for several kilometres, stopping to scoop water from shallow puddles. He ran until the last light disappeared over the horizon, until the rain set in as a peaceful blessing, he ran until he had no more running left in his legs and then he stumbled on the ruins.

The phone rang in Gubu station. With the chaos of the day over, PC Khumalo had settled into her night shift routine. Nothing happened at night, so she slept or crocheted. She unwound wool from several old pullovers bought from the second-hand bendover market in Bulawayo and was fashioning squares for a winter blanket. The rain-cool evenings made this a pleasant and relaxing task. The repetition was soothing, the growth of the work steady and satisfying. She stopped from time to time to admire her handiwork and to smooth and shape the curling edges. She crocheted one square at a time so she could stuff the wool under the counter in case of a night-time crime spree in the village.

Who was ringing at this time? Poking the hook into the ball of wool, she picked up the receiver. In many ways she wished she hadn't. As the phone call progressed, the blood drained from her face until she was as grey as the grubby paint on the police station walls and her eyes were as wide as a terrified cow in an abattoir. At that moment, detective Chanza walked through reception.

'Are you alright, PC Khumalo, you look terrible.'

She stood, but her legs gave way. She leaned on the counter to stop herself falling, 'I'm… I'm not well, sir. I must go home.'

'You should go to the clinic.'

'The clinic?'

'Won't Sister Angel Better be able to help?'

'Yes, Sister Angel,' her eyes focused, 'I must go now.'

'Wait, who'll cover your duty?'

She turned, 'Find someone, you're in charge.' A hint of steel returned to her voice.

PC Khumalo walked out of the station, leaving Detective Chanza scratching his thinning pate and shoving his recidivist glasses back up the bridge of his nose. As she walked, Zanele Khumalo felt her strength returning. She had to find Detective Sibanda or Sergeant Ncube or better still, both. Detective Sibanda wasn't answering his phone and since the shoot-out, no one knew where he was or even if he was still alive. Her best bet was Sergeant Ncube. He'd followed his wives to their rural home with Miss Daisy to get ready for the rains. The silly man didn't have a mobile phone. She'd have to go and find him in person. To do that she'd need time and to buy time she'd need Sister Angel and a sick note. She hoped her pale appearance would pass for the onset of a summer cold. Should she add to the mix by complaining about pains in her chest or some woman's ailment? She hoped her BP had gone through the roof. It seemed to explode from time to time and Sister Angel was always on at her to lose weight.

As it turned out, she didn't need to lie to Sister Angel or search for her. Detective Chanza had phoned ahead to tell the nurse to be at the clinic, 'PC Khumalo is in a bad way, she must be coming down with the flu.'

'You don't seem to have a temperature.' Sister Angel was thorough with her checks. 'Your blood pressure is up and you do look pale. You haven't had a shock or some bad news, have you?'

'No, nothing like that,' PC Khumalo lied.

'Should I do a pregnancy test?'

'What? Are you kidding? Old mother Emmerentia at St Monica's has more chance than me!' PC Khumalo contemplated her current lack of partner with regret. She'd sent Zenzo on his way with a black eye after she caught him stealing her savings from behind the loose brick in the kitchen. He drank too much anyway, and had become part of the furniture at The Blue Gnu.

'I'm at a loss to explain what's happened but perhaps you better have some rest. Come back in three days and we'll see how you are then.' Sister Angel went to her medicine cupboard and took down the container.

'Paracetamol?' PC Khumalo guessed.

'Yes, paracetamol.' Sister Angel shrugged her shoulders in apology, 'It's all the clinic has. Take two every four hours.'

PC Khumalo had already made plans. She would be up before the cockerels tomorrow although she doubted she would get a wink of sleep with the news she received twisting her guts like monkey rope. She would take the first bus to Umgusa. Sergeant Ncube would know what to do or at least he would know where Detective Sibanda was. She must get the message to him. Lives depended on it.

Detective Sibanda hacked through the undergrowth of shrubs and the creeping vines of wild grape, *amajambe*, lacing his path like a cat's cradle, snaking around the fallen stones of the ruin. He was lucky to escape the helicopters but now his priority was to find somewhere dry to hole up for the night. His clothing was soaked, he shivered, close to hypothermia, in an African summer's night. He hadn't been aiming for Bembusi ruins, the mid nineteenth century capital of the Nambya kingdom, almost forgotten by history, had stumbled on it by accident. Few people ever visited. The stone structures in the middle of the park had been left to crumble and rot. Who knew what hidden archaeology those walls could reveal? Right now they offered the possibility of shelter.

He climbed the hill to the most intact building he could see, a circular, tapering structure of dry-stone walls. The detective clambered up the sandstone cliff to a sentinel African fig whose creamy coloured roots snaked across the rock face, clinging in places like a baby night ape to its mother. The roots insinuated themselves into fissures in the rocks, widening the cracks. The trees weren't nicknamed the boulder-splitting fig for nothing. Sibanda made use of the handy footholds to scale the cliff face. The ruin at the top looked as though it might have been an iron smelter. Bellows holes at the bottom allowed him to crawl inside.

He checked every rock in the curved wall with his flashlight, having no intention of sharing his bed with a black mamba. This was their territory. The deadliest snake in Africa loved rocks and crevices and whilst a night adder bite might have been debilitating, a mamba would kill him. The enclosure was circular, with enough space to lie down. Inside was dry, littered with loose baboon faeces. The fig tree outside was in fruit, not red ripe yet but the baboons didn't care. They enjoyed biting into the tart, scouring green berries, discarding the sourest bits and suffering the gastric consequences. Unsurprisingly, his thoughts turned to sergeant Ncube as he cleared the debris away. He hoped his sergeant was safe, ploughing his fields with his wives. The detective slumped with his back to the ancient walls.

Sibanda had to risk a fire. He was soaked to the skin. Gathering dry kindling from inside his shelter, without wind and rain to hamper him, he started a blaze in minutes. The rain eased, the clouds cleared enough for the moon to make an appearance, not full and busty but with enough light for Sibanda to examine his feet. They had been wet for two days and he was wary of infected blisters. He removed his boots and peeled off his socks. The heat of the fire on his sodden skin was a relief. He massaged the prune-like wrinkles. Once his feet were dry, he pulled a fresh pair of socks from his backpack. His jacket, hanging from a branch jutting through the walls, was steaming. He changed to the dry shirt he'd grabbed from his laundry pile. Within minutes, a few strips of kudu were sizzling on the coals, and he was munching some of the wild grapes growing nearby. Time to make a plan.

He was at Bambusi ruins so Sinematella camp couldn't be far away; maybe three hours jogging as the crow flies. That meant tourists in vehicles on their way to Victoria Falls. The helicopter attack told him he had to get to Vic Falls faster than his own legs could carry him. Those choppers would be back when the weather cleared, searching in ever widening circles. Before turning in, he slithered back through the vent in the wall and climbed to the highest point of the citadel. From there, and with the moon now high up in the sky, he could see for miles.

Far in the distance, three fires burned in three different locations, all in the west. His pursuers had split up which meant they hadn't got on his tracks yet. How long before they twigged he was travelling north? As he slithered back down to his shelter, moon beams bouncing off the sandstone highlighted a series of round shadows, a regular pattern of shallow holes worn from the rocks. He recognised the rows of an ancient *Tsoro* board. More than 150 years ago, sentries scoured these hollows, amused themselves with the age-old game as they squatted and kept watch from this vantage point. The rules dictated you move counters along the rows, clockwise, until you ran out of empty holes and the next man took his turn. Had those ancient guards used seasonal fruit from this very fig as counters or at least an ancestor of the fig? Sibanda crouched and ran his fingers over the rounded depressions. He felt a connection with the past and this forgotten civilisation. Ghosts were about, men who lived and died defending this refuge, men who failed to protect their leader, Chief Whange, from the brutal and torturous attentions of a young King Lobengula who skinned the chief alive. He shivered as though someone walked over his grave and thought again of his sergeant.

Ncube reached Victoria Falls, Miss Daisy's watery headlights flickering into the gloom. He planned to stay with his sister, Smilo, but that was as far as his planning went. The realisation dawned, as he watched one of the Bulawayo coaches pull in and disgorge its passengers, that the town bustled with people. How would he connect with detective Sibanda, the pin in the fodder? He would sleep on it and eat on it. After all, great thoughts come from good food. Even the locust knows when it's time to settle and focus on the maize. He smiled in anticipation; his sister, Smilo, could whip up a pot of maize porridge with the deft hand of his mother.

Chapter 20

'Not here, you say?' PC Khumalo tried to keep the concern from her face.

'He's not in trouble, is he? Has something happened? Should I call the others?' A heavily pregnant Nomatter had been left with the younger children. The older ones, along with Blessing and Sukho, were in the fields, hoeing in the cool morning.

'No, nothing to worry about. I er... was sent to ask him to return from leave. PC Tshuma has called in sick and the station is short-handed.' Zee Khumalo was lucky to be talking to Nomatter. Blessing, Ncube's senior wife, would have rumbled her lies straight away. That one was as sharp as a mouth full of kitten teeth.

'Leave? He never mentioned he was taking leave. Where is he?' Nomatter sounded worried. She shifted the baby from one hip to the other and took the hand of the toddler at her feet.

PC Khumalo attempted a reassuring laugh that came out as more of a snort, but it served its purpose. 'Probably with Detective Sibanda. You know those two, guinea fowl with the same spots.'

'But isn't detective Sibanda in trouble? We heard…'

'…Oh that. That's all sorted now,' she fluffed, 'a mistake. Well, I'd better get to the bus stop. I'll be needed back in Gubu.'

'You must stay for refreshment. Blessing and Sukho would love to hear all the news.'

'Thank you, but we're short staffed. I must get back.' PC Khumalo turned and ran along the track to the gravel road and the bus stop. Any more questioning and she might have blurted out the truth.

Sibanda spent a comfortable night. The old stones radiated their stored warmth, security and sense of belonging. He woke mid-way through the night to a nocturne of owls, the mournful fugue of the eagle owl, the monotone toccata of the scops, and the spooky accelerando of the pearl spotted. The bright night inspired their singing. Looking up as he turned to rotate one hip for the other, he caught a movement, a rusty-spotted genet mother and two kittens silhouetted against the moon on the dry-stone lip of his shelter. Her long back, tail hoops and large ears made the cat the very embodiment of an Egyptian hieroglyph. She fitted in well amongst the ruins. Her kittens jumped and played on the rocky ledge until a signal from their mother caused them to freeze like statues. The cat looked down into the space below. Her wide-eyed nocturnal vision spotted him. She stared for a moment before disappearing with her little ones to search for beetles and bird's eggs and maybe a mouse or two. The detective, content for the first time in days, turned over and slept again.

Sibanda was up long before dawn and on his way. This rockier terrain was trickier to run across, but it left few signs behind, meaning pursuers would have trouble tracking him. He made good progress. The land still felt cool as she towelled herself off in the breeze and dawn broke into a cloudless sky awash with gold, silver, fresh green light on clean leaves and the promise of a drier day. Sibanda could see the camp up on a hill in the distance and reckoned he had an hour to go at a steady jog. Enough time to scout the camp to find a suitable vehicle to stow away in.

Sergeant Ncube slept later than usual. There were no babies crying, no bustling in the kitchen and no domestic chitter chatter, but there was a sensational smell wafting up his nostrils and assailing his gurgling stomach.

His sister was cooking up a favourite childhood breakfast of *amaqebelengwane* morning bread. He could picture her taking *umnyii*, the brown and yellow spotted beans that grew wild. She would have washed them, dried them and pounded them to a powder, picking out the seeds. Next came the addition of maize meal with a touch of water to blend the powders. The dough-like mixture was rolled into balls. The crowning moment was the making of thumb holes in the morning bread. His mother sometimes allowed him that task if his hands were clean, and then she threw the little blobs into boiling water until they bubbled to the surface as a fluffy delight. Could he smell peanut sauce to go with it? He hurried to get dressed. The family had spent last night planning, he, Smilo and his brother-in-law, Prince. Over a stew of lake sardines cooked in milk steeped with coconut, garlic, onions and tomatoes, Prince came up with the idea. Ncube had been regaling them with stories of his adventures with the detective as he mopped up every last drop of the delicious juices when Prince jumped up, 'That's it!'

Ncube and Smilo said 'What?' in unison. They had been in tune since childhood.

'You're worried about meeting up with the detective, that he'll get caught if they see you together. So why don't you park that Land Rover in the middle of town and sit somewhere you can keep an eye on it. He's bound to recognise the old *skoroskoro*.'

'The CIO and police know who I am. They will have been told to be vigilant with two border crossings close by. They believe the detective has the diamonds and is trying to escape. If they spot me...' Smilo and Prince both guffawed.

'They'll spot you alright,' Smilo laughed, 'You're like a pink hippo in a sea of Zambezi mud.'

'You'll be in disguise,' Prince interrupted.

'No, no, no, not again.' Ncube understood Prince's plan

'It's the answer and you know it. You're the same size as Smilo so you can borrow her clothes. Being dressed as a woman worked for your previous case. You've told us so yourself. '

'*Bantubenkosi*,' was all Ncube could utter with a sigh of resignation.

PC Khumalo sat at the bus stop for over two hours. Rural buses were like banded mongooses. They arrived in a huddle, pursuing one another like mercury rolling down a hill until they blended into a ball of charm, welcomed by some for their war on snakes, despised by others for their predation on chickens, but nowhere to be seen when a cobra was ready to strike. When the ball of bus dust came barrelling down the road, an anxious

PC Khumalo forgave the delay. Her relief was enormous. The information she harboured made any spitting cobra pale into insignificance. Besides, sitting gave her time to think. Where had those two gone? The phone call had shocked her, made her weak at the knees. Halfway through her wait, with no distraction other than to sift through what she knew of the murders, she had her light bulb moment. Of course, all the clues pointed to one place, Victoria Falls. The detective, if he was still alive and free, would be in pursuit of the murderers and Sergeant Ncube would be after him. PC Khumalo boarded the bus and paid for a ticket as far as the main road. After that, she would catch another bus past Gubu and up to Victoria Falls.

Sibanda underestimated his journey. Reaching Sinematella camp took an hour longer than he'd thought. He'd run into a small cow herd of elephants, twitchy, defensive and alarmed, their ears flapping despite the cool morning. One cow shook her head, another was swinging her feet, clear signs of irritation. Their calves were milling, aware of their mother's stress. The cows' temporal glands streamed. Small, pinched eyes with white flecks in the corners were another measure of mood. This was a plentiful time of year and with pools of standing water, protein levels high and new leaf on offer, the herd should have been more relaxed. Sibanda was disturbed to note how jumpy they were. Maybe they'd been shot at or had a run in with lions. He wasn't the cause of their drama, but his sudden appearance didn't help. He backed away and took a wide berth around them. When he did reach Sinematella, it was already 9am. He made it into the campground undetected. With little time to find his mark, he couldn't indulge in the panoramic view the camp offered from its clifftop site. Instead, he cleaned up as best he could in the shower block and walked around like a tourist. At the shop, he bought milk and a tin of bully beef. He wolfed them down.

He reached the chalets as an older, white couple were packing up from a late breakfast. Their vehicle, a pick-up, sported a taut canvas covering on the back, held in place by elastic stringing pulled over lugs. With any luck, the pair were heading north. He'd tuck himself under the covering after they'd stowed their bags, and hope the roadblocks weren't too thorough. The police let white people pass without problems, particularly old white people. The perception was *mukiwa*s were too well off to be criminals and old white people were saints. Sibanda was thankful few of his colleagues had worked overseas because they might have had a different picture. He positioned himself so he could overhear their conversation.

'Come on, dear, shake a leg, you're holding me up again.'

'We could have moved off an hour ago if you'd helped with the clean-up.'

'I didn't come on holiday to be a houseboy.'

'Then don't expect me to help with your packing.'

'I'm already packed.'

'Your razor is still in the bathroom, there's a pair of your underpants under the bed and a sock wrapped in the bedspread.'

'Thank God we're staying in a hotel in Vic Falls. I don't need this irritability from you.' The man stormed back into the chalet. The woman placed her bags by the back of the pick-up and sat in the front seat, stony faced, looking ahead. Sibanda left them to their domestic wretchedness and headed to the boom gate. All vehicles stopped at the office to check out. He'd try and jump on board then.

PC Khumalo reached Victoria Falls. She didn't know the town well having only visited once before when she and Zenzo were in the first flush. She smiled at the delicious memory. Sergeant Ncube's sister lived here but she had no idea what her name was and didn't dare go near the police station. She wandered down the main street, taking in all the travel shops and adventure booking kiosks, avoiding the touts offering her river cruises and gorge swings. Did she look like the sort of person who would launch herself into space on the end of an elastic band? This was hopeless. How did she imagine she was going to arrive in Vic Falls and find two men in hiding? Desperation set in. The news was weighing on her. A deadline loomed and if she didn't find one of them soon, then... well she couldn't bear to think of the consequences.

Suddenly, in front of her was an ancient Land Rover, that hideous, broken-down old wreck parked on the side of the road. No mistaking the identity. She could have kissed the battered, paint chipped body all over. Even the lavatory green door looked appealing. She almost cried, but PC Khumalo didn't do tears. Her head swivelled from side to side. Where was Sergeant Ncube? He wouldn't leave his beloved Miss Daisy for long, yet there was no sign of him. She would wait. She would wait all through the night if that's what it took. Ncube would come back for this vehicle if it was the last thing he did.

'Psst,'

PC Khumalo wasn't expecting anyone she knew. She didn't even look around.

'Psst, psst.'

The hissing became insistent. An old lady a few feet away was beckoning her.

'Salibonani, Mama, do I know you?'

'Of course, you know me. It's me, *ngimi*, Sergeant Ncube.'

'Sergeant Ncube, but what....'

'Shh, don't make a fuss. I'm undercover waiting for Detective Sibanda and hoping he's headed in this direction. Have you seen him? What have you heard?'

'Nothing. But no news can tell a happy story, can't it?' She looked him up and down, her lips twitching, battling not to laugh given the seriousness of the situation, 'Nice skirt.'

'No one will recognise me like this.' He adjusted his headscarf and fiddled with his handbag to conceal his embarrassment, 'But what are you doing here?'

'Oh Ncube,' her voice broke, 'It's a mess, a terrible mess. I received a phone call last night from a neighbour of detective Sibanda's brother. Xolisani and his wife have been taken into custody by the CIO. The neighbour has the children with her, but she's heading to Botswana tomorrow for a wedding. She tried to get hold of their grandmother, but Sibanda's mother is in South Africa. The neighbour doesn't know what to do with the children. She's frightened of being associated with the family and wants the little ones gone. Why have they done this? Why have the CIO arrested them? He's a lawyer. Those poor parents, those poor children. What should we do?'

Ncube shuddered, and his stomach sank. 'They've arrested them to get Detective Sibanda to hand himself in. Let me think.'

'We don't have long. Those children are about to be dumped.'

Sibanda slipped under the canopy. The old man disappeared into the office, his wife remained, staring ahead. She looked back when the car rocked but Sibanda was already under the canvas. Getting in was the easy part; getting out undetected would be more difficult. Once on the road, he kept an eye on progress by lifting the side of the canvas. They sailed through the first roadblock. The second was trickier as the police wanted licences.

'Give me my licence,' he growled to his wife

'Where is it?'

'In the glove box.'

'No, it's not.'

'You've got it, I gave it to you.'

'Why did you do that?'

'What?'

'Give me the licence?'

'I don't have time for silly questions.'

'And I don't have the licence.' She folded her arms.

The licenc e was found at the last minute as the police were gesticulating for the old man to pull over. Sibanda wasn't sure he'd picked the right couple. They might dismember one another before they reached Victoria Falls.

The last roadblock was even trickier. The police wanted to see what was under the canopy, but the old man had reached breaking point. His wife had pushed him over the edge with her silence and obstinance. Now this Police whippersnapper wanted to delay him further. 'Do you see this face?' he asked them, 'Does it look like the face of a criminal? I'm an old man. Would you talk to your grandfather like that? My suitcases are in the back and that's all.' The police officer smiled and waved him through. They'd dealt with cantankerous old white men before; they weren't worth the effort. He diverted his attention to an overloaded bus approaching; here were rich pickings.

The distance from the airport to the town was long and the speed limit low. Sibanda hoped the driver would be extra cautious so he could slip out, but the old man was irritated. His foot remained on the accelerator. The possibility of exiting the vehicle was getting trickier. He loosened the canopy and risked a peak out. The town couldn't be far now; he'd have to make a move. Sibanda's luck changed when a herd of elephants walked across the road. The pick-up stopped. There were no other cars in sight. Sibanda jumped off and disappeared into the bush, but not before he caught some of the couple's conversation.

'Be careful you'll get us killed. Back up!'

'Oh, shut up, you stupid woman.'

Chapter 21

'We have to get to a phone.' Ncube hurried, abandoned his old lady rolling walk and marched as if on parade, a row of popping squeaks and farts following him.

'Wait, wait, I have a phone.' PC Khumalo was trailing in his malodorous wake, 'Who are you calling?'

'The only person I know with a reliable vehicle. She will drop everything to come to detective Sibanda's aid.'

'Who's that? '

'Berry Barton.'

'The rumour is they've broken up.'

'Hmmm, that's what they think. They're mistaken. Sometimes even baboons fall out of trees. We are phoning Kestrel Vale school, she teaches there.'

Sibanda arrived in the town about an hour after his drop off. He made straight for the shops and kitted himself out in a pair of cargo shorts, a vest, sandals and a cheap Chinese, multi-function, rubberised, army-style watch – the uniform of the white-water rafting guides who owned bragging rights around town. He stuffed his old clothes in his backpack and headed out to the municipal campgrounds to check for the Rugged Rascals truck. The overlanders were due to arrive in two days. They would be nervy about their passports. He wanted to be waiting for them before they pitched up at the local police station demanding the return of their documents. The political party conference was taking place at Hippo Hills, a large hotel overlooking the Zambezi River some distance from the town. Cuthbert Muchacha would be in the thick of the shoulder rubbing, toadying his way back to the heart of the pond slime with the rest of the bottom dwellers. He was charming and resilient with animal cunning, you had to give him that.

Sibanda scouted the curio market, keeping his distance. The Manhombo twins, Talkmore and Talkless, chipped away at a block of stone. Large, well-muscled men wearing identical clothes, grinning from ear to ear, indistinguishable from each other and unmissable. What was their role in the diamond dealing? Thomas Mabiza was around too, also unmissable, still in his number nine Ronaldo shirt, sticking out like a thumb full of yellow pus, talking to a young man with a disfigured face. They were having an argument. Mabiza jeered and pointed at the young man's facial defect, showing off to a gathered audience. The argument was heating up. He pushed the mutilated man and received a well-aimed punch in return, flooring him. Scarface knew how to handle himself, had probably been in many fights before. That mutilated face would have brought him a lifetime of taunts. Ncube mentioned a henchman with a deformed top lip hanging around Cuthbert Muchacha. This was too much of a coincidence. Nearby traders gathered around the melee but kept their distance from the young man who stalked off, massaging his fist. Sibanda followed him as he hurried towards the town centre. The man walked with his head down but seemed able to negotiate oncoming pedestrians with a sixth sense. One of the pedestrians stopped, a white woman. She hugged him with affection. They knew one another, but the young man was uncomfortable with the familiarity. Sibanda moved in closer and listened.

'Godwishes, what are you doing up here?'

'Hello Madam, I'm helping the big chef , Minister Muchacha. He's up here for a conference.'

'I've told you, call me Caro. Everyone does. I didn't know you worked for a politician. I thought you lived with your uncle.'

'Same person. And you, Miss Caro, why are you here? I thought you and boss Rupert were leaving for England.'

'Rupert changed plans... again. Heaven knows what we'll be doing next, heading for Timbuktu at this rate. He's off somewhere scheming, all very cloak and dagger these days.'

'Cloak and dagger, Miss?'

'Underhand, you know? Secretive, has been like that since we arrived in Africa. And drop the Miss, call me Caro.'

'I'm Wishes,' he said.

'That's a deal.'

'Will you be selling the house mi... Caro?'

'I'm not sure yet, Wishes. Are you worried about noisy new neighbours?' she laughed.

'No, no. I hoped you might be living next door. I could fix your garden.'

Caro went quiet. 'No decision yet. Why don't you come and have a coffee? I'd love to tell you about a journal I've found.'

'I can't, I have an urgent message for my boss. He's staying at Hippo Hills. It's quite a way.'

'We're staying at the Victoria Falls Hotel if you want to get in touch.'

Sibanda began to wonder how Muchacha's henchman was involved with this English couple.

Godwishes nodded but he wouldn't be visiting that place for rich tourists. He was still thinking about the hug. He hadn't known an affectionate touch since he was a child. 'Thank you,' he smiled, 'I must go now.'

'You can't walk all that way. I'll get a taxi for you.'

'It's okay, Caro, I'm used to it.'

'Rubbish,' she insisted, 'I'm paying, it's the least I can do. You rescued me from a snake!'

As the taxi disappeared along the road on its way to Hippo Hills, Sibanda contemplated following Caro and finding out about the underhanded Rupert, their relationship with Godwishes and Cuthbert Muchacha, but she wandered in and out of shops, picking up ethnic jewellery, table cloths and wall hangings, feeling them and putting them down again. Shopping and its associated customs were a mystery to the detective, but Sibanda understood enough to expect it might go on for hours. Besides, he had overheard which hotel they were staying in. His focus shifted instead to the deformed lad. What message did Godwishes have to deliver to Cuthbert Muchacha in such a hurry as to give up a decent coffee and a cake thrown into the bargain? Godwishes didn't look as though he got any of those sorts of treats often.

Sibanda would use this time to find a base, somewhere to sleep, hole up and plot. Somewhere low key, maybe in the township to stretch his seven hundred dollars. He didn't know how long he would be there or what contingencies would arise.

Seeing Miss Daisy parked in the middle of town jolted him.

'What the...' he swallowed the expletive, turned his back to the vehicle and stared into a shop window, watching the old Land Rover in the reflection of the glass. This was a trap. Had the CIO worked out he would head for Victoria Falls and dragged the vehicle up here as bait? He slid into the shop and peered through a display of shirts in the window, scanning the street. Nothing, no obvious set up, no bulging jackets, no twitchy operatives staking out the vehicle. It took a few minutes to locate the culprits. Sitting together on a bench, nattering away like long lost sisters were PC Khumalo and his rotund sergeant, 'Precious' Ncube.

'What do you two think you're up to?' Sibanda came up on them from behind. They both started. Sergeant Ncube's gut rumbled, expelling gases that caused his skirt to billow. PC Khumalo's eyes rolled like dice in a casino.

'Sir, we've been...' Ncube almost swallowed his tongue.

'Keep calm, Precious. This time, I'm your son, Joe.'

'Are you alright... Joe?' PC Khumalo was recovering from the shock. 'We've been so worried.'

'Don't know if I'm glad to see you two or not. We need somewhere more private to talk.'

'My sister's house. She won't mind... and we have news.'

'No, we can't get your family involved, Ncube. We'll meet in plain sight. Where they'll least expect me to be.'

'Where's that, sir... Joe?'

'The Devils' Cataract. One hour. Travel separately. Precious, take a taxi.' Sibanda peeled off five dollars and disappeared.

'How will we tell him?' PC Khumalo stood to start her walk down to the waterfall.

'Leave it to me, I'll think of something.' Sergeant Ncube pottered off towards the taxi rank. He would have to swing past his sister's house to borrow her identity card. No one entered the Victoria Falls National Park unless they produced a Zimbabwean ID or paid a week's wages in American dollars.

Sibanda couldn't show his ID. He didn't know how far the warrant for his arrest reached. He headed to the Zambezi River, upstream of the falls, to a spot closest to the Devil's Cataract. A three-metre-high fence topped with razor wire enclosed the national park. No one was gazing on the wonders of the Victoria Falls without paying. The fence was buried deep in the ground, making wriggling under impossible. He skirted the enclosure, looking for an easier climb and found his spot. A portion of fence had been hit and buckled by a wayward vehicle or an angry elephant. Sibanda used the bent stake to get to the top of the lowered fence. The razor wire was trickier to negotiate. He balanced on the top of the mesh fence and with the aid of an overhanging branch, steadied himself and stepped over it. He spent a moment unpicking his vest from the sharp blades before climbing down the other side.

A baboon barked annoyance at the invasion of his territory whilst overhead, a pair of African palm swifts raced by in a helter-skelter pattern, fast and furious, screaming in a thin, piercing pitch as they flew. A frantic breed, eating and drinking on the wing. Sibanda knew his next few days would be similar. Despite his precarious position, he couldn't resist glancing across to a stand of ilala palms. The swifts glued their nest with saliva to the underside of the leaves, a frail, shallow construction cobbled with feathers. Even the nestlings clung on for dear life. Palm trees and water drew the swifts to this spot. Murderers, diamonds, and corruption drew him.

Sergeant Ncube and PC Khumalo found a bench in the shadow of David Livingstone's statue whose bronze-cast, heavy thighs fascinated PC Khumalo. All her men so far seemed to have legs like chickens.

Sibanda approached with his single lensed binoculars in hand. He watched a reed cormorant on the rocks, cruciform, hanging his wings out to dry, wearing his breeding plumage of glossy black and bronze-grey. Sibanda's strolling, bird watching camouflage was no hardship. He eased himself onto the bench next to the agitated pair.

'Relax, we're safe here.' Sibanda kept an eagle eye out on his journey. He was sure the town CIO and police were tied up with security at the party conference. They weren't looking for him yet.

'It's not us, Joe, we're alright…'

'Then what is it? Spit it out Ncube. The pair of you are as fidgety as a troop of baboons in a clump of buffalo beans.'

The mention of beans of any variety would normally have delighted Ncube, but he'd been attacked by buffalo beans as a child and the memory brought back hours of itching agony from the tiny poisonous hairs the beans used to defend themselves. He lifted his skirt and scratched his thighs.

'It's your brother…' PC Khumalo spluttered.

'Xolisani?'

'He's been arrested, along with your sister-in-law, Thandie.'

'Is this a joke? Are Lisana and Umkhonto okay?'

'The next-door neighbour phoned Gubu police station when she couldn't get hold of anyone else. She had the children with her.' PC Khumalo was anxious, her voice softer than usual.

'Had? Where are they now?'

'Sergeant Ncube phoned…' her voice trailed off.

Ncube took up the story, 'The neighbour is going away. She couldn't keep the children, so I phoned Miss Barton, the first person I thought of.' Ncube was apologetic.

'Berry?'

'She drove to Bulawayo and collected Lisana and Umkhonto. She's trying to contact your mother.'

Sibanda was quiet, staring into the distance. Everyone gazed into the deep well looking for the missing penny, but few would go down to retrieve it. Sibanda was one of the few. Ncube didn't like the detective's attitude. He preferred being peppered with difficult questions to this silence of the stalking leopard.

Sibanda snapped out of his reverie. 'You did well Ncube. I got Xolisani and Thandie into this mess, they're being held as hostages against my giving myself up. The sooner we solve this case, the sooner I can get them released. Zee.' He turned to the quivering PC Khumalo.

'Yes, Joe.'

'Take this,' he handed her a wad of dollars. Go back into town, buy a new phone and number. Leave it on the front wheel of Miss Daisy. Then I want you back in Gubu.'

'Can't I be of use here?' PC Khumalo was disappointed. She wanted to be in the thick of the investigation.

'Do you remember where you put the carving of the dancing lady?'

'Yes.'

'Still safe, I hope?'

'It should be', she fudged. PC Khumalo had forgotten the carving. She'd left it under the counter, never logged it in as evidence. 'Is it important?'

'She's the key to everything. And one more thing.'

PC Khumalo was keen to change the subject of the abandoned statue, 'What's that, Joe?' She liked the informality of 'Joe'.

'Get the address of Cuthbert Muchacha in Bulawayo and see if you can find out anything about his immediate neighbours. And then bring the statue back here as soon as you can.'

At the mention of Cuthbert Muchacha, Sergeant Ncube's skirt, now indecorously above his knees, began to billow again. He flattened the floral swirl as best he could.

'What should I do?' Ncube had no idea how this mess would be solved.

'Head home to your sister. Tonight, collect Miss Daisy and the phone. Time to get her off the street. Tomorrow we're heading after the curio sellers.'

An old couple walked past them and stood at the point where the water plummeted down into the gorge below, a great raging torrent of white frothing spittle.

The Devil's Cataract was the first, narrowest and most powerful of the five different falls. The water levels hadn't yet reached their peak and married them into an overpowering crashing tumble of deafening water. The couple were holding hands, giggling like teenagers with eyes full of stars. They looked to the trio on the bench.

'Would one of you mind taking a photo of us?' they shouted above the roaring din, offering a camera.

'No, we can't.' Ncube shouted back, forgetting to pitch his voice in the female range. He didn't want to disturb the detective and his planning.

'I'll do it. I owe them.' Sibanda took their camera and snapped the blissful pair whilst the pounding water behind formed its famous prism and spun a fairy tale rainbow that spanned the torrent and framed the couple in kaleidoscopic happiness.

'Thank you. We came on our honeymoon fifty years ago and today is our anniversary,' the wife looked at her husband with adoration.

'Every minute has been perfect. I can recommend it, young man. Are you married?' Sibanda shook his head. 'Ah well, there's still time.' The couple walked off, he with his arm around her shoulder, she with hers around his waist.

'What do you mean you owe them, sir, who are they?'

'They gave me a lift to the Falls.'

Chapter 22

'There's a link, Ncube, between Cuthbert Muchacha, the man with the disfigured face, one of the curio sellers and a white couple staying at The Victoria Falls Hotel.'

'A white man was hanging around Madani Haddads's place on the night of his murder.'

'What has he been up to? How does he fit into all this?'

The pair were strolling on the outskirts of the township, having arranged to meet under an advertising hoarding boasting the remarkable cleansing properties of a bar of green laundry soap. There wasn't another soul in sight.

'Do you think the *mukiwa* murdered Madani Haddad and found a way to get through the closed door?'

'He didn't murder Haddad, but I know who did.'

'Who?'

'I'll explain later, but there were no ghosts or baboons involved. For now, let's concentrate on Jaafar Bastany.'

'Jaafar Bas...Bas... Who's he?'

'AKA Laurent Kasongo, our masked man, shot in the alley. The white man could have murdered him.'

'How did you find out his real name, sir?'

'Let's just say I met an old acquaintance on my way here who let me in on the identity of the victim.'

'How... Who?'

'No time for explanations, Ncube. I helped him, he repaid the debt with information and some rather angry and unwanted visitors. Let's leave it at that. Have you got the phone?'

Ncube fished around in his skirt for the device and handed it over.

'Where's Miss Daisy?'

'Garaged in the back of the fire station yard. My brother-in-law's sister is married to the fire chief. What's our next move? Shall we continue to peregrinate?' Ncube felt a welling of pride. What a word. He learned it, remembered it, and found the perfect moment to launch it. The word had something to do with birds. That should cheer the detective up.

Ncube was alarmed when the detective looked at him with flared nostrils. This preceded a spewing of impossible words delivered with the sting of a hornet.

'Ncube, do yourself a favour and throw that dictionary away. While you're at it, ditch the disguise. You look more like a rhino in drag than a respectable Ndebele Gogo. '

'I'll be recognised, sir.' Ncube sensed Sibanda had insulted him again. At least he had bettered the detective with a word as long as a monkey's tail, although maybe it should have been longer. Did he leave a bit off the end?

'Stay out of the main streets, Ncube.'

'How can I help with the investigation if I'm hidden away?'

'You have a network up here. They can be your eyes. Can you get me the guest list for the Victoria Falls Hotel?'

'Leave that with me, sir. Prince, my brother-in-law, works in the laundry at the hotel.' Ncube waddled off pleased with the important task at hand.

PC Khumalo's bus ride back to Gubu was fraught, not by screaming babies or overweight, overburdened seat-sharers but by two worrisome problems – would the statue still be where she left it, and how was she going to get Cuthbert Muchacha's address? There was little she could do about the statue except pray no one had taken a fancy to it. She had to be safe in that regard. Who would want a fat, shapeless, colourless, lump of stone to dust? Finding Muchacha's address was more complicated. Could she risk returning to the police station to make an official phone call where everyone would see she was well enough to go back to work? She mulled over the problem as the bus pulled up at yet another roadblock and vendors shoved oranges, bananas, popcorn, and roasted maize cobs through the window. She ignored them. Detectives never seemed to be hungry, she noted.

One of the more persistent vendors sported a wart on the side of his nose. As she yet again swatted away a bag of home-roasted peanuts, the nasal wart reminded her of her uncle, Efficient, an Uber driver in South Africa. He was home, having a break from the taxi wars raging in the streets of Johannesburg. Two weeks ago, Efficient experienced a moment of madness. Red mist descended after a hot day negotiating knotted traffic, endless road works and a faulty air conditioner. He had rammed a mini-bus attempting to burst into a long traffic jam. Her uncle retreated to his Zimbabwe rural home to contemplate the folly of road rage and to escape reprisals. Efficient, nose wart and all, was a stalwart supporter of the ruling party and if anyone could worm information from those in the know, he could. PC Khumalo settled back in her seat. One problem solved. Now who could she find to smuggle the statue out of the police station?

Sibanda left Ncube and headed for the curio market, having arranged to meet up later in a remote corner of the township. The market was beginning to fill with tourists wishing to avoid the steaming mid-day humidity. Sibanda wanted to interrogate the sculpting twins.

'Nice stuff.'

'Thanks, we try.' The twins answered in unison; inseparable in feature, they talked as one.

'How's business?'

The twins shrugged and shook their heads. 'Not good,' said one. 'We get by,' said the other, a rare dichotomy.

'A friend of mine bought a sculpture here. Do you have any similar?' Sibanda showed them the photo of Mama Ecstasy.

'Good choice.'

'We don't do repeats.'

'We're not into mass production.'

'Each piece is unique.'

'I remember that statue.'

'Yeh, we sold it to a Congolese guy.'

'Odd man, loaded with cash.'

'He never haggled.'

'Accepted our price.'

'We ate well last week.' They both rubbed their stomachs in a clockwise direction.

Sibanda interrupted the duo's conversation, 'Laurent can be strange, but I'm surprised he possessed so much money. He's usually broke.'

'Well, not last week.'

'He showed us wads of USD notes.'

'Crisp and clean.'

Sibanda rubbed his chin, 'Not like him to buy art. He's more of a gambling man.' He fingered the notes in his pocket that belonged to Jaafar Bastany.

'We can understand that.'

'He was not interested in the look of the sculpture.'

'No, he wanted the weight and the girth. Didn't he almost measure them, Less?'

'You're right, More, he chose the fattest lady.'

'Maybe he had a thing.' They said this in unison. The pair were an extraordinary double act.

'A thing?' Sibanda queried.

'Some guys prefer their women with a lot of flesh.' They laughed again, glancing at one another, sharing some joke only they understood.

'Sorry, guys. So rude of me, I'm Joe Dube. I have a gallery in Bulawayo. I'm looking for classy art and your sculptures fit the bill, do you have a business card?'

'No card, but you can always find us – Talkmore and Talkless Manhombo, we're twins,' they stated the obvious.

'Manhombo?' Sibanda had waited for this name. 'Aren't you from the same area as Cuthbert Muchacha?'

The twins fell quiet. The permanent smiles plastered across their faces crumpled, the four eyes closed to a squint and their skin darkened from polished teak to ebony. One of them spat. Sibanda was surprised they didn't spit in unison.

'Do not paint us with the same spots as that hyena.'

Sibanda spent a few moments feigning gallery-buyer interest until he spied an irresistible piece, Mama Ecstasy's sister. Instead of dancing, she was carrying a basket of maize on her head, each pip defined, wilting leaves overhanging. The twins captured the sway of her hips, the weariness of her walk and a slight stoop in her back, eased with a resting hand. Above all, she spoke of the pride of African womanhood. Sibanda bargained them down. She was worth every penny of the fifty dollars he settled on. The seven hundred dollars was diminishing, but the purchase was not one he would regret. He would love to give it to Berry. She would be as enchanted as he was. 'Thanks, Jaafar,' he whispered under his breath.

The detective walked away from the twins, convinced they weren't part of any diamond dealing plot. Mama Ecstasy was chosen for size not beauty. Did she have a role in all this?

Sibanda turned his attention to Thomas Mabiza. The man had been watching him from a distance. Sibanda had been aware of his constant gaze during his conversation with the twins. Mabiza might recognise him. Did he know who he was, that the CIO was after him? Tourist police patrolled the curio market, employed to keep the touts and pesterers a healthy distance from visitors. They could be summoned in an instance. Sibanda had to take the risk he'd be spotted. He dallied by the refreshment stall, drank a bottle of water, and watched Mabiza whilst chatting to the stall holder. She had no idea who he was, just a handsome face in a queue of thirsty ones.

'Been busy?' he asked.

'Can't complain,' she replied with a yawn. This man with the muscles of an iron man and the face of a movie star was the most exciting thing in her morning.

'That stall looks interesting.' He pointed to Thomas Mabiza's stand. I'm looking for some curios for my gallery in Bulawayo.

'Stay away.' she muttered under her breath.

'Why?'

'He's *yisigebenga* and a rubbish carver. Look at all the broken stuff at the back of his stall. His carvings crack and break. Why would you choose him?'

'A crook?'

'Always leaving his stand and wandering off with known shady characters. The Falls is full of them. Look, he's off again now.'

Sibanda watched as Thomas Mabiza struck up a conversation with a seedy looking man who'd arrived at his stall. Mabiza's eyes swivelled as he talked.

'I might have a look at his wire work, it seems appealing. But thanks for the warning.'

Sibanda wandered to Mabiza's now abandoned pitch. He was left on his own to take a closer look. The drinks' vendor was right, Mabiza was up to something. His stock was from other stalls. He had tried his hand at stone carving, but the results were disastrous. The back of his stand was littered with chipped and broken figurines and animals. Mabiza was no artist, had no touch or skill with a chisel. He seemed to find the wrong vein in the stone. This business was a cover for underhand dealings. Currency? Drugs? Diamonds? The man with the scarred lip, Cuthbert Muchacha's henchman, seemed linked to him. Could Mabiza have followed Jaafar Bastany to Gubu, shot him, and stolen the diamonds at Muchacha's command? He was one to keep an eye on.

PC Khumalo realised she would have to retrieve the sculpture herself. She needed to make herself appear ill and unfit for duty. No use rubbing ash or clay on her skin to look paler; everyone would notice. Working on her eyes was a possibility. First, she found burned wood and used the charcoal mixed with face cream to rub into the area under her eyes until she developed dark rings and bags to rival Barghees grocery counter. She applied red lipstick around the rims, a move she regretted as the grease spread across her eyeballs, making the world fuzzy. She blinked. Before leaving home, she took a slice of onion and poked it in the corner of her eyes and then up her nostrils. Her eyes stung like nettles, and streamed, her nose did the same. Onion was an old foe. She sneezed in a gasp of sneezes until her handkerchief turned soggy.

When she reached the police station, PC Tshuma was on duty. He looked at her in horror, 'Should you be here in that state? We'll all get infected?'

'Sorry,' she sniffled, 'but I have to collect some things and then I'll go back to bed.

'What things?'

'Personal stuff.'

'Oh,' Tshuma blushed. Women were still a mystery to him and their personal belongings, scary.

PC Khumalo staggered a little and held onto the charge office counter. 'Are you sure you should be here?' The more PC Khumalo approached, the more Tshuma backed away. Germs terrorised him.

'I could use a glass of water, I'm feeling faint.'

PC Tshuma hurried into the bowels of the station, glad to distance himself from the germ-ridden, snot snorter.

PC Khumalo rummaged under the counter as soon as his back was turned. The space underneath was narrow, deep, dark, dusty and cluttered with many years' accumulation of odd papers, dog eared files and a mountain of unclaimed, useless lost property. Anything desirable was pilfered by the staff after the requisite three month waiting period. One recent, homeless file had pushed Mama Ecstasy to the back of the cavity behind a single shoe of indeterminate age and odour. As her fingers curled around the statue's neck, PC Khumalo breathed a sigh of relief. She stuffed her in a bag and leaned on the counter, head in hands as if in extremis. Tshuma returned, placed the water on the counter and took a healthy step back.

'You've missed all the excitement around here.'

'What's happened?' she sipped the water for effect, her least favourite liquid.

'CIO came in and turned this station upside down looking for a statue.'

'A statue?' She held the bag closer.

'Evidence in the Detective Sibanda murders. They wrecked his office.'

'Did they find it?'

'No trace. He must have it with him wherever he is. I wouldn't like to be in his shoes.'

'To think we've been working with a murderer all this time.' She sneezed again. The onion was relentless.

'Go home!' The distaste on Tshuma's face was a picture; one hand covered pursed lips and a scrunched nose. With his free hand, he waved her away.

Detective Sibanda's phone rang. Only two people knew this number. Ncube and PC Khumalo.

'I borrowed this phone from my sister, sir. I thought I'd let you know as soon as possible.

'What have you got, Ncube?'

'The guest list from the Victoria Falls Hotel. I've been through all the names. Nothing stands out except for a Mr and Mrs Rupert Templeton. Isn't Templeton the name of one of the suspects on the overland truck?'

'Meet me under the soap advert in half an hour. We'll pay a visit to Mr and Mrs Templeton.' Sibanda stroked his chin. How many other Ruperts could there be in Victoria Falls. Was the surname a coincidence?

The phone rang again. 'Zee?'

'Sir, I have the statue. I'll be back on tomorrow's bus.'

'Muchacha's neighbours?'

'On the one side, the Patel family. He owns a hardware shop. The other is a house empty for years. The owner, Isaiah Jacobs, died. They've been trying to trace his relatives. A Mrs Templeton has inherited it. She was there until a few days ago, cleaning up.'

'Excellent Zee, that ties in. Get back safely with the statue.'

'I'm guarding it with my life.'

Chapter 23

Caroline was sitting with Rupert on the terrace of the Victoria Falls Hotel, sharing a rare moment together with her husband. Since their arrival in the tourist town, Rupert was on his own mission. God knows what he was up to. Caroline stared into the distance, to the old bridge dusted with spray from a waterfall that amazed and dazzled her. No wonder the locals named it "the smoke that thunders," she thought. Even the dour, humourless, irritable missionary, Livingstone, had been moved to dabble with the lyrical in his journal: "Scenes so lovely must have been gazed upon by angels in their flight." Last night, as the sun sank behind the bridge, a steam train crossed, its smoke challenging the spray and the low clouds until all the vapours met, layered and illuminated with the gentle light of evening. Pink, yellow, rose, every shade of dragon's breath hovered over a shimmering Zambezi. Livingstone never saw the train but maybe his angels did. This morning, the sheer size and power of the biggest waterfall in the world left her breathless. The grand old Edwardian hotel was now providing both her and Rupert with a delicious lunch and a moment of reflection.

Rupert took a long swallow of his wine. The time had come. 'I'm leaving Caro.'

'What do you mean, leaving? You haven't even seen the Falls yet?' She slammed her glass down. Rupert was becoming impossible. People on the adjacent tables fell silent, looked around, wiped their mouths with starched napkins, tucked back into their meals and resumed their chatter.

'Leaving you. It's over between us, has been for some time. Don't tell me you haven't noticed. We've changed...'

'... This is sudden. Couldn't this announcement have waited until we got home. Shouldn't we at least talk?'

'No time to talk. I'm getting out of this accursed country... on my own.'

'Why on your own?'

'I've got myself into a spot of bother.' Rupert dragged out the last word in a long, low, typically English, understated tone. 'I've been researching my exit and I think I've found a way.'

'Can't I help?'

'I don't want you involved. It's tricky.'

'I'll be left here alone. What do I do?'

'What do you do? Oh, Caro, you're far better equipped to deal with these situations than I am. Your genetics are more... more robust.'

'What are you saying?'

'Look at you, you've always done well in a crisis, maybe it's the blood of Africa in your veins. No point denying it.' He looked into her eyes. She didn't flinch. 'What DNA do I have? A public-school father with a stutter, receding chin, popping eyes and whose greatest claim to fame was playing Bottom in a Midsummer Night's Dream. You've met my mother…' he sneered, 'I was born to stuff up, that's my inheritance. Yours, my darling, is the world.'

Caroline didn't refute any of this. She focused on Richard's stomach, expanded to unappealing flab in recent months, 'What sort of bother?'

'The police are after me. I have to skip across the border. It'll be easier here to do that. I have two choices, Zambia or Botswana. If I can't manage those, Namibia is a stone's throw away.'

'For heaven's sake, why are the police after you?'

'I've done something stupid and unforgivable. Don't ask me to explain.'

'Something to do with Bilal?'

'Yes.'

'That man is shifty. I picked him from the off.'

'Maybe I would have too if I wasn't so caught up with a failing business.' He looked down, 'And on that note…'

'…You want the ring back.'

He gave her an apologetic look and laughed, 'You can still read me like a book. The diamond will help.'

Caroline slipped the engagement ring off her finger and placed it on Rupert's side plate. 'When are you leaving?'

'Tomorrow morning. I've booked a cross-border excursion. It'll be easier to get through immigration with my passport tucked in amongst those of the rest of the travellers.'

'To where?'

'Better you don't know. I am so sorry, Caroline,' he took her hands.

'Me too.' She stared at Rupert for a moment. He looked away. Her gaze was unbearable. She stood and gave her husband a rueful smile, turned and walked back to the room. She didn't wish him ill, wasn't shocked at the declaration, had in fact been expecting it. She had even been hoping for it. Massaging the impressed, branded flesh on her finger, the spot the ring encircled for eight years, she smiled again, a secret smile, a smile of triumph.

From the table where he sat, Rupert thought he heard his wife laughing. He dismissed it as wishful thinking. She was probably sobbing her eyes out in her pillow by now. He sighed, popped the ring in his pocket and waited for the bill.

I saw the war coming. I didn't need the barking dog and roaring lions of Umlilo's cave to tell me that. Men are driven by greed and by the desire for land and more land after that. Enough is never enough. One day the world will have no more land to give and what will they do then? Colonialism is war by stealth, but the British were now gearing for an open war with horses, swords, rifles, and gun carriages. They had seen the riches of Matabeleland, lusted for the gold in the ground, seen how the crops grew tall, green and richly tasselled like the tails of wildebeest. They smelled the rains that brought life and caused the rivers to run and play. They feasted on our herds and wild meat that swarmed the plains and forests, they witnessed the great gatherings of elephants with the riches of ivory curving from their jaws. They had a passion for the hunt, an unquenchable blood lust. They were never going to leave us alone. I tried to convince the King to prepare his impis, to fire up his regiments but he was tired of living by then, his body weighed down by the dripping fats of his cattle that settled on his heart and around his girth, his health hindered by breathlessness and the unbearable pain that plagued his feet and joints. The last time I urged him to be prepared he said this:

'Did you ever see a chameleon catch a fly, Jacobi? The chameleon gets behind the fly and remains motionless for some time, then he advances very slowly and gently, first putting forward one leg and then the other. At last, when well within reach, he darts his tongue and the fly disappears. England is the chameleon and I am that fly.' A long speech for the King.

I knew then it was over, that the king had given his land to Rhodes, to the rapacious English milord. Oh, for the cunning of the umlaladwayi, *the tree that looks like an umbrella, the tree that provides spear shafts for our warriors, the tree with one straight thorn to repel enemies and one hooked for those that penetrate the first defences. Lo Bengula was born without a hooked thorn.*

When one of his senior indunas, Magwegwe, summoned me and told me the King wished to travel, I was heartened. Maybe he had a plan, maybe he possessed a hook after all.

Caroline awoke to a knock. The journal fell from her grip. She opened the door.

'Mrs Templeton?'

'Yes...'

'We're police officers. We'd like to ask a couple of questions.'

'Police officers?' She stared at the two men at her door. One looked like a mythical god and not at all like any police officer she'd ever seen here or anywhere else for that matter. And the other, well... he was a tub of lard. Neither wore uniforms. 'Are you sure?'

'Yes, madam.' Sergeant Ncube showed her his ZRP I.D.

'Oh, right, how can I help?'

'Is your husband here?' The good looking one spoke in a voice like warm brown honey. She shivered.

'He's out at the moment.'

'Back soon?'

'I'm not sure.' She noted the tall man was taking the lead.

'Can we come in?' Sibanda felt uneasy in the corridor. Ncube and his rotundity stood out like the bright blue mating testicles of a vervet monkey.

Caroline hesitated but there was something trustworthy about the pair, something in their eyes and she held herself a good judge of character. Was she being swayed by good looks and rotund affability? She opened the door.

'Mrs Templeton,' the tall one began, 'have you visited Gubu?'

'Gubu? Near the park? Yes, we spent three nights there. Fabulous place. It rained a lot, but the elephants were amazing.'

'When was that?'

'About a week ago, arrived on the 21st, left on the 24th.'

'Where did you stay?'

'Gubu Safari Lodge.'

'What were you doing on the evening of the 23rd?'

'Watching elephants.'

'And your husband?'

'Rupert had an appointment in Gubu with a business associate on one of the evenings. The 23rd, I think. Yes, I remember because it was the night before we left for Bulawayo.'

'The name of the associate?'

'He never mentioned it. What is this all about?'

‘Two men were murdered in Gubu on the afternoon and night of the 23rd. A white man was seen in the vicinity.’

‘Murdered? Do you suspect my husband? Is that why you’re here? He’s an investment banker in London, for heaven’s sake, not a murderer.’

Sibanda ignored the questions. ‘Do any of these names mean anything – Cuthbert Muchacha?’ She shook her head, ‘Laurent Kasongo?’

‘Never heard of either of them.’ Caroline was wringing her hands. What had Rupert done? What sort of mess was he dragging her into? A spot of bother, he said. Well, murder was more than a spot of bother.

‘Jaafar Bastany? Madani Haddad?’

Caroline’s eyes flickered, ‘No, sorry.’

‘Are you sure, Mrs Templeton?’ Sergeant Ncube had picked up on the eye twitch.

‘My husband has a business associate in the UK called Bilal Haddad, but I’ve never heard mention of Madani Haddad.’

‘An unusual name to be a coincidence?’ Sibanda pressed.

Caroline never replied. Her eyes were fixed on the door behind them as it opened.

Rupert stepped halfway into the room, took in the situation, turned and bolted.

Sibanda was after him, racing down the long, carpeted corridors, disturbing the decorum of the noble explorers, aristocracy and royalty who peered down from their sepia-dusty portraits. Rupert Templeton was something of an athlete in his youth, but his recent stresses and lack of exercise took their toll. Compared to Sibanda, he was lumbering. The detective knew he couldn’t afford to make a scene of the chase, couldn’t bring attention to himself for fear of his own arrest. This pursuit had to end soon, or he would have to give up on the man. The corridor dash had already raised a few portly eyebrows and pursed a few wrinkled lips on their way for a nap. Mid-afternoon was a quiet time for the elderly and well-heeled. The younger set were still sipping lunchtime Pimm's on the veranda. When Templeton dodged sideways into the Bingley Room, Sibanda cornered him, slamming the door behind him. They were alone.

'Don't be stupid, Templeton, I just want to talk.' Rupert Templeton grabbed a silver-plated letter opener from a large, Edwardian desk in the corner. No one wrote letters any more whose envelopes needed slitting but its very placement added style to the hushed atmosphere of the reading room.

'I haven't done anything,' he hissed.

'Then why are you running? Put the knife down.'

'You've been chasing me from Bulawayo all the way up here. You don't do that if there's no crime to answer. I know Africa, you'll pin something on me. I'll rot in a rat-infested jail for years. There'll be no justice here. Third world courts are a joke. I won't be fitted up.' Templeton lunged. The knife missed Sibanda's ribs by less than a whisker on the octogenarian face of Lady Montague Bingley whose portrait dominated the room as her life had dominated the early days of Victoria Falls.

The men circled one another, Templeton feinting with his silver weapon, Sibanda jibbing and watching, waiting for his moment. All the while, Lobengula, last King of the Ndebele, looked down on the fight from his portrait on the opposite wall. His fat stomach gleamed. His chieftain's circular head knot, his *isidhlodhlo*, tilted in a hint of the sorrowful end that awaited him, a metaphor for future suffering, like the infant Jesus' falling sandal in the famous Madonna and Child icon. Lobengula looked with scorn on the miniature spear in the white man's hand and mocked the lack of bloodlust and killing in either man's eyes. Is this what his kingdom had come to, a pair of grown men playing warriors like children? When Templeton lunged again, the detective sidestepped and tripped his assailant. He wrestled him to the ground and subdued him with a few well-aimed punches. In moments, Templeton's arms were pinned under him, and the knife pointed at the banker's throat, almost piercing the flesh.

'If it's any consolation, Templeton, I believe you,' he hissed into the gasping man's ear, 'no one has been chasing you.'

'What? Then why...?'

'...Crossed purposes and an unfortunate coincidence. Now get up, we'll walk back to your room. Don't attempt to escape and remember to smile at any guests we pass. This knife might be used for cutting paper, but I'll wager it'll slice into your kidneys just as well.'

Rupert Templeton did as he was told. The last time he'd been involved in physical affray was at school when a lower sixth beat him senseless for failing to reveal the location of his Nanny's famed chocolate mud cake. Since then, he'd done his best to avoid both confrontation and chocolate cake. Every cocoa laden crumb could bring back nightmares. As he walked, blood dribbled from his lip, his throbbing eye would turn into a shiner by tomorrow and he was aware of a sharp point in the small of his back.

Back in the room, Sibanda barked orders, 'Ncube, go to the manager's officer, he may have complaints coming his way. Pre-empt them, apologise for the disturbance, tell him you've arrested a well-known drug dealer and it's best for the hotel's reputation it stays under wraps. Mrs Templeton, your husband needs a glass of water.'

'What have you done to him?' Caroline was dabbing at Rupert's cuts and bruises.

'Less than he deserves.' He turned to the battered man. 'Templeton, why did you run when you saw us?'

Rupert waited until his wife finished fussing to reply. 'I know you've been snivelling around my wife's house; I know you are trying to pin a murder on me.'

'Whose murder?'

'Madani Haddad.'

'Tell me about Madani Haddad.'

'I never met him. I was supposed to link up with him but...'

'... when you arrived at his house, he was already dead.'

Templeton perked up at this lifeline, 'How did you know?'

'If the detective says he knows, then he knows. Do not question him.' Ncube had slipped back into the room during the interrogation.

'What was the meeting about?' Sibanda resumed his questioning.

'I was supposed to collect a package from him.' Templeton head lay in his hands. 'I was assured the pick-up wasn't drugs. I would never have agreed to being a drug mule.'

'You didn't know what was in the package?'

'No, but I didn't think it would be above board.'

'Run me through your movements that day.'

'I left Gubu Safari Lodge after lunch and found Haddad's house. I parked some distance away and walked the rest of the way. No one seems to have numbers on their house. I arrived later than planned.'

'Everyone knows everyone in Gubu, Mr Templeton, we don't need numbers. Each village has its own way of cutting up a chicken. Go on.'

'I knocked on the door, no one came. I went around the back to have a look. Maybe Haddad hadn't heard me. I saw him, through the bedroom window lying flat on his back, eyes wide open. He was dead. I panicked.'

'Why?'

'Because Haddad was a crook. His cousin, Bilal Haddad, the man who sent me to collect the package, is Lebanese Mafia. It was obvious Madani Haddad had been murdered. Mafioso don't die of natural causes on their bedroom floor. Whoever polished him off might be looking for me.'

'Did you see or hear anything?'

'Nothing. I hid for a while to make sure no one was around and then snuck to my car and raced back to the lodge.'

'Did you see anyone at all?'

'A few people walking. Neighbours chatting over fences, some kids playing in the street. Went straight back to Caroline.'

Sibanda moved closer to Templeton and stood over him. 'You're lying. You didn't go straight back to Gubu Safari Lodge, because you had to rescue the deal. You waited till after dark, walked into the centre of the village and traced another of your contacts, Jaafar Bastany. You killed him and stole the package of diamonds he was couriering.'

'Diamonds? Oh God. I never knew I was to carry diamonds. Jaafar Bastany? I've never heard of him. You've seen me in physical contact. I'm useless, how could I murder him? Throttle him? Stab him with a paper knife?' Templeton was almost hysterical.

'You shot him with a 9mm, a clean shot to the back of the skull.'

Caroline let out a shriek. 'You didn't bring your grandfather's weapon over here, did you? Oh, Rupert, you're more stupid than I thought. Is this your "spot of bother"? Gun running, diamond smuggling and murder?'

'No. How would I have got the pistol past all those X-ray machines. I promise you, Caro, I haven't murdered anyone. You can't believe that of me, can you?' His marriage was further gone than he thought.

'You had a fair go at me, Templeton.'

'I was desperate, trapped. I did not murder Madani Haddad or Jaafar Whatever. I'm a failed smuggler, a courier caught in a trap who was coerced into picking up a package with no idea of the contents. This is all Bilal Haddad's fault. He's the one you should be after.'

'Blackmailed?'

'Pressurised is a better word. I'm in financial trouble,' His voice dropped. 'Bilal Haddad offered me a way out.'

'I remember now, Rupert,' Caroline butted in. 'You got back to Gubu Safari Lodge before nightfall, as the storm was about to break. We talked about the elephants at the waterhole. There would have been no time for you to go back after dark and murder someone in the village.' She hesitated, chose her next words and delivered them with finality, 'Rupert can't have murdered Jaafar Bastany, detective. He was with me.'

Chapter 24

'What was all that about the newspaper, sir?' Sibanda and Ncube were walking away from the hotel.

'A ridiculous coincidence, Ncube. I found a sheet of folded newspaper in Jaafar Bastany's backpack. It had to be significant. I went over that page with great care. I couldn't understand why he'd kept it so neatly folded and then I found a small mark on the back amongst the classifieds. That mark was next to a deceased estate. The house turned out to be the one Caroline Templeton inherited but the clue was a classic red herring.'

'Ah yes, I remember. That's the fish that isn't a fish?' Ncube smacked his lips.

'A false lead. When the CIO took the backpack from my office, they also saw the mark on the paper and came to the same conclusion. They visited the house and that set Rupert Templeton on the run. He never murdered either of the suspects, but he was up to no good and his guilty conscience got the better of him.'

'You've let Rupert Templeton go, sir. Shouldn't we be charging him...'

'...With what, Ncube? He hasn't committed a crime in this country. He'll be arrested as soon as he sets foot back in England.'

'How do you know that? Your ancestors have spoken?'

'No spooky spirit voices, Ncube. Just a voice on the end of a telephone. He'll get what's coming to him.'

'So why did Laurent or Jaafar have that piece of newspaper?'

'The reason Jaafar Bastany kept the folded sheet of newspaper was nothing to do with the classifieds. Leave it at that.'

'What next, sir?'

'I'm heading to Hippo Hills to talk to the young man with the damaged lip. You wait here, in town. PC Khumalo is arriving this evening. See what she has to say. Make sure the statue stays safe and hidden.'

'You should stay safe and hidden, sir, you are swimming in dangerous waters. The Party Conference is at Hippo Hills. Remember not to bait the crocodile until you have crossed the river.'

'A wily crocodile stays submerged, waiting until prey comes to drink, then it lunges. Don't worry about me, Ncube, it takes a croc to know a croc,' Sibanda replied, as he walked towards the taxi rank. He halted after a few steps and turned back. 'One other thing, Ncube, phone Miss Barton. Check if there's any news on the children or my brother and his wife.'

'I'll do that, sir. And you stay deep down in those murky waters,' muttered Ncube, as he set off for Smilo's house.

Sibanda asked the taxi to drop him off at another hotel about a kilometre from Hippo Hills. The large conference centre would be crawling with police and

CIO for the Party meeting. He couldn't pull up at the front entrance.

Separating the hotels was thick bush. Sibanda negotiated it with caution. He smelled the brittle, alien scent long before he caught sight of the troops, a camouflaged nest of them, huddled down in the grass, bristling with weapons. One of them was on a smoke break. The smell of exhaled nicotine stood out. Sibanda thanked the gods of addiction. The army was here defending their generals and the Party faithful. He should have expected that. Outposts were staggered around the hotel. Sibanda snaked through the bush on his belly, his nerves stretched. When he put up a covey of Swainson's spurfowl, he flinched. He had almost revealed his position. The birds screamed kwahli, kwahli, kwahli as they ran, low profile, through the grass, squawking an alarm call frighteningly human in its pitch. The high-volume shrieking warned a family of bush pigs. The nocturnal bush pigs in turn, thundered through the undergrowth, causing a nervy trooper at the next outpost to yell 'Lions, watch out, they've caught one of us.'

Sibanda made great headway as a result of the stampeding chaos. Pigs and men alike scattered and stampeded. Soldiers trampled each other. Blood ran. The bush pigs escaped and Sibanda was able to pinpoint and avoid every sniper's nest. Minutes later, leaving the mayhem in his wake, he reached the edge of the golf course. A cool manicured swathe of fairways greeted him, along with munching warthogs who were as attracted to the greenery as the golfers. A troop of baboons on the fairway groomed one another. Sibanda reached the eighth green. From thick bush he watched a foursome tee off for the ninth and shadowed them as they progressed down the course. The sun was still high, hot and humid and these golfers were no athletes. Sibanda was banking on them taking a break at the bar on the ninth hole.

As the foursome gulped their drinks, the detective made off with a set of clubs abandoned for a beer. No one noticed. He raced through the bush with his booty. Sibanda played the eighteenth with the ease of a professional and sauntered back to the clubhouse as though he owned it. He purchased a peak cap and golf shirt with the Hippo Hills logo, pulled them on, the cap low over his face. He walked, clubs on his shoulder, towards the hotel. The twitching operatives in reception never gave him a second glance. He headed for the bar. Barmen, in his experience, were rogues, owned heads of cattle that belied their earnings and knew everything about everyone. He ordered an expensive cocktail to get attention, a *pink crocodile*. The sugar-edged glass delivered a disgusting taste, all roses, syrup, vodka and maybe a hint of vermouth. He slapped his lips after the first sip to cover the desire to spit the vile mouthwash into a nearby pot plant, but the noise passed for approval.

'One of our popular drinks,' the barman commented.

'I can imagine,' Sibanda replied with as much enthusiasm as he could muster.

'Good game?' The barman stopped his glass polishing and gestured towards the clubs.

'Average.'

'You with this lot?' He indicated a group of suited MPs gathered in a huddle, a side bar to the main party-political event. 'What do you suppose they're scheming?'

'I'm the driver for Minister Muchacha. He's given me the afternoon off.'

'He must pay well.' The barman nodded towards the pink glass.

'There's overtime, other incentives...' Sibanda winked and tapped his nose, 'almost as good as a barman's perks.' The barman laughed so heartily his dimples nearly bored a hole through his cheeks. The huddled group of politicians halted mid conspiracy.

'Another?' The barman continued to chortle. The pink glass was empty.

'No, thanks. I need to locate the boy with the hare lip. Have you seen him around? Minister Muchacha asked me to look out for him.'

'Maybe in the car park towards the helicopter launch pad. Most of the off-duty support staff congregate there.'

Sibanda collected the golf clubs and headed through reception. He had no choice but to walk openly through the car park and hope his disguise held. There were more operatives around the fleet of ministerial Mercedes' than a spy convention. Sibanda strode past the onlookers, head averted, a golfer in search of his car. Several sets of eyes followed him. He almost made it past the rows of black gleaming bodywork and polished chrome when a voice called out, 'Hey, you.'

Sibanda kept walking, hoping the interest would pass. But this operative was bored, new to the job and wanted to make a statement.

'I said, you,' the man repeated in an authoritative voice, 'what's in that bag?'

The detective halted, trying to hide his tension. He was primed to sprint and had already worked out his escape route. Enough trees dotted the fringes of the road for him to dodge a fusillade until he could get to thicker bush. With every muscle on edge, he exhaled and turned to face his interrogator. He hoped the Pink Crocodile reeked on his breath. 'Golf kit,' he slurred.

'Empty it.'

'Here? Now?'

'Right now.' The suited man walked closer and peered in Sibanda's face. 'Don't I know you?'

'From the golf course? Sibanda grinned like an idiot. He had to think on his feet, needed a diversion. If any of the other CIO contingent came over, one might recognise him. He took out the clubs and fumbled. They clattered to the ground. A few balls rolled out. He chased them, falling on his knees, scrambling under a large four-wheel drive to retrieve them. Out of sight, he pushed them further, missing them at each stretch. The man was irritated and wanted rid of this buffoon making a show of him. A few nearby colleagues were beginning to laugh at the antics. When the atmosphere changed and a stiff silence descended, Sibanda glanced over his shoulder.

Cuthbert Muchacha was leaving the hotel, heading for one of the cars. If he came close, the Minister would pick him out straight away. Of all the faces in the world, Sibanda's would be burned in his brain. Sibanda pulled the cap lower over his face and rummaged in the bag. Cuthbert Muchacha passed within metres, barking orders to call his driver. Sibanda kept his back turned, fished out an outsize pair of Y fronts which anyone with any sort of an eye could have figured didn't belong to him, and a packet of condoms. The CIO man snarled, eager to make way for the minister and avoid further embarrassment. 'Get on your way before I arrest you for drunkenness. You'll sober up inside a jail cell.'

Sibanda repacked the golf bag with remarkable speed and loped off towards the helicopter pad. He stumbled a couple of times for good measure until he reached the helicopters. The politicians' men were sitting around, some smoking, some sipping from cool drink cans. Godwishes was alone, his back propped against a large baobab tree. Sibanda sat down next to him.

'Mind if I share your shade?'

Godwishes shifted to accommodate the new arrival.

'Hot day.' Sibanda let the golf bag slide to the ground.

Godwishes didn't reply.

'Lost my car in this maze. It must be here somewhere, but I can't remember where I put it. Hey, didn't I see you in a fight at the curio market?'

Godwishes faced Sibanda. 'He got what he deserved.'

'I saw that. You can handle yourself.'

Unused to praise of any sort, Godwishes grinned, 'Thanks.'

'You don't look like the curio buying sort.'

'I'm not. My boss asked me to talk to that man.

'Your boss collects sculptures, does he? Got a lot around his house?'

'No, he wanted me to check if anyone delivered his parcel and if there were any more sculptures coming.'

'Coming from where?'

Godwishes shook his head in bemusement, 'The vendor got angry. He said he wasn't getting paid enough. People were starting to ask questions. The trade was becoming dangerous, and he wanted to know where his money was. And then he started pushing me around. You saw what happened then. '

'Quite a fight. What did your boss say when you told him?'

'He was fuming. I wouldn't like to be that vendor or the person asking questions. My uncle has the temper of a man eater.'

'I know too well,' Sibanda muttered under his breath. He stood, 'Time to look for my car again.' Either Godwishes was playing dumb, or he was naïve. Sibanda chose the latter. But the conversation confirmed his suspicions. Mama Ecstasy was a player in more ways than one, a prime suspect in fact and Cuthbert Muchacha was up to his eyes in murder and diamonds.

Chapter 25

Extract from John Jacob's Journal:

The wagons were large, well-constructed and took a span of eight mature oxen. The sturdy carts trekked here from South Africa and had already proven themselves up to the task of the wilderness journey that would be asked of them again. The wheels were four feet in diameter, shod with metal rims half an inch thick, the hoops seared and beaten onto the wood by master blacksmiths. Most wagons were 15 feet long, constructed of good South African hardwood. Each joint showed the artisans' skill and understanding of the battle to be waged against rocks and gullies, flooded rivers and fallen trees. It was a fine spectacle as the wagon train assembled, albeit hastily, with sail cloth coverings stretched. The great wooden hubs glistened with the rendered fat of sheep tails, riempies and harnesses, repaired and greased, rotting disselbooms chopped and replaced. Yokes assembled and the iron loops to guide the reins hammered and checked. The King and his entourage were travelling. Lo Bengula was taking his treasure where no Englishman would ever find it.

I and some of the senior indunas were put in charge of the loading. First the ivory was carted from the storehouse by an army of men who toiled under the weight of the massive tusks. The cavity of each tusk was packed with dry grass to protect the thin shell of the nerve cavity. One poor soul who dropped his precious cargo had his own teeth knocked out one by one. He would suck his food like a baby for the rest of his life. The packing of the ivory took hours, but the transporting of the safes from the treasury was a more delicate and nerve-wracking mission for all involved, stuffed as they were with gold and four-gallon tins of diamonds.

Mid-task, I was once again summoned to the King's kraal. 'Jacobi, we need to move. How is the loading progressing?'

'Very well, oh, great one. We only have the safes left to move.'

'I have been thinking, Jacobi, these are difficult times. We may yet need gold to buy off our enemies. See that 1200 gold sovereigns are left behind and 12 large diamonds of the finest quality.'

This was to prove a disastrous move. The King had become wise in the ways of the English. He knew they were a rapacious nation, but he could not have foreseen the destiny of this money. None of us could. That gold, stolen by the messengers, was to lead to the death of the King, the massacre of a troop of brave, if misguided men under the leadership of Alan Wilson, and the end of a great nation.

Caroline threw down the journal. She was wasting her time reading about some distant history lesson every Zimbabwean school child knew by heart. The English, the land of her birth, were not squeaky clean at all. Her ancestor thought them colonial bully boys. The read was becoming more and more unpalatable.

Rupert had left for the border – which one, she didn't know – but she was now alone. He had handed her the ticket home and she had her credit card although Rupert was unsure it would even work. He shared with her the few dollars remaining, counted them out into two piles as if to underline his fairness. He left, saying very little. No big goodbyes, no emotional hugs, no regrets. Caroline reflected on her failed marriage. The sensible option was to get back to Bulawayo and rebook her ticket home.

Chapter 26

'Why did they ransack your office for this old thing, sir?' Constable Khumalo passed over the statue of Mama Ecstasy. She, Sergeant Ncube and Detective Sibanda met in the car park of a large supermarket. They sat on a crumbling wall, eating pies the detective had bought them for breakfast. The trio blended with the wash of diverse humanity traversing the busy parking lot. Even Sergeant Ncube's bulk seemed to have diminished despite the fact he had already eaten one breakfast – Smilo's *indumba* bean porridge, made from those glorious, spotted, colourful beans. The preparation was an art, of course. First the smooth multi-coloured protein parcels were dry-fried and crushed to powder, mixed with stamped peanuts and a touch of salt, all boiled into a delicious porridge, accompanied by fried bananas. Ncube had no words to extol the delicacy, so he belched his appreciation. This seemed to prompt a reply from the pensive detective examining the sculpture.

'Look at this large nibble on her base. I'd stake my reputation, tattered though it is, if forensics ever examine this statue, they'll find traces of Madani Haddad's blood and tissue in these chips.'

'But how...?' Sergeant Ncube was shaking his head in disbelief.

'...Did she get in and out of the locked room? I'll explain later, right now we need to get to the overlanders before they complain about their missing passports and head to the Police.'

'Won't it be dangerous to meet up with them? They'll turn you in, sir?' PC Khumalo's eyes held concern. Sergeant Ncube wished the look was meant for him.

'I'm gambling they've been out of circulation, over in the middle of the country. They won't know I'm on the run.'

'The detective's right, MaKhumalo.' He turned to Sibanda. 'You'll have to look like a detective, sir. Shorts and a vest are a little...'

'.... Informal? I'll change.'

'And me? Should I stay undercover?' Despite the danger, PC Khumalo was enjoying the adventure.

'Zee, I need you back in Gubu. Go home and make a miraculous recovery. You can be my eyes and ears in the station. Keep me posted if you hear anything about my family.'

'Sorry, sir,' Ncube apologised. He'd been unable to contact Berry. 'But Miss Barton is a good friend and if you give a friend a goat, you have to let go of the leash. She and the children will be fine.'

'Keep your home-grown advice to yourself, Ncube, I'm in no mood for platitudes. But I'll make those bastards pay a terrifying price if they've laid a single finger on my brother or his wife and kids.'

Ncube had heard his boss angry before, had witnessed his seething frustration and himself been the butt of Sibanda sarcasm, but he'd never heard words delivered with such steel, never seen sparks flashing from eyes that could have killed with a glance and never before watched as his muscles stiffened and his fists curled. The moment was fleeting, but Ncube was relieved he wasn't on the wrong side of the detective. The man was a lion, a Sibanda by totem, the king of beasts by birth. No one could take him on in a mood like this.

'Come, we must head to the camping ground. I'll meet you there, Ncube. Travel safe, Zee.'

Passing a cheap clothing store, Sibanda purchased a shirt and a pair of chinos. His vest and shorts kept Mama Ecstasy company in his backpack. He reached the camp before Ncube. As he did, the Rugged Rascals truck pulled in. He observed the occupants for a while, watched as they set up tents. The dynamics of the group had changed. James Templeton and Becky Grasston, paired up, were setting up their tents very close to one another, laughing, with a camaraderie that spoke of more than friendship. Geneva and Alair Van Dalen kept themselves at a distance, working methodically, knowing where the other one was as they passed poles and pegs and cooperated in the construction of their tent. Marlie was the odd one out. Alone she battled to erect her bubble. She threw in her bed roll and zipped up the door. Barney Jones stuck his head under the bonnet of the Rugged Rascals vehicle.

Where was Ncube? He couldn't wait for him much longer. Barney slammed down the bonnet and headed for the cab. He revved the engine. A plume of black smoke exited the exhaust pipe in a murky fug to put Miss Daisy's irritable emissions to shame. Barney kicked the tyre and spat on the ground. Now, Sibanda decided, was the time to confront his rival, sweating and challenged.

'You got here, I see.' Sibanda approached the overland driver.

'Limped in, but you've arrived in the nick of time.'

'Why?'

'Whatever made me think overland safaris were a good idea? This lot have driven me mad, particularly her.' He gesticulated to the lopsided, sagging tent of Marlie Scalzo. 'She wants to leave, has wanted to leave almost since Thunduluka and your visit. I trust you've brought the passports.'

'I have, but the investigation is not over. There is still the matter of the unsolved murder of Laurent Kasongo. How many nights are you here for?'

'Two. This is supposed to be the farewell party, you know, a couple of nights out on the town... Party time! Whoopi.

'What went wrong?'

'First the vehicle played up, over heated. And then everyone paired off except Marlie, and her eyes were on me.

'A fine-looking woman.'

'Maybe, but I'm a lover of blonds myself and I'm taken. You detective?'

Sibanda ignored the question, aware he was now becoming the irritable one. He could feel Barney Jones getting under his skin again. Was jealousy eating him? 'I'll start my enquiry with Marlie first,' he snapped. Barney roused her from her tent.

'Oh my, the handsome detective. What a nice surprise. Got a pair of handcuffs for me?' Marlie proffered her wrists and flicked her tongue to moisten her lips. 'This has been a long, long lonely trip.

'No handcuffs, but plenty of questions. The afternoon and evening of the 23rd, the night Laurent Kasongo was murdered, you were with him in the village. Do you know his real name was Jaafar Bastany?' Sibanda wished his sergeant was here. Where was he? He might have picked up on the body language, a fine reader of tell-tale tics.

'Never heard that name, but nothing surprises me about the man. He was cold and distant and a few pickles short of a barrel. We were all together in Gubu village. Barney told us we should sample the simple African life and dropped us off around 3pm. He looked like he wanted to get rid of us all for a while if you ask me.'

'Did the group split?'

'Sure. Those Belgian girls are 'bout as exciting as a mashed potato sandwich and naïve, like they fell off a turnip truck. They found themselves a bench and sat and whiled away the evening. Laurent told us he was going his own way and leaving the trip. Becky and James, well, they were already close and gittin' thicker than fleas on a farm dog. I didn't want to play gooseberry. They planned on heading to a diner for a peri peri chicken liver burger, a local speciality – can't forget that. It sounded like shit on toast. Barney was off somewhere in the truck visiting with a friend, so I headed to the Blu Gnu.'

'The cocktail bar?'

'Yep. It seemed cute, but let me tell you that ain't a good name for it. That bar hadn't seen a genuine cocktail since my granpappy gave up his guitar for a harp. They drink some kinda opaque beer. More like warm vomit with bits in it.'

'And Laurent Kasongo, when did you last see him?'

'Late afternoon, I guess. He said he knew someone in the village and was going to visit. He crossed over the railway line.'

'Did anyone follow him?'

'Couldn't say. I turned and headed for the high life, the Blue Gnu.'

'Can anyone give you an alibi for the time you entered the bar until the time you left?'

'Detective, that bar hasn't seen a white girl in it, *ever.* Ask anyone, they'll all remember Marlie. I drank most of the old men under the table.'

'What do you know about diamonds?'

'Everything, that's my job.'

'How did you fund this trip?'

'I worked and saved hard.'

'Not a lot of money in being a park ranger is there?'

'How do you know I was a park ranger?'

Sibanda raised his eyebrows. 'Manage to find a few diamonds, maybe not declare them to your bosses? Or did you tell someone their find was rubbish and pocket the stone for yourself? You lost your job didn't you.'

'Yes, but I never stole no diamonds. Diamond finds are as rare as hen's teeth anyway. In all my time there I assessed one and it was a chip.'

'So why were you dismissed?'

Marlie stared at the detective with large brown eyes, debating how much of the truth to tell. 'You might not like handcuffs on the bedhead detective, more's the pity.' She sighed, 'You and I coulda reached great heights... but my boss sure liked to be hog tied and ridden like a rodeo bull. His wife found out and...'

'... Fine, Marlie, spare me the details.'

'Anyway, my boss funded this holiday as long as I kept my mouth shut. Guess I've let him down.'

'His secret's safe with me.' Sibanda's irony was to the fore. 'And your companions on this trip, any of them discuss diamonds or The Congo or were hostile to Laurent Kasongo?'

'Nope, they're just kids. Innocent, immature kids, Detective, all bacon and no sizzle.' She sneered in the direction of James Templeton and then Barney Jones

'What time did Barney collect you that night?'

'He was late. We were supposed to meet at 9 pm. All of us were there, except Laurent. Barney pitched up about 10pm, apologised, said he couldn't get away sooner, his friend needed him.' Marlie underlined *needed*. Sibanda wrestled with his jealousy. The thought of Barney and Berry together hurt his heart. He could almost feel his fingers squeezing Barney Jones' throat, throttling the life out of the handsome guide.

If Barney was absent from the group when Jaafar Bastany was murdered, he had the time and the space to commit the crime. Sibanda left the southern girl, convinced her alibi would check out, and headed towards Barney Jones who'd returned to tinkering under the bonnet. The guide was wiping his hands with a greasy rag. It made him wonder again where Sergeant Ncube was. Probably had his face planted in another pie. Damn him.

'This old girl is a goner. One bloody trip and she's cracked the cylinder head.' Barney slammed the bonnet down and leaned against the bumper. 'Guess I'll have to look for a new career. I hear importing goods from China is the way to go.'

'Have you made enough to finance a new business?'

'I've got a cushion. I'm thinking women's high-end shoes.'

'With diamond encrusted heels?'

'What do you know about women's shoes detective?' Barney wore a guarded look on his face.

'Nothing, but I do know about diamonds.'

'Diamonds?'

'You wanted them didn't you, Barney? Understood this overland business was a non- starter, needed funds to capitalise a new venture.'

'What are you saying? Spit it out, Detective.'

'Let's take another tack. You found out Laurent Kasongo, also known as Jaafar Bastany was carrying diamonds, so you dropped everyone off in Gubu, tracked him down and shot him. But you didn't find the diamonds, did you? Must have been frustrating.'

'Rubbish. This isn't the first time you've accused me of murder. What is it with you? What have you got against me?'

'Do you have an alibi for between the time you left the group in Gubu until the time you picked them up at 10 pm?'

'I do. I was with Berry Barton. I went to Kestrel Valle school, she's a teacher there. Ask her.'

Despite himself, and his desire to punch the smug, self-satisfied look right off the man's face, he asked, 'Berry Barton will give you an alibi?'

'She will.'

'Have you heard from her?'

'A text to say she's busy babysitting. Some stray kids got dumped in her lap.'

Sibanda, for once, was at a loss for words. He was relieved the children were safe. A cough interrupted his unease. 'Someone's looking for you, detective.' Barney indicated over the detective's shoulder and Sibanda turned. PC Khumalo was a few metres away. The detective could read stress all over her face. She was shaking. Why wasn't she on the bus back to Gubu?

He walked towards her, 'What is it, Zee?'

'It's Sergeant Ncube, sir,' she whispered, 'he's been arrested.'

Sibanda strode away from the campground, PC Khumalo jogging to keep up and Barney Jones following in their wake. 'Our passports?' he queried.

'I'll be back before you leave,' he swatted the guide away with a dismissive wave.

'What happened, Zee?'

'Sergeant Ncube left the car park before me. We planned it that way. I watched him walking towards the road. Out of nowhere, an unmarked car pitched up, three men leapt out and confronted the sergeant. He should have stayed in disguise.'

'My mistake. Where did they take him?'

'They bundled him into the vehicle. A tight squeeze, I didn't think they'd lever Ncube in, but they managed. In the end, one of the men gave up his place. They opened the windows smartish, then the car took off. I followed the man evicted from the cab. He went straight to the police station. The car was already there, but the occupants had disappeared into the building.'

'So, they've got Ncube in the lock up In Vic Falls police station. What do you know of the lay out?'

'Not a lot. I was up here a few months ago, introduced myself. They gave me a quick tour. If I remember, the lock up is around the back.'

'We'll have to move. They'll take him to Bulawayo, to their own truth-extorting domain for questioning. Tonight, Zee, we have to act tonight.'

'What can I do, sir?'

'Marshall the troops.'

CHAPTER 27

Sibanda spent the rest of the morning in his rafting disguise, casing the police station, his phone glued to his ear or to his thumbs, receiving imaginary calls, tapping out messages to no one. He did make one genuine call to Eddie in the UK, to learn the tentacles of the Zimbabwe CIO had reached the distant island.

'Buggar, Jabs, you're in trouble, I shouldn't even be taking this call. There's an Interpol alert out for you. I can see from the phone code you're still in Zimbabwe. Get out, you're mincemeat, mate.'

'You've got to trust me, Eddie.'

'What have you been up to, Jabs? They're talking a double murder and diamond theft.'

'Not me, I swear innocence by the mole on the inside of Casta's left thigh. I've been set up.'

Eddie was silent for a moment. 'So, you've been there too?'

Sibanda laughed, 'No, Eddie, you told me about that mole. You said it was sexy, remember?'

'Oh, okay.' Sibanda heard the relief in his friend's voice. 'You got me there, you bastard. Not like you to make a joke.'

'Sometimes you have to laugh, Eddie. It's all there is.'

'What do you need and make it quick? I'm due in the briefing room.'

'Firstly, a trade. I'll give you something, but I want something from you in return.'

'Your info first.'

'You can tell your mates at immigration Rupert Templeton is on his way home. Secondly, there's a much more dangerous character you need to watch. Bilal Haddad. He's one of Templeton's associates, up to his dodgy eyeballs in money deals and diamond smuggling, Lebanese mafia.'

'Right, thanks for the tip. What do you need, Jabs, what's the trade?'

'Anything else you've found on those names I gave you? I'm closing in on the murderers and the diamonds, but I need a break.'

'Nothing. Jabs, I have to go, I'm getting the beady eye.'

'One last favour, Eddie. Another name on the list, the murder victim – Jaafar Bastany, Lebanese national. Send me everything you've got on him too.'

'So not much then?' he laughed.

'Thanks, Eddie, I owe you one.'

'You owe me more than one, Jabs. I'll be in the shit myself if anyone monitors this call.'

The Victoria Falls police building stood on the main road into the town, a large blue and white edifice with all road-facing windows screened by a brick trellis, a legacy of the bush war when the missiles from Zambian based cadres lobbed across the border from time to time, the police station a prime target. The building dominated the street, a far cry from the modest Gubu station. Sibanda concentrated on the back of the compound. Sergeant Ncube hadn't cracked yet, given him up. The town would have been swarming with police, CID and CIO, checking everyone's IDs, stopping all suspects. How long could the sergeant hold out?

By afternoon, a plan was beginning to form. His stakeout had provided useful information. He'd watched as two officers armed with keys and a dustbin lid of day-old, crumbled mealie meal, headed for a building not far from the back fence. The building was fenced within the sturdy perimeter and topped with razor wire. There were bars on each cell. The officers entered the lock up area and threw the dustbin lid down. Much of the dry mealie meal spilled onto the sandy ground. The first jailer unlocked four of the holding cells whilst the second, armed with a rifle, kept guard. Three men exited their cells and leapt on the unappetising food in front of them. The fourth, from the end lock up, a very large and shaky Ncube, had to be pulled from his cell. His head wound, barely healed from the pistol whipping, reopened. His round face was rounder than ever, swollen and bruised from a heavy pasting. He was limping. Ncube stood for a moment unaided, glanced at the scraps of remaining sand encrusted mealie meal and ignored the offering. 'I am not a dog,' he said and returned to his cell.

'Have it your way, Fatso,' the guard with the keys spoke, 'but trust me by tomorrow you'll be scrabbling in the dirt with the rest of them.'

'I don't think so, young man, I am impermeable to your heckles and revulsions. Disabundance is not my enemy nor cornucopia my friend. My lips remain constricted.'

The guards looked at him as though he was mad and pushed him the rest of the way into his cell with a rifle butt to the kidneys. 'Shut up, Mafuta, you'll be screaming for your mother in plain language by nightfall.' Sibanda's fists were clenched, his jaw grinding. He wanted to rescue his sergeant now, but that would blow their best opportunity tonight. Normally, he would ridicule Ncube for his ludicrous tirade, but in that moment, hearing those mangled words, he never felt prouder of anyone.

PC Khumalo pondered the detective's words. 'Marshall the troops,' the detective had said. But which troops? Sibanda had told her about Sergeant Ncube's extended circle in the Falls: 'Smilo and Prince. There can't be too many couples with those names. Track them down. There's a connection to the fire station. I'll need their help and the keys to Miss Daisy.'

'Miss Daisy? What use can that old wreck be?' she asked

'She's our getaway vehicle.'

'Then Heaven help us all. *Ithemba kalibulali.*'

'You're right, Zee. Hope doesn't kill and *kaligejwa igodi umuntu engakafi.*' That saying highlighted the danger of the situation. The detective's reminder not to dig the grave before the person died, shook her with its mention of funerals. Ncube could become one of the 'disappeared' like the detective's brother. She hurried back towards Chinotimba, the dusty high-density township that serviced the high-living glamour of Victoria Falls. Smilo and Prince would be resident there. Her task was to find them. After an hour of enquiries and a couple of false leads, she was directed to the right house. She knew she had found the sister's house the moment she set eyes on Smilo. Here was Ncube's double with a skirt on.

'Oh Mama,' she said, 'I have bad news. Your brother has been arrested. I am here to get help. Detective Sibanda has a plan. He is breaking him out of the lock up tonight.'

Smilo didn't fall in a heap or wail and gnash her teeth as might be expected. Instead, she stood, her full height and weight dominating the room, 'Arrested my brother, have they?' There was menace in her voice, 'They'll live to regret that. No one messes with my family. I swallowed the stone of courage at birth, all who know me, know that. The CIO better watch themselves.' She leaned into the corner and picked up a large, lethal looking knobkerrie, slapping the well-worn weapon into the palm of her hand as though she was smashing the skulls of her enemies.

'No, no, Mama.' PC Khumalo was alarmed and a little intimidated. 'Detective Sibanda has it worked out. He needs us pulling together, your husband, Prince, and his brother-in-law from the fire station.'

'Ha! That will all be talk. We must act now.'

'No, you must trust the detective.'

'Is this the same detective my brother always speaks of?'

'Yes, Detective Jabulani Sibanda. He works with Ncube. Together, they have solved many crimes, he… he has powers.'

'Powers? What powers are these? I know power.' She slapped the knobkerrie into her hand.

'This is different. He knows things he cannot know, he sees things no one else can. The ancestors speak to him. He has fire in his blood to both warm the hands of the innocent and burn the bones of the evil and he's far too handsome for his own good. If anyone can get Sergeant Ncube out of jail, it's him.'

'Humph, sounds too good to be true, like the dew has blessed him.'

'Wait until you meet him, you will see. He's soaked in the stuff.'

The meeting was arranged for late afternoon behind the fire station, in thick bush, away from prying eyes. Six of them gathered, Sibanda and Zee Khumalo, Smilo and Prince, Fire officer Johnson Nkala and his son, Khuba. Smilo was very quick to give PC Khumalo an appreciative nod in the direction of the detective.

'Are you sure about this?' Sibanda looked at all of them. He gave them a detailed run down of his plan.

'We can't wait. Those police *amasela* stole the Zambezi Cup from us. Robbers! Khuba slammed that goal into the back of the net, harder than a falcon hitting a dove. The police goalie couldn't get near the ball. He'd met his match.' Johnson Nkala was bitter.

His son continued the tale, 'Their crooked coach appealed to the ref, who turned out to be the son-in-law of the Officer-in-Charge and he called off-side, disallowed the goal, didn't he, Baba?'

'*Ndodana*, this is our chance to get revenge against those thieving cheats.'

'Right. Let's go over the plan one more time.' Sibanda wanted to make sure his strategy was as organised as possible given the urgency and some of the dubious motives of his accomplices. 'I'll set fire to the large rubbish heap at the back of the station.

'Should go up like a blaze from Hell. The rain hasn't reached us yet and I've warned the OIC about the dangers of that pile of leaves, paper, and plastic for months. All those wooden pallets are a fire hazard.' Nkala was a well-trained fire officer.

Sibanda glanced at the gathering clouds overhead. The atmosphere was thick, hot and muggy. The rain had to hold off for another few hours if his plan was to succeed. 'Let's hope so, Nkala. I'll have some petrol to help the blaze on its way. Smilo,' he turned to Ncube's sister, 'at 9 pm you'll call the fire brigade to attend the fire. We need an official log of the call. Before that, I want you to prepare your brother's favourite food, enough for a couple of days. He'll be hungry.

'...But can't I be there? I want to *gongoda* those men until their brains come out of their nostrils.'

Sibanda took a deep breath. This sister who looked so much like her brother was a different personality altogether from the gentle and conciliatory sergeant. 'Smilo,' he placed a reassuring hand on her shoulder, 'we need the police to think this whole escape is an accident, no recriminations against anyone. Just make the call.'

The detective's touch melted her anger. 'I'm not happy. Ncube is my brother. Pain to those who have inflicted pain on mine is the rule I live by.'

'Not this time, mama, leave that to me.' But he sympathised with her sentiment. *If anyone hurt Xolisani and Thandie...* He turned to Smilo's husband, 'Prince, you're with me. I may need help getting Ncube out of the cell and into the Land Rover. He looked a little unsteady on his feet when I saw him. Sibanda glanced towards Smilo, but she kept her peace. The detective had put a spell on her.

'No problems.' Prince replied. Sibanda hoped he could control his wife's emotions.

'Khuba, fill the Land Rover.' He handed him a wad of dollars, 'drive it from the fire station and position it at the back of the police station. Leave it running. As soon as the fire goes up, I want you away from the scene and in your bed. That vehicle is a tricky madam, by the way, so give her the once over before you leave.'

'I know vehicles Detective. You can rely on me.'

'You might, but this *skoroskoro's* a real challenge. She answers to Miss Daisy and is as cantankerous as a swatted hornet.' Sibanda shook his head and allowed himself a wry smile. 'Nkala, you know your role. Come in, all sirens wailing. Manoeuvre the fire engine towards the blaze. Reverse into the last cell on the right, knock down the fence and damage the wall so we can get Ncube out.'

'I'm as happy as a man who goes hunting a rat and catches an elephant. A fire to fight and revenge to inflict. This will be a night to remember,' the fire officer beamed from ear to ear. Sibanda once again wondered if he'd chosen the right companions.

'One more thing, Nkala. I need wire cutters for the perimeter fence.'

'You'll have them. Khuba, they're in my office. Get them now.'

'What about me?' PC Khumalo waited to hear her role in the breakout.

'You can't be anywhere near this, Zee, you know that. You're too close to Ncube. If you're caught committing arson or aiding a prisoner escape, you'll never work in the force again. I want you on the next bus out of here and back at work tomorrow. Besides, there's a couple of alibis needing checking.'

'What's going to happen to Sergeant Ncube once he's released?'

'I'm taking care of that. The less any of you know about those plans the better. Now, go home, all of you, get some rest and let's hope for luck tonight.

'We are with you,' they replied.

Chapter 28

Night fell with a watery moon and a stiff breeze for company. The rain held off, but the sky threatened diluvial mayhem. The gathering wind was a warning. By 8.30pm Sibanda was in place; Prince, wire cutters and *isighubhu* of petrol at his side.

A fidgety Prince checked his watch again, 'What time are we moving in?' he whispered.

'Ten minutes.' Enough time to cut the fence, chuck the fuel over the dump, light the fire and watch it flame. Nkala and the fire truck will be here at 9.10. By then the blaze will have taken hold.'

'What about guards?'

'I haven't seen any about the cells, but there are officers sitting outside those houses too hot to go to bed yet.' He pointed to a row of police accommodation within the compound. 'They're the danger. The fire should distract them but keep your eyes open.'

The pair fell silent. Sibanda checked his watch one last time and moved towards the perimeter. Earlier in the day he'd thrown a pebble at the security light covering this patch of fence. He'd hit it first time, smashing the bulb. His skill hadn't deserted, he could still pitch a cricket ball on a five-cent coin. Snipping the cyclone fencing, he made the entrance larger than needed. Sergeant Ncube was no sylph. Sibanda and Prince slithered through the slit, keeping as low a profile as possible.

'Stay back, Prince.' Sibanda doused petrol over the blind side of the dump, throwing the container for good measure. The wind began to gust, lifting leaves from the pile, swirling them into the night. When lightning sheeted across the sky, illuminating the whole area, Sibanda and Prince ducked back behind a bush in the corner. A second strike followed and the sky was lit with a brilliant light show, balls of luminescence bouncing off every cloud. Sibanda checked his watch. Timing was crucial. They dared not venture into the open now. They would stand out like elephants bathed in sunlight.

'Stay here and stay out of sight, Prince. Watch my back.' Sibanda slithered on his belly towards the dump. His first match failed to ignite as did the second, and the wind blew out the third. He cupped the fourth like the face of a precious child. It flickered and caught. He removed a twist of petrol-soaked rag from his pocket. The fire-starter torched. He lobbed the flaming rag onto the pile. A squall of wind encouraged the flames. Within moments, the debris was blazing. The fire was away, flames running into the sky, sparks reaching further, dancing like fireflies against the menacing clouds.

'Bonfire night.'

'What's that, Sibanda?' Prince slithered next to him.

'An English tradition. I hope none of us are going to be the Guy.'

Prince shrugged his shoulders. Ncube had told him the detective rambled at times. Sibanda's mind flicked to a huge bonfire, Berry at his side, the orange light bathing her perfect features, turning her white hair golden as she laughed and ate a toffee apple. Fireworks shot into the sky - rockets, Catherine wheels, Roman candles showering the crowd in a ballet of light and sound. He should have kissed her then, at the very beginning, maybe...

'What next?' Prince broke the spell.

'We wait for Nkala.' They heard the siren in the distance almost as soon as he had finished speaking.

Some of the police officers from the accommodation block were beginning to show interest in the flames. There were shouts and a group of them were approaching with buckets. The fire was getting out of hand already.

'Now, Prince. Run for the corner of the lock up fence.' Sibanda watched as his accomplice left the fire, reached the fencing around the cells. In the mounting confusion, he followed.

'Ncube,' he hissed towards the sergeant's cell. No reply. He whispered again, but this time louder, 'Ncube.'

A groan, 'Who is bothering my sleep? What more do you want? I have nothing to tell you. My lips are glued.'

'Ncube, it's me, Sibanda. We've come to get you out.'

'You, sir, what are you doing? Get away now, you are in danger.' He sounded alarmed. 'They are after you.'

'I'm not going anywhere without you, Ncube, and Miss Daisy is pining.'

'How can I get out of here, sir? Have you got the key to the lock up?'

'Something bigger than that. Go to the far side wall. We are knocking this one down.'

'But...'

'No questions, Ncube, there's no time.'

The fire engine was now in the police compound. The fire was bigger than anyone envisaged. Old tyres and years of waste and plastic rubbish made a perfect smoke screen. Nkala did a fine job of positioning the fire tender. Sibanda glimpsed Nkala's face in the burning glow. His ecstasy was almost manic, eyes shining over a lop-sided smile as wide as the Zambezi River. A good fire to him was better than a night at the bar with a pocketful of pay.

All police eyes were now on the blaze. Embers were flying. Fear of the fire spreading to the accommodation block was real. Nkala fuelled the rumour.

'Go and douse your houses,' Nkala shouted to the watching mob. 'This blaze could get out of hand.' He hoped it would. In another life, Nkala would have been a match-carrying arsonist. The gathered police officers dispersed to take care of their own possessions. Nkala reversed the large fire tender at full throttle. He made short work of the lock up fence, but it took two firm shunts to get Ncube's cell wall to crumble. Having achieved his allotted task, he made for the fire. His crew had the hoses ready. This fire wouldn't take much extinguishing, but the whole excursion was fun and a good exercise for his men.

Sibanda grabbed at some of the loosened blocks from the damaged lock up wall. Ncube moved a few more from his side. Between them they enlarged the hole enough for the sergeant to clamber out. Prince was keeping guard. 'Hurry,' he stressed, 'the fire is dying and some of the cops are coming back.'

'Ncube, let's go.' With his arm around the sergeant for support, Sibanda, Ncube and Prince hurried, using the smoke and shadows for cover, to the opening in the fence. Sibanda had underestimated the sergeant's bulk. Ncube got stuck in the fence like a moth staked with pins in a lepidoptery collection. Even Prince pushing from behind failed to budge him.

'Leave me, sir, get away. You have no idea what they will do to you if they catch you.'

'Ncube, you are coming with us and if we don't get you through this fence then Prince will be stuck on the wrong side.' Sibanda clipped away at a few more diamonds. Prince pushed, his shoulder under his brother-in-law's buttocks. Sibanda pulled. Ncube popped through the fence, shredded like a cheese in a grater.

'Miss Daisy,' was all Ncube could splutter as he looked up to see his favourite vehicle purring.

'I suppose she'll get all the gratitude.' Sibanda's comment went unnoticed, but his plan had worked so far. 'Prince, get on home, I'll take over from here.'

With sergeant Ncube in the passenger seat, Sibanda set off in Miss Daisy, slow at first as though he was a spectator come to view the excitement, but once away from the police station he sped up. The pair made a clean getaway as the clouds burst. The rain put paid to the fire and swept them on their way.

'Where are we going, sir? There's no escape, nowhere to hide.'

'Botswana.'

'I don't have a passport.'

'Neither do I, but when has paperwork ever stopped me?' Ncube put his head in his hands, groaning. 'Are you okay sergeant? Should I stop, look at your head wound?'

'No sir, it's not my head I'm worried about. How are we ever clearing up this mess? We are in more danger than a one-legged chicken in a den of jackals. Will I ever see my family again?'

'Look at me Ncube.' The sergeant took his head from his hands. 'Have I ever let you down?'

'No sir, but...'

'I promise this: if I haven't solved these murders in the next two days, I will turn myself in and clear your name. It's me they're after and the diamonds. When they couldn't get to me through Xolisani and Thandie, they went after you.'

'Are you any closer to solving the murders, sir?' Two days seemed a short time to sort out this tangle knotted like a fishing line in the hands of a child.

'I do know who killed Madani Haddad.'

'Tell me who, sir. And how did they get out of that locked room? I can't work it out.'

'Jaafar Bastany.'

'Laurent Kasongo murdered Madani Haddad?'

'He was the link between the Congolese diamonds and Madani Haddad, the middleman, the diamond broker. Bastany was on the run from a slew of people he'd crossed. He disguised himself as Laurent Kasongo, came into the country on the overland truck so his face and passport wouldn't be scrutinised.'

'His disguise would have fooled anyone.'

'But not you Ncube, you picked up on his eyes.' Ncube sat a little more upright. 'Bastany broke away from the overlanders. Wearing that disguise all day and night became too difficult. The oppressive heat, wrapped up in rubber. He hadn't thought of that, so he planned to move on alone.'

'What motive did he have for murdering his middleman?'

'That I don't know Ncube. Perhaps they argued over payment for the diamonds. We found no money in Haddad's house. Maybe the end buyer hadn't paid Haddad and he in turn couldn't pay Bastany. Whatever the reason, there was a fight.'

'How did Bastany kill Haddad?'

'The disagreement became violent, so Bastany grabbed the sculpture and bludgeoned Haddad to death. Those chips in her base are a giveaway. I should have picked up on those sooner. Mama Ecstasy was the murder weapon. A couple of blows with her would have done for Haddad.'

'But so little blood. Shouldn't there have been more signs around? That house was almost as clean as a pauper's cooking pot.'

'Bastany cleaned up the house and the victim to make the murder look like an accident.'

'Everyone would have believed that explanation if it wasn't for you, sir.'

'The official conclusion is still suicide, Ncube. Bastany was clever. He burned his gloves with all the blood and mess on them and a sponge he'd used for the clean-up then left the room locked, hoping to put us all off the scent. He almost succeeded.'

'So how did he get out of the room and yet leave it locked?'

'The piece of folded newspaper gave him away. Another clue I overlooked. I got sucked in by the content of the newsprint rather than the page itself. After the clean-up, Bastany left the room and locked it from the outside. He must have torn a sheet from a newspaper in the house. He slid the key back under the door using that folded newspaper.'

'But the key fell out of the lock on the inside. PC Khumalo and assistant detective Chanza swore they heard it fall.'

'What they heard, Ncube, was the metal latch plate being wrenched from the jamb and falling when the door was forced open. The key was already on the floor. It was a natural assumption the key was in the lock.'

Ncube shook his head. 'I do not know how you worked this out, sir. Your ancestors must have helped.'

'Not this time,' Sibanda laughed. 'A childhood read, but if Bastany hadn't kept that piece of folded newspaper in his backpack and I hadn't found myself in the bush with a folded bit of tin foil from my backpack, I may never have arrived at that conclusion.'

'So, who murdered Jaafar Bastany?'

'I don't know, but I'm getting closer. Marlie Scalzo and Barney Jones both appear to have watertight alibis. PC Khumalo is checking on those.'

'What about those twins at the curio market? The ones who carved the statue?'

'The Manhombo twins are in the clear. They loathe Muchacha more than I do.'

'And the other suspects?'

'Rupert Templeton, the white man with the pointy nose and translucent ears has been duped, played like a *mbira*. He doesn't have the stomach for murder. I'm not sure about his relative, James. He could be in business with Bilal Haddad. James worked for Templeton's investment firm so who's to say he didn't get sucked into the Mafia's plans. The girls from Belgium seem unlikely murderers and there's no suspicion attached to

Rebecca Grasston but I'm waiting for more information. Thomas Mabiza's been up to something though. He's somehow linked to Cuthbert Muchacha via the lipless henchman. The minister's up to his armpits in diamonds.'

The sergeant's stomach gave an enormous rumble at the mention of Muchacha's name, a clap to rival the thunder gathering overhead. 'Here, Ncube,' Sibanda reached over to the back seat and produced a bundle wrapped in a clean t-towel. Your sister sent food. He reached back again for one of the many cans of Ncube's beloved sticky orange drink he stocked for his gastrically challenged sergeant.

Ncube lost all interest in talk of murders and culprits, opened the can and glugged the contents in one swallow. Investigation of the food led to an appreciative sigh. Smilo made all his favourites. The first delight he dived into was a paste made from the soaked and cooked white kidney-shaped *indumbu* pounded with garlic, herbs, lemon and kapenta, the salted, dried lake sardines he loved so much. To accompany this non-drip travel friendly sauce, he found still warm *isitshwala*. He pinched a portion of the thick porridge and rolled it into a neat ball of white stickiness, ready to accept a swipe of relish. He almost finished the entire dishful before coming up for air.

The rain was lashing hard as they drove towards the Botswana border. The occasional flash from a distant sheet of light gave eerie definition to the heavy clouds and a silver tint to the road ahead. Sibanda would have delighted in the daylight trip, heading west on a road lined with forest and valleys, groves of tall teak trees mixed with miombo woodland. The possibility of elephants and antelope, even lions, would be a bonus.

At night, he had to concentrate hard to avoid a crossing herd or unwary kudu. The skittish antelope were often confused by headlights, drawn to them like moths to a candle flame, leaping towards the light. Even impala were not immune to being dazzled. Miss Daisy was battered enough. He didn't think she would survive another encounter. He leant into the windscreen, scanning the road ahead.

'Nearly there, Ncube.'

'What is your plan, sir?'

'I'm turning off the headlights. We're going in blind from here.'

Chapter 29

Caroline turned over in her camp bed and stretched her back. The old house creaked and groaned as the wind whistled around the eaves and across the ancient tin roof. They could build in the twentieth century. Not one drop of the pouring rain made the interior. The bus trip down to Bulawayo had given her time to reflect on how her next chapter would read. Without Rupert and any known living relatives, she was on her own for the first time in her life. She relished the privacy. Her mother always advised her never to mistake solitude for loneliness. Solitude was a rare gift, she would say, while loneliness was a common affliction. How many women ever experienced this glorious frisson of self-determination? She resolved to make the most of it.

Caroline threw off the sleeping bag and greeted the day with enthusiasm, splashed her face with bottled water she lugged from a nearby supermarket, and lit a fire in the old wood stove. The ancient kitchen boasted a black enamel kettle and a few dubious pots and pans. She would survive. Rupert's divided dollars provided enough to buy the camp bed, sleeping bag and food for a few days. Getting water and electricity connected would be a priority.

Caroline was far from destitute, had money of her own, significant money. James had taken care of that. James was the wiliest and most astute of all the Templetons by a country mile. He could even run rings around her mother-in-law, Bobo. Maybe she would phone him and access some of their ill-gotten gains, get this old house functional again. Might be a fun challenge.

A cup of tea in hand, bread toasted over the flames and slathered with butter and marmalade, Caroline settled down on an old chair dragged from the veranda and opened John Jacob's journal to amuse her while she ate.

Getting Lo Bengula into his transport was the most difficult of all the tasks. He was hoisted and hauled, pushed and shoved into the King's wagon by several tribesmen. An undignified episode for a great king, but by then his knees were useless hinges in the fight against the mound of flesh they needed to lever. Finally, the King settled on his karosses and the wagons began to roll. There were twenty of us in the party: Lo Bengula, myself, four indunas, led by Magwegwe, the King's most trusted ear and advisor, and fourteen Matabele tribesmen skilled in the driving of oxen.

First, we headed north for several days and then, at the King's command, we veered eastwards, avoiding difficult river crossings. All rivers run east to west in the kingdom of the Matabele. And thus, we progressed at stately pace. The King could not be rattled or shaken on rocky or uneven ground, his bones and joints ached so. Many days passed. The King never ventured from his wagon. On the morning of the eighteenth day, Lo Bengula called a halt to our journey. 'Here,' he proclaimed, 'We shall bury my treasure.' Standing on the wagon, he pointed with his intonga (this was intricately carved and acted as his royal sceptre for he hadn't fought with a stick in years) to a steep rise in the ground.

The men leapt from their wagons and outspanned the oxen in fearful haste. The wise could already smell blood in the air. With amahloka, amakhuba, *and even the short, stabbing* imikhonto *they began to break the ground, turning the hard, dry sods of winter, loosening the heavy clay with every muscle straining. Soon they sang in rhythm to the pounding of the earth for we were far from human ears and the sound would never be heard except by the beasts that lived in this wild place. We had not seen a village for days. Then the* amafotsholo *were brought from the wagons and the men began to dig, deeper and deeper until a cavernous trench ran alongside a steep wall. The skin of the men glistened. No one dared call for water or show fatigue. The King was in no mood for weakness.*

The men slept deeply that night, exhausted from their labours, but were up at first light, to deepen the trench until a man standing on the shoulders of another would disappear into its depths and all fourteen men lying head to toe would not stretch the length of the ditch. Lo Bengula again stood upon his wagon and pointed to the steep wall, 'The safes shall be buried in this wall,' he commanded. The men began to dig, carving out two holes large enough to take the safes. Once the safes and their treasure were in place, Lo Bengula commanded that a stone rampart be built to conceal them. The men dragged rocks from a nearby gully and piled them like the dry stones of the sheep pastures in Scotland. The structure was fortress-like, a castle wall in the bush. Next came the tusks. The wagons were offloaded, and the heavy sticks of creamy ivory were laid in the trench on top of one another, a great gathering of precious wealth like a mythical elephant graveyard. When the whole of the treasure, wall and all, was buried again and disguised against prying eyes, we set back for KoBulawayo.

I know now as I write this account that the safes and ivory hoard have glimpsed the last light they may ever see. I am the final one alive to know where the treasure is buried, for the very next night, whilst the tribesmen slept the sleep of the dead, weary from impossible toil, the King had all his men slaughtered with assegais, the very ones used to break the earth. The screams were disturbing to hear, but the deaths were swift. I and the Indunas were spared. Lo Bengula was a gentle man at heart, so he spoke with regret when he said, 'I have no prisons like the white man, Jacobi, so I am obliged to frighten and kill people to keep order and secrets.' As the youngest of the party I, John Jacobs, am now the only one left to tell the tale. Magwegwe, the last of the indunas, perished with the king and since the death of Lo Bengula and the ascendance of the white man and his government, I am banned from the country and vilified, unable to return. But there is more to tell, my story does not end here. Read on my children for these hidden riches may one day be yours...

Caroline's tea had gone cold but she munched her way through the marmalade toast. *Good heavens*, she thought, *it doesn't look like anyone but me has read this journal for years*. His children must have found their way back to Zimbabwe and were embarrassed by their boastful ancestor who seemed to have insinuated himself into the history books. They probably barely looked at the journal, dismissing the writing as the ramblings of a deluded old man. Maybe they were, but then again... She had already noted how, apart from the water damage, the spine of the book was still stiff with binding starch, how the pages were unmarked, had no dust, and the cover, albeit a little faded, remained in remarkable condition. The account was interesting with its talk of diamonds. Could this be her destiny, her signature, her second Diamond Lil moment? What sweet irony.

She picked up her phone and dialled James. 'James, you're still in Zimbabwe aren't you? Are you alone? Can you talk?'

Chapter 30

'I can't see anything, sir, isn't this dangerous? It's as black as a burnt pot out there.'

'Not if we stay on the road.'

'But where is the road? This is like driving with a blindfold on.'

'Look ahead, those lights are at the border post.'

'We'll never get past the booms and gates. They'll spot us straight away.'

'We won't risk the main offices. There's a road to the left, Ncube, running along the border. We're taking that. A couple of kilometres along we'll cross over into Botswana. The road is unpatrolled, but we'll have to be careful. There are villages. No lights from now on.' Sibanda cut the engine. Miss Daisy cruised downhill towards the border.

'Will we make it?' Ncube was whispering now. He did not want to return to a jail cell and starvation rations.

'Momentum should get us a few metres onto the dirt road. After that we'll start up.' He swung Miss Daisy onto the border road. 'So far so good,' he muttered, but Ncube could hear the strain in his voice. A dog barked, setting off a neighbouring response. There was no sign of Immigration or Customs.

'Miss Daisy's behaved so far, sir.'

'Don't say a word, Ncube, you might jinx us. This old rattle trap is your transport home.'

Ncube objected to "rattle trap" but the detective had risked his own freedom to get him released, now was not the time to scold him. Sibanda was a lost cause when it came to Miss Daisy.

Miss Daisy began to slow. Sibanda turned the key and put her in second gear. He took his foot off the clutch and jump started the Land Rover. She purred to life. Ncube smiled with pride, a smile wiped off his face a moment later as the old girl belched with such force that she could have blown a nest of hibernating mambas from their underground burrow.

Ncube glanced at the detective whose face was set in grim lines. There was shouting and a vehicle started up behind them. Sibanda slammed his foot on the accelerator. 'Hang on Ncube,' he hissed, 'here we go again.' He drove like the wind. With no lights, Sibanda was hitting potholes, dips and wash-aways. Miss Daisy's springs groaned. Her shocks were in shock. She careened down the dirt road like a ping pong ball.

'Take care, sir, Miss Daisy isn't built for bouncing.'

'She's a Land Rover, Ncube, this is her job. And if you don't want to end up back in that flea pit, cross your fingers she can muddle through. Hang on.' He looked back. The headlights in the distance were gaining.

Sibanda drove the vehicle into the bush, stopped, leapt out and headed back to the road. He had enough time to drag a fallen log across the path of the oncoming vehicle undetected. In a flash, Sibanda was back in Miss Daisy and driving off road. Ncube marvelled at the detective. The log should have taken three men to move but somehow Sibanda found superhuman speed and strength. Miss Daisy set off again, ploughing through undergrowth. Ncube covered his eyes. His stomach couldn't take the strain of knowing a tree or deep ditch could be in their way.

'We've delayed them for a while and we're technically in Botswana. If we criss-cross between the two countries and avoid the border road, we might give them the slip... Uh oh...'

Ncube eyes shot open. 'What is it?'

'Buffalo. A big herd blocking our path. Could be to our advantage.'

'If you say so, sir.' Ncube gazed at the gathering of horns, each one lethal and sprouting from a heavy stippled bosse on the forehead. No wonder buffalo had such thick necks and massive bodies. Those horns together with the mighty muscles could toss a grown man like a leaf in the wind. Milling on the road, they appeared like a herd of placid cows, but the animals were amongst the most dangerous beasts.

'The buffalo will obliterate our tracks, Ncube. I'll manoeuvre behind the herd and drive them towards the vehicle if it's still following. I haven't seen their lights for a while, that log has held them up.'

'Aren't buffalo very dangerous? Won't they turn on us?'

'They kill more hunters than any other animal. They circle back and ambush their tormentors after they've been wounded, but we're safe in Miss Daisy and this option will buy us time.'

Sibanda drove in a wide circle around the herd and then shepherded them from behind. Soon Miss Daisy herded the whole mob, chased them towards the following vehicle. Sibanda turned off the road, left the buffalo charging and headed deeper into the bush.

After half an hour Sibanda pulled up, 'This'll do Ncube'

'Where are we, sir?'

'In Botswana, about a kilometre from the border road. Behind these bushes no one will find you.'

'Find me? What about you, sir?'

'I'm heading back to Victoria Falls. I should make the border post by daylight. I'll hitch a lift back to the town.'

'The CIO will know you're about after my escape. Vic Falls will be crawling with officers like worms in a child's guts.'

'I have to find the murderer, Ncube. It's the key to getting us both out of this mess.'

'What am I supposed to do?'

'Wait here until the day after tomorrow. There's enough food and drink to keep even you alive. Don't go far from the vehicle and listen for border patrols.'

'But...'

'No buts, Ncube. You're safe here. No one will find you. The morning after tomorrow, head into the rising sun. You'll reach the border road. Go back to Victoria Falls. I'll be waiting, or...'

'Or what, sir?'

'Or head home to Gubu.'

'And you?'

'I can take care of myself. Who knows? I might just get demoted again, this time to Magwegwe township. I hear they have wooden boxes for a police station.' Sibanda laughed, Ncube was alarmed.

'It's midnight, sir. Stay and share this food with me.'

'If I head off now, Ncube, I'll make the main road by daylight. There'll be traffic coming through the border.

I'll hitch a lift. I have to get back to those overlanders and find out what Muchacha is up to. Stay safe, Sergeant.'

The sergeant looked into the detective's eyes and for a moment as slender as the eye lash of an acacia mouse, they held each other's glance. At the centre of those deep black pupils and handsome nut-brown eyes Ncube recognised the mixed emotions of concern and regret.

'Don't worry about me sir, I have food and Miss Daisy for company.' Ncube was terrified of being left alone in the bush, was already shaking inside like a child's jelly at a Christmas party, but the detective had enough worries without him adding to them.

Sibanda nodded and set off towards the dirt road. Moments later he was back. 'I forgot to give you this, sergeant.' He handed Ncube a hundred dollar note.

'What's this for, sir?'

'Use it to get Miss Daisy fixed.' He disappeared again into the night.

The last Ncube saw of him was a silhouette. The clouds parted and a full moon bathed him in a golden light. Ncube stared hard, hoping to catch another glimpse, but the moment was gone and so was Sibanda.

'Watch out for the buffalo, sir,' Ncube called out, but his words were lost on the wind, in the whispering grass and in the answering leaves. He settled down for the night, but not before sampling more of Smilo's cooking.

Sibanda jogged as best he could in the dark, grateful the rain was holding off. He had advised Patson Mwembe never to move at night. He didn't have time to heed his own advice. Within an hour, he reached the place where the buffalo gathered, moving with care, stopping to listen for clicking horns or the occasional grunt, or to catch the acrid whiff of steaming hides and wet droppings. The buffalo herd had moved on into Zimbabwe. Further down the road he noted where the pursuing vehicle had turned back. They lost Miss Daisy's tracks under the churning mix of buffalo hooves. After another hour, the clouds cleared, and the moon came out, making the going easier and less dangerous. He could now see spoor on the road - day old elephant tracks; baboon pads showing a troop heading to a roost; various rodents' claws scampering after beetles, and beetles scampering after procreation - tok tokkie beetles that banged their fluted carapaces on the ground to attract a mate, dung beetles pushing their precious incubating balls of rotting waste along the road, looking for a safe nursery site; each one leaving tiny marks in the wet earth. The bush was a highway of life if you could read the signs.

In this way, the trek passed for Sibanda, kept him awake and alert and took his mind off the problems ahead. When he detected a rattling sound, he stood for a moment, trying to decipher the noise. Not something he heard often, porcupine, the biggest rodent in Africa. The creature with a hyper keen sense of smell had got wind of him and was rattling the hollow quills of his tail producing a drum-like hissing. Porcupines couldn't shoot their quills, that was the stuff of legend, but come too close, touch them and they seemed to have a mechanism for loosening their sharp spears. The tips stuck into flesh to fester like poisoned darts. With every spine and quill upright, the porcupine, haloed in moonlight, presented a formidable opponent. The spiny rat threatened with his rays of black and white bands, each one sharpened to a point. Sibanda gave him or her – impossible to tell the sex – a wide berth. Porcupines were monogamous, mated for life. Unusual in the animal kingdom, unusual in his own kingdom these days. His thoughts strayed to Berry and what might have been. He distracted himself from gloomy impossibility trying to remember more facts about the loyal rodent, the *inungu*, to distract his brain.

Dawn rose over his right shoulder and swept across the tar road ahead as he came up with the last detail: porcupines could weigh up to thirty kilograms.

Chapter 31

The truck driver accepted his dollars and told Sibanda to hop on the back. The detective sat next to a woman with grocery shopping. They nodded in greeting but otherwise remained silent. Sibanda wanted to sleep. He braced his back against the cab, head on his chest, backpack under his knees. He opened one eye. 'Please, wake me fifteen minutes out of Vic Falls, mama.' The old lady smiled. He sagged into a deep sleep.

When Sibanda woke he was covered in a blanket, his head resting on the old woman's shoulder. 'Where are we?'

'Not far now. You slept through the roadblock.' She gave him an intense look, the one his mother gave him as a child when examining his features for dirt. 'You must be exhausted.'

'Pretty tired, mama. No sleep last night.'

She continued to stare. Her voice dropped. 'They were looking for you.'

'At the roadblock?'

'Yes, and an old *skoroskoro* Land Rover. They were showing pictures. It is you?'

'Yes.' There was no point in lying, 'But how did they not see me?'

'I said you were my son, that you were serious, sick with flu and covered in a rash. I put the blanket over you. They stayed well clear.'

'Why did you do that for me, mama?'

'The ears and eyes reach the heart, not the voice of others. Your face speaks of innocence. You remind me of my late son, Peace.'

'What happened to him?'

'He was murdered by the army in Marange.'

'The diamond fields?'

'Peace wanted to make his fortune. I begged him not to, but he said there are no jobs. "I cannot stay at your hearth forever, Mama, I have to provide for my children," he said. He may have been mining illegally but didn't deserve to be killed.'

'Marange is more a battlefield than a diamond field. Everyone is scrambling for those stones and there's blood on them.'

The old lady nodded, 'Peace went to live in a deserted hut and excavated the floor. Many locals were doing that.'

'I hear some people dug out huge underground warrens. Word got out when the big shiny new 4 x 4's were parked outside those modest huts.'

'I don't know if Peace found anything, but they killed him anyway. They burst into the hut and shot him in the ground as he worked.'

'I'm sorry, Mama.'

'It's okay, *mtanami*, he has left me grandchildren. They are my joy now. What have you done that the police are looking for you?'

'Nothing, I promise on your son's precious memory. But I am caught up in a diamond plot. Maybe the same diamonds your son died for. I must go now, mama, but thank you for your kindness. He thrust fifty dollars into her hand. This is for your grandchildren.' Sibanda banged on the cab roof, the sign to stop. The driver pulled over and he hopped off. The last he saw of the old lady was on the back of the truck, waving to him, her skin furrowed with the lines of unimaginable grief, tears in her eyes. Sibanda reflected, and not for the first time, that Africa was a harsh place to live. Life was cheap, a flimsy child's paper boat on a fierce flood of autocracy and greed. Some of those boats absorbed the waters of despotism and sank. Some tipped on a wave of tyranny and disappeared. Some beached in the wrong place and were trampled by the ungulate whim of the powerful. Even the robust, the well-constructed that sailed on the political winds were not unscathed. They collapsed on the bank, soggy, waterlogged, exhausted by sycophancy. When would it change? Who would be the one to change it?

Sibanda found himself on the outskirts of the town. This was no time to philosophise. He had a murder to solve and his own fragile paper boat to re float, his own rocks, snags and whirlpools waiting to sink him. And there was the first of them, another roadblock. Cuthbert Muchacha and his minions were pulling out all the stops in their search.

He stepped off the main road and into the forest. The morning was cool and clear, leaves were still dripping from their night-time shower. Through each drop, the sun revealed a rainbow prism before evaporating into the humidity of the day. Sibanda skirted the roadblock, moved through the bush until the searchers were far behind. When he reached a small clearing dominated by a single ochna pulchra in full bloom, he rested. The small tree liked to live alone, and in contrast to most of the natural world, had adapted to make germination difficult so offspring couldn't compete. Blossoms hung from this specimen in magnificent bouquets of yellow-hued, orchid-like clusters. The twisting trunk cracked in silver flakes to reveal a pearl bark beneath. The air was scented with the gentle, sweet perfume of the blossoms.

This was as good a place as any to consider his options and as good a burial site as he was likely to find for Mama Ecstasy. A spot easily located again. He took the panga from his backpack and began to dig beneath the tree, Linnaeus, the botanist, named *beautiful wild pear*. The tree turned out to be no relation to the pear at all. The Afrikaners got it more accurately if less poetically right. They called it Lekkerbreek because the branches were so brittle. For Sibanda it would always be the umnyelenyele, the childhood tree that reminded him of home. A fine specimen grew in the centre of his parents' kraal and for a few weeks of the year carpeted the hard-swept earth in yellow confetti. He and Xolisani, gathered up the fallen petals, made garlands for their mother or pounded the flowers to make a perfume for her. Those yellow days were happy, signalling the arrival of the rains. The maize would grow, fruits and berries sprouted in the bush and his father's stress seemed to melt as he recognised they had food security for another year.

With Mama Ecstasy underground. Sibanda took a couple of moments to plan his next move. The yellow flowers reminded him of who he was, where he came from and what he must do next. An option that couldn't be ignored, that he owed to his long dead father, a man who put family before anything else. Sibanda would be taking a huge risk, but the stakes were high.

Heading back to town, his first advantage was that Muchacha and his cronies expected him to be driving Miss Daisy. His second; no one else knew of the Rugged Rascals truck and its connection to Jaafar Bastany and the diamonds. That wouldn't last long when the overlanders started complaining to the local police about their missing passports. The window to unravel this mess was closing fast.

Half an hour later, Sibanda reached the town. In his rafting outfit he blended in. The next move would be in his own time and on his own terms. Passing one of the adrenalin adventure shops, he snaffled a pile of loose flyers and made his way down the street, offering them to passers-by. The area was being watched. He observed a few operatives lounging on street corners, in shop doorways, and in a corner café, thinking they were camouflaged. Their khaki was too new, their attitudes too authoritative and their shoes too pointy. These were men trained in the dark arts of the spy, not safari operations. What safari guide sat in a café pretending to read a newspaper wearing leather soled shoes? Disguise was all in the detail. No one noticed him walking by. He slouched, swaggered and high-fived a few other rafters who thought he was a new boy in town working for one of the opposition rafting companies. The sooner he got off the streets the better. He couldn't push his luck. He made it back to his township base, washed and changed. He was now himself, comfortable in his own skin, Detective Jabulani Sibanda, a man in no mood to be messed with. He hailed a taxi

'Where to?' The driver asked.

'Hippo Hills and pull up at the front entrance.'

'Are you sure? That place is crawling with cops, security is tight. You don't have lanyard or a badge.'

'Get me there.'

Sibanda made it as far as reception before they pounced on him. Three of them at first, then others. Despite him not resisting arrest, they roughed him up with a couple of punches. He was bleeding from the lip and his left eyebrow.

'We've been looking for you, Detective Sibanda.'

'And here I am, *madoda*.' He held his wrists out to be handcuffed whilst trying to wipe away the dripping blood with his upper arm.

'You've led us a merry dance,' said the lead man, as he punched Sibanda in the gut. 'Take that from me. I've had enough sleepless nights and extra duty.'

Sibanda bent double and took a moment to regain his breath. 'I apologise,' he gasped through still winded lungs, 'but I've been here all along, in plain sight. You must have missed me.'

'They said you were a smart one, Sibanda, that you have magic powers,' he laughed. 'Deserted you, have they? Magic yourself out of this.' This time he delivered a blow to the side of Sibanda's head. The detective fell on all fours.

A uniformed police officer joined in and kicked him in the ribs, 'And that's for trying to burn the police station down. Where's that fat sergeant? Run away I bet. Useless piece of *mafuta yengulube*,' he snarled.

'I take it your anger is based on the fact you couldn't break him. Not such a useless piece of pig fat after all,'

Sibanda spat through gathering blood. The police officer kicked him again.

'Take him away,' he sneered, 'there won't be anyone to break him out of the lock up. No incompetent fire brigade this time. We have a special cell for people like you. Cosier you might say. We don't like murderers.'

'I don't think so.' Sibanda stood and spoke with authority, 'I'm not going anywhere. I have an appointment with Minister Muchacha.'

'Ha, He's the last person you'd want to see Sibanda, no love lost there. Go quietly before *he* makes the plans. They won't be as... considerate as ours,' the lead CIO officer with the eager fists spoke.

'You're right, I don't want to see him. But I'm certain he'll want to see me when you tell him I have something he's been looking for.'

'Hand it over, *uSathane*.' The operative cuffed him across the face.

'I don't have the item on me, and neither will anyone unless I see the minister. He'll be angry when he knows. Heads will roll and it won't be mine.'

A conference convened. The man at the centre of the violence walked away to make a phone call. When he returned, he snapped out orders, 'Take him to the minister's suite and don't leave him alone for a second. If this man escapes, then I'll have your *amasende* sliced on toast for breakfast.'

Chapter 32

'Detective Inspector Jabulani Sibanda. We meet again,' a short bespectacled, barrel-like figure, little neck, all torso with the fleshy pink lips of a woman entered the suite.

'Minister Cuthbert Muchacha, I'd like to say it is a pleasure but we both know I would be lying.'

'Too smart for yourself as ever, I see, Sibanda.'

'Much too smart for you, Muchacha.'

The accompanying CIO officer, the one who'd picked Sibanda out in the car park and was still smarting from the humiliation, smacked the detective hard with the butt of his pistol, opening a cut on his cheek, 'Mind your manners in the presence of your superiors.' Sibanda managed to hold his ground. The infuriated officer took another swing. This time Sibanda ducked, the operative lost his balance and staggered across the room, his weapon clattering across the floor. Sibanda had made another life-long enemy. Double humiliation didn't sit well with anyone.

Muchacha put up his hands to indicate an end to the violence. 'I can take it from here, thank you, Charamba. You can leave us now.'

'But, sir, I was told...'

'I can handle this man alone.' The minister brushed away the operative. 'Wait outside the door. Now, I need a drink.' He opened the mini bar and poured a hefty tot of whiskey sweetened with coke. Sibanda ignored the sacrilege. 'Take a seat detective.' The minister settled himself in to an easy chair.

'I prefer to stand.'

'Then let's get down to business. You have something belonging to me and if you don't want to end up drowning in the pit latrine at Chikurubi maximum security prison, I suggest you hand it over. You see, there's a lot worse than demotion to Gubu police station,' the minister laughed with a croak like a mating toad.

'Being appointed Minister of Rural and Cultural Affairs wasn't any promotion either, I seem to remember. Not a cosy cabinet post, not in the inner circle anymore, Muchacha. That must hurt. I wonder who has the most to regret?'

'I'll be back there soon enough, whilst you, my friend, will rot in that Gubu backwater.' Muchacha dribbled whiskey as he spat out the words.

Sibanda smiled. If Gubu was a rotting backwater, then bring on the putrefaction. 'There'll never be the opportunity to milk the system so easily in another ministry, will there Muchacha? Mining is the top prize.'

The minister swirled his muddy drink and took a hefty swig. 'I don't know what you mean.'

'Yes, you do. How much was lithium back then? $5000 a tonne? A dream come true, a machine for printing money until I caught you dealing out leases to companies nominally owned by relatives. I hear the ore price has shot up to $17000 and is about to double.

More lucrative than diamonds.' Muchacha's face crumpled.

Sibanda continued. 'When I prised the lithium from your grasp, you got a serious rap over the knuckles. Minister of Rural and Cultural Affairs is not a powerhouse. Think of this, Muchacha, if those leases weren't cancelled, you'd be rolling in cash by now.'

'You filthy piece of floating shit.' Muchacha stood and threw the rest of his drink in the detective's face. Sibanda winced as the alcohol ran into his cuts. 'If you hadn't interfered, if you hadn't rocked the boat life would be good. Why didn't you let it go like I asked? There was money in it for you. Did you really think your antics would stop me?'

'Not for a minute. Politicians like you are in it for power, the corrupt opportunities. That isn't likely to change, whatever the ministry. It's just the scale of the fraudulence that varies. So now you're dealing diamonds, using your old mining connections to wash the blood off them and legitimise their origins.'

'And if you get in my way again, you and your whole family will go down this time.'

Sibanda took a step towards the minister, his anger rising, 'You touch my brother or sister- in-law, I will...' the menace in Sibanda's voice was chilling.

Muchacha recoiled, 'Don't threaten me, Sibanda. One word and the man outside that door wouldn't need much encouragement to come in and shoot you where you stand. He'd claim you were threatening my life. I'll back his story.'

'If he can keep his weapon in his hands,' Sibanda scorned. 'And then you'd never see those diamonds.'

Muchacha stared through the window. The man had him. With the current smell of political uncertainty in the wind, he needed those diamonds now before he lost his connections, before power shifted from one faction to the other. He turned, took a calming breath, 'What are you suggesting, detective? We appear to have a stand-off.'

'A swap. The diamonds for the safe release of my family and the dropping of your hounds from my heels.'

Muchacha walked to the mini bar and poured another drink, appearing to consider the trade, 'You know where the diamonds are?'

'First, how do I know that Xolisani and Thandie are safe? I need proof of life before you get your hands on those stones.'

'And I need to make sure you have the diamonds.'

'They're yours as soon as I see my brother and his wife alive and well. I take it you've imprisoned them in Bulawayo?'

Muchacha nodded, 'You've asked for two things Sibanda: your freedom and that of your family.'

'And I'll give you two things in return. The diamonds and your courier's murderer.'

Muchacha nodded again. 'Fair enough. Bastany was a good man, reliable, true to his word, and he delivered high quality diamonds. I take it whoever murdered him stole the diamonds he was carrying?'

Sibanda shrugged his shoulders and noted his bruised ribs. 'Your reliable courier was no saint, Muchacha, he murdered Madani Haddad. The man didn't commit suicide. Bastany covered his tracks. Clever the way he did it. I doubt Haddad was his first victim.'

Muchacha swirled the liquid in his glass, composing his reply. 'I suspected as much. No love lost there, it was just a matter of time.'

'Or money?'

'What do you mean?'

'You failed to give Haddad the cash to pay for the diamond delivery, maybe even for previous deliveries. This underground diamond railroad has been running some time, hasn't it? That's why you were racing down from Vic Falls. You needed to get to Gubu before Bastany, to make excuses, calm the situation, but you were too late. Bastany lost patience with Haddad, assumed he was cheating him.'

'Seems I've scored some free diamonds then, doesn't it?' The minister snorted. Sibanda's fingers twitched. He wanted to erase that slimy grin and one day he would, but not today. There was too much at stake. 'Do you know who murdered Bastany, who has the diamonds?' The Minister continued.

'I didn't remove them from Madani Haddad's house if that's what you think, but I'm closing in on the killer. I take it we can rule out your goons?'

'I didn't order the murder, it was not in my interest. No deaths on my conscience… this month at least,' he smirked.

'Thomas Mabiza from the curio market, what's his role in all this?'

'That's my business, but he's no murderer. He can't even handle a chisel let alone a weapon. How did you get on to him?'

'And that is *my* business Muchacha.'

'Fair enough. You have 24 hours to produce those diamonds, or your family will be beyond your help.' Muchacha opened the door and called in the CIO officer, 'Uncuff Detective Inspector Sibanda. He can go.' As the hand cuffs were coming off, he added 'If you're not back here by tomorrow then it's open season, Sibanda.' The detective wasted no time getting on his way. The sooner he solved this murder the sooner he could get his brother released and the children back to their parents. He wondered how Berry was coping. Something told him despite her revulsion of him, she would be brilliant. His nephew and niece would be well cared for. She owed him nothing, but he knew her well enough. She would be loyal when it counted. And it counted now.

Berry Barton drove her pickup into the village and admired the flowering ochna pulchra in the centre of the yard dominating the neat arrangement of huts. No sooner had the vehicle stopped than the children in the back were fiddling with their seatbelts. The young boy unsnapped his and was out of the pickup in seconds.

'Wait Lisana, I'll help,' Berry laughed, as the younger of the two children struggled with the metal fastening. 'There you are.' She set the child on the ground, her legs pedalling to make up for lost time.

'Gogo, Gogo we're here,' they shouted, running towards an old lady emerging from one of the huts. Berry watched as they flung themselves into her arms. She bent to hug them and then straightened.

'Come. We must greet our guest.'

'That's Berry,' Lisana offered.

'We've been playing cricket,' Umkhonto's eyes were shining with delight.

'At a big school,' Lisana's small pudgy hands reached as high as they could.

'And swimming. I can do a whole length now.' Umkhonto's arms windmilled in a practised rhythm.

Berry walked towards them, listening to their excited chatter. The slender lady in front of her stirred a raft of uncomfortable emotions. She might not have Jabu's build, his strong shoulders, tall frame and rippling muscles but she had given him her eyes - rich, polished mahogany swirls etched with depth and mystery, flecked with strength and hypnotic in their appeal. Berry caught her breath. That's what she'd fallen in love with.

'Hello Mama,' she held out her hand, 'what delightful grandchildren you have.'

The old lady took both of Berry's hands, 'I cannot thank you enough for taking care of them.'

'My pleasure. I've had loads of fun, they're a lively pair.'

Sibanda's mother shooed the children away, 'Go to the kitchen hut, *abantwana*, you will find juice.' She turned to Berry, 'Let us sit in the shade. You have had a long journey.'

'Not as long as yours, Mama. You are the one who has just returned from South Africa.'

'To take care of my grandchildren. I cannot find enough warmth in my heart to thank you for what you have done. I'm not sure how they came to be in your care.'

'Sergeant Ncube contacted me. He's busy on a case with your son, Jabu... Jabulani. The sergeant told me that Xolisani and Thandie left the children with their friend next-door who was called away on family matters to Botswana...' her voice trailed off. She could see Jabu's mother was distressed. 'Have I said something to upset you?'

'No, my child. It is as you said, my journey has been long and hot. The bus was crowded, and I am an old woman with all my children far away like stars in the distant heavens, untouchable and unreachable. They are both a light in my eyes and an ache in my heart.'

Berry clasped the old lady's hands. She felt an instant connection. She shared her distress. The break-up from Jabu was as the old lady described; he was untouchable and unreachable but still a light in her eyes and an ache in her heart. She had no mother to confide in. Her own mother had died in childbirth.

'But I cannot hear their voices,' Sibanda's mother keened, 'and the memory of their words gets fainter every day like a whisper to the deaf, like a leaf falling on soft sand. I can sense them. Xolisani is blessed like the earth after summer rains. Jabulani is strong with the heady fragrance of African winds that brush the wilderness. Sabatha is lost to the tangle of a city but here in the remembered scent of these yellow blossoms.' She shook her head to rid it of troubling thoughts.

'But they will all be home soon.' Berry was alarmed. Was there something happening she didn't know about?

'Yes, of course. I am a silly sentimental old *salukazi*. But tell me, Berry,' Mathilda Sibanda took control of her emotions, 'How did you become friends with Thandie? Did you go to school together?'

'I don't know the children's parents at all.'

'Then how...?'

'...I do know Sergeant Ncube. I met him during the Black Sparrowhawk investigation. I was one of the girls attacked on the train.' Some sixth sense told Berry to tread carefully about her relationship with Jabu. It was over, no use digging up old ground.

'Oh, my child, were you hurt? That murderer was an evil man.'

'Your detective son, Jabulani, saved me from the worst of it. I told both he and Sergeant Ncube then if either of them ever needed a favour...'

'...So, Sergeant Ncube called you?'

'Yes, he did.'

'Do you know where he is now? I don't have his number.'

'He hasn't got a phone, he borrowed one to call me. You should call your son, they will be together.'

'He's out of range.'

'And the children's parents?'

'Out of the country.'

Their eyes met, brown and troubled, blue and concerned. Berry suspected Mathilda Sibanda was hiding something. She hoped her own eyes weren't giving away secrets.

Chapter 33

Extract from the journal of John Jacobs:

We returned home and the wagons were kept at hand, the oxen outspanned and penned nearby. The King was ready to escape when the moment arrived. Lo Bengula had long been raiding Mashonaland for women, slaves and cattle but he was cunning enough to avoid conflict with white settlers until Chief Gomara from the region of the British Fort at Victoria refused to pay him tribute. The King, already harassed by his cousins and advisors for being as weak as a woman, had to make a statement of strength. He sent thousands of warriors to the area to teach the chief a lesson with the stern dictum: 'If you shed one drop of the white man's blood on this raid into Mashonaland, I will have every one of you killed when you return'. The King did not understand that the opportunistic British, whatever colour blood was spilled, would use this disciplinary action as a flimsy excuse to start a war, the spoils of which are swelling the British coffers to this day.

'Hindsight is a wonderful thing, but foresight is better.' William Blake was a canny wordsmith indeed. But the

tragedies of history are forged from such happenstance. Peace might have been maintained if only Lo Bengula had ignored his advisors and the zeal of his young warriors; if only war monger Major Allan Wilson, a man set on vainglorious reputation, had not been a troop commander in the Fort Victoria region, agitating for martial response (in this he was soon to be satisfied, insisting on a suicide mission in his pursuit of the king which led to his death and that of thirty-one of his comrades); if the two old white men Rhodes and Jameson had not been addicted to the drug of colonial greed and the lure of Mashonaland gold (and they had always wanted an excuse to get their hands on the gold). If only...

I do not write here of the burning of KoBulawayo by our own regiments, of the battles of Bonko or Egodade. The victors have written adequate accounts of the slaughter of the Matabele although they name the battles, Shangani and Bembesi.

'I cannot speak too highly of the pluck of the Ingubo and Imbizo Regiments,' wrote one witness, Sir John Willoughby, 'I believe that no civilised army could have withstood the terrific fire they did for at most half as long.' The American scout, Burnham with all his experience of the wild west frontier and the Indian wars had not been prepared for such scenes of unholy massacre. He described the battlefield as a slaughter with a 'combined stench of human piss, shit and death.' I must remain grateful not to have witnessed those last battles. Our warriors were not defeated, mutilated or eviscerated by lack of valour, by lack of numbers, by lack of strategy, by lack of Martini-Henrys, (Rhodes bought the mineral rights with a 1000 of the latter) no, we were humbled by that fearsome invention the isigwagwa, the Maxim gun, and its first ever outing on a battlefield. Those, like me, who survive into the twentieth

century have read of longer, bigger and bloodier battles, although none with such blanket bravery. Wave upon wave of our regiments, the Imbizo, Ingubo, Isiziba, Ihlati, Avavene, Icobo and Insukamini swept forward to be felled, and according to Burnham, 'mown down like grass.' Those words will haunt me to my grave. The Maxim's glowing reputation in the Matabele killing fields was firmly cemented in the Great War.

'A pity we didn't meet up in Vic Falls, James. I thought we might, but then I wasn't sure I could afford another night in that hotel, so I came back here to Bulawayo.'

'Rupert wouldn't have been happy to see me, we didn't part on good terms. I was tied up anyway. I've hired a car to get down here. What's the rush and why am I reading about some obscure battles, Caro?'

'Forget the battles, James, it's what happens before and after that's interesting for us. That's why I need access to some of the money.'

'Tell me what's written here, precis it. My eyes aren't used to deciphering handwriting, particularly this ancient, spidery joined-up sort.'

'Well, the local King, Lobengula, gets on his horse, and I have to say he must have lost loads of weight in between his first and second journeys or else John Jacobs is a bit of a romancer. There are inconsistencies in his account. Maybe he's made the whole thing up.' Caroline pinched a roll of flesh on her stomach. 'I wouldn't mind his diet, this holiday-making is too relaxing.'

'Come on, you're as beautiful as ever and you know it.'

Caroline frowned. 'Anyway, Lobengula is travelling on horseback, on a saddle given to him by Queen

Victoria no less, his own baggage train of Queens in tow, his throne along with him. He left most of his warriors behind to blow up his arsenal to keep it out of British hands, raze his town and fight his battles.

'Bad move. He would have been easy to follow with a big entourage.'

'No, he was a wily old fox to the end. The wagons with the Queens went in a different direction to the King to throw off the baying colonial army. After the defeats in battle, the morale of the Matabele was low, but at least three regiments stuck with him to protect his back. The King realised the game was up, so he ordered my ancestor, John Jacobs, to give a thousand sovereigns they'd kept in reserve to two tribesmen.' She flicked the pages over until she found the right spot, 'Petchan and Sehuloholu. That's them, with the instruction they were to hand the sovereigns to the British as a peace offering.' She snapped the book closed, as she did a loose piece of paper from the back of the book fell out, unnoticed and slipped under the old chair.

'Impressive,' James whistled in appreciation. 'That was a shed load of money in those days,'

'And someone succumbed to temptation because although the box of sovereigns was handed over to two British troopers, the gold disappeared and never made it to the commanders. They never knew of the offer.'

'Would it have made a difference?'

'Who knows? Maybe not, maybe the die was already cast. The British tried some suspects for the theft and found them guilty, but then exonerated them.

'Imagine if you'd invested that amount back then, when was it?'

'1894.'

'Look for some super rich colonial whose family was around at the time and bingo, you've got your thieves. You said this King went on a journey, ran away. Some leader to abandon his army.'

'Lobengula wasn't a bad lad by contemporary standards. Everyone he met liked him. Soft-spoken, commanding presence, witty, they said. He was a saint if you compare him to the brutal justice meted out by our crowned heads. Confrontation wasn't his forte.'

'So, he didn't behead his Queens when he no longer fancied them or find a new religion to suit his adultery?'

'Of course not. And he owned no tower to imprison felons in either. His justice was more immediate. He might have been tough, but at least he was fair. According to John Jacobs, in the Matabele tradition, a King had to be kept safe. He couldn't fall into foreign hands, nor could his body. All some mumbo jumbo, juju stuff about strangers stealing power from the dead corpse of a king, so his courtiers insisted he flee. His first journey was to bury his vast hoard of gold, diamonds and ivory to keep it out of the hands of the British, wagon loads of the stuff.'

'And his second journey was to collect it?'

'No, he was escaping our militia and they couldn't catch him. Try as they might, he got away. Lobengula never came back for his treasure as far as I can make out. He died soon after, poisoned himself and was buried in a cave. That's as far as I've read.' She opened the journal at a page with a pen sketch, waving the drawing in front of James. 'I've got the treasure map,' Caroline sing-songed, 'John Jacobs was the last man standing to know the location of Lobengula's hoard.'

'And now you want money to go treasure hunting?'

'You've got it in one, Jamie darling. This could be a real adventure and I'm footloose, fancy free and up for it. What did you do with my diamond money?'

'Invested it in Apple stocks. Your £150,000 investment has done well in the last twelve months. You should see a significant gain.'

'Wow! Clever you.'

'I took some commission. How do you think I afforded this holiday? But Rupert will learn the truth when he hocks that ring. And if Bobo finds out, she'll sue your arse off.'

'Rupert's gone, James, and taken the ring with him, fake, worthless diamond and all,' she laughed, 'Why would they check? No one will ever notice the switch and even if they do, they'll never realise I substituted the stone. I'm too mumsy, too working class to do something so daring. Bobo will never believe it.'

'What if Richard sells the ring to shore up the business?'

'Despite what Rupert thinks, Bobo won't let him sell the ring. It's her precious heritage. No, Rupert's saviour is squint-eyed Sappy Washington.'

'Poor bastard.' There was genuine sympathy in James' comment. 'Sappy Washington... Rupert's gone where?'

'On his way home.'

'Why? He could have waited to drop the divorce bombshell until you got back to London. Zimbabwe is an amazing destination.'

'He somehow got mixed up in a murder investigation, to do with diamonds. Isn't that a neat irony?'

The colour drained from James' face. 'Who was murdered?'

'A cousin of that awful Bilal Haddad and some other bloke with a weird name, Jaafar Bast... something or other. A tall, black, scary and far too attractive policeman came to investigate. Rupert did a brief runner, but he was caught. I was able to give him an alibi. They let him go.'

'Detective Sibanda? Bit of a cold fish?'

'Yes, but how do you know him?'

'Because I'm in the frame for that murder.'

'What?'

'Laurent Kasongo, real name, Jaafar Bastany was on the same overland trip. I was with him hours before he was killed. That detective has confiscated all our passports. I'm a suspect and I'm down here in Bulawayo, the cousin of Rupert Templeton, with you, the wife of Rupert Templeton, the man who's up to his eyes with Bilal Haddad and this whole mess. This doesn't look good for me, Caro.'

'But you don't even know Bilal Haddad. You've been out of the firm for months.'

'Don't I? Who do you think brokered the sale of the Hudson diamond and got us the fake? Bilal Haddad has his fingerprints all over diamond fraud.'

'Bilal did the diamond swap?'

James nodded and furrowed his brow. 'He's a genius at fakes. You must have read about that case in New York. A rare blue, similar to the Hope diamond revealed as a white diamond with an almost undetectable composite blue coating sprayed on.'

Caroline shook her head.

'Or the five-carat stone from the Prague Museum collection that, on recent inspection, turned out to be a lump of glass?

Caroline looked bemused. 'No, never heard anything.'

'That's all Bilal's work.'

'Oh, for heaven's sake, this is like a plot for a thriller...'

'Except it's not fiction. Bilal is moving away from dealing naturals into the synthetics market. It's now impossible to tell a genuine diamond from a fake. Yours isn't the only diamond he's fiddled with or swapped.'

'How are you involved with him?'

'I know what he's up to and that makes me an accessory after the fact, maybe even before. He dragged me into his schemes Caro, for the price of your freedom. And that's not even the half of it... I...' He bit his lip. '...best you don't know any of this. Let me think.'

'Oh God, James, what are you going to do?'

'I'm heading back to Victoria Falls. This is not Scotland Yard we're talking about. Let's hope that detective is more stupid than he looks.'

Chapter 34

'Eddie, thanks for calling. Have you solved my murder?' Sibanda made his way back to the campground. The kicks had done some damage, his ribs were stabbing each time he moved. The Rugged Rascals truck was parked in the same place, but with very little activity, no tents and no people.

'Do you want the good news first?' Eddie chirped, 'Your name just came off the Interpol Red Notice. I can talk to you.'

'That was quick. And the bad news?'

'Not much to tell you about your suspect list. No one stands out as a possible murderer, no motives. But I do have some information on your victim.'

'Jaafar Bastany?'

'He's a whistle-blower gone rogue. A couple of years ago, he contacted the Antwerp Police with a tip off about the Federal Commissioner in charge of the diamond investigation unit, the fraud squad. Aric De Vos had been swindling for years. Bastany informed on him, told the police to check out De Vos's villa in the

South of France and the yacht moored nearby. When they raided De Vos's house, they discovered a cache of diamonds and wads of Euros. Bastany asked for immunity.'

'I remember reading about that case, high profile. Hard to believe the guy in charge of fraud was a crook. I don't recall mention of a whistle blower.'

'They kept that under wraps.'

'What made Bastany grass up the head guy? There must have been something in it for him other than immunity.'

'Revenge. He and his Lebanese mates invested in synthetic diamonds. De Vos double crossed him even though he'd been paid good money to turn a blind eye. De Vos realised he had to achieve a high-profile bust to shore up his position and cover his tracks. He liked to swagger in front of the cameras, so he staged the exposure of hundreds of synthetic diamonds sitting at the Gemstone Foundation.'

'I take it the gemologists bought those fakes from Bastany and his mates.'

'Yes. De Vos claimed hero status and the so-called experts came out of it with egg all over their faces. The raid made the commissioner look good and put Jaafar Bastany in the cross hairs of some dangerous people.'

'Because he'd sold the fakes in the first place?'

'Ripped the Foundation off and humiliated them at the same time.'

'Heavy stuff,' Sibanda whistled under his breath.

'Bastany was under a witness protection scheme for the first year.'

'Witness protection? That's serious. Who was after him?'

'Everyone. His own guys because they thought he'd sold them out in collusion with De Vos, and that mob don't like grasses.'

'The Gemstone Foundation can't have been happy.'

'No and they have their own protection force not averse to a bit of heavy leaning to keep everyone honest. And the Diamond Squad themselves. Remember, Aric De Vos ran the squad for ten years, was a fixture and well liked.

'He took the fall?'

'There were others in the squad involved. They're still mopping up.'

'What happened to De Vos?'

'He killed himself. Jumped off a bridge before his trial, but no one makes the heady rank of police commissioner without cultivating criminal contacts.'

'He may have set his own revenge in motion, set the dogs on Bastany, before he committed suicide.' Sibanda could see a picture building.

'You're right. Word is, there was a contract out on your Lebanese murder victim.'

'No wonder Bastany was in disguise. Must have spent months looking over his shoulder. What happened to his safe house, new identity?'

'Bastany skipped out. Once a dealer, always a dealer. He wanted back in the game. His minders lost him. No one will be stunned at the outcome. He was a marked man.'

'Thanks for all this, Eddie.'

'Don't thank me, Jabs. I've probably opened a bigger can of worms and extended your suspect profile to include half the hard men of Europe.'

Sibanda took a few moments to process the phone call. Jaafar Bastany had serious enemies. He'd known all along this murder smacked of a revenge killing with a motive that lay beyond the village of Gubu. Did a hitman wait until Bastany got all the way to Gubu before executing him? Unlikely. He could have been picked off by a professional anywhere along his route. So why was Jafaar Bastany murdered in a village backwater? Why did the murderer wait?

During his time with the diamond fraud squad, he'd skimmed through the report on the Antwerp scandal Damien Bartle handed him. Something in that report was niggling, some detail stored away, some clue hovering beyond his reach. A name? A place? Just as he was thinking he might haul the recalcitrant memory to the surface, a car drove in and parked next to the Rugged Rascals truck. James Templeton got out. Sibanda walked over.

'Detective Sibanda, you've come to return our passports?'

'When I'm satisfied none of you were involved with the murder of Jaafar Bastany.'

'Then I'm in the clear, detective. I didn't even know his real name until two days ago. I thought he was Laurent Kasongo from Congo.' Templeton was on firm ground, sure of himself.

'But you do know Bilal Haddad.'

'Not a familiar name.' Sibanda didn't need Sergeant Ncube's interpretation of face twitches, the man's discomfort was obvious.

'You worked at Templetons?'

'Yes, but I left months ago.'

'Why?'

'Rupert and I disagreed over the direction of the firm.'

'In what way?'

'He was too cavalier, took unnecessary risks with other people's money. It'll all end in tears.'

'Was Bilal Haddad one of those risks?'

'Look, detective, I've already told you I don't know the man.'

'I think you do and I think you know his contact in Gubu, Madani Haddad. My connections tell me you were at the investment firm for some time. Long enough to have met a frequent visitor. Bilal Haddad haunted those offices. Rupert Templeton is in custody in the UK right now. He'll be blabbing all he knows.' Sibanda took out his phone. 'Should I dial my contacts?'

James leant on the car and shook his head. 'I haven't murdered anyone.'

'Why did you hire the car?'

'To get around and see the sights. I'm on holiday.' Templeton was confused by the change of questioning.

'You can walk to almost every tourist spot in Vic Falls or get a transfer cheaply enough. I can check on the mileage. Where did you go?'

'Okay, so I went to Bulawayo, but that doesn't make me a criminal.'

'Why Bulawayo?'

'To visit a friend. She's inherited a house. She wanted my advice.'

'Caroline Templeton?'

Templeton seemed to sag, his body needing the support of the hire car. How did this detective know about Caroline's house? He was sunk.

'Don't move an inch, Templeton. I haven't finished with you.' Sibanda walked a few metres, keen for space to explore the scenario building. Jaafar Bastany was supposed to deliver diamonds to Madani Haddad. Bilal Haddad was expecting Rupert Templeton to collect a package of diamonds and take them back to London and yet Cuthbert Muchacha thought *he* was buying those diamonds. Who was getting their hands on those stones? One of them was going to be double crossed. Sibanda was certain there was a connection between Bilal and James Templeton. Was Caroline involved as well? Was he wrong to let Rupert Templeton travel back to the UK? What was he missing? He ran through everything he knew about the case, every detail he'd gleaned from Eddie. He rubbed his chin to ease the tension in his jaw.

And then the link clicked into place. The perfect con, and a lesson in how to crook a crook. He strode back to James Templeton and took a good look at the man's feet, at least a size 12. He had found Bigfoot.

'You visited Madani Haddad's house on the afternoon Jaafar Bastany was murdered, didn't you?'

'No, no…'

'There were footprints under his bedroom window and your large size shoe puts you there. Don't bother denying it.'

'I didn't kill anyone,' he sagged further and then caved under the glare of the detective. 'Okay, I was at Haddad's house. I saw his body lying in the room. I was terrified, so I legged it. I've never seen a dead body before.'

'Why didn't you phone the police, report a death?'

'And be involved with statements, evidence, court cases and dodgy foreign police?'

'Did you meet your cousin at Haddad's house? Were you colluding with one another?' Sibanda was questioning him shrapnel sharp. He was tired of the assumption that all Zimbabwe police were corrupt.

'What?' James Templeton's surprise was genuine.

'Rupert, your cousin.'

'Do you think he murdered Haddad? He might be an idiot, but I wouldn't have thought Rupert could kill a fly. Didn't even enjoy pinging birds. He went along with the shooting parties to drink the sloe gin and network with the rich and the worthy.'

'Did you know Rupert and Caroline were in Zimbabwe?'

'Yes, I heard they were coming out, but I thought they were in Bulawayo.'

'You're right, Rupert didn't kill Haddad. But he was supposed to collect a parcel from him to take back to Bilal and you were supposed to deliver one, weren't you?'

James shook his head in denial. 'You're on the wrong track, Detective.'

'I don't think so. And when you went to deliver your parcel that afternoon, you saw Jaafar Bastany at Haddad's house, followed him back to the centre of the village and then killed him for the genuine diamonds you knew he was carrying.'

'Oh God, real diamonds? Is that what this is about? I swear… Bilal never said…'

'…You had the opportunity; you were at the scene and you have a motive.'

'I came straight back from that house. I couldn't get away fast enough.' James was beginning to sweat. His eyes were darting, looking for safety.

'What time was that?'

'Early evening. It was still light. I met up with Rebecca. There was a storm brewing, so we went to find some shelter. We ended up in an eatery.'

'Mama Elephant's?'

'I think that was the name.'

'You never saw Bastany?'

'No, not after he left us, when Barney dropped us off.'

'He was murdered in the alley way outside the diner. You were there.'

'No, we didn't stay long. We had burgers and left for the meeting place. I never saw Bastany. We were the first ones there. The others came later.'

'And Rebecca will vouch you were with her?'

'She'd better. I was shaken. I told her I'd seen my first dead body. She was consoling. We agreed to keep it all secret, spent the time together until Barney arrived at around ten-ish. I didn't want to be alone.'

'So, you weren't able to deliver your parcel. Where is it?'

'What parcel are you talking about?'

'Come clean, Templeton. The synthetic diamonds Bilal Haddad told you to deliver to Madani Haddad.'

'How...how did you know?'

'If he says he knows, he knows,' Sergeant Ncube's reassuring voice boomed from the background. He appeared from nowhere and was hovering over Sibanda's left shoulder. 'Sorry, sir, I couldn't sit in the bush any longer. What happened to your face?'

'Another time, Ncube.' He turned to Templeton, 'The diamonds?'

James Templeton threw his hands up, 'Okay, I was carrying a delivery for Haddad.'

'Why did you agree to courier the synthetics, Templeton?'

'Bilal threatened blackmail. He'd done me a favour and he wanted payback. Look he's plausible, charming, impossible to mistrust until he's sucked you in, until it's too late. Am I in trouble? The synthetics are worthless, fakes, copies. I won't be arrested, will I?'

'Aren't you arresting him, sir?' Sibanda and Ncube were walking back to Miss Daisy parked on the edge of the campgrounds. Sibanda was weighing a bound parcel of synthetic diamonds in his hands.

'I've got a lot on my plate, Ncube and this guy was a stooge. Why didn't you obey orders and stay put?'

'Miss Daisy was fretful. A herd of elephants surrounded us for most of the night and in the morning when I visited the bushes, there was a huge snake with triangle splodges all down its back...a mamba.'

'Not all snakes are mambas, Ncube, what colour was its mouth?'

'It's mouth? Ncube was aghast. I didn't look in its mouth, sir, why would anyone look a snake in the mouth? That's like sharpening a lion's claws with a rasp or picking stringy sinew from a hyena's fangs. Crazy...'

'Never mind,' Sibanda rolled his eyes, 'those markings sound like it was an adder, a night adder and it can't have been huge. They grow to a metre.'

'It looked huge. I nearly fainted. Ncube's stomach gurgled at the memory of the evil, beady eyed, tongue-flicking creature. It might have been years before anyone found my corpse in that wilderness. I could have wasted away to a shadow and Miss Daisy to a rotting hulk.'

'Your shadow is in no danger of fading, Ncube and Miss Daisy is already a rotting hulk.'

The sergeant wasn't sure if he'd been insulted. Miss Daisy certainly had, but he made no comment. He was enjoying the banter. He and the detective were back to being a team, sitting together in Miss Daisy, the detective being rude about her, the pastel deckchair upholstery comforting, a murder investigation rumbling around the detective's brain, the mouldy smell of the rotting roof lining reeking with familiarity, even the plugged bullet hole becoming an affirming part of their working environment. He reached up and ran his fingers over his handywork. This was a mistake. He had devoured Smilo's two-day supply of food in a single night and was relaxed after the stress of imprisonment and the escape to Botswana. His extended stomach began a series of odour shedding reverberations. Sibanda rolled down the windows.

I'll check the tyres, sir, Ncube mumbled as he made a hasty exit, leaving a little taster behind as he slid off the seat. Sibanda opened the door and wafted it backwards and forwards, fanning Miss Daisy's interior until the air became breathable. He used Ncube's absence to reassemble his old phone and number. The first number he called was his mother.

She was crying. 'Oh my son, I was so worried when no one could reach you by phone. Do you know about Xolisani?'

'Xolisani will be home soon, Mama. I promise you will hear from him by tomorrow.'

'How can you make this happen, Jabu? They tell me the CIO has taken both he and Thandie.'

'I have connections Mama, you know that.' Sibanda had no connections in high places, had lost any influence when he'd exposed Cuthbert Muchacha's schemes, but it didn't hurt to let his mother believe he could lean on people.

'Where have you been? I am desperate. Not knowing is like death - silence, darkness and suffocation. I am sorry to burden you with my fears, my son, if anything was to happen to either of you...'

'I was away on a job, Mama, an important case. I have to solve it first and then I will come to visit. Xolisani and Thandie will be released. Do you have the children?'

'Umkhonto and Lisana are here with me but wanting their mother and father.'

'Tomorrow, Mama, Tuesday at the latest, we will all be reunited.'

'You are a blessing my son. You have the strength of your father. The white girl...'

'...Berry?' Sibanda held his breath.

'Yes, she looked after the children until I arrived from Johannesburg. She...she seems very kind, the children love her. My son, if she is the one, then I would not be unhappy. We got on so well, chatted, drank tea, laughed. She seemed almost like one of us, like a Ndebele girl, respectful of our culture. I have come to realise milk and honey have different colours, but they can share the same house peacefully.'

'No, Mama,' Sibanda faked a laugh, 'She is out of my league. I wasn't involved with Berry,' he lied to his mother a second time, but his pain was intolerable and hers would be double, if she knew Berry was lost to him forever. He ended the call, but he couldn't end the ache in his heart. He thought of the girl he loved who had somehow charmed his exacting mother and overcame her racial prejudices.

'The tyres are fine, sir, a little worn, but they'll get us home to Gubu.' Sergeant Ncube felt enough time had lapsed to disperse his signature hum. 'One question though; why was James Templeton delivering fake diamonds to Madani Haddad? It doesn't make sense. Haddad dealt in real ones.'

'Perfect sense Ncube. The Haddad cousins planned the deception. Bastany was to deliver the real diamonds from the Congo to Madani Haddad to sell on. When no money was forthcoming, he killed him. James Templeton was delivering synthetic diamonds and the bastard who thought he was buying the consignment of real diamonds from Bastany via Haddad would get the synthetics. The real diamonds being couriered back to London to Bilal Haddad, via Rupert Templeton.'

'Clever. Who was being set up with the fakes?'

'Cuthbert Muchacha.'

Ncube's stomach roared. 'The minister is being double crossed?'

'He who empties his gut on the road meets flies on his journey and Cuthbert Muchacha has deposited a mound of excrement in his time. Here, Ncube, phone your wives and let them know you'll be with them soon.'

'What will you do, sir?'

'Stay here as long as it takes to solve Jaafar Bastany's murder and sort out the manure the good minister has spread.'

'I'm staying too sir. I can help with the dung.'

Sibanda laughed, 'Ncube, I never thanked you for coming into town. I'll need your help in the hours ahead.'

'Out there in the bush, Miss Daisy and I both felt as uncomfortable as a torn toenail in a tight shoe. We were worried. I trust you, sir. This nightmare will all be over tomorrow. I'll let my wives know.'

Chapter 35

'You're back from the Falls, Wishes?' Caroline negotiated her way past the guarded gate, down the path to the battered door.

'Yes, Miss Caro.'

Caroline frowned at the name. Habits were as resilient as the weeds colonising the rain-soaked cracks in the pathway. 'Could you give me a hand with the old house? I'm staying for a while. I'll need a handy man from time to time, nailing down floorboards, cleaning gutters, maybe a bit of gardening. Can your uncle spare you?'

'He's still up in Vic Falls at the conference.'

Caroline wondered if James was also still in the Falls and if he'd encountered the gorgeous detective and come away unscathed. What on earth possessed James to get involved with Bilal Haddad? She'd always thought he was smarter than Rupert. The apples hadn't fallen far from the grandfather's tree, it turned out. 'What were you doing up there, Wishes?'

'Running errands. My uncle has some sort of business, he uses one of the curio sellers to handle goods for him.'

'Your uncle deals in curios?'

'No, but the curio guy is in trouble. When he sent on the last shipment of whatever my uncle was expecting, it got lost. I've never seen my uncle so angry and stressed. He has money troubles, like everyone. He gambles a lot and he hit Martha the other day.'

'Martha?'

'His domestic. Her eye is still closed.'

'She has stayed?' Caroline was horrified.

'Where else could she go. She has children to feed. There are no other jobs.' Godwishes shrugged his shoulders. Violence was part of his landscape.

Caroline made a decision, 'Would you come and work for me, Wishes?'

'Full time?'

'I'll pay you, of course. I need someone local. I have a quest.'

'A quest? What's that?'

'A sort of treasure hunt, but we'll talk about that later. First, we're going to fix your lip.' Wishes' hand went to his mouth. 'I'm sorry, have I embarrassed you? Have you seen a doctor?'

'The clinic, when I was smaller. They gave me some liquid to paint on. It didn't help. Can this be fixed?' He pointed to the suppurating sore under his nose and the missing piece of his lip.

'I've been checking online.' Caroline was bubbling with enthusiasm, her brown eyes shining, 'I think it's something called Noma, a type of infectious disease that attacks the mouth, cured with antibiotics and good food.'

'But the hole in my lip?'

'There are visiting charities and surgeons who'll help with a bit of plastic surgery.'

'Can that happen?' Godwishes was amazed

'I'll make it happen, Wishes. We'll find a doctor tomorrow. Come over to the house this afternoon and we'll start on the clean-up.'

Godwishes grinned, no longer attempting to hide the disfigurement. His miserable life was about to be changed forever.

Caroline returned to her house and settled down with her ancestor's journal. She read again about the death of the Lobengula, taking in the detail, hoping to glean more clues to the location of the treasure.

The King knew the day had come. He stood before those of his people still faithful to him and spoke, 'Go now, all of you to Rhodes and seek his protection. He will be your chief and friend.' He praised his warriors, 'You have done your best, my soldiers; you can help me no more. I thank you all. Go now to your kraals. Mjan, the greatest of you all, will go to Rhodes, who will make things all right for you. To all of you I say Hambani kuhle.' Mjan, the commander-in-chief and leader of all the impis, took these words on his shoulders with the sorrowful mantle of unwanted leadership. All eyes now fell on him.

It was a moment of unbearable sadness and the last public words of a great King. I, half white, half black as I am, would not have entrusted my followers to a white foreigner, the very man who had stolen the land, stolen the minerals and enslaved the tribe. But Lo Bengula was a better judge than I, for Rhodes proved not to be a waspish leader. He held great vision for the future of the land and showed compassion in his dealings with a conquered people, but alas, no justice. The Matabele never ruled their kingdom again.

Once the King made good his escape, he halted in Pashu's country. It was there I left him for the last time and accompanied Mjan, having been dispatched thus with the rest of his followers. The Commander and I bade our farewells not far from the site of the King's destroyed kraal. It took me several days of riding to reach the Limpopo and several weeks of waiting before the river subsided, and my journey back to the Republic concluded. The momentous news travelled faster than my horse. The king was dead within 24 hours of his final speech. He drank from his own bottle of arsenic. Magwegwe, his faithful induna, took the potion in equal dose. They died together, speedily and painlessly. I knew that bottle had been given to him by the missionary Moffat for intestinal disorders, to be administered a few drops at a time (he suffered from digestive issues due to his vast intake of meat and beer), but Lo Bengula understood well its potency.

I learned Lo Bengula had been interred in a cave nearby, seated on his wooden throne, wrapped in the skin of a black ox, surrounded by those items he treasured most in life: his rifles, the Martini Henrys and the Wesley Richards monkey tail; his dear little Flobert gallery pistol that amused him as he targeted lizards and doves when he could no longer hunt; his silver trimmed hemp pipe; his saddle and other accoutrements.

Like Egyptian Pharaohs, Ndebele royalty could not be laid in the ground. The people believed the flesh of the King to be imbued with the power to destroy the next King. It could never fall into evil hands. For the continuity of the house of Khumalo and the stability of the nation, it was imperative the King's flesh be rotted from his bones before interment could take place. I was later advised that the grave had been opened and his bleached bones removed from the cave to the gravesite of his father, the great King Mzilikazi. Secretly, in order to foil grave robbers, those who hoped to scrape even a small piece of flesh from the King's remains, the bones of a large young man of Lo Bengula's height were disinterred and scattered in the cave in his place.

I wonder now if that is the truth, given the fall of the Ndebele nation and the failure of a new King to rise, to claim the throne and to stir up a proud nation. If I believed these stories of witchcraft (which as a good Christian I do not) then surely some enemy entered the cave and stole that precious flesh, for a spell has been cast over this land from which it has never recovered. The Ndebele people are asleep. They await their prince in vain.

Have I ever returned to that glorious land, that piece of God's earth that stole my soul, I hear you ask? Yes, I have been back three times. I have led three expeditions to recover Lo Bengula's treasure in which attempts I have been foiled. It is true I have been paid well for my services at a time when I am down on my luck, but I have offered adventure to these treasure seekers beyond their wildest dreams. It is enough. The white government, now set up far from Kobulawayo in the land of the Mashonas, has forbidden me to enter the country, sentenced me to hard labour for trying and deported me when they could. They are frightened, they know I know...

Caroline closed the journal and pondered her next move. Was John Jacobs real? How reliable was this journal? Her possible three times great grandfather seemed to have insinuated himself into all the major events in local history, a bit like the fictional Victorian scoundrel and cad, Harry Flashman, bully of Tom

Brown's schooldays and hero of the 11th Light Dragoons. How did Jacobs manage to be there when the King buried his treasure and accompany him when he fled on his death march? How did he have conversations with the leaders of famous battles? How was he entrusted with his peace offering to the British and yet she'd never heard speak of him in the family? Was this journal a mock-up to tempt potential investors in his expeditions? What did he mean by "it is enough"? Her brain was spinning. What to believe? She was trained as a rational scientist and yet the lure of a diamond cache was irresistible. She witnessed first-hand, the riches that one diamond could generate let alone fabled safes full of the stones.

Caroline looked at the map again. What the hell, she thought, who ever got to follow a treasure trail in real life? She had the resources thanks to Bobo's diamond. This could be a real King Solomon's mines moment. She placed the journal on the table and smiled, 'Alanna Quatermaine, here I come,' she said to the walls of the old house.

Up in the attic, a night adder came looking for her mate. She smelled his presence on her flicking tongue, but the trail was old. He had moved on. She curled in the corner where a break of sunlight washed across the old wooden floorboards and caressed her diamonds that shimmered and undulated like granite pebbles under wind ruffled water.

Chapter 36

'Your phone, sir.'

'Thanks, Ncube, how are Blessing, Nomatter and Sukho?' Sibanda had his fuzzy one-eyed binoculars trained on a lourie. Was it the Knysna or the purple crested? Both possessed distinctive red primary feathers caused by a copper pigment said to dissolve in water. Was it true they got washed out and paler in the rainy season? He'd caught a flash of red as the bird flew, now he was waiting for a clearer view through the thick foliage. He hoped for the rarer Knysna.

'They are well and happy, sir. The lands are ploughed and planted. Blessing tells me the little one will be arriving within days. I am looking forward to seeing the children.' Ncube was waiting for the detective's regular lecture on birth control and how the sergeant's contribution to overpopulation was ruining the planet. Sibanda didn't respond. He'd put his binoculars down and checked his phone. Ncube had accidentally hit a button and brought up a photo on the screen of Berry and her father, Buff. Sibanda's heart skipped. He wanted to curse his sergeant for digging up unwanted memories. How long did it take to mend a shattered, heart he wondered? He took one last moment to gaze on the face he loved before getting rid of it. His finger hovered over the delete button, but some instinct stopped him...

'Damn it, Ncube, the murder suspect has been staring me in the face.'

It can't be Miss Barton, he thought, she has the innocence of an angel. Ncube saw the wistful look in the detective's eyes as he gazed at the screen and decided there and then to get Blessing to concoct a potion. Maybe something that worked slowly. After all, love was misty rain, arriving softly but eventually flooding the river. Blessing would have the detective's river overflowing in no time with the right *muthi*.

'Do you really suspect Miss Barton, sir?'

'What makes you think she is involved?'

'The photo you were looking at?'

'It's the likeness, Ncube, between Berry and her father. Remarkable. Two peas in a pod.'

'I know. Two pins in the fodder.'

'Where did that pin nonsense come from, your dictionary?' Sibanda scoffed.

'Cold War,' Ncube was defensive. 'It's the eyes, sir. No one else in the world can have those eyes the colour of a deep blue winter sky. They both have them. Miss Barton would make a very fine first wife.'

'Stay out of it, Ncube.' Sibanda warned. 'The murder had nothing to do with the Bartons, but their likeness has reminded me of another photo I've seen. Where are those passports?' Sibanda flicked through the documents' photo pages. 'That's it! An uncanny resemblance to a disgraced diamond fraud officer. It all fits.' Sibanda rubbed his chin. 'I had a hunch this was a revenge murder. I never forget a face. The file photo of Aric de Vos I saw when I was working with the UK diamond fraud squad is a giveaway. I don't know how I missed it until now.'

'Are we looking for a relation of the bad officer, this Aric de Vos, sir?'

'Yes. Jaafar Bastany brought about the man's downfall, his shame and his suicide. De Vos was the head of the diamond fraud squad in Antwerp, a highflyer corrupted by diamonds. In shopping him, Bastany crossed the Lebanese mafia, a corrupt cartel and some naïve diamond buyers. Bastany had a contract out on his life which put me off the scent. I thought we were looking for a professional hitman not a family member. Aric de Vos's children came after Jaafar Bastany. They wanted revenge.'

'We don't have any suspects with the name De Vos.'

'It's easy to change a name. Come, Ncube.'

'Where to, sir?'

'To arrest our murderers.'

'Murderers, sir? There are more than one?'

'Oh yes, Ncube, we have a pair of culprits and they're in cahoots.'

'Where's that? I've never heard of Cahoots. Is it near?'

Sibanda clicked his tongue in frustration. 'These two are working together, had a plan from the beginning. De Vos's mates in the squad would have kept them up to speed on Bastany's movements. The killers trailed him to Zambia and onto the overland truck.'

'Sir, there's Barney Jones, is he one of them you're after?'

'No, Ncube, more's the pity. But I need to question him.'

Sibanda jumped out of Miss Daisy and raced to intercept the safari guide.

'Jones, where are your overlanders?'

'Mooching around waiting for their passports. They want to move on.'

'You can have them back. Here.' Sibanda thrust the passport collection at the safari guide, 'but I'm hanging onto these two.'

'What... never... those two, together?'

'Yes, where are they?'

'I left them with some of the others at the café overlooking the gorge.'

Sibanda sprinted back to the Land Rover, holding his injured ribs as he ran. Ncube trundled after him as best he could, scrambling into the passenger side. Half his body was still outside as the vehicle took off. The day heated up, steaming and heavy. Rain was coming, the build-up was suffocating. Miss Daisy's door flapped and creaked as Ncube reached to close it. His shirt was soaked, his brow dripping.

'Who are we after, sir?'

'The Belgian girls.'

'The Van Dalens?' Ncube blinked the sweat from his eyes.

'Hang on, Ncube.' Sibanda swerved off the main road onto the track leading to the gorge and the café.

'How do you know it's them?' The sergeant's body slammed against the door and shed more droplets like a laundered sheet being bashed on rocks.

'They look like their father. You said it, two pins in the fodder. Check the passport photos, look at those square jaws, the narrow set eyes, the thick blond hair. Those feathers haven't fallen far from the rooster. They're Aric De Vos's daughters, there's no doubt.'

'They're girls, how did they manage to overpower a grown man?'

'You didn't feel their handshakes, Ncube. They both had a grip a python would have been proud of. My guess is their circus performance was some kind of strong woman act. The Van Dalen's, must have changed their names from De Vos because of the high-profile fraud case in Antwerp. Belgium is a small country. They couldn't work under that name, so they took on a stage name.'

'And the weapon with the stupid, snail bullets, where did they get that?'

Sibanda didn't ponder over the ridiculous description, there was no time. 'They smuggled it in or bought it in Africa but my bet is they found it in Bastany's backpack. Remember the lining was worn and frayed by something hard. Bastany carried that weapon with him to protect his back. He didn't know who was coming after him from one day to the next.'

'Why didn't he just shoot Haddad if he had a weapon all along?'

'He chose to bludgeon his contact with the statue hoping he could disguise the killing by cleaning Hadadd's face, locking the door and returning the key to the inside. He very nearly succeeded. The death has been recorded as suicide. Plus, I don't think he went to the house with murder in mind. His anger got the better of him when there was no money to pay for the delivery. The statue was at the ready in his hand, the weapon in his backpack.'

'Why did he have the statue in his hand, sir? A gift for the middleman?'

'A gift of sorts, Ncube, of more value than your wildest imaginings.'

'Bastany didn't see those girls coming.'

'No, who would suspect a couple of girls. They befriended him even though he was strange. Everyone else on the trip avoided him.'

'How did the girls grab his weapon and overpower a big strong man?'

'After Barney dropped them off, they followed Bastany to Haddad's house and witnessed the murder. So many tracks outside that bedroom window it could have been Barghees on sale day.'

'Those girls followed him down Mama Elephant's alley and shot him. This is hard to believe.'

'Believe it Ncube. Have you never heard the saying that the female of the species is deadlier than the male? We can thank Rudyard Kipling for that.'

'Who, sir?'

'Mowgli, The Jungle Book, If?'

Despite his best efforts, the sergeant's eyes widened, his mouth dropped open. The detective was speaking his strange language again.

'Plenty of examples of ruthless women. Some take their lead from the insect world. The female praying mantis bites off her mate's head after intercourse and munches her way through the body. The extra nutrition ensures a good crop of eggs. There's a poor midge who gets all his blood sucked out during sex and his genitals broken off inside the female for his troubles, not to mention the black widow spider...'

'... No more sir, please, I have three wives... my legs are feeling weak.'

'Relax Ncube, Geneva and Alair Van Dalen killed for revenge, not sexual cannibalism. We're nearly there. Remember, they're armed.'

Miss Daisy pulled up in the car park. 'We'll move in casually. Too many other diners around. Don't do anything that might alert the girls we're on to them.'

'Right, sir.' Ncube was trying hard to concentrate. The stakes were high, but this was a restaurant, and the lunchtime smells were irresistible. His stomach was in rebellion.

'Focus, Ncube.' Sibanda watched his sergeant's eyes follow a waiter to a nearby table and serve a platter of unimaginable treats. All Sibanda's senses were concentrated on the edge of the gorge with a breathtaking view to the Zambezi hundreds of feet below. The river sliced a passage through the basalt. 150 000 years ago, the cooling lava contracted and cracked east to west. Water found the weakness, as water does, nibbling and eroding, millennia after millennia, until the river ate through and formed a gorge. Time and water were relentless. This carved ravine formed the border between Zimbabwe and Zambia. Sibanda's eyes scanned the rugged, ochre-splashed walls of the gorge for a Taita falcon. A sighting would have been a lifer for him. And here he was at the Taita's Zimbabwe haunt. Instead, his eyes scrutinised the busy tables. He could no more allow himself the indulgence of birdwatching than Ncube could food watching.

'Sir, over there.'

Sibanda's gaze followed Ncube's. At the very edge of the gorge, sitting at a table were four girls, their eyes fixed on a platform nearby jutting out into the chasm. A giggling couple rigged to a rope were about to launch themselves off the lip on a long swing that would plummet them in a stomach-churning ride almost to the water below. Every instinct was telling them not to jump, their bodies were leaning backwards and yet on cue they leapt forward. Yells and screams bounced off the walls of the gorge, echoing along the river as the tandem pair pendulummed back and forth, losing a little momentum with each swing until they came to a dangling stop, their feet almost in the river. Brilliant lunchtime theatre.

Sibanda moved between the tables set out on a lawn. Ncube followed him, nudging diners, squeezing between spaces his body was not designed to negotiate, muttering apologies, torturing himself with the sight of gourmet cuisine and dishes he could never hope to sample. This was the domain of the well-heeled tourist.

'Look girls, it's the cop that makes Samson look sensitive.' Marlie was the first to spot him, 'Come and join us. Have you been in a scrap with a bob cat, Detective Sibanda? Your face... Feisty girlfriend? Get a bit rough, did she?'

'This isn't a social visit.' Sibanda's response was hard and uncompromising.

'Well, I'm real sorry 'bout that. Great spot for a lazy lunch.' She waved her arms towards the view, 'You sure? You and I have unfinished business.'

'It's Geneva and Alair I want a word with.'

'Be like that then,' Marlie pouted, a fake pucker practised to highlight her cheekbones. 'C'mon Becky, let's go launch ourselves into the Zambezi.'

The two girls disappeared back down the dusty road. The gorge swing platform was a hundred metres to their left, but a ravine cut across the path and there was no bridge across. They would have to walk around.

'Detective,' Geneva acknowledged his presence, 'how can we help?'

'To begin with, tell me your real names.'

'Geneva and Alair. That is how we were baptised,' They looked at one another and shrugged shoulders.

Sibanda raised his eyebrows, 'Your surname?'

'Van Dalen.'

'The name you were born with. Van Dalen is the name you perform under.'

'What is this? Why these questions?' Geneva was leading the defence. Alair was nervy, blinking and breathing raggedly.

'Alair, what do you have to say about that?' Sibanda turned his glare on the younger, more vulnerable sister. She remained silent, picking at her fingers, looking down at the table. 'Your father was Aric De Vos of the Antwerp diamond fraud squad. De Vos is your surname, isn't it?'

'We are Van Dalens,' Alair stuttered.

'Where's the gun, Geneva?'

'I don't have any gun, Detective.'

'But I do, and my name is Alair De Vos.' the younger sister whipped the 9mm out of her backpack and trained it on Sibanda. He cursed, not having anticipated Alair would have the weapon. He'd been blindsided by her shyness and reticence. 'Tell that fat plug not to move,' she gestured to Sergeant Ncube.

The tables of diners nearby were alarmed, chairs were tumbling, people were scrambling and yelling. A terrified waiter tossed his tray full of laden plates into the gorge and headed for the safety of the restaurant. In a short time, the area was deserted except for the four of them.

'Don't do anything stupid, Alair, there's no escape.' Sibanda was calm.

'That's for us to decide, Detective.' Geneva took the weapon from her sister and trained it on Sibanda's forehead. He never flinched, never took his eyes off the girl. 'Sergeant, she pointed the gun at Ncube, 'get here. Sit down next to the detective and don't move.'

'Do it, Ncube,' Sibanda ordered.

'If you're interested, we did what we had to do. Jaafar Bastany deserved to die. He killed our father and put our mother in a mental institution. We lost our house, everything's gone,' Geneva spoke. Alair stripped a few tables of their coverings, ripped them in strips and began to bind Sibanda and Ncube to the chairs

'Whatever the motive, however corrupt the victim, murder is still a crime.' Sibanda wanted to keep the girls talking, delay them. One of the diners would surely have dialled the police by now.

'Bastany was never going to jail for his crimes. What was his sentence? Immunity, witness protection and an easy life.' Alair, snarled as she tightened the cloth on Sibanda's wrists. He'd been right about the sisters' strength. He experienced the full brunt of the power in those hands, could already feel the blood constricting below the tie. She began work strapping his legs to the chair.

'The police will be here in a moment. Put down the weapon. Zimbabwe Police shoot to kill.' Sibanda tried to imagine Ncube's bumbling captors racing to the site. He couldn't picture a speedy, accurate or successful outcome.

'We'll be gone soon, don't worry. Give us our passports.'

'They're in my inside pocket, but they'll be no use to you, we'll have an alert out.'

'This is Africa, Detective Sibanda. Does the right hand even know what the left hand is doing?' Sibanda refrained from agreeing. The girls couldn't be allowed to leave Zimbabwe.

'How did you do it?' Ncube asked. He understood Sibanda was trying to delay the sisters.

'Murder him?' Geneva laughed, 'He stowed this weapon in his backpack.' She waved the 9mm in Ncube's face, 'Made it easy for us. You know he killed someone in the village?'

'Madani Haddad,' Sibanda offered, already trying to loosen the binding. Alair was tying up Ncube.

'We followed Bastany to the house and watched through the window as he smashed the man's face in with a statue and then cleaned up the mess. We trailed him, caught up with him near the diner. It was dark, no one was around. There'd been a violent storm. Must have kept everyone home, thunder was still rumbling so he didn't hear us coming. Alair tripped him, we both overpowered him, stuffed a cloth in his mouth. He wasn't in the best of shape. We planned to strangle him with our bare hands, practised for months but then we found the weapon in his backpack and boom!'

'We made sure he knew he was being killed, we made sure he understood we, the daughters of Aric De Vos, were his executioners. He pleaded with us, even cried, as if his contrition could make up for our pain.'

'Ready to move?' Geneva asked.

'Both secure, Genny.' Alair finished tying up Ncube.

'How did you track Bastany to Zimbabwe?' Sibanda kept the conversation going. The girls were proud of their achievement, satisfied with their revenge and his gut told him they wanted to share it. Where were those useless Vic Falls Police?

'We heard he was up to his old tricks, trading diamonds, heading via Zambia to Victoria Falls and some contact in Gubu. We made our way here, hung around the border post. He booked on the Ragged Rascals trip and so did we.'

'And the disguise? How did you know he was wearing a mask?'

'That would be telling. Let's just say we got our hands on his fake passport photo. We have our sources. We received information he was travelling under the name of Laurent Kasongo and that's all the facts you're getting. Okay, Alair, allons-y.'

'Au revoir, Detective,' Alair gave him a triumphant smile as she followed her sister towards the restaurant. Geneva had gone ahead, the 9mm in her hands, threatening anyone who moved.

CHAPTER 37

'Ncube, any chance of loosening your ties? Can you get your hands free?' Sibanda grunted from his own efforts.

'This binding is tighter than a tick after a week on a dog. You were right about those girls, sir, they are strong.'

'Keep trying Ncube. Sibanda was working his wrists, but he'd made little progress. If I can reach that knife...' On a table behind Sibanda, close to the cliff edge, lay a couple of steak knives. Sibanda began to bunny hop on his chair, scraping over the lawn in a see-saw motion until he arrived at the table.

'Can you grab one?' Ncube, facing the restaurant building, was looking over his shoulder.

'Not yet, the table is too high.' Sibanda manoeuvred the chair so his back was parallel to the table, but his hands were too low to reach the knife. The drop in front of him was vertiginous. Acrobatics on the edge of the gorge were folly, but he had no option. Sibanda stretched every sinew until sweat bubbled on his brow, the knives were tantalisingly beyond his reach. He needed another tactic. He leant forward and placed his feet on the ground, his body almost bent double, the chair on his back like a tortoise shell. If he could jump up and back, there was a chance. On his first attempt his cracked ribs hit the table. He fell back close to the gorge edge. Pain shot through his lungs and torso. He yelled and cursed.

'Are you alright, sir?'

'No, but I will be.' After a moment's rest, he tried again. This time his fingers touched one of the knives but he pushed it further away from the table's edge, out of his range. He had one shot left.

Overhead, thunder cracked. The sky was the colour of flint, poised ready to strike and spark. Leaden clouds swam across the landscape, grey Zambezi sharks, diving over the gorges drowning the sun. With every muscle primed, Sibanda jumped again. This time his fingers grasped the last steak knife. He fell forward, his head dangling over the gorge, upside down, a chair on his back pushing him forward. Rocks dislodged by the movement plunged. Sibanda watched as they travelled down into the distant churning water. Below him lay a grade 6 rapid, one of the most violent on earth. Here, the Zambezi tumbled and fought with the rocky outcrops, swirling and leaping in foam-filled anger. Sibanda assessed his position.

'I'm coming, sir!' Ncube was alarmed at the angle of the detective. He was about to disappear over the edge.

'Stay where you are Ncube,' Sibanda shouted, 'Don't move. If you tip your chair, we'll have no chance.' Sibanda tried to manoeuvre himself away from the edge by wriggling his shoulders and knees, but more rocks loosened. He slipped further forward. Another inch and his weight would throw him to his death. He lay stranded, as still as possible, watching sandy basalt grains and pebbles dribble and fall from under him down the gorge face, bouncing off sharp outcrops until they plummeted into the river. This would be his fate, smashed or impaled on the rocks beneath. He couldn't hang on much longer, the trickling sand was eroding his position. He had to move from the edge. This time, agonisingly slowly, he shuffled, every movement miniscule and calculated. Time stretched like the river beneath him as he crawled and finessed his position until his head was no longer dangling in space. Using his forehead, he made more progress until his toes found the lip of a path. He prised hard and threw himself backwards, the chair wobbled, almost tipped over the wrong way and then settled him back in the upright position. He bunny hopped to Ncube.

'Can you see those girls?'

'I can see them sir, but you aren't going to like it. Look.' Ncube swivelled his head to the right of the restaurant. Strung across the gorge was a cable anchored to a granite pillar on the Zambian side. The girls were shimmying their way across the gorge on their stomachs with the agility of star circus performers. The Van Dalens were a balancing act, used to dancing on high wires, performing all manner of daring-do in the lights of the big top. Moving commando style along the cable was child's play to them. They were making steady progress.

'A clever pair, Ncube, I underestimated them. They are as resourceful a set of killers as we have ever met.'

'Getting clean away, sir. We'll never track them down over the border.'

'Not if I've got anything to do with it. Here, Ncube.' Sibanda was now back to back with his sergeant. He passed him the knife, 'Saw away and make it quick.'

'I can't see, I might cut you, sir.'

'Get on with it, Sergeant. Slit wrists will be the least of my troubles if I don't get those girls.'

Ncube worked hard at severing the ties. but his own wrists were tightly bound. 'Try and rip it now, sir,' Ncube gasped, his fingers begging for a rest.

'Not yet, Ncube, cut some more. Why has no one come? Where are the police?'

'I don't think they know, sir. I suspect everyone is locked up in a storeroom. I can see a pile of cell phones on the bar counter. Those girls made sure they were going to escape.'

Ncube heard a ripping sound, Sibanda's hands were free. The detective untied his legs. Once free, he sliced through Ncube's bindings and then ran to the cable line. The girls were halfway along. He would never catch them. Geneva and Alair de Vos were agile and athletic. He needed a quicker way across the gorge.

'Ncube,' he yelled, 'get over here.'

Ncube was rubbing his hands to restore feeling. His legs stumbled; they lacked blood. 'What can I do sir?'

'Watch those girls and release the staff and guests. Phone your ex-captors. We'll need police back up. Take my jacket, be careful with it our lives depend on the safety of its contents.'

'What are you going to do?'

'Find a quicker way across this gorge. I want to intercept the Van Dalens on the other side.'

Ncube watched as Sibanda sprinted to the lip of the gorge, the site of his near disaster. 'What are you doing, sir, this is madness?' Ncube warned. At that moment, the Heavens opened in a deluge that would have shocked Noah himself. Sibanda disappeared over the edge.

The detective was making his way to the gorge swing by the quickest possible route. He sidled along the gorge wall, feeling for hand and toe holds, aware of the steep drop beneath him. He'd nearly plunged to his death once, but he couldn't afford caution. The girls were nudging along the cable one after the other at a steady speed. Although their muscles and balance were circus trained, Sibanda hoped they would flag, a big top and a windy, storm-blasted cable crawl were different environments.

The rain was teeming in spears. The wind was gathering strength, making his own traverse perilous. His climb was hard enough without being pummelled and battered by the weather. The basalt was slippery, but a few cracks in the igneous rock offered reliable handholds. Halfway to the platform, Sibanda found a ledge with enough width to allow his toes some grip. He made good progress until he came to a sheer section with no obvious holds. Nothing for it, but to take a chance. With one foot grounded and the other splayed at a wide angle, searching for a toe hold, he reached as far as he could, pivoting off the grounded foot. For a second, he thought he was done for, could feel the fingers of his left hand slipping. Berry's face flashed before him, followed by his niece and nephew, his brother... He had to hang on or Xolisani would disappear forever. Muchacha would see to that. His mother would never recover from the loss of two sons and the children would be orphaned. Every sinew strained, every muscle aching, he stretched beyond the reach he thought possible, ignored the severe stabbing pain in his ribs and leaped for a jutting shard. He grabbed the rocky outcrop with his right hand, dangling in space until his feet found foot holds and his left hand found a crevice that saved his life. He rested for a moment and sucked in a steadying breath. The rest of the traverse was less complex, littered with bushes growing from the rock face and stepping-stone ledges. Despite the gusting wind, driving rain and his own expectations, Sibanda reached the wooden platform.

'I was watching you. That was crazy, man,' the guide tethered to the edge of the wooden platform helped him clamber up, 'What are those two doing over there on that old cable? This must be the day for the *penga* people, something in the air. The updrafts are lethal. I doubt they make it.'

'They'll make it. Those two are armed killers. I have to arrest them before they reach Zambia.'

'Good luck with that, how do you plan to get down the gorge and over the river and up the other side. It's full of crocs down there.'

'You're going to help me.'

'What?'

'I'm taking the gorge swing.'

'You can't, there's a safety talk and a queue.'

Sibanda shrugged, 'Too bad for the waiting crowd. Now, hook me in so I can release myself at the bottom.'

'You mean drop into the water?'

'I do.'

'Too dangerous, man. It's all crocs, rocks, whirlpools and unpredictable currents. You'll be a dead man.'

'I'll be a dead man if I don't, now hook me up and be quick, those murderers are three quarters of the way across.'

'We don't allow the swing to proceed in high winds and rains.'

'Let me guess, too dangerous?'

The guide shook his head and prepared the tack, 'Step in here.'

'No harness, just the belt and the hook.'

'That's insane, you'll slip out when the rope straightens. The jolt is serious and stomach churning.'

'I'll be fine.'

'Have it your way,' the guide shook his head.

'Hurry, I've still got to swim to the other side and find a way out and up.'

'There's a sort of beach over there and a path up. It's steep but passable, try and steer for that.'

'Thanks.'

'I'll lose my job. For God's sake don't die on me, the publicity would be ruinous.'

'I'm not planning on it.' Sibanda walked back a few paces and understood why the jumpers he watched leaned backwards, the pull forward of the swing rope was inexorable.

'I've cinched the belt tighter than usual. Your ribs may end up in your mouth. Normally it's your stomach that ends up there. Good Luck. One, two…' The guide never made three, Sibanda ran to the edge and leapt into the vast emptiness.

CHAPTER 38

Sibanda tumbled through the air. Seventy feet of free fall was mind altering and life changing. Every instinct was to fight, but the brain accepted struggle was hopeless. Time stood still. Even the thrashing rain and pounding wind were excluded. Sibanda plunged in silence. The detective's descent was eternal as though he was sinking into Hell, and yet there she was again, Berry, with her wide smile, her flawless skin and her wild white hair billowing as she fell with him. He reached out to touch her. In that moment, he knew he would do whatever it took to get her back. He wouldn't give up, wouldn't take no for an answer even if she was standing at the altar with Barney Jones. He would be the one with his hand up when the minister asked if there were any objections to the marriage. He would fight Barney Jones to the death.

The jolt, when it came, was as shocking as the guide had warned, wrenching him from his reverie. He was winded and his cracked ribs felt as though they were squeezed into his chest. He bounced upwards. Another shock came as he plummeted again, about thirty feet this time, and received another jar to the ribs. He clung hard to the rope above his head. And then he was swinging over the river like a child in a giant's playground. The water beneath was dark grey and menacing, swirling, flecked with spume and stippled with the prickly spite of the downpour. When his pendulum came to a stop, when his lungs reinflated, he reached for the cleat, unhooked himself and dropped the ten feet into the river below, sinking beneath the violent water before surfacing and grabbing a quick breath. He turned towards the guide and gave him the thumbs up. Adrenalin from the plunge raced through his body.

The survival endorphins didn't last long before the river grabbed him and tumbled him in a washing machine of churning, sudsy water. He didn't know which way was up, where the light was. He fought hard to surface. The vortex hawked him out long enough for him to gasp before he was swept further downstream at an alarming speed. Sibanda was a strong swimmer, but the river was stronger. Once again, he was somersaulting, cartwheeling under water, the current relentless. He surfaced, half drowned, gasping.

Ahead, there was a hazard so risky and treacherous as to spell certain death, the rapid itself. Sibanda steeled for impact, tried to present himself feet first and fought with every stroke to avoid the danger but the water sped up, carrying him like his flimsy paper boat to the rocks. He kicked hard at the last moment and steered away from the worst of the murderous, jagged edges to a less perilous track - a mini waterfall between two boulders. He slithered over eel-like to be imprisoned in its whirlpool. As he circled like a leaf in a dust devil, sometimes under, sometimes above the water, he saw the Van Dalens overhead.

One of them had slipped and hung beneath the cable. Alair was shedding their back packs. Sibanda watched their belongings fall to the water and drift off downstream. The wind and rain were taking their toll on the circus girls and the mistake gave him extra time. The beach was ahead but he'd never make it unless he could free himself from this maelstrom. The river sucked him under again. Near the end of his endurance, out of breath, he stopped fighting. This agitated eddy would choose whether to let him go or not, struggle was pointless and merely energy sapping. The river was a giant, a raging torrent, his captor, and it had him at its mercy. He was tossed and twisted in ever widening circles until he reached the fringes of the suction and the pool spat him out. Exhausted, he swam hard. Before him was a patch of calmer water. A last spurt of energy and he might survive. When he reached the gentle water, he turned on his back and paddled towards the river's edge. He made the beach. The Zambezi was finished with him.

He lay face down for a while but he couldn't rest for long. The river had eyes, yellow and green ones attached to massive jaws and merciless, flesh ripping teeth. All his thrashing and splashing would have alerted the crocs in the area. He'd done battle with one before and he had no energy for a repeat performance. He dragged himself upright and headed for the steep cliff path.

Shaking from his battle with the river, Sibanda moved as fast as he could up the near vertical incline. The rain continued to pound, sucking oxygen. At times, the climb was sheer. He grabbed at tenacious roots and shrubs to hoist himself, scrambling on all fours. In other sections, he made good speed. His lungs burned, his muscles screamed, but the top was in sight. Had he made it in time to intercept the killers?

He glanced across to the Zimbabwean side. There was movement. The police had arrived and were ushering the diners away from the scene. The fire engine was there. But there was no sign of Sergeant Ncube.

Sibanda headed to the cable stanchion, but the Belgian girls had reached the Zambian side before him and were gone. Which way? He could outrun them if he knew their direction. The downpour was easing up. The rain wouldn't obliterate tracks. The damp earth would in fact make tracking easy. He checked for the sisters' spoor heading inland, the safest and best option, but the girls had chosen to follow the course of the river along the boundary with Zimbabwe. They obviously didn't understand the terrain, and hadn't foreseen a chase – seven river gorges stretched for over a hundred kilometres between the two countries. Although lengths of peaceful water occurred in between the raging torrents, a river crossing back into Zimbabwe remained treacherous and foolhardy and there were no more cables.

What were the pair up to?

Sibanda ran on their tracks. The sisters had made no effort to disguise their spoor, not expecting anyone to be after them so quickly. They were careless and he could see they were tiring from their imprints which were getting heavier, more ragged. Geneva and Alair may have been built for strength and balance but not for grace and speed. Broad shoulders and heavy bones were weighing them down.

Within a kilometre, he had them in his sights. With an extra spurt he could circle, overtake, and set an ambush. He was wary of tackling them head on. He'd witnessed their instinctive cooperation when together, how they'd made easy meat of subduing Jaafar Bastany and if they were still armed, he was in no doubt they would kill him. He'd go for their knees, come out of nowhere with a good heavy branch and fell them, take away their main weapons: spring, agility and balance. That was his plan at least.

The plan almost worked. Alair was running in front. He put her down with one blow, left her writhing, but Geneva, further behind, had time to sidestep the ambush. She turned, grabbed his throat and in seconds, her strong fingers were blocking off his windpipe.

'You shouldn't have come after us, Detective, we warned you,' she screamed in his face.

Sibanda broke the grip with an upward thrust of his arms. He had no time to go on the attack. Alair grabbed his legs in a vice grip.

'I've got him Genny! ' she shouted. Sibanda toppled. Within seconds they were both on him; Geneva, her strangler's grip on his throat and Alair lying across his abdomen, taking his legs out of play. He grabbed each of Geneva's hands in his and forced them away from his neck. He had to get her away from his throat, he was starting to see stars and struggling to draw breath. Geneva had the advantage of downward force. The Belgian girl showed impressive strength. Keeping his grip on her wrists, he pushed Geneva backwards, let go and struck her, a double blow, each fist delivering a knock-out punch. His third smashed her in the solar plexus. Geneva fell away and sat, winded and battered.

'Keep at him Alair,' she gasped, 'like we practised.'

But Alair didn't have the strength of her sister and Sibanda was more of a match than Jafaar Bastany had been. He thwarted the younger sister's attack, lifted her off him by the scruff of her neck and hurled her into the bush. She landed with a thud. The sisters appeared to no longer have the weapon. He wouldn't have stood a chance against the 9 mm. Geneva, regaining her breath, came at him again. He swatted her, twisted her body, and pinned her in a wrestler's hold. Alair could barely stand. She would be going nowhere without a crutch.

'Give up, you two, you won't get away.'

'How do you think you're going to keep us both pinned down in this wilderness? You've got no handcuffs and no back-up.'

'Help will be here soon.'

'Who?' she sneered. 'And how? They'll never get across the gorge.'

Sibanda had to admit the situation verged on impossible. He could have tried to frogmarch Geneva back along the cliff top but then Alair wouldn't be incapacitated for long, and he had no way of tethering her. He looked back across the Zambezi and smiled.

'I think you're wrong Geneva, look.' On the Zimbabwe side, the fire crew had followed their flight, pinpointed their position and lowered their ladders down the opposite side of the gorge. The ladders didn't reach all the way to the bottom, but they did reach an accessible slope. At the vanguard of men climbing down the rungs was Sergeant Ncube. A flotilla of tandem kayaks bobbed in the river at the bottom of the slope. He couldn't imagine how Ncube was ever going to fit into one and stay upright, but Sibanda knew he would, just as he knew he would make it up the impossible slope on the other side. The man's loyalty was unshakable. When Sergeant Ncube reached the bottom of the ladder, he turned, looked across to his boss and waved. Detective Inspector Jabulani Sibanda waved back.

Chapter 39

Sergeant Ncube collapsed on the restaurant lawn. A cool breeze was fanning his body. He ached in every muscle, his lungs were raw and his heart was whirring like a hyperactive cicada. The river crossing had been hair- raising. He never wanted to attempt that again. Scrambling up the gorges was torture. He couldn't have climbed back up the ladders on the Zimbabwe side without Prince shoving him from behind and Khuba pulling him from above. Perhaps he should exercise a bit more if police work was going to require all this effort. He lifted his head to see the Belgian girls being led away in handcuffs.

'We got them, sir,' he gasped between sips of his favourite orange fizz.

'You did a fine job of organising the rescue, Ncube.'

'Thank you, sir, but Prince and Nkala got the fire engine ladders set up, and Khuba thought of the kayaks.'

'They did well to retrieve the backpack with the 9 mm. Forensics will make the link to the slug retrieved from Bastany's body.'

'Case closed, then, sir. We can go home.'

'I have one last visit to make. You rest here, have a meal, anything you want on the menu. I'll pick up the tab.' Sibanda checked his jacket pocket. He still had a crisp fifty dollar note in his wallet. 'I'll be back in an hour. If I'm not, head home alone.'

'But sir…'

'No arguments, Ncube.'

Sibanda jumped into Miss Daisy. For the first time, he noticed what a wrecked state she was in. Ncube would get her fixed. With a hundred dollars, his sergeant could work miracles. He wondered what colour wing she would end up with. Pink?

He pulled up at the front of Hippo Hills. Miss Daisy made a disturbing contrast to the few ministerial cars that remained. The conference was winding down. She, herself, was purring. After all, everyone knew a British built Land Rover, no matter what age or condition, had more status and dignity than those tarty, black, shiny, useless, fragile, low slung people carriages.

'You can't leave that heap of rattling rubbish here,' a uniformed concierge accosted the detective.

'Police duty,' Sibanda replied, 'I can, and I will.' The concierge huffed off to find higher authority. He was used to dealing with this sort of situation, but he was intimidated by the man's stature and assurance which contrasted with the vehicle he had emerged from.

Sibanda made his way to the Cuthbert Muchacha's suite. Charamba was standing guard outside. 'I've been told to let you in,' he snarled.

'Then do it,' Sibanda snarled back, his face inches from the CIO officer's. Charamba backed off and opened the door.

Cuthbert Muchacha was sitting on the sofa, whiskey and coke in hand. 'Detective Sibanda, as promised, come to deliver my package, I hope. We did make a mess of your good looks, I see.'

'Cuts and bruises heal, Muchacha, reputations rarely do.'

'Hand them over,' the minister snapped, his good humour dissolving.

'You can have the package as soon as I know my brother and sister-in-law are safe and only then.'

Muchacha made a phone call while Sibanda listened to the instructions. 'They are being released now, Sibanda. They'll phone you in five minutes. You see, I keep my promises.'

Sibanda walked to the window and stared at the golf course, waiting until Xolisani and Thandie made it out of whatever hell hole they'd been incarcerated in. It gave him time to think.

Sibanda's phone rang.

'Xoli, are you okay.'

'Filthy, sweaty, flea infested and dying for a glass of red, but yes, Thandie and I are fine. How are the kids?'

'With our mother, happy and well. They think you two are on holiday. Where are you?'

'Hailing a taxi. We'll be home soon. I can't wait to sleep in a real bed.'

'I'm sorry Xoli...'

'...This is Zimbabwe, my brother, nothing to be sorry about.'

'I'll meet you at our home tomorrow. It'll be easier to talk then.'

'Satisfied?' Muchacha was standing, his hand outstretched.

Sibanda reached in his pocket and took out the parcel he'd prised from James Templeton. Muchacha opened it and beamed. Sibanda walked to the door.

He gambled Muchacha's diamond knowledge was sketchy , and he likely didn't have a loupe. If these synthetics had fooled the Antwerp Gemstone Foundation, they would fool a greedy amateur like Muchacha. Bilal and Madani Haddad thought they could get away with the swop and they were the cheating experts. The real diamonds lay under the ochna pulchra in the hollowed-out shell of Mama Ecstasy.

The broken shards and ruined carvings at the back of Thomas Mabiza's stand spoke of his failed attempts to hollow out his own sculptures for smuggling. Bastany was obliged to buy Mama Ecstasy from the Manhombo twins. Her robust structure and superior stone meant Mabiza could hollow her out and stash the diamonds inside, camouflage the opening and keep them safe from the prying eyes of the overlanders. Mabiza might have been a useless sculptor, but he disguised the base of the hollow statue with skill.

The real diamonds were buried. He had no use for them, but these were difficult times in his country. Maybe one day they would come in handy. He turned back towards the minister, but the man was absorbed, running the diamonds through his fingers, chuckling. Sibanda strode away. His mind focussed on his family. His heart focused on winning back the love of Berry Barton.

Epilogue

It was too wet to work in the garden. The storm was fierce and lashing. Godwishes sheltered inside, pushing a broom around the old kitchen floor. Caro had gone out to buy supplies. She was planning some kind of cross-country trip. Together, they'd visited the doctor who confirmed he didn't have leprosy. The course of antibiotics seemed to be clearing up the oozing sores eating away at his lip. He pushed aside the old chair. Amongst the fluff, dust and dead flies, there was something stuck underneath. A piece of paper. He picked it up. The document was torn and yellowing, a discarded letter. He was about to bunch it up when he noticed a circle of red wax stuck on the bottom. On closer inspection there appeared to be two elephants impressed into the surface. Some child's art work he thought. Miss Caro wouldn't want it. He screwed the paper up and threw it in the flames of the old wood stove.

Jacobi, this is my final letter, written by the boy at my side you have trained in your ways. It is you who will write my story, scribe it for eternity, for you have the words the English will understand. Do not lie, be honest, but treat me well in your account, as I have treated you. I have made mistakes, but the English would not have been stopped whatever course I took. They wanted the treasures of our land and the toil of my people. Therein lies my true wealth, not in the diamonds from the Kimberley mines or the tributes from the hunters and explorers. Too late, I realise this. With death comes wisdom.

In your final accounting, know the few sovereigns I had left, after the bribe to the English, were spent on securing my grave and the events that must happen after my death to inter my bones. The ivory store was destroyed when my impis burnt my capital, Kobulawayo. The two safes containing the tins of diamonds and the Mashona gold have been sent to my son Nyamande. It is he I anoint as my successor. I leave him a broken land and a subjugated people. I pray to the god of the missionaries he may rise up and succeed in his kingship.

Farewell my faithful servant. When you receive this letter, I will already be with my ancestors. I am going to a pain-free peace and an English-free land.

Lo Bengula King of the Matabele and Mashonas

Printed in April 2023
by Rotomail Italia S.p.A., Vignate (MI) - Italy